Beautiful

Sylvia Hubbard

CONTENTS

CHAPTER 1

MADISON OLIVER STAYED mostly to herself, but Nikki Powers had been her best friend since junior high. Since Madison had moved to the west side of Detroit, Nikki occasionally visited from the suburbs where Madison used to live with her mother.

Her father gave Nikki the suspect eye as he allowed her in his house. A man of the church, he looked over at his daughter. "I thought you had a lot of studying to do tonight?"

"We do," Nikki said in Madison's defense. "Mr. Dowell, your kind daughter is helping me with my final thesis."

Her father looked hard at Nikki. "I would like a private word with you in my study, Nikki Powers, before you corrupt my daughter." He looked up at Madison. "I'll send her upstairs when I'm done, Madison."

Madison looked worried. It wasn't the first time her father had wanted a private word with Nikki.

Nikki looked up at Madison at the top of the stairs. "Don't worry, Maddie. He'll just preach to me about not corrupting his daughter once again." She winked at her to assure her friend things would be fine.

Madison relaxed and watched Nikki go into her father's study. Instead of going into her attic bedroom, she waited in the hallway. After twenty minutes, Nikki came bounding out the office and up the stairs. She grabbed Madison's hand and dragged her to the bedroom to ensconce themselves inside.

"Why'd you even move here?" Nikki said, annoyed. "He treats you like a child. You're three years shy of thirty."

"He's a pastor," Madison said proudly in her father's defense.

Nikki austerely corrected her. "An assistant pastor, Maddie, and a control freak. He wants to punish you because he's still angry at your mother for leaving him." She snorted. "I need to use your bathroom." She closed the door before Madison could say anything.

Taking a moment to push away Nikki's harsh words about her father, Madison wasn't going to discuss how she needed to stay with him because she was broke while trying to finish her master's, unlike Nikki, supported by her semi-wealthy parents who bought everything and anything for their only daughter.

Unfortunately, Madison wasn't Cyrus Dowell's only child, just his oldest. After her mother left him when Maddie was only five, Cyrus married another woman and had two kids by her, plus cared for three of the woman's other children. Madison's stepmother was even more controlling than her father, and their children were cruel and spoiled as well.

Yet, Cyrus didn't want it rumored that he'd turned his daughter away when she needed help. He liked his religious persona, so he gave her a room in the attic. But it had barely enough light to help her study, and she was so far from the internet box she could barely get a signal on her laptop.

Cyrus had made it difficult for anyone to even see Madison, because he didn't want her mother's 'people' in his house. Nikki was the only one allowed in their home, but always had to be preached to.

Madison knew that once her project was accepted and the grant given, her days of living in this place would be over. She'd be able to step out on faith with her lifelong research, and do things on her own.

Time was just going very slow and painfully for her.

Madison pressed her ear against the bathroom door and listened. Water ran and then… she heard Nikki throwing up.

"Are you okay?" she questioned.

"Yeah," Nikki panted. "I haven't been eating right." She came out of the bathroom. "Your final thesis, how's it going?"

Madison pursed her lips together, not wanting to speak of her project. "It's fine. Professor Barfield believes our samples will come out right this time and the grant will be all ours."

"Is he just saying that because his tenure is on the line and all the personal money he's invested in it?"

Shaking her head, Madison said, "No, Nikki, he believes in me. I know it should work this time."

Nikki sighed. "When are you going to give me more details? It sounds so interesting."

"Soon. I don't want to jinx it." Madison pretended straightening up her vanity table was very important, but really it was just a way to not look at Nikki.

Nikki was gorgeous. She reminded Madison of the model Iman, tall, dark and elegantly beautiful. She carried herself so regally and exquisite, making men lustful and women jealous. Standing in her shadow most of her life, Madison felt honored to be her friend, yet slightly wary.

As they grew up together, Madison had come to the realization that Nikki wasn't so smart in books, and perhaps envied Madison's intellect and fast learning skills. Madison didn't mind explaining things to Nikki, at first. But then, in high school, Nikki convinced her to let her copy papers or even do them for her.

Madison wasn't stupid. She knew Nikki needed her, and Madison didn't want to give up on the relationship. In her mind, she hoped she could learn from Nikki; be brave, confident and courageous.

Be beautiful.

Nikki interrupted Madison's pondering. "Let's hurry up and get me to understand this. I have to meet someone tonight at Club Henry downtown."

It was true, Madison had to help Nikki with her studies that night. Nikki decided to go after her master's degree at a private college, while Madison barely got a scholarship to get in at Wayne State University in Detroit.

Once Nikki was gone for the night, Madison stayed up and studied more, updated databases and reports.

She was dedicated to her project, and nothing would get in the way of her accomplishing her goal—nothing!

At five in the morning, her alarm clock woke her from a dead sleep. Somehow, she had ended up face-down in her books. The slobber from her mouth had adhered the paper to her face.

Moving quietly as a mouse through the sleeping home, Madison washed her face and body by the sink. Her stepmother, Hazel Dowell, hated when shower ran any earlier than seven A.M.

Yet, with no car, Madison had to get up early for school. The bus she had to take to past the New Center area of Detroit was three blocks away from the house.

The morning was cold as hell for April. A light snow had fallen, despite the fact the season was going into spring. Yet, her father refused to let her wear pants. He said God never wanted a woman to wear pants, so no woman in his household was allowed.

To help her legs not suffer the bitter, brutal wind of Detroit, Madison wore thick, thigh-high stockings. She'd found early on she was allergic to nylons, so thick skirts with thick stockings kept her warm enough, as long as the wind didn't blow.

With a bottle of water and a toothbrush, Madison never bothered to brush her teeth at home. After taking a piece of dried roll from dinner the previous night out of the refrigerator, Madison hurried out of the house in the cold morning air and made her way down the street.

At the bus stop, she had to keep her senses alive, because the stop was in front of empty duplexes that had been torn apart, and often had wild animals or even vagrants squatting inside. She always tried to time her walk to the bus stop so that she didn't have to wait long. Although some days she cut it close, and if she missed the bus, it was an hour-and-a-half wait. She'd miss her lab time at school, but would still be on-time for class.

She hated missing lab because it would mean she would have to stay at school longer afterward.

Even as the sun rested on the horizon, it didn't stop a strong wind from whipping about her, picking up the thick fabric of her skirt and showing her legs to anyone near.

She pushed her skirt down, caught off-guard, and looked around frantically, hoping no one had seen. The only cars parked on the street near her were an Explorer, a bus, and a1970 teal Lincoln Continental in pristine condition.

All of the vehicles seemed to be empty, although the Lincoln had darkened windows, except on the windshield, so she couldn't be absolutely sure.

The wind blew again, lifting her skirt up and exposing a good amount of her stockinged thighs. This time, she forgot if anyone was around and looked down the street impatiently for the bus.

A door slammed from a home across the street and a young girl ran out of the house and jumped into the passenger side of the Lincoln.

The lights turned on, the engine roared, and a window on the driver's side slowly rolled down. A dark man wearing a baseball cap and dark hoodie looked her way. He had seen her. He had been watching her!

Embarrassed, Madison looked away, praying the bus would come.

Thankfully, the huge city bus pulled in front of her and she quickly got on. Sitting on the side where she could see the Lincoln, she saw the driver again…

He took off his sunglasses and looked at her.

He had a thin goatee, clear chocolate skin, and sensual lips that curled into a wicked smile.

The bus drove off, but their eyes stayed connected through her window until she couldn't see him anymore.

That lustful look in his eyes… It had made her feel…beautiful.

CHAPTER 2

FORCING HERSELF TO CONCENTRATE on her work that day, Madison was too overwhelmed with her project to really think about the gawker…the handsome gawker.

Yet, as she rode the bus home and her mind finally relaxed, she remembered a lot more. The Lincoln Continental was a big car. She remembered her mother had one when she was young. Albeit, it wasn't as old as this one. The older ones stood out among other cars as a smooth ride.

Had she ever seen him there before?

No, she would have remembered that vehicle. She would have remembered him!

So why now had he been sitting there?

The bus dropped her off at about the same location across the street where the Lincoln had been parked.

An older woman got off the bus with her and started to walk in the opposite direction, until she paused and turned back around.

"Do you know Deacon Cyrus Dowell?" the woman inquired.

Madison judged the woman would've been as old as her mother, if her mother was still alive.

"My father is Pastor Cyrus Dowell," she said.

"I knew it! You're Madison?" the woman proclaimed. "Oh, my goodness, you have your mother's eyes. I knew it."

"You knew my mother?" To find someone who knew her mother was a goldmine. When her parents divorced, her mother had moved to the suburbs and decided not to interact with family, friends or anyone from their former life. She never talked about why she left Cyrus Dowell, and she never talked to anyone else for that matter.

"All too well, but you said your father is a pastor now? Of what?" The woman's tone sounded insulting.

"Of Mount Zion Missionary Baptist Church."

The woman looked confused. "That church is huge. Who made him pastor of such a large congregation?"

Madison corrected herself, not used to talking about her father. "Well, he's assistant pastor. He was just appointed."

"I do newsletters for various churches and maybe I should speak to someone at Mount Zion—"

Madison cut her off. "I don't mean to make trouble for my father. I live with him now until I get out of school with my master's."

The woman looked a little wary. "You moved in with him?"

"I've been unable to support myself and go to school full-time." She didn't feel all the way comfortable telling this woman all her details of her miserable life. "Her estate paid off the debt from the hospital bills, so I really didn't have anything."

The woman seemed a little more disturbed. "Well, Madison Dowell, I never thought I would see you again after everything."

Feeling some disdain for the way the woman spoke about her father, Madison stiffly corrected her, "My mother changed my last name to Oliver."

The woman looked regretful. "I guess I can understand, when she found out the truth."

"What truth? My parents divorced over irreconcilable differences," Madison said. "I'm sorry, but who are you?"

"Me? I'm Sister Onetta Nate. Your mother never spoke about me?" She looked offended. "I was your godmother. I remember when you were first born. Your mother and I were best friends." Guilt was heavy on her face. "But once Mattie realized… well, I guess I can understand her not telling you anything. And she most likely told your father never to say anything to you."

"Say what?"

"I'm sorry, child. You should talk to your mother. I shouldn't be telling business she most likely never wanted you to know."

Frustrated, Madison said, "My mother is dead. Died of cancer a few years ago, ma'am."

"Mattie Oliver is dead?" the woman asked in pure disbelief. "Oh, my. She didn't deserve that. Not after what your father put her through."

"What did he do? What 'truth' did my mother find out?"

The woman looked around as if people were listening in, but there was no one around.

"Well, your mother didn't find anything out until the majority of other church members at which the head deacon accused Cyrus of embezzling church funds to support his sex addiction."

Madison's mouth dropped open. "His what?"

"I'm sorry, Madison. Maybe you shouldn't be finding this out from me."

Madison said defensively, "Maybe you shouldn't be lying."

The woman stiffened. "Why would I lie when it was all in the papers? You be blessed little girl, and be careful, because your mother shouldn't have died penniless." The woman walked away from her.

Madison didn't know how to feel as she walked home, forcing herself to forget the lies she had just been told.

By the time she was shedding off her coat in the house, she couldn't stop thinking about the stranger and what she'd said.

"Dinner's cold," her stepmother, Hazel Dowell snipped. "And since you're the last to eat, clean up the kitchen and don't run the dishwasher."

Madison knew Hazel made a point of trying to have everyone eat early, knowing Madison would be home late. Everyone else got to use the dishwasher, except Madison.

"Hazel," she asked before the woman closed herself away in her bedroom. "When did you meet my father?"

Hazel cut her beady black eyes at Madison. "That's none of your business." She walked away.

Madison hurried to eat her dinner and finish cleaning the kitchen, then went up to her attic bedroom to lock herself in for the night. Once she'd turned on her laptop, she realized she had to sit in the far corner in order to pick up a strong enough Wi-Fi signal, but Madison was able to use the Internet finally.

Typing in her father's name, articles came up from around the time she was just being born.

"DEACON ACCUSED OF EMBELLIZING OVER 2.5 MILLION FROM MEGA-CHURCH TO AFFORD HIS SEX ADDICTION."

She read on, stunned, to see her father trying to cover his face in shame in the pictures, and her mother walking into the church. Her mother was carrying a small baby, whom Madison could only assume was her.

The church had burned down in a fire after a large, cash fundraising function had taken place, and in the melee, over 2.5 million dollars came up missing, at first believed to have been destroyed in the fire.

Yet, assistant secretary Sister Onetta Nate testified Deacon Dowell admitted he stole to support a sex addiction. "He's owed some debts to some pimps—more than he has in his bank account—and he needed the money fast. Otherwise, they had threatened to hurt Cyrus' wife, who is my best friend."

When asked why she'd come forward with this information, Sister Onetta Nate admitted, "Because I was one of those women he slept with, and it was fine until I caught his diseases, just like all the others."

Madison looked around for more articles of incrimination, shocked to discover her father was the man Sister Onetta Nate said he was. Unfortunately, the only other article was about charges being dropped by the prosecution for no evidence to pin on Cyrus Dowell. However, he'd been removed from the church after his wife filed for divorce.

Saving the articles on her flash drive, Madison tried to finish the schoolwork she hadn't gotten to in the lab, and sent her results to the professor.

Going into the bathroom, Madison looked in the mirror at her acne-scarred face. For years, she had tried to remove the scars, but nothing seemed to work. The chemicals made her itch and the natural soaps weren't effective.

She'd tried everything, and was always looking right at some kind of pimple about to pop on her face.

After scrubbing her face for her nightly routine, she lay in bed. Madison wondered if the guy in the Lincoln had seen her up close, would he mind the adult acne? Probably. She minded.

Closing her eyes, she tried to wonder if she'd walked up to the car, would he look just as cute. And what if he got out and pulled her in his arms?

What if?

Madison could almost imagine his hands on her thighs, moving higher between her legs.

Parting her thighs, she moved her hands between her legs to ply through her already moistened folds.

Biting her lips, she knew this was wrong, and was mortified at the idea of ever being caught, but that didn't stop her from circling lightly around the tip of her arousal and producing even more essence to dribble down on her bedsheets.

She continued to imagine the stranger's hands doing what she was doing to herself, and Madison didn't care if her skirt was hiked up, her ass pressed up against his Lincoln Continental while he whispered in her ear, "Let me bend you over my hood and…"

That was all she needed as she exploded, wetting her sheets and hand, gushing out her release, while using her other hand to cover her mouth so no one would hear.

Finally, sleep came.

Most likely, she'd never see that stranger again, and most likely Madison would forget she ever saw him or that look in his eyes.

CHAPTER 3

HER SCHEDULE HAD always pretty much set in stone. That morning, she got up and got dressed. This time was different.

There was an urgency in her mind to hurry up and get out of the house.

Just as she reached the front door, Hazel came out of nowhere to block her exit.

Without all the heavy makeup Hazel usually wore, old age at almost sixty and life was starting to take a toll on her face. She looked like a rundown, black version of Martin Short, without her long-haired wigs she always wore. Now her hair was short and brittle. Damaged by perms and coloring, she barely had any left. And the makeup hadn't helped her skin. Hazel's flesh was dry as a bone. It appeared no amount of lotion or moisturizer could help her.

Taking a drag on a cigarette, Hazel snipped, "Do you have to make so much noise in the morning?"

Madison had been quiet as a mouse just like any other day. Matter of fact, she'd only washed her face in the sink and jumped right into her clothes so she could get out of the house quickly.

She hadn't even gone to the kitchen to grab anything to eat. Was this just a bad day for Hazel?

Yet, Madison didn't want to argue. Docilely, she apologized, "I'm sorry, Hazel. I'll be quieter."

Hazel pursed her lips together, as if she wanted to say something else nasty, but instead asked, "Why you being so nosy all of a sudden? Who's in your ear, girl?"

Madison wondered why Hazel suspected this, and why it had taken all night for the woman to figure she had been talking to someone. Was that the real reason her father tried to make sure none of her mother's friends ever came in his house, so she couldn't find out the truth about his past?

"I was on the bus and I met a Sister Onetta."

Hazel now looked uneasy. "That cunt. She's always been a little sour Cyrus picked me over her."

Madison gasped, never having heard Hazel curse before, especially since Hazel tried to walk around the house and even at church as if she was a first lady already.

"She's got nerve to get in your ear and talk anything since she was sleeping with your dad too. And don't act so damn shocked. I'm sure she told you everything."

Not sure how to react, Madison fumbled, "I-it doesn't matter. It's the past."

"Really? The money didn't matter, either?"

That was the second time money had been mentioned, and this time Madison paid attention. "My mother's money?"

Hazel snorted. "Her money. Your money. Any of the money."

"How much?"

"Two million," Hazel said, taking a final drag on her cigarette. "Your father hates for me to smoke in the house, you know that? He says it reminds him of the night his church burnt to the ground." A secret smile came to Hazel lips as if she was hiding the secret of the century. "I don't know why Cyrus' worries. My old man was a fire fighter. I know all about fires."

Madison didn't want to change the subject. "Where's the money?"

"Gone. Paid all the bills. My bills." She smirked. "When I knew the type of man your father was and who his wife was, I knew I had a ticket to freedom. Using his religion and guilt was just a way to get it. I did." She smiled wickedly. "Sometimes you have to do whatever it takes to get what you want. Getting pregnant was the easy part. And I knew one baby wasn't going to do it. For a man like Cyrus, you have to own his soul." Again that menacing secret smile crept over Hazel's lips.

If Madison had eaten, she probably would have thrown everything up. Hazel was becoming sickening to look at, and the no makeup or wig didn't help.

"Your mother knew the children were his from the moment she saw them, and I knew she'd file for divorce immediately. But she didn't expect me to be smarter, with intentions of taking the money. By the time she confronted your father with the affair, way before the church suspected, I had convinced him to transfer her money into my accounts. He was already stealing from the church, so stealing from his wife was easy. I didn't care she kept you. I had enough."

"Enough of what?" Madison said, feeling her throat going dry.

"Money."

She narrowed her eyes, needing to get out of Hazel's sight. "I have to leave. I'll miss my bus." She started to walk away, but Hazel grabbed her arm, digging her nails into her skin.

"You just stay away from people like that bitch Onetta. And you'd better act like you know nothing if you want to stay under this roof. Your innocence is the only thing saving you. I can make your life very hard, if you push me; just like I did for your mother when she threatened to tell the church about the money."

Madison snatched her arm away and walked out the door, not even bothering to close it behind her.

She pushed what Hazel said out of her head and hurried to the bus stop. Most likely, she'd missed her coach, but hopefully she hadn't missed the stranger in the Lincoln Continental.

Getting to the corner where her stop was, she found no one was there and she became upset; Not just because she had missed her bus, but because she'd also missed the possibility of seeing the stranger again.

She was being silly, she knew.

Yet, it was the only peace of mind she knew she would feel.

Why now? Why was all this coming out?

Why was she remembering her mother's dying words?

"Your face. I'm sorry. I'm so sorry. I was going…and they took everything."

Pulling out a compact, Madison looked at herself. The acne was always ever present on her skin, and most days she stayed away from her reflection so as never to see it.

Anything affected her. Too much of this. Too much of that, and never enough water.

But, she felt, maybe as she got older it would disappear…though it never did.

She wanted to pretend that morning and the day before had never happened, but everything was pouring into her brain on repeat like a tape recorder that could not be stopped.

Her bus came half an hour later, but there was no Lincoln, and no Sister Onetta.

Getting to class on time, she took out her heavy old laptop that used to be her mother's. She connected to the school's Internet and looked up Onetta

Nate. Amazingly, she had a profile page on the popular social network and even a phone number listed.

Madison didn't send her a friend request, but she did put the number in her flip phone.

She had tests and could barely concentrate on them. Good thing she was studious and had her easy classes that day.

Afterward, she went to the lab. Only one intern was there, and the professor was in meetings all day.

"Watching it won't make the results come any faster," she said, seeing the intern leaning over the pods.

"How do you know?" he asked.

"I used to do the same thing, but after round twelve, I realized that I could look all I want and there was nothing going to make it work until it felt like working." She walked up to him and checked his name badge. "Joshua? Are you new?"

"Yes, I interviewed with you at the beginning of the semester, but was just placed on a waiting list."

She'd been really involved in the intern process at the beginning of the year, but with the possibility of a major grant coming up, she'd devoted all her brain cells to this.

"I thought our intern quota was filled."

"It was, until one dropped out of school and the other changed schools. I was next on the list." He smiled proudly.

Joshua reminded her of a younger version of Bradley Cooper, except with dull brown eyes and a grim expression. He kept his brown sugar colored hair very short and straight, as if he was in the military.

"You think all this is going to work?" Joshua asked.

"I know it's going to work. I've been working on it since high school and the professor really believes it will, too."

"I hope so too," he said.

She pulled out the chart to update the growth process. Everyone was banking on this work. Her creation. Her idea.

She wanted to hope, too.

Yet, there was so much on her mind to deter her from getting anything done, she was almost grateful for Joshua and his hovering, even though normally she never liked that.

That day was different.

That day, she needed someone to take her mind off of everything.

"You really like this," Joshua said, as she entered her results for the daily report.

"Yes, I do. Creating something that could change lives makes me happy," she confessed. "I like knowing I can make the world beautiful." In her mind, she finished off, *Even if I can't be.*

"What?" Joshua asked, as if he'd heard something.

"Nothing," she said quietly.

After she was done with the lab, she went to catch her bus. Joshua pulled up beside her in his Honda Civic. "You want a ride?"

She knew if she pulled up at the house in his car, her father would have a fit. "No, thank you. I'm fine."

"It's late and still cold," he said. "I don't mind."

"I do."

A horn honked across the street. "Hey, Maddie!" Nikki called.

Glad to see her, Madison walked away from Joshua's car and got into Nikki's Chevy Malibu.

The brand new car smell assailed her nose immediately as she shut the door and Nikki took off. "How'd you know I'd be out there?"

"I know you stay in the lab late and I was actually going to come by tonight and keep you company."

Madison smiled meekly. "Really?"

"Yeah, but then my daddy said he had a surprise." Nikki slapped the steering wheel. "You like my new car?"

"Yeah, sure…what happened to your other car?" Madison inquired, a little flustered and trying not to be jealous.

"Oh, I don't know," Nikki said. "What's been up?"

There was so much on her mind, she actually really needed to talk to someone about what was going on with her.

Starting with seeing the Lincoln Continental, she then progressed to Sister Onetta and then the odd conversation with Hazel that morning.

Nikki drove toward Madison's house and they both looked a little relieved that her father wasn't home. Hazel was somewhere in the house, but didn't come out, and Nikki followed Madison up to her room in the attic.

"What does this stranger have to do with anything?" Nikki questioned.

Out of everything she had told Nikki, Madison wondered why Nikki had focused on the guy and not on the fact that her mother died penniless when the money could have paid for medical bills and healthcare. Also, the fact that her father was a sex maniac and her stepmother was a gold digging whore.

She answered Nikki. "I don't know. It was weird that he was just watching me."

"Are you sure he was looking at you?"

Feeling doubtful, she said, "Well, no, I don't know, but it felt like it, even when I got on the bus."

Nikki wrinkled her nose. "You're acting like you wanted him to be looking. That's pretty slutty, Madison."

Feeling ashamed, she denied, "No, I'm just saying it was odd."

"He's probably some old geezer doing a one-time favor of taking a young relative to school." Nikki shrugged it off. "Just be careful. You're in Detroit now, Madison, and you can't be nice to these people. Go look for the devil and you're bound to find him."

Madison nodded, but changed the subject since she was feeling silly for even bringing it up to Nikki. "How's everything going with you, Nikki? Other than the new car?"

This, of course, opened the door for Nikki to talk about herself, and Nikki LOVED to talk about herself.

With her full scholarship to Western University, nice new car, and parents paying for an apartment near campus, Nikki gabbed on about all the new fun and friends she was experiencing without a worry in the world.

Madison really tried not to feel jealous. Instead, she forced herself to feel happy for her friend.

"Maybe you should get serious about your face," Nikki said offhandedly. "Maybe remembering what your mother said on her deathbed after the encounter with Hazel was just something you need to concentrate on instead of concentrating on all this other stuff that's in the past."

Confused, Madison questioned, "My face?"

"Remember in ninth grade, you wanted to go to a dermatologist but your mother said it was too expensive, and then shortly after that, cancer came, so you stopped pressuring her about it?"

"That's because all the money was going to the bills and her new boyfriend told me to stop crying about my face when my mother was dying."

She remembered that time. "He said, if God made me ugly I should just accept it." The memory brought a bitter taste in her mouth.

"You could go to a dermatologist now," Nikki suggested.

Rolling her eyes in exasperation, Madison said, "I'm not under her healthcare anymore, Nikki. I'm too old to be added to my father's and the cheap insurance I have through school just covers annuals and generals. Nothing covers dermatology for free."

Nikki snorted. "Aren't there some natural treatments online you haven't tried?"

"I have other research to do right now to be worried over my face."

"I think you should look into it, and your dad is shit for not helping you out."

"Please, Nikki" Madison said, worried. "I don't want him or anyone of his other house spies to hear anything."

"Ugh…" Nikki sighed. "Then let me go before I say something that will get you kicked out of here."

They hugged, and Madison watched as Nikki pulled away in her brand new car.

Going back to her room, Madison went on her computer and looked up home remedies. Most of them she had done already, but she found one she had never tried, and knew she would never, EVER try.

The reason she had never explored the option when she was younger was because she was just too young to be reading anything like the new research she now pulled up.

Yet, the idea of this…it was farfetched, and no one would help her. Well, no one she knew.

Madison didn't know a lot of men to help her or who wouldn't think she was absolutely insane for asking.

CHAPTER 4

THERE WAS AN ARTICLE by a skin doctor, which spoke about how male reproductive fluid was often used in expensive skin creams and promoted healthy collagen when applied to the skin. Women swore by the various creams the doctor touted.

Madison knew there would be no way she could afford those elixirs for her face.

She could always find a guy and make her own elixir. This thought left her as soon as it came. That would be stupid and very unsafe.

Madison was innocent, but not stupid.

***

The following morning, she was even quieter to get out of the door, praying she wouldn't run into Hazel, her father, or even one of her siblings. Getting to the bus stop, Madison looked eagerly around for the Lincoln, but to her disappointment didn't see anyone.

It was sad the stranger in the Lincoln was the only thing she had to look forward to in her life.

Rushing out the house very quietly went on for a week, and she decided Nikki was right. She was foolish to hope to see this guy again.

As for her father's secrets and the high possibility he took the money that could have saved her mother, she pushed that to the back of her mind, erasing her computer history just in case her father tried to see what she'd been looking at.

To get her mind off everything, Madison threw herself into studying and nothing else.

The following Sunday, her father suddenly came up to the attic. With each step he took, her heart slowed with dread. He usually tried his best to avoid her, while his new wife just gave Madison dirty looks but hardly said anything to her.

Madison was startled to see her father, who looked around her small room as if he didn't know where he was.

When she had moved in, he'd told her she could have the attic, but when she went up there, no one had touched the place in years. It had taken three months to clean a corner, get a makeshift room together, and just be able to call it her living quarters. A previous owner of the house had used it to rent out and added a guest bathroom, so she didn't have to leave the attic to get anything else in the house, except for food.

"I was getting ready for church," she explained, when he looked disapprovingly at her in just a slip.

Her father was already dressed in a black polyester suit. "I'm not here about that, but we're leaving soon. I just thought you should know with the added expense of you living here, Hazel sees there's a need for more income in the home." He paused as if she had said something to upset him. He harshly cleared his voice and straightened his tie. "I know you've got a full load at school, but taking you on is a big expense for the extra food and utilities, and we need some help. Alice is still in high school and, this being her last year, I've realized we got a lot of bills about to come in. Just something part-time should cover the extra expenses."

She didn't know what to say. With two of her scholarships, Madison was doing internships, and with a full workload at school, she was worried a job would get in the way of everything–including her doctorate project.

Did he realize what he was asking?!

"No disrespect, sir, but it's going to be real hard to get something that's going to work around my full school schedule," she explained.

Cyrus stiffened. "Well, maybe you should think about taking a couple years off. Save up until you can afford everything, and then return to school."

Madison was horrified at his selfishness. She could lose her scholarship! Stop her education? Was he crazy?

Cyrus cleared his throat impatiently, straightened his tie, and walked out.

End of discussion–on his part.

No way to avoid the inevitable.

Madison sunk to her bed, wanting to cry. What was she going to do?

***

When Madison returned home from church, it was too late for her to do anything. Her father literally stayed all day at church, and by the time she got home, she barely had enough energy to get her homework done, do a little work on her research, and then go to bed.

So exhausted from worry, Madison slept restlessly and woke up late. Barely stuffing herself in her clothes and grabbing her hoodie, she burst out of the house in full dash mode. She hadn't even combed her hair and was glad the hoodie hung low so people wouldn't see what a hot mess she was before at least could use her fingers like a comb to do something her bed head.

Running to the bus stop, she missed the first bus and groaned, knowing she was going to have to wait for the second one.

"Psst," someone hissed behind her.

She looked and gasped at the Lincoln, which was parked perpendicular on the side of the abandoned buildings. Turning around quickly, she pretended she hadn't heard a thing.

In the past, Nikki told her Detroit was strange and to be careful.

"Psst," the driver said again.

Madison tried to fight not looking, but being able to see the driver close up was what she had longed for.

Her curiosity won out. She turned to him and took in his features as she warily walked up to the car.

He was handsome. Too handsome.

"I shouldn't talk to strangers," she said sternly.

The stranger cajoled, reaching out to touch her sleeve innocently. "What's the harm in talking?" His hand moved down to her hand and rubbed on her knuckles.

He was touching her. Were his eyes bad? She wondered. She looked down at her hand where his fingers rubbed against her fingers. "N-No, harm, I guess."

"How old are you?" he inquired.

Looking back at his face, she answered. "Twenty-eight. Umm, my birthday's coming up next week."

She didn't know why she told this stranger personal information, but she hadn't told anyone about her birthday coming up, and rambling through her nervousness with a cute guy looking at her so closely made her less anxious.

He licked his thick bottom lip slowly. "Really?" he sounded fascinated by that information. "You on your way to school or work?"

Too nervous to talk, she only nodded.

He chuckled. It was a sensual sound that made her ear drums tingle. "Which one, little girl?"

"S-School."

He gently started to massage her hand. His touch felt like warm electricity. "I could give you a ride," he offered.

CHAPTER 5

HE LOOKED TO BE about in his late thirties or maybe forties with this Michael Ealy flair, but without the unique eyes. This guy's eyes were dark amber brown, but still made her feel something. He looked happy to see her. He was thickly built, but not fat. A man. A real man talking to her.

"I was born at night, but not last night," she said, moving to stand a foot away from the car. Something had to be wrong with him, because she knew exactly what he was looking at.

He smiled. "Because I see you waiting on the bus and I wanted to offer you a ride?"

Madison turned away, too overwhelmed because he was actually talking to her with sincerity. This wasn't a joke. He didn't lose a bet.

Why?

Why now?

"Hey girl, come on," he urged. "Come back here. We can just talk."

Madison looked back at him and shook her head. Determinedly she said, "I'm not a little girl." Obviously, his vision sucked and he couldn't see her very clearly, but she knew if she got any closer, whatever illusion he saw would fade away and she'd see a familiar look of horror. The hoodie only hid so much. He'd see the bumps and craters, the pimples and redness on her face, then most likely speed away.

"I can't get to know you if you don't come closer," he persisted. "Give me your name if you want me to not call you baby girl."

"I shouldn't talk to strangers," she snipped again.

"I won't be a stranger if you tell me your name. See, it's easy." He touched his broad chest. "I'm called Jamar."

That name definitely didn't sound made up. He was serious! Why did his name sound so sexy? Madison went into panic mode. "I can't do this with you."

"Do what? I haven't suggested anything…yet," he chuckled.

HE WAS FLIRTING?

She stepped back some more. "Please stop it."

"Stop what?"

Madison rolled her eyes. She might as well walk up to the car and get this over with.

Leaning into the window, in a firm tone, she said, "I can't play games with you, sir. Stop what you're doing or think you're doing."

He licked his bottom lip hungrily, not at all bothered by her proximity. "You don't look twenty-eight. You aren't lying about your age?" he questioned skeptically.

There was a teasing light in his mahogany eyes, but she became defensive. "Of course I'm twenty-eight. What purpose would it serve me to lie to you?"

"You're on your way to school, you're carrying a backpack and you just look young."

"Your observation skills suck," she said.

Jamar chortled. "You sound like my brother." He reached out again and covered his hand over hers. "You're really on your way to school?"

That warm electricity pulsed from his palm into her knuckles and flowed up her arm into her body. She became too nervous to speak. She nodded in answer to his question. Being befuddled hardly ever happened to her.

Now he was back to massaging her hand. His touch felt like a warm pulse shuddering through her veins. "I could give you a ride to wherever you want," he offered.

"I-I…I shouldn't. I don't know you."

"You're right," he agreed, and extended his free hand. "I'm Jamar Ross. And you are?"

"Madison…Madison Oliver."

"Well, now we know each other," he said warmly.

She was feeling the pulse quicken. "I'm okay," she said. "I'm fine waiting for the bus here."

"Well, it is a dangerous neighborhood. I saw you the other day and saw lots of cars slowing down to check you out. My god-niece says this isn't a safe neighborhood."

"I can handle myself," she said, faking confidence, although she never remembered any cars slowing down to look at her.

"Well, how about as a friend, I sit right here and wait, and you can just stand right there, huh? Just to make sure you're safe," he suggested.

Madison wondered if he was really just there to keep her safe, but then again, this was kind. The kindest thing any guy had done in a long time.

"Kind of early to be going to school." That skeptical tone was still in his voice.

She pulled her hand away. "I have lab work to do before class."

"I've never seen you around here before this time of year."

"I'm from Grosse Pointe Woods, before my mother died a few years ago."

"That's out by the east side," he noted, slightly impressed. "The upper suburbs, right?"

She never liked to brag that she grew up around wealth, and moving back to Detroit, losing everything felt like the rug had been pulled from under her. "Yes, I grew up there in that area, most of my life. My mother had a rich boyfriend. After she died, when I came home from the funeral, all my things were packed up on the porch waiting for me."

He actually looked devastated on her behalf. "Wow, I'm sorry about that."

She shrugged it off. "Nothing for you to be sorry about. You didn't throw me on the streets and sell all my mother's stuff to pay off her bills. He did."

"Maybe losing her was heartbreaking."

Bitterly, she said, "That wasn't love. He didn't love her. He loved the money she gave him because he didn't have to use his own. Money she worked very hard to make."

"Love, money, sometimes it's all the same thing," he said with a wry smile, trying to make her feel better.

Did he see her pimples? The craters on her face? She wondered because when he looked at her he didn't flinch or try not to look at her face. That was usually the case when guys looked at her. As many times as she had to practice presenting her research in front of people, she could remember everyone's stares.

"Your bus is coming," he said abruptly.

"What?"

"Your bus." He pointed.

So consumed with actually talking with him, she had forgotten about everything else.

"Bye, Madison," he said.

"Madison waved and jogged the short distance to catch her bus. When she got on the bus, she looked back at him. He waved his right hand, but his left hand was inside the car, down in his lap. Now it seemed non-important, but when she had been standing there, where had his other hand been?

Yes, down in his lap.

Why did this seem important now?

The bus pulled away as she sat down, and Jamar watched her the whole time until he couldn't see her anymore.

Would he be there tomorrow? Madison wondered.

CHAPTER 6

"**Y**OU'RE DISTRACTED MORE than normal," her environmental professor, Neville Barfield, observed.

Of course she wasn't going to say it was because of a guy. Instead, she said, "I met the new intern yesterday in the lab."

"New Intern?" he asked confused. "Oh yeah, that guy that…yeah…he said…really strange…he was here?"

The professor seemed flustered.

She answered, "He said he was on the waiting list and finally got in."

"Yeah," the professor said. "He was inquisitive. Too inquisitive."

The professor was always too paranoid about everyone, but Madison really did have a good feeling about Joshua. She didn't think this student was trying to do anything to hurt the project. "He seems as if he's going to do well for us on this project," she assured the professor.

Madison decided to change the subject. "My father needs me to get a job to offset my living cost."

Professor Barfield frowned. "You've taken a full schedule, plus your internship in the lab, and with no car, the time for transportation… How are you supposed to get a job, keep your grades up, do your internship and work on the project? You can't take any more time away from this project, Madison."

She shrugged. "I don't know."

"I see why you're distracted." He sighed. "If I find anything that can work around your schedule, I'll send it your way."

"Thank you, Professor," she said gratefully.

He went back to work and she went back to trying to work.

The project they were working on regarded environmental sustainability due to unstable climates. Her research and work were recognized nationally and she had been given many accolades and rewards for her work even before she had graduated from high school.

Unfortunately, her family really didn't understand how important her work was, or they didn't care. Madison often deluded herself into believing her family just didn't understand the importance of agriculture and how passionate she was about it. She wanted to believe maybe what she was studying was too complex for her family to grasp. So they didn't, due to fear of being confused or bored.

Forcing herself to concentrate, Madison tried to do as much work as possible. In less than four months, she would present to an international committee about plant reproduction. If she could convince them to fund her project, she wouldn't have to worry about getting a job.

But until then, she knew her father couldn't wait that long and wanted money now.

Getting home that night, instead of writing her research up, she had to go to bible study. Her father had ordered that as long as she stayed in the house, she had to fit her schedule around his heavy-attending church schedule.

As frustrating as it was, she found comfort that she could write long hand in the back of the church without her father knowing. Her stepmother would occasionally walk by to spy on Madison to see if she was paying attention, and Madison had to hide her small notepad under her bible so Hazel wouldn't run back to her father and tell on her.

True, this was childish, but she felt her father would forever treat her like a child and not care that she had responsibilities that had nothing to do with family or church. Her mother had understood, but her father couldn't have cared less.

Her thoughts kept straying to Jamar. When she couldn't stop thinking about him, she'd bite her tongue to punish herself.

Work, Madison! Work!

Bible study didn't end until after nine P.M., and they didn't get home until after ten. As usual, Madison stayed up until eleven to type her notes, and she spent another two hours looking up verifying information to support her work.

After showering and preparing for the next day, she finally snuggled down in her bed and closed her eyes.

Through all of this, Jamar was still on her mind. Would he be there again? Why was he interested in her? Why couldn't she stop thinking about him?

Maybe Nikki was right. He could be some weirdo, and maybe Madison needed to stay to herself.

Yet, when Madison awoke the next morning and washed her face, staring back at herself in the mirror were the ugly white pimples, the dark discoloration and the red marks. How could she not think about the quick remedy and wonder if Jamar would help her? For research purposes only.

Getting out of bed was difficult because sleep had not come to her easily that night and her stepmother made her even more late by making her put the garbage out.

Of course, she ended up missing her bus again, but Jamar was parked between the abandoned buildings, smiling as she walked up to him.

"Looks like rain, Madison. You sure you don't want to get inside?" he suggested.

Today, he wore a T-shirt and some loose jogging shorts. She could tell he was fresh out of the shower because she could still smell soap on his skin, even standing two feet away from his open window. His teeth shone like brand new. He looked like he was genuinely happy to see her. She couldn't understand his fascination with her.

"Why me?" she asked.

"Why you for what?" he asked. "I'm being a friend. Making sure no weirdo bothers you," he explained.

"Why do you want to be my friend?" she insisted.

He shrugged. "You look like you needed one and you look like a pretty nice girl."

"I'm not a little girl, Jamar. I'm just about to turn twenty-nine."

"I would agree you're not a little girl," he said.

The sky seemed to open up and rain came down.

He motioned for her to hurry and get in the passenger side, and she didn't hesitate because other than running into an abandoned house, there was no cover.

Once she was ensconced inside his vehicle, she could see him at perfect eye level. His legs were long and she could see the muscles in the arms. Jamar had to be mid-thirties, but she wasn't absolutely sure.

"Do you often stalk girls at bus stops?" she questioned.

He smirked guiltily. "I don't, but my mornings are free and I saw you out there a couple of times when I picked up my god-niece and just wondered..." He let his voice linger, looking at her.

"Wondered about what?" she pressed, listening for the bus, but the pellets of the rain on the car got in the way.

"The other day you were…well, you had on these stockings and pleated skirt, and when the wind whipped about, your side was to me…" His voice wandered off and he smirked wickedly this time.

"What?" she urged.

"You wear those clips on your stockings," he noted.

Madison blushed explaining, "I can't wear full stockings. They make me break out."

"But you can wear them on your legs?"

"Yes, but my thighs and backside will break out." She was becoming more embarrassed, speaking about this to him.

His eyes wandered down to her legs.

She was wearing another heavy polyester pleated skirt with a black top. This was one of her stepmother's old dresses, two sizes too big for her, with lots of safety pins to keep it at least on her shoulders.

"Do you have them on now?" he asked.

Pressing her legs together, she knew answering could take her down a very naughty road. Yet if she didn't, she would never know, and curiosity was killing her.

"I have to wear them," she answered. "Every time I wear a dress or skirt."

"Can I see?" he asked.

"I-I don't think…" She could feel her cheeks burning.

The panic sensation came upon her suddenly.

The bus was coming. It was a perfect time to jump out of the car.

Jamar only waved and, as usual, waited until she was out of sight.

CHAPTER 7

SLUMPING IN HER CHAIR, Madison was definitely more confused about Jamar Ross.

After class, she went to change her clothes in the nearest bathroom. That day was field work, and she would have to get dirty.

Her father hated when women wore pants, but field work required her to get on the ground, so Madison carried extra clothing on those days so she wouldn't come home a mess.

Joshua poked his head in the bathroom while she was in the stall. "Hey, Madison, where's yesterday's analysis for the professor? He wants to look it over while you're out in the field."

"It's in my field bag," she said.

"Where's that?"

Coming out of the stall, tying the scarf around her head, she said, "Over…" Her field bag was not over in the area of all her bags. Retracing her steps, she gasped. Had she left it in HIS car?

Oh no!

Madison paced for a minute, knowing she still had to get the analysis to the professor, but she didn't want anyone knowing she had lost work important to this project. The professor was already too paranoid. "Can you go on the computer and access the Cloud documents? I updated it on the server last night."

"I haven't gotten my passcode yet," he said disappointedly.

She really didn't have time to print all that out again, and she needed to think about the fact that she had lost her field bag in some stranger's car. How stupid could she be?

Coming out of the bathroom, Joshua followed her back to the lab where she avoided bumping into the professor to get to the computer. Signing into the server and getting to the files, she turned to Joshua. "Can you just wait while these print off and give them to the professor, so I won't miss the transport to get out on the field?"

"No problem," he said happily. "That's why I'm here."

"And don't forget to sign me off," she warned as she left the room to run to the transport that would take her and other interns to the field.

She heard Joshua yell out, "Don't worry, I'll leave it in his basket."

She wasn't worried about that anymore. Now she was consumed with never seeing her field bag again.

It was so hard to concentrate while she worked out in the field that evening because all she thought about was Jamar looking through her bag. What if he took her reports and used them?

Impossible!

Ninety percent of people didn't even know what those analyses were, unless they were familiar with her work. In the hands of someone like Nikki, yes, those reports could be dangerous. They'd studied together and albeit, Nikki may have not been book smart, she could still access what those reports could mean.

Also, a stranger with too much free time named Jamar!

***

The next morning, Madison needed to scramble out of the house as quietly as possible.

Her father had texted her late the previous night while she was on the bus and asked how was the job search was going, and whether he could expect any money in the next couple of weeks.

Madison wanted to scream. The stress of living with her father had increased exponentially with the demand to get a job, and now her field bag… gone!

Damn her curiosity!

Getting to the bus stop, she didn't even look to see if the bus was coming. She was looking for the Lincoln.

The bus passed her by, but she didn't care as her eyes landed on the Lincoln sitting between the two abandoned buildings.

Madison walked up to the driver's side of the car and Jamar put the field bag out the window with a smirk on his face.

"Thank you," she said gratefully, taking it.

"If I didn't know better, I thought you left it in the car to guarantee I'd see you today, just when I thought you never wanted to see me again."

She blurted out, "I really didn't want to see you again."

"Then I definitely deserve a reward," he said disappointedly.

"I don't have any money."

Jamar patted the seat beside him inside of the car. "Then we should discuss the terms of another reward, Ms. Madison Oliver."

She had missed the bus, so she knew she had time before the next one came. Sliding in the passenger next to him, she wondered, had she really left the bag on purpose, subconsciously, just to see him again?

He wore the same thing as the day before, but a different T-shirt with the name *Ross Groceries* on the right side of his upper chest, where the ridges of his muscles were defined. She wondered if he had ripples in his stomach…

Stop that!

He's a stranger.

But he looked like a healthy specimen!

Stop that!

Dang, her thoughts!

"What reward, Jamar?" she inquired.

His eyes looked down at her legs.

She wore a thick green shirt with a matching blouse and light jacket underneath her coat. Again, another hand-me-down from her stepmother, and with her hair pulled back in afro puffs, she most likely looked like a dizzy little girl. He couldn't possibly see her as a woman.

Because of how badly it exacerbated her acne, Madison wasn't a makeup girl, and although her ears were pierced she rarely wore earrings.

He had the heat on in the car and the temperature was becoming hell-hot, even on the low setting. She unzipped her jacket to give herself some air to combat the sweating that had started.

His expressive amber almond eyes hungrily looked at her thighs.

"Why is seeing my garters so important?" she questioned.

"You don't see that type of underwear on a woman often, let alone a black woman these days. It's a rarity, but when I was ten there was this neighbor, Ms. Kelso, and she would get in and out of her car across the street from my house all the time. Beautiful older woman with young features. She'd open the car door and her dress would be hiked up past her knees, and I could see her garters. I used to kill myself trying to look at her whenever she got home. I'd jerk off that night, wishing she'd call me over to help with her groceries, and then just as she was getting out the car, she'd let me put my hand on her bare thigh."

Never in her life had any man ever told her a fantasy. She knew men had them and loved to fulfill them, but no one man had ever confessed something so personal to her.

For some reason, she felt closer to Jamar for his erotic revelation and honesty.

That had been a very deep secret confession. "Did Ms. Kelso ever let you touch her?"

"Nah," he said with more disappointment, but trying to keep casual. "My younger brother told me she died in my second year of college, from breast cancer."

Madison looked around nervously. "What if someone walks by here and sees me?" she asked. "Aren't you worried?"

He smirked wickedly as if he'd thought of this already. "I've got tinted windows. No one can see in if they walked by, except through the front. Plus, no one comes this way, over by these buildings," he assured her, shifting in her direction.

Madison looked around worriedly once again. This was insane, but his request seemed salaciously fun.

She put all her bags at her feet and then put her fingers at the hem of her skirt. What could it hurt? She was grown. He was grown. Nothing could possibly happen any further, right?

CHAPTER 8

HER FINGERS DIDN'T MOVE from the hem, and she almost liked the way his eyes danced about in expectation.

"You sure this is what you want as your reward?" she asked.

He nodded, gripping the steering wheel column so tightly, the leather cover seemed to scream in agony.

Madison convinced herself no harm ever came from just looking as she started raise her skirt one centimeter at a time. His eyes danced in delight as each piece under her stockings were revealed and she was finding herself breathless, watching his serious arousal. The physical science behind her body's own arousal intrigued her and made her wonder more about this stranger and the possibilities.

She wasn't a virgin. The worst night of her sexual life was when she gave up her virginity painfully to a boy at school she thought liked her, but later found out he had just taken pity on her. When she came home from the encounter, it was to meet the police leaving her house to tell her that her mother was dead.

She had tried a second time when hanging with Nikki, who had brought some guys. Nikki thought plying Madison with a lot of alcohol would make her easy, but it only made Madison depressed. She still went along with the encounter and just allowed the boy to rut on top of her, glad there was a condom protecting her and keeping them from really touching. When he was done, he got up immediately, put his pants back on, and just left her.

Other than those two encounters, Madison's sex life had been about masturbation, and once on a horse as the saddle rode against her body.

Now she was here, with a stranger. How far was this going to go?

Madison raised her skirt slowly, trying to overcome her own embarrassment as each centimeter was revealed. Soon her skirt was bunched around her waist, and he could see everything.

His eyes went from her mid-thigh black stockings, red garters and even a peek at her white grandma underwear.

Maybe she should have worn something else, but how was she to have planned something like this?

She continued to raise her dress slowly, loving the heightened look of adoration on his face. Was she crazy?

No, she was sane and feeling amazing. Was it because of his arousing visual caress?

Jamar looked at her as if she were the most beautiful woman in the world. His face glowed in amazement and she thought she saw his lip tremble.

Yet, she had to be realistic, and this was a man she had only known less than twenty-fours, and now he was seeing parts of her hardly anyone had ever seen—that included the sorry guys she had slept with. They hadn't paid any attention to her thighs at all.

"Are you okay?" she asked, concerned, when it looked as if Jamar might've stopped breathing.

"Yes…" He cleared his throat. "Thank you," he said, appreciative.

The tease in her came from out of nowhere as she asked, "Would you like to touch them?"

Jamar looked as if he was about to pass out. There was sweat on his brow. "Can I? Are you sure?"

Madison reached over and pried his hands off of the steering wheel to lay them on her knee. Now his hand definitely trembled. His palm seemed incredibly hot on her skin despite the thick layer of stockings between his hand and her flesh.

Slowly, his hand started to ascend without her encouragement, moving over each side and even underneath, as if he were trying to remember every millimeter of skin. He licked his lips greedily, which made it her turn to tremble as she envisioned him using his lips and tongue instead of his hand on her thighs.

This was so naughty, but she felt like Little Red Riding Hood being held hostage by the wolf. An animalistic nature radiated from him, touched her soul, and she was almost powerless to stop him.

Yet, as his hand moved past her middle thigh, alarms screamed in her head as if there was a point of no return and he was almost there.

Jamar met her eyes, and she knew he could see her fear, but it wasn't fear of him. Madison was fearful of what she might do.

"You're beautiful," he said.

Coming completely to reality, she rolled her eyes in disbelief.

"What was that for?" he asked.

"My thighs are beautiful," she corrected him.

"No, your thighs are sexy as hell, Madison. You, as a person, are beautiful."

She snorted, not believing one word, and moved his hand back to his lap with clear disinterest. His verbal dishonesty was too much for her. "You don't have to lie to me to get me to do things, Jamar."

He looked shocked, and then had the nerve to look insulted. "I mean what I say Madison." His tone was filled with sternness. "When I look at you I see a beautiful woman. Why do you have a problem with that?"

Madison shifted in her seat, completely uncomfortable now, but she decided to be honest with him. "Because I see my face every day and I know what I see."

"Come over here," he ordered, patting the space right next to him.

Hesitantly, she scooted over. With this being an older vehicle, there was nothing between them. Not even an arm rest came down.

When she was right beside him, he put his arm over her shoulder, pulling her even closer, while his other hand pulled down the mirror in front of him.

"Beauty is in the eye of the beholder, Madison, and though you may have heard this before, you really should believe it. Your innocence, heart and soul shines through, enhancing your perfect nose, luscious lips, and just about the most beautifully expressive eyes I've ever seen on a woman."

She looked away from the mirror and looked at him. "You must know a lot of ugly women to speak so eloquently about beauty, Jamar."

"No, Madison," he said as he held her hand. "But I can see you haven't been told enough how beautiful you really are."

"That's just evidence that I'm not that beautiful."

He looked flabbergasted. "What makes you think you're ugly?"

"My face," she said obviously. "My skin. My pimples."

"That's all cosmetic. Fixable. Just a matter of finding the right regiment and products."

Rolling her eyes, she said, "I've tried everything. Up until my mother's death, she tried everything too and was going to take me to this guy in Canada, but we needed the money for her medical bills. I was hoping I could get my own insurance, but it's too costly and I need the money for school. No insurance plan I can find covers a dermatology visit in full. But if my grant goes through, I'll be able to really pay off anything for my face, get my own place, and finally live." Madison fidgeted nervously, because she had never discussed her skin condition and how much she hated it, except with her mother. Suddenly from her lips, she burst out, "But I found a low-cost natural method."

CHAPTER 9

JAMAR AT FIRST LOOKED AS if he wanted to suggest something else, but at her statement, his look changed to curiosity.

"Really?" he asked, raising a brow. "What method?"

She almost wanted to bite her tongue for even thinking of saying this out loud to man she barely knew. "Well, it's a stupid idea," she said, shying away.

"Oh no, you have to tell me," he insisted. "You've fully piqued my curiosity on this."

She caved. "I was doing research on products used to make skin healthy and strong," she said, twisting her hands together. "There's a lot of bull crap out there and I remember a lot of times my mother was spinning her wheels on what worked and didn't work…well, I read that a man's semen prevents skin conditions like mine."

Jamar stared at her for a long moment, and then asked, "Would that be internally or externally?"

Blushing to high heaven, she responded, "I don't know. I see it a lot in expensive skin creams–really expensive creams, but when I read more about it, it looks like you have to buy a lot of it and use it religiously for it to work." She sighed in disappointment. "I barely have two cents to rub together for transportation now, let alone get money for cream for my face."

"And I guess no boyfriend, either, to help with the supply?" he surmised, smirking.

"Of course not, plus if I did get that kind of money, I'd have to give it straight to my father, so I'll have a place to stay for a couple of months, so I won't have to get a job. He doesn't care that I have classes, research and grant endowment field study."

"And does he know this? Does your father understand how really busy you are?" Jamar asked, concerned.

It was really nice to speak to someone about her problems without them cutting her off and starting to focus on themselves, which is usually what Nikki did, making Madison feel like her problems didn't mean anything. "I've mentioned my schedule in passing, but honestly, I'm coming to the realization that I don't think he cares. It's just about him and making his new wife happy, which means making me miserable. As long as I go to church at least four times a week, he couldn't really care less about me."

"Care less? Four days? That sounds like a job. I'm shocked you can afford that much time to do something like that."

"I really can't," she admitted, pushing her skirt all the way down to her knees. "That's why most times, I'm exhausted in the morning and miss the bus because I stay up so late with research and making notes."

"So how do you plan on acquiring semen, if you could?" he asked.

She was speechless, unsure of how to respond to him. "I don't know. I haven't thought that far into the idea of even being able to obtain any."

"But you've thought about obtaining it. You did the research."

"That's because I do love to research and discover how to do things feasibly. In this case, I didn't think when doing the research that a specimen would be hard to obtain, if I...well, if I asked someone. There are a million men out in the world; I'm sure not all of them want to keep it all to themselves."

"Were you asking me for mine?"

Could she blush anymore before exploding? "I-I haven't thought that far."

"Ah, but you did think of asking me." This wasn't a question, but a statement.

"It crossed my mind," she admitted.

He stretched his arm over the back of the seat. "And what benefit would I get, allowing you to procure my sample?"

"Are you healthy?" she questioned suspiciously. "Healthy, in not just no STDs, but health-wise."

"Pretty healthy. Low cholesterol, blood pressure, but maybe a slice of German Chocolate Cake every once in a while. What are my benefits, Madison?" he demanded to know.

"You'd be helping a friend?" she tried.

He chuckled. "You're my friend now?" Jamar rubbed his chin. "This sounds like another reward."

"Really?" she asked incredulously.

Before Madison could say anything else, he said, "Your bus is coming."

Reluctantly, she gathered her bags and jumped out of the car.

He said before she got on the bus, "I'll know tomorrow what reward I'll collect from you once I find you a suitable job."

She rolled her eyes again and got on the bus. His reward system today had certainly done things to her biologically.

Her panties were drenched and her heart was still strangely palpitating. None of which had ever happened to her before.

Getting to school, Madison went about her day in a haze. She arrived home late, and despite her father's irritation at her lack of participation at the bible study he held Thursday nights in his home, she wasn't fazed.

She was really just distracted about the idea of using real sperm for her skin regime.

That night she really went to work on the research to know how to obtain a viable specimen, how would she utilize it, and what other ingredients she would need?

The idea that, after she got the specimen, her plan might actually work, made her eager to see Jamar the next day.

Unfortunately, when she arrived at the bus stop early the next morning, Jamar was nowhere to be seen. She even let the bus go by but he never showed up.

Getting to campus again, her Friday was altogether different from the previous day. Now she was agitated and touchy. She couldn't get out of her field work fast enough to get home and get her mind off of not seeing him.

Before leaving, she'd grabbed some items from the supply closet. Hauling everything home was a struggle, but once she was in her room, setting up made her giddy.

It was almost like before when she had first come into her grant project at the beginning. The research, the potential of working, and the possibility of failure stirred her to happiness. She actually had a goal in mind instead of turning her wheels trying to figure out why everything didn't work. All she needed was the specimen.

Maybe she was rushing things in her head and becoming too wrapped up in all the attention Jamar was raining down on her. She wasn't logically seeing this through.

Nikki would have told her she was foolish and stupid to have gotten in the car with a complete stranger and then to reveal all her business to him was even more stupid. Her father would have outright beat her. Her mother would have just scolded her and said she was weak, just like her. That was something Madison never wanted to be compared with.

All weekend, Madison got to think over not seeing Jamar again, and she forced herself to put her brain in check, keeping her emotions out of it. This also gave her time to think over the new project–something she had not done in a long time. Since high school, she'd worked on her initial project. It was what had paid for most of her college and gotten her the recognition. Yet, the idea of working on something new made her feel so alive.

She spent most of her weekend getting the formula together. If she could economically replicate the expensive creams using all natural ingredients, she could clear up her face in six months' time. She'd even calculated how much sperm she would need.

"One point five what?" Hazel asked in annoyance, slamming the refrigerator door.

Madison was sitting in the kitchen to get some air, hoping her stepmother was out with her church ladies, since it was Sunday evening.

"I was just whispering out a calculation," Madison said.

"Do it quieter. No one wants to hear that stupid drabble." She grabbed her purse off the counter. "I forgot my purse. Your dad is in his study and he said under no circumstances to bother him."

Her father usually stayed in his office Sundays after church, and no one ever went in there unless they were ordered to.

"Yes, ma'am," Madison said obediently, but even as she spoke, a sour feeling in her gut came upon her; even the sweet orange juice she sipped didn't make that feeling go away. Though she had been concentrating on her new project and her old project, in the back of her head for the past couple of days was that living at her father's home was really not conducive to her sanity, nor her happiness.

Being stuck was frustrating, and all she hoped was that she got her grant and moved as far away as possible.

Hazel left, but Madison no longer wanted to be in the kitchen anymore, and decided to adjourn to her room.

She walked out of the kitchen just as her father's study door opened, and Nikki walked out, applying lipstick.

CHAPTER 10

"HEY YOU," NIKKI SAID, as if she wanted to bump into Madison, while closing the door quickly to Cyrus's study.

"I didn't know you were here," Madison said, holding all her work close to her so Nikki wouldn't see.

"I just arrived and you know your father." Nikki rolled her eyes and mimicked Cyrus. *"Don't corrupt my daughter* speech ensued."

"Oh," Madison said, and continued up to her room where she could put her research down.

Nikki looked around as if she hadn't been there in a while. "You bring your work home now?"

Madison was too embarrassed to tell Nikki exactly what she was working on. "No, I just started a side project. Something personal."

"Would you like to go shopping with me?" Nikki asked.

It wasn't odd for Nikki to ask Madison to go shopping with her.

"I need some makeup," Nikki announced. "And I hate going to that Mac counter by myself."

Madison would rather stay home. "Why would I go with you? I don't even wear makeup."

Nikki shrugged. "I just want company, Maddie. Just go ask your father. I know how he feels Sunday is so holy and made a big thing last time you went out on a Sunday with me."

Madison sighed, feeling like a child, hating her life in this house, and Nikki followed her back downstairs. Cyrus was coming out of his office, adjusting his tie. His eyes went to Nikki first before he looked sternly at his daughter.

"Dad, Nikki needs me to go help her at the makeup counter," Madison said. "I didn't want you to blow your cap like last time."

"It's just the two of you?" he asked.

"Yes, sir," Nikki said with an over-exaggeration of good girl.

He looked at Madison distrustfully. "You know curfew is ten, right? It's a school night."

"Yes, Father," Madison answered obediently, feeling that sour feeling in her gut again.

Nikki grabbed Madison's arm and dragged out of the house.

When they were getting in the car, putting on the seatbelts, Nikki said, "They really treat you like a child. I don't know how you can be so respectful all the time." Nikki started driving. "I wouldn't be able to put up with that man or even how you put up living in that house."

Stating the obvious, not really wanting to get into this with Nikki, Madison said, "Unlike you, I don't have a choice where can I live. I have to make do with what I have."

Madison also wasn't in the mood to hear Nikki brag about the apartment her father was funding her.

"Oh, boy," Nikki said, surprised. "You're snippy today, Madison. What's gotten into you?"

"Just tired," Madison said, refusing to apologize for what she said or her attitude. "I've been working really long hours, trying to prepare for the presentation for the endowment."

Nikki actually looked concerned. "Do you think you'll be ready?"

"There's still a lot of field work I want to accomplish to solidify the project. The professor said if we can accomplish it, we've got more than enough to get the endowment, but you what a perfectionist I am."

"And an overachiever," Nikki teased. "You know, if you need some new insight, I don't mind looking anything over."

Madison knew Nikki had chosen the same field of study as she had. It was as if Nikki was trying to be her.

Choosing the same course of study, Nikki had applied for the same scholarships as Madison, especially large and prestigious ones, and somehow, Nikki had mysteriously won.

"It's hard to keep up with you anymore, Madison, but you are such a sweet person and very hardworking," Nikki complimented her.

This was odd for Nikki, but Madison didn't point that out. "Thanks, Nikki."

"I bet you still keep your flash drives in your bag, Ms. Overachiever."

Now she didn't know if Nikki was being complimentary or secretly making fun of her.

Smiling guiltily, Madison admitted, "I never know when I might find a way to work, being out and about."

Nikki chuckled in agreement. "Never know." They had arrived at the mall, and Nikki diverted to a small store selling women's casual clothes.

Madison noticed it had long dresses her father would approve of.

"Go ahead and get something for your birthday," Nikki urged her. "Since it's coming up, I can spot you a couple of them."

Madison hadn't gotten new clothes in so long, she quickly picked up a couple of dresses and went into the dressing room. It wasn't unusual that Nikki came in, because since high school Madison had always joined her when Nikki tried on clothes.

They talked a lot about college life for Nikki. Of course, Nikki was the life of the campus and all the girls were jealous of her.

"There's only one girl in my study group who thinks she knows it all. I can't stand her," Nikki sneered as Madison pulled a dress over her head.

"Do I know her?" Madison inquired.

"Nah, she went to some Detroit public school, but her parents were loaded so she walks around and acts like a martyr for public school systems. I don't even see how anyone could possibly learn anything or know anything coming from the Detroit Public School system. Her name even makes me want to throw up. *Mercy*." Nikki made a gagging noise. "She reminds me of you. She's a little shy, but she has this street confidence. It's weird. Make her mad and she turns into a bitch."

"Kinda like you," Madison teased.

Nikki shifted uncomfortably. "Yeah, but she's worse. She's like a Jekyll and Hyde. On top of that, she has this best friend that sticks by her like white on rice, named Pheare."

"That's a pretty name."

Nikki sneered. "Pretty deadly. She's also from Detroit and looks like she'll cut you in a heartbeat."

Madison was tempted to tell Nikki about Jamar, but changed her mind and just kept their talk all about Nikki—as usual.

Nikki used her father's credit card to purchase everything, and an hour later returned Madison home.

Eager to get back to her research, Madison went to her room and dug in her purse to get her flash drive, but when she couldn't find the little coin purse she always kept her flash drives in, she started to panic.

Running to the house phone, where her sister was hogging it, talking to some friends on a three way, Madison had to wait an extra ten minutes before her sister finally got off. She called Nikki.

The first three times there was no answer, but the fourth time Nikki finally answered.

"What's up?"

"Did I leave anything in your car?" Madison asked apprehensively.

"Um, no, I don't see anything."

Her stomach felt like it was about to drop out of her body. "Please look around, Nikki. I lost something."

"Oh, wait. I see a coin purse. An ugly green coin purse."

Sighing in relief, Madison said, "Can you bring that back? Please, it's important."

"Let me stop for gas and I'll be back."

Madison didn't say anything, even though she had noticed Nikki still had a full tank when she had been dropped off after shopping. Maybe Nikki just wanted a full tank.

Maybe.

Almost an hour later, Nikki pulled in the driveway, and Madison ran out to the car.

"I was almost home, you know," Nikki said grudgingly. "But I know how important your work is. Sorry it took so long, but I met this cute guy at the gas station, though, so thanks." She flicked her hair back.

Madison thanked her and took her coin purse. When she went back inside, her father was standing at the door.

"You shouldn't be outside this late," he scolded.

"I left my stuff in Nikki's car, Father…" She was immediately silenced by the slap on her face.

"I didn't ask for an explanation or any backtalk, girl."

Her senses were still rocked, and it took everything inside her not to cry.

"I just want to hear two words," her father demanded.

"Yes, sir," she said in a shaky voice.

"Did you find a job yet?"

"No, sir."

"No more Nikki visits until you are gainfully employed, Madison. Now get to your room," he ordered.

She hadn't eaten dinner, but she wasn't going to backtalk or say anything, terrified her father would discipline her again.

When she was younger and came over for visits, he would discipline her by putting her over his knee, pulling down her panties, and spanking her butt.

Cyrus did it so much, she thought that was actually how he showed his love, because it seemed the only way to get his attention.

Madison had thought she was too old now to be disciplined, but that slap to her face reminded her there were other ways her father could make her obey; ways she wouldn't like and maybe worse than a slap on her behind.

Getting to her room and digging into her research, Madison tried not to remind herself she was hungry or to think about Jamar.

That night, when she lay in bed, her thoughts returned to him and his hands on her thighs. He'd looked at her garters like he wanted to tear them off with his teeth.

To make herself feel better and to help her sleep, she moved her hands between her legs and manipulated herself to pleasure.

All the while thinking of Jamar, the way he licked his lips, the way his touch made her shudder and the way he looked at her... looked at her... looked ... at... her!

Yes, she came quietly, burying her face in her pillow so no one would hear.

Her face still hurt, but sleep finally came.

CHAPTER 11

HER THOUGHTS WERE already occupied when she awoke Monday morning. Madison dressed quietly, as usual, but when she came downstairs, intending to grab something out of the refrigerator, she heard her father in the kitchen, fiddling around.

He didn't hear her because he was on the phone.

Madison found it odd, as he was usually never up that early, and it sounded like he was looking through the cabinets. She approached the kitchen, not bothering to turn on any lights. She was worried about getting caught eavesdropping.

"How would I know, or even care about anything like that? She does what she wants to do, as long as she obeys the rules of my house."

Madison couldn't stop listening now, because she knew her father was speaking about her.

"I don't care… No, you need this… Listen I'm really getting tired of bending over backwards for you. Who the fuck cares? The woman is dead and gone, and so is all the money. Hazel went through it like she was drowning. There's nothing else to pay you."

Whom was he talking to?

"I'm going to forget this conversation ever happened, and if you know what's good for you, you'll get whatever you need, however you're used to getting it, and stop thinking you can just use people to get what you want."

Madison heard his voice getting close to her, and she backed away.

Moving to the front door, she waited a moment before leaving, disappointed that she had not gotten anything to eat.

She wondered whom her father had been talking to and why had he mentioned her mother's money, just like that older woman from her parents' past had done. Where could she find out about her mother's estate? It had to be public?

She made a mental note to look into this when she was at the lab that day.

There was still the problem of getting a job, and she was confused as to how she was going to find something with less hours, easy to get to, and then work around her busy schedule.

She came around the corner to see the Lincoln parked alongside the abandoned townhouses.

She tried hard not to look happy to see him or to run too quickly the car.

He was smiling brightly. "You mind missing your bus for me, beautiful?"

The new nickname caught her off-guard.

Madison got in the car with him.

"I'm mesmerized by what I see," Jamar said, leaning over and hugging her.

She hadn't been expecting him to press his body against hers, but damn if he didn't smell like fresh soap and evergreens.

"What was that for?" she questioned when he drew away.

"I'm sorry. I actually really missed you. I know what you're going to say, Madison. We haven't known each other long enough to really miss each other, but I found my thoughts kept drifting and I'm not a drifter." He looked down at her skirt, and she saw him shift again.

"You thought of my thighs," she teased him. "Not me."

He shrugged, blushing. "I occasionally thought of your thighs and the treat you offered me last time, but honestly, I thought about you. I haven't been mesmerized by someone in a long time. You're smart, funny and–"

She put a finger on his lips, knowing he was going to say 'beautiful' again.

This time he took her fingers from her lips and held her hand. "I didn't come by on Friday to see you, because I got caught up at work. My godbrother and I opened up a pop-up grocery shop and one of the carts broke. I run maintenance and it was a bigger job than I thought. Damn the potholes in Detroit."

"Oh, wow. That sounds fun. The pop-up shop, not the pothole."

"Yeah, but it's a lot of hard work," he said. "You miss me?"

"No," she lied, and giggled.

He shifted his weight again. "I was also working on your stuff, too, over the weekend."

"My stuff?" she asked, confused.

"Well, you mentioned you needed a job, and I had to think of a way for you to reward me." His eyes moved down briefly to her thighs again. "I love your rewards."

"I can't reward you if you haven't done anything," she said sternly. The man was incorrigible. She couldn't believe how much he had enjoyed looking at her thighs. Did he actually want to look at them again?

The bus slowed down in front of them, then continued on without her.

She still had time to decide whether to get out of there, once the second bus came to take her to school on time.

"What do you have for me?" she asked, getting back on subject.

"How good are you with your hands?" he questioned.

"Very good. I'm always gardening, cleaning and-"

He cut her off. "You like to garden?"

"Yes," she said excitedly. "I'm somewhat majoring in it."

"Seriously? Because my god brother just bought a new house for this girl he's been trying to catch. I think she's got his mind twisted, but so what. I want him to be happy" He looked away, as if debating something internally, and then said, "So you'd be okay working in a greenhouse? Cleaning it up? Doing actual gardening there?"

"Yes," she said eagerly.

"My god brother can pay you fifty dollars for five hours a week. It doesn't matter when you choose to work, but he'd like some progress at least by the end of the summer. He said he's trying to surprise this girl who works with plants."

Odd that his god brother was dating someone who worked with plants, just like her, but Madison didn't dwell too much on that thought.

Reviving a greenhouse would make a great addition to her portfolio and a perfect job for her. "So where is it located?"

"Out in Grosse Pointe, edge of Detroit."

This was becoming more and more of a dream come true. Fate was finally smiling down on her. She was familiar with the city where she had grown up.

"Will transportation be a problem?" Jamar questioned.

"Sometimes," she admitted. "Getting there from campus could be challenging depending on the day."

"Here's the address and the key to the greenhouse. My cell number is on there. I get done with work after four in the afternoon, so give me a call if you need a ride. I'm usually far west and head past the campus to get home on the east side."

She asked, "Why are you being so nice to me?"

Jamar smiled wickedly. "Maybe I want more rewards."

CHAPTER 12

BITING HER LIP NERVOUSLY, Madison was at a loss. She saw the intensity on his face and couldn't believe how responsive her body became to his needs. "Would you like your reward now, for helping me get a job?"

The lustful twinkle shone in his eyes. "I think raising your skirt is just a portion of a reward, for obtaining you a job. Don't you think?"

Incredulously, she asked, "Are you negotiating rewards, Jamar?"

He chuckled, unabashed by his proposal. "I am also in charge of customer contracts in our company. Two years of contact law, woman. I didn't take the bar though, so this is all unofficial between you and me."

She was impressed. "I can agree that raising my dress is a meager payment for helping me get a job, but any other rewards have to be approved."

"Wow. Approved? You are a negotiator also."

She downplayed her skills. "I wish I was better. I'm just cautious."

A small flinch came over his face, right before he looked at the clock. "I'll agree to that, but before we go on, are you going to give me the first part of my reward?"

She giggled nervously, then started to raise her skirt. He caught her hands.

"Wait," he said. "Can I?"

Alarms went off in her head, but she really wanted to see how he would raise her skirt.

Yes, in the back of her head, she wondered what Jamar's deal was. Did he just go around and act this perverted with anyone? Or was this all about her? She was dying to know, but she wouldn't ask…not right now.

Madison nodded, giving him permission.

Jamar reached the end of her mid-calf-length skirt and slowly raised it up over her leg, to her knees. He paused for just a moment, took a deep breath, and then continued raising the skirt up her thighs. His breathing increased the higher her skirt moved. He gasped, finally seeing the top of her garter.

When her skirt was past her garter straps, midway up her thighs, she put her hand on top of his to stop his ascent. His eyes meet hers, disappointment clearly reflected.

"You are driving me crazy, Madison," he whispered. "I like that."

She laughed. "I told you, I'm cautious."

"But also curious, I see," he noted. "That could be a good thing for me."

"You do keep me guessing," she pointed out. "Is that what you like, Jamar?"

He smirked. "I like a lot of things. Things I shouldn't. I don't want to scare you." He still had his hands on her thighs, where her skirt had stopped. He squeezed. "You made me remember things I haven't felt in a long time."

He closed his eyes and took a deep breath, shifting uncomfortably. "Do you want your sample now?"

The question threw her for a loop. She hadn't expected him to bring up what they had discussed the previous week.

"There's a lot involved with getting a sample," she said, reaching in her bag and retrieving her collecting kit she had stolen from the lab.

"Look," he stated, becoming businesslike. "I'm clean. I just had a doctor's visit and got a clean bill of health." He raised his arm to show her a puncture mark proudly. "I even got a blood test for you. I thought you were loony, but I looked up what you said on the Internet. You're still little crazy, but I can see the meaning to your madness if you're good at this science stuff."

"And how would I collect your sample?"

He spread his arms out resting on the back of the seat. "I have a suspicion you've never done this before by that blatant blush on your face."

Could she blush any harder?

Turning away slightly to compose herself, Madison thought everything was becoming insane, yet at the same time this was exactly what she wanted. "No, I've never requested sperm from a man. Most times I'm extracting a necessary sample from an inhuman source with a very large needle."

"That doesn't sound enjoyable," he teased. "You'll first have learn my body, won't you? Otherwise, I don't think you'll get a good sample."

"Couldn't we… I mean, a cup should do it, and returning it to me…right?" she asked, flustered, picking up the cup from the kit.

"The fresher the sample is secured, the better, and since this IS your experiment, you should retrieve the sample to make sure you get it right."

How could he make so much sense?

Why couldn't she think straight?

Jamar added, "Plus, it's the other part of my reward. I think I should enjoy giving you the sample."

"Here?" she questioned frantically, looking around. "Won't someone see us?"

"My windows are tinted, Madison," he reminded her.

He reached over and gently took her hand. "No one will see a thing. Now close your eyes, before you have a panic attack."

Madison hesitated, but decided to trust him. He moved her hand towards him.

"I'm only doing this," he explained, "because you are too tense to do this with your eyes open, and you could hurt me."

How could he know that?

It was true. She was very tense, and she had to fight to keep her hand relaxed in order for him to be able to control her.

She could stop him. At any second, she could stop him and say no, that this wasn't what she wanted.

Yet, it was. Not just for the new project, but because she wanted the distraction of this sexual encounter to get her mind off of her own world. When she was with Jamar, everything else that was happening to her didn't matter, and she needed that.

She needed him. His attention. His eyes on her. His voice talking to her. The touch of him… the touch… his touch… her touching him…

Madison had to lean over to follow her arm. "W-what are you doing?" she asked.

"You're going to touch me and listen to my voice. Open your palm."

Was she too young to have a heart attack? Trying to sound like she knew what she was doing, she said, "I'm not a virgin, Jamar. I've touched… you know, a penis before."

He chortled. "I don't doubt it. But have you ever used your hand to pleasure a man until he came?"

"No," she said, insulted. "I don't go around giving hand jobs."

"If you want a decent sample you need to get it right, correct? You need to know how to get the sample from me. No man is the same. I know I'm different."

There he went, making sense again.

Her eyes were still closed, and he was still holding her hand.

"Are you ready?" he questioned.

She really did want this, but at the same time, felt she should turn back. Yet, not only curiosity was fueling this agenda, but the potential of obtaining the sample she needed.

"Yes," she acquiesced, forcing herself to relax and scooting closer to him.

She remembered her skirt was still hiked, and started to use her free to straighten her clothes.

"Stop that," he reprimanded her. "I do need visual aid. At least give me that, Madison."

She moved her hand away from her skirt and nodded. Taking a deep breath, she said, "Show me, Jamar."

CHAPTER 13

J AMAR TOOK HER HAND firmly and began to guide her toward him. She held her breath until she felt her fingertips touch the warmness of him.

Immediately, she snatched her hand away.

"I can't. I can't!" she said covering her eyes. "This is so wrong."

She could hear him adjusting something, but then it was quiet. Slowly, she peeked between her fingers and looked over at him. He looked relaxed, his long arm stretched out on the back of the seat, while his other rested on the steering column. His pants were closed, and she relaxed too, putting her hands down in her lap.

Noticing her skirt was still up, she pushed that down too. It wasn't going to happen, even though deep down inside, she wanted it to.

"You're thinking too much," he said calmly.

"Of course, I am. I'm over thinking this," she reprimanded herself. "I can't understand anything that's going on."

"What don't you understand?"

"Why are you doing this?" she blurted out.

"You want the truth, or just something to make you feel good?"

She paused, hesitating. "The truth?"

"Are you asking or telling me?"

"Telling," she responded determinedly.

He shifted his weight again. "Fine, I'll tell you the truth. I have lots of problems. Successful as I am in business, I'm fucked personally."

Now she was more confused about Jamar, and a little bit frightened. "You aren't a serial killer, are you?"

"Afraid not, and that's not good. At least if I were one, I'd only have one wrong thing with me instead of many."

"What's wrong with you?"

He looked away for a moment. "I've never told anyone, except my brother. Why I need to tell you... well, I think I should."

Madison didn't know if she wanted to know, but of course, her curiosity was insanely powerful. "Tell me," she insisted.

Jamar looked at her seriously. "I used to have a problem. A sort of sexual hang-up. I mean, I still do, but I was ... am, trying to get control of everything."

Not understand his flustered, garbled explanation, she asked, "You're going to have to be a little more specific. What type of sexual hang-up did you have?"

"Well, I mentioned my god brother, right?"

She nodded.

"Jason's parents died when he was young. Prior to this, I was never... well, my mother never was fond of me. My father was abusive. He died when I was five in the same accident that killed Jason's parents. My mother adopted him and ... well, she loved him like the son I couldn't be to her, because I reminded her so much of my father."

That was just awful; worse than her situation.

"Except," Jamar said, "she loved him more than just a son. When he was thirteen, she went up into his room and... well, she didn't know I was in the closet, because I'd sneak in his room after bedtime and play games with him. She... she...touched him and then got on top of him. You know, sexually, and I watched the whole thing. And the next time, and the next time."

Madison was shocked, but also felt a closer to Jamar for revealing this to her. "Did he tell?" she asked, also feeling a little closer to Jason even though she had never met him.

"Tell who? We didn't know who to tell, and we didn't know how really wrong it was. She was the only parental unit we had. Without her, we didn't know what was going to happen to us. My mother was this powerful force in the city. A philanthropist to the arts and sciences and... we didn't know what to do."

"You always watched."

"She caught me," he said guiltily. "The fourth time, she caught me. In the middle of being on top of him, she suddenly got off of him, came right to the closet, and dragged me out. Pushed me down in a chair and slapped me hard."

"She punished you, and she was the one who was wrong," Madison said incredulously.

"She saw I was affected by what I saw. You know, hard. And she slathered Vaseline in my hand and told me to finish it off. If I didn't, she would beat me within an inch of my life, and hurt Jason."

Gripping her chest, Madison's heart lurched at the atrocity Jamar suffered. "D-Did you?" She was barely able to get her questions out. "Were you able too?"

"Barely."

"Did you tell someone after that?"

He shook his head. "We didn't. And it happened again and again."

She gasped in disgust.

"She'd make me sit in that chair and perform while she…finished off on Jason. This went on for years and years. No one ever knew. And we never told, even after her death."

"Now that she's passed away, how did you overcome her abuse?"

"I got help," he admitted. "Therapy. I'm not that fucked up…" His voice trailed off and he looked away again.

"But?" she asked, feeling there was something more.

"But I do have hang-ups."

"Sexual hang-ups," she finished, remembering what he said. "So you told me this to say…?"

"I can't perform unless… well, I need assistance. I couldn't masturbate on my own, so I used to spend a great amount of money on hand jobs. And then I got therapy for my problem and stopped, but … well, now with you…"

"You really are still sick," she blurted out.

He looked directly at her. "I'm not afraid to admit it, but at least it's only you that brings out this sickness. With you needing this sample, I figured…" His words trailed off, and he confessed, "It's pretty much all I could think of last weekend."

She looked at her hand. "I'd only be encouraging what therapy helped stop."

"Probably," he agreed. "But you do need a sample."

"You're incorrigible, Jamar. And wouldn't Jason be disappointed in your regression?"

He shrugged. "Probably, but if he met you, I think he might understand."

Rolling her eyes at that compliment, Madison said, "I shouldn't help you."

Again he reiterated, "But you do need a sample." There was clear excitement in his voice.

She looked at his crotch, and then her hand again. Now that she knew the truth, she needed to get out of the car and never see him again.

First, she looked at the door handle, and then down at the sample cup. This guy could have been giving her a load of crap. Why should she believe him?

Yet, this was very personal to her. Touching her face, she could feel the imperfections.

His story could be a farce just to get her to feel bad for him, but her imperfections weren't lies, and she really wanted to do whatever she had to do to get rid of them.

He was willing to help. Whom else could she ask?

"So if I help you, I'd also be helping myself," she determined.

"We'd be helping each other," he agreed. "I know it's sick, but the opportunity to be able to have what you can give me is incredible to me."

She turned to him and then slowly pulled up her skirt until it was mid-thigh again.

Already his sensuous brown eyes were dancing in excitement before she reached over her hand and said, "Show me how to please you, Jamar. I'm serious this time. I won't stop you."

CHAPTER 14

HER EYES CLOSED TIGHT, hearing him adjusting himself as he took her hand again. Her fingertips grazed something warm, velvety but firm. Every wrong sexual encounter went through her head, and she never remembered handling a man. They would guide themselves in. She would just lie there and wait for it.

Madison tensed her arm slightly, as if she had been brushed by fire. "What was that?"

"It's me," he assured her.

"You're hot," she blurted out.

He chortled. "Thank you?"

Realization of exactly what part of him she had touched overcame her, and she wanted to hyperventilate as he spread her hand again.

"Gently hold me, Madison," he instructed, moving her palm up against him.

His shaft against her palm was unbelievable heated.

Her fingers curved around the base of his rod. Madison could feel his hair and her fingertips barely touched it. He was at full arousal–hardened completely.

Excitedly, she held him tighter.

When she'd slept with men in the past, the room was always very dark – upon her insistence and the guy usually handled himself. She would just lie there and brace herself, too worried about if he could see her face and not really enjoying herself.

Jamar winced and she loosened her grip just a little, worried she was hurting him.

"Now move up and down, slowly," he instructed. His hand guided hers, taking her palm to the tip of him where she felt the tight bulbous head thickening and pulsing in her palm. When he returned her hand to the base, he repeated this action several times until she took control and started doing the motion on her own.

Feeling him pulse and grow even more in her hand was absolutely fascinating. She could feel his body move with her motions, urging her to go faster, but allowing her to have the control.

This was power. Her power over him. She loved this feeling.

His hand wandered over to her thighs and started feeling her garter, loosening and tightening his grip on her leg, moving higher and higher up her thigh.

She didn't stop him.

"Fuck!" he exclaimed. "Beautiful! F-fuck!"

There was a moment she felt connected to him, and his words touched her soul.

She felt wetness cover her hand suddenly, and he gripped her thigh so tightly, she knew there'd be a mark later.

His body finally relaxed, and she could feel his manhood starting to become flaccid. He took her hand, and she could feel the sample cup against her skin. She flinched, but then felt him using tissue to clean between her fingers.

"You can open your eyes now," he said, amused.

As she opened them, he was just finishing straightening his clothes. Her sample cup was on the seat between them. There wasn't a lot, but she could probably extract what she needed.

"I'm going to need more fluid from you," she said excitedly closing the cup and shoving the sample deep in her bag.

"Lots of them, but not today," he said with a mischievous wink. "Your bus is coming."

"What?"

"Bus," he said again.

Quickly, she gathered her items and jumped out of the car. Her dress was barely straightened as she got on the bus and paid her fare. As usual, he watched her leave.

Touching her hand that had manipulated him, she noticed the softness about her skin and lifted her nose to smell him. She didn't find his scent vulgar.

After getting her journal out, she scribbled down notes dedicated to concocting a "potion" for a cream she could possibly use with her specimen.

Briefly, she wondered how he tasted. Licking her lips, she almost felt inclined to taste her fingers, but resisted the urge. What was wrong with her?

The whole experience was changing her, and the scary part was that she was liking the way she was changing.

When she got to the lab, she stuck several empty specimen cups and labels into her bag. Her thigh felt sore and she raised her skirt to see if there were marks near her garter where Jamar had been gripping her. Not yet.

"Are you okay?" Joshua asked behind her.

Madison almost jumped out of her skin as she pushed her skirt down and turned around to zip her bag shut. "I-I'm fine." She knew Joshua had seen a decent amount of skin under her skirt, and hopefully it had distracted him enough not to see the supplies she was stealing. "You scared the bejesus out of me. I thought no one would be here this early."

"I was coming to straighten up the lab," he said. "I wanted to get in before everyone else does."

She frowned, coming to her senses. "I didn't know interns had clearance passes to just come and go."

"The professor approved and told me to ask the guard for entry."

Since he put it like that, she only shrugged off her suspicion. "You must sure love this place. Almost as much as I do," she noticed.

"Love? I admire your work. I always have. I transferred to this school just because of your work, actually. I've been passionate about world food consumption for a long time and I think you are on the precipice of something great."

Wow! No one had complimented her about her work in so long since the professor first had. "Thank you, Joshua."

People started coming in and Joshua returned to cleaning up. Madison resumed her research of different homemade acne creams, feeling more confident that she could perfect her own using natural ingredients and her newly-acquired specimen.

"Lemons?" the professor asked, looking over her shoulder and seeing what she was looking up on the search engines. "They're good for your skin," he suggested.

"Thank you," she said, only slightly embarrassed he caught her.

"Could those be in the study?"

"Possibly," she answered evasively.

He nodded in approval. "This is going to turn the food community on its ear." He walked away mumbling more things, as was his nature when he was excited.

She checked her lab samples before leaving for the day and heading home.

Monday night Bible study took way too long, and she was eager to get back to her research.

But her father blocked her way up to her room that evening. "We need to talk, Madison."

Eager to get to her room to her research, she forgot all about the respect she was supposed to be giving. "Not tonight, Dad. I have work to do."

He looked shocked. "We have to talk now, Madison. There's no money left."

Rolling her eyes in exasperation, she said, "Yeah, I know. You used it on your new wife and now possibly your bimbo? I'm not stupid. And now you want to squeeze any last dime I have in order to stay afloat, while you haven't asked any of my other half-breeds for one cent. I'll get your money as soon as I can. I got a job. Now please, just leave me alone. I have research to do." She walked around him and took the steps two at a time, leaving her father speechless.

She took a quick shower in her attic bathroom, and when she stepped out she looked down at her thigh. There were small bruises where Jamar had gripped the garter and the plastic had bruised her skin. This made her smile, being marked by him.

Once back in her bedroom, she cleared her mind, and then an area near her bed, and started her personal project. She had stopped at the grocery store before coming home from school and had picked up everything she needed. The amazing part was that all the other ingredients were easy to obtain.

Once she had more of the "final" ingredients, she could start making the cream. She really needed more. A lot more, and she was willing to do anything to get it from Jamar.

She could hardly sleep in bed that night, excited to extract more specimen from him the next day.

Seeing his car there the next morning made her heartrate accelerate.

"Good morning, Madison," he said pleasantly as she slid in the passenger side without any prompting from him.

"Good morning, Jamar," she returned, smiling. "I bought more cups, and I think this time I can get a full sample."

"Oh, really? You're quite studious."

"I try to be."

"Today, you're going to learn a new way to extract your sample," he said with that mischievous grin.

"A new way?"

"Yes, Madison. With that gorgeous mouth of yours."

What had she gotten herself into?

CHAPTER 15

"**M**Y MOUTH?" SHE QUESTIONED, flustered. "What's wrong with my hand?"

"It's part of my reward."

Sucking on her bottom lip indecisively, she looked down at his jogging pants, remembering what she had felt the day before. Would it fit in her mouth?

What the hell? How could she even entertain the thought?

"Didn't we agree that any reward had to be pre-approved first?" she reminded him.

"We did?" He feigned innocence.

"Jamar! You're acting like you don't remember."

"I think I should teach you all the ways to collect my specimen, right?"

"I think we should take this slow," she said, poking his chest.

"Then are you ready?" he asked, starting to unloosen his jogging pants.

She turned away quickly and removed the cups from her bag. "I-I brought the cups."

"Good," he said, taking one, opening it up slightly and resting it on the seat next to him.

She knew he was sitting back with his arm resting on the seat, while the other one was resting on the steering column, but she kept her eyes forward as she reached down to him.

"You're way off," he said with a chuckle. "You know it doesn't hurt to look."

Taking a deep breath, she slowly turned her head.

Her hand was on his thigh, resting right by his manhood, which lay flaccid. The coloring was the same as his face, and he was cleanly circumcised.

Hesitant, she touched the tip and then remembered how he had shown her how to grip him. As soon as she had the base of him in the palm of her hand, he hardened just a little.

She smiled, liking how his manhood responded to her touch. Moving her hand up to the tip of him and then back to the base, she saw more of the effects she was having on his body.

Now he was breathing hard, and each breath in seemed to make his manhood stiffen more. She saw him wince just a little, and noted the down stroke was dry.

Now she understood why he wanted her to taste him. He needed lubrication. Slowing her stroke, she asked, "What would tasting you involve?"

His head had been resting back, but his eyes popped open to look at her. Clearing his throat, he said, "Are you sure?"

"No, I'm not sure. I've never done it before," she admitted, blushing.

He pulled a condom out.

She frowned. "Won't the lubrication from that thing interfere with the specimen I need?"

"These are natural lubrication. Chemical-free. I thought we should use this initially, and you can test to see if it affects the strength. Plus, it's lubed on the inside and not the outside."

Amazed he'd done his homework, she nodded and let him put the condom on. "So, I don't need to … use my mouth."

"No, but I really could use the help, because the condom lessens the feeling for me."

Twisting her lips in frustration, she hated not knowing how to do something she should know how to do. "What do I do?"

"Stroke me like you were doing, without going over the tip. With your tongue, lick around the tip slowly, and then suckle me into your mouth as deep as you can."

"How will it taste?" She looked at the condom.

"I don't know," he said honestly.

It seemed simple, and she took a deep breath to prepare. Grasping his manhood again, she could feel he had gone down some. She began her stroke, concentrating on exciting him again.

Leaning down, being this close to him, she could smell him. Soap and… pecans. His natural scent reminded her of the fresh Georgia pecans her mother used to get from the grocery store when they were in season. He stiffened a little more in her grasp as her mouth closed in over the tip.

Madison coordinated her initial lick with a downward stroke. His thigh tightened as if she had licked there.

After three licks like that, all around the tip, she delved further, and took him in her mouth in an upward stroke.

"Yes," he whispered, sounding almost pained, but he wasn't.

She could feel him radiate from what she made him feel.

With every upward stroke, she descended further on him. Madison forgot everything and just thought about how much she could take before she felt like she was going to throw up.

Listening to his body though, there was a silent language she never knew existed. With each stroke she gave, his body seemed to throb in ecstasy, and each lick elicited trembles. He made her want this. His delight was infectious and soon…

Suddenly, he pushed her off, grabbed the cup, ripped the condom off and, with two more strokes from her hand, pulsated into the cup.

There was a lot more than the previous day, and it hadn't taken that long for him this time.

Had it been because of her mouth?

She knew the answer, and smiled at her accomplishment.

He handed the cup to her and wiped himself down. The condom had been thrown down onto the floor of the car. He retrieved it and wrapped it up in the tissue. She made sure the cap on the specimen jar was nice and tight. She couldn't wait to get it to the lab.

"Enough?" he asked quietly.

"No," she said. "I'm going to need some more."

He raised a brow. "I don't think I can go again, right now. Let me breathe first."
She blushed. "I meant, another day."

He chuckled as he reached inside of his coat and pulled out an envelope. "Before I forget this again, take this."

Hearing her bus coming, she grabbed the envelope and her sample and stuffed them in her bag, excited about getting to the lab. Without thinking, she leaned over and kissed him abruptly, right on the lips.

Immediately, before either had time to react to what she had just done, she jumped out of the car and ran for the bus.

After getting on and paying her fare, she looked back through the windows to see if he was still there. He was, and he was looking at her through the windshield, but he was rubbing his lips fondly.

She rubbed her lips too, trying to remember how his had felt on hers.

You kissed him! She scolded herself.

And you liked it.

She didn't know how she should feel, but she knew she wanted more.

***

Joshua, along with other interns, greeted her when she came to the lab that day. The professor was out at a staff meeting, but Joshua had taken the lead and made sure everything was ready for her.

First, she met Jamar, and now there was Joshua.

How as she so lucky to get these great guys in her life?

"You okay?" Joshua asked. "You seem distracted."

"I've got a lot on my mind," she said. She couldn't go into detail about what she was thinking about – Jamar's lips, and really tasting him.

"Really? Well, I've been thinking a lot about you too," he said.

She smiled fondly, not believing Joshua was actually trying to flirt with her. Guys just didn't do that, and it was silly to believe two guys were liking her at the same time.

"You mean the project, right?" she questioned.

"Yeah, of course," he said with a shrug. "I mean, you're working hard, all alone. I was going to ask if I could help out with the reports or something like that."

She knew the professor would have a heart attack if someone else got access into the accounts. The man changed the password practically every day and had created some crazy algorithm to figure out where the file to all their research was at all times, just to ensure no one took anything.

"I'm fine, Joshua," she assured him. "We're in the home stretch anyway, and I need to have my hands on everything to make sure it all goes right."

Another intern came up to them. "Madison, there's some women outside of the lab here to see you?"

"Did they say they were looking for me or the professor?"

"No, and they asked specifically for you."

She never had guests. At college, she was nobody.

Maybe it was one of her half-sisters or something. Maybe it was Nikki and another friend?

"I could go with you," Joshua said. "You know, for protection."

"I'll be fine. Get everyone's samples back in and you're free to go. I'll lock up when I'm done with them."

"You sure?" he asked. "I could stay and we could go out for burgers after."

Was he really flirting?

Nah!

"That's alright, Joshua. See you guys later." Going out in the hallway, she almost had a heart attack to see a young girl who looked exactly like her mother.

CHAPTER 16

THERE WAS ANOTHER BLACK, full-figured female standing next to the young lady dressed in a boyish dark green outfit.

She nudged the woman who looked like her mother and snorted. "I think her jaw dropped far enough, Mercy. You'd better say something before she starts to drool."

They exchanged glances, seeming to share an ability to speak to each other nonverbally, and the girl in dark green walked away, but no more than eight feet.

The young lady that looked like her mother was modestly dressed in a Sunday-type outfit, almost like Madison, but with brighter colors, and she wore dark grunge boots as if she'd gone to war. A very odd combination as if she were trying to conform, but her personality was to stand out.

"I'm not your sister," the young lady said, clearing that up from the get-go. "Your mother could only have one child. It was the only way to receive her measly fortune your father blew through."

Madison blinked as if coming out of a daze. Her face most likely said it all.

The woman continued. "I'm your cousin, Mercy Oliver. My mother is dead too. Murdered, actually, and my sister and I were raised ... well, we were raised, and that's pretty much all I have to say." She was a little bit taller than Madison, and instead of the soft, brown almond eyes Madison had, Mercy had this sort of harsh look. Skeptic, rough and cruel.

"Mattie Oliver was disowned when she married your father. Took a payout and walked away, thinking she was in love with the man that gave her a baby, and thought the family would never accept her because of what she did." Mercy walked closer to Madison, then started to walk around her, looking her up and down from head to toe. "Sister Onetta found me and my sister. She said I would be pleasantly surprised and disgusted at the same time."

"So, is that my cousin, too?" Madison asked, nodding to the other woman a few feet away.

Mercy snorted. "Nah, that's just Pheare. She's my sidekick." Leaning close to Madison, she said, "She's a bitch, but I love her like a sister. We were kind of raised together."

"Then where is your sister? My other cousin."

"Grace is most likely in church somewhere. It's how Sister Onetta found us. Grace is a diehard zealot, while I'm just barely on God's good side." She seemed to find this funny. "Said Mattie Oliver's memory was still alive, but under the sex demon's control."

"She referred to my father as a demon?" Albeit from what Madison found out about her father, she couldn't believe Sister Onetta would blurt that out to someone else just like that.

"Among other things that weren't very 'Christian' of her to say. I see you must know about the sex part, huh?"

Madison chose to not say anything on that matter. "So, how did you find me?"

"I just needed a name. Madison Oliver. And I knew your age, so I figured you were a hooker or a very smart cookie. I looked at the schools, hoping you were being awesome first and lying on your back last."

"I'm glad I turned out alright. I'm not very good on my back."

"The jury is still out on that," Mercy commented, as if she knew more than what she was saying.

Joshua peaked his head out of the lab's security. "Madison, we're going home. I turned off everything for you."

"Thanks, Joshua. I'll lock up," she said, and wished him goodnight.

When she turned to look back at Mercy, the young woman's face was turned fully away, as if she hadn't wanted to be seen.

"What was that?" Madison questioned the awkward behavior.

"I just don't like to be on the radar like my sister," Mercy said. "You want a ride home?"

"Sure," Madison agreed. "I'll meet you outside the main doors after I lock up and we can finish up your need to find me." She went back into the lab and shut down everything, making sure she added the professor's extra security on the computers, and then secured the greenhouse.

Mercy was sitting in the back of a Ford Escape. Pheare was driving. Getting in the rear, Madison noticed Pheare was looking at her.

Pheare nodded and started driving.

"So, are you old as I am?" Madison asked.

"I'm twenty-six, and both my parents are already gone. My dad died of lung cancer because he smoked like a train," Mercy answered.

"How was your mother murdered?"

Mercy shrugged. "Yeah, that's not something we know a lot about, but afterwards, the family didn't really want to associate with us. We were orphans and no one had time for that, so I met someone who didn't mind having orphans and could help us."

"Who?"

"We can talk about that later," Mercy said, and handed Madison a piece of paper. "I went by your house earlier and met your evil fat-ass stepmother."

Pheare chuckled.

"My contact information is on there. Memorize it, just in case. That father of yours is stupid as shit and he's going to dig his own grave. I hope you get that grant to get out of there soon."

"How'd you know about the grant?"

"I can do a little research too, Madison. We're from the same blood. We're smart-ass chicks. That's why Pheare hangs around me. She can't deal with stupid people."

Pheare snickered.

Madison felt this was an inside joke between the two of them, but she didn't question it as they pulled up to her father's home.

"Also, I wouldn't tell your old man that you have more family. He separated your mother from our side on purpose because they would have told her to get the hell away from him. He's doing the same to you."

"Really?"

Mercy rolled her eyes. "Look, Maddie, I'm not trying to tell you what to do, but get your life together and give me a call when you do. Otherwise, I might punch that dirty sex demon in the mouth. He'll deserve to lose some teeth."

Madison got out after Pheare parked in front of her house. When they drove away, she watched them until the Ford Escape turned a corner and was out of her sight.

Her life was changing.

For good or bad, she didn't know.

Getting in the house, she hurried upstairs to calculate the effectiveness of the new sample she had obtained from Jamar. She had used the machines at the lab to purify it, but now she needed to gauge the results.

CHAPTER 17

WHIPPING AROUND TO HIM, consumed by her whole week, she let everything go. In her impatience, she forgot respect and snapped, "You're really asking me to talk, Father? You mean to order me to stay here and deal with drama again, right?"

Cyrus slapped her so hard, she bit the inside of her mouth.

Everyone except Hazel left the study, trapping Madison inside with her father and stepmother. Madison could taste blood in her mouth, but refused to cry.

"You will not talk to me like that in my house, little girl."

Fury grew inside her, despite the threat of getting slapped again. Speaking up would almost be worth the pain.

"And you'll start giving us the respect we deserve," her father continued.

It took every ounce of her will not to scream at him in defiance. She was a grown-ass woman and she was sick and tired of this treatment. She had done absolutely nothing to deserve what they were giving her.

"Ask her, Cyrus," Hazel ordered him, locking the study door.

Madison looked at Hazel sharply, and then back at her father. The fact that her stepmother had locked the door set alarms off in her head. "Ask me what?" she questioned bitterly.

Cyrus gritted his teeth. "You'd better not lie to me, child."

"Lie about what?" Madison demanded.

"Are you letting some little boy between your legs?" Hazel demanded to know.

The audacity of the accusation startled her. "No!" she screamed.

"She's lying," Hazel accused.

Her father grabbed her by her arm and dragged her over as he took a seat.

"Stop!" Madison cried. "No!"

"Do it, Cyrus. Teach her a lesson. A good lesson," Hazel urged. "Show her who's boss!"

Cyrus yanked her over his knee and hiked up her dress.

"Nooooo!" She screamed hysterically and almost broke free from her father's hold, until Hazel came over with a death grip on Madison's arms, holding them out, rendering the ability to get away impossible. Madison screamed hysterically.

The first slap to her raw skin knocked the air out of her, but by the fifth one she had regained her voice and tried to wrench away, yet still couldn't. She sobbed harder and harder, mortified at the shame she endured as her father continued until about twenty firm slaps were delivered to her posterior.

When Hazel and Cyrus released her, Madison fell to the floor, sobbing in grief and pain.

"I'd better not find that you're spreading your legs, little girl," Cyrus threatened. "You'll be sorry. You hear me? I won't have a whore in my house. And you'd better hurry and get a job, or I'll be sure to make your life a living hell around here."

As quickly as she could, she straightened her clothes and trudged out of the study, past Hazel's smug little smiling face.

Before going upstairs to her room, she grabbed the backpack she'd left by the door with the most important research.

Her room had been trashed by her half-siblings, who'd done it just to be evil. Her research had only been kicked around, but the machine she had stolen from the lab had been knocked over and, she was sure, damaged.

She worried about how she was going to explain its brokenness to the professor, but if they got the grant, no one would know the older machine was broken because the professor would buy new machines. Luckily though, Jamar's sample was still safe inside her bag.

Wiping the tears from her face and trying to get mental control of her life, Madison told herself she would make the best of her situation for now and figure out everything else later. That's what her mother would've said.

Cleaning her room somewhat, Madison did what she could, but most of the items she didn't care about. She wasn't invested in material items and she was glad her siblings didn't know how much her backpack meant to her.

Going into a secret compartment by her dresser, she pulled out the groceries she'd bought. She had used dry ice from the lab to keep some of the items cool, which was why obtaining the samples quickly was so important, because she didn't want the other ingredients going bad.

During the bible study earlier, she determined she had enough specimen to make two types of creams, both with the same effectiveness.

Mixing everything together, she smiled proudly at her creation. Whether it worked or not, Madison was happy she had stuck with her resolve, despite what had happened to her.

After scrubbing her face to death when she got out of her shower, Madison applied each cream to the sides of her face and wrote down her experience in her journal.

Going to bed, she couldn't wait to see Jamar the next morning.

***

To her disappointment, Jamar wasn't there, but she had gotten to the bus stop early enough to catch the first bus. On the ride to school, Madison found the envelope he had given her last time deep in her backpack. Inside the envelope was a piece of paper with an address and simple instructions:

I'd like the nursery to look professional and healthy. Jason.

There was a key card, and on the back were four digits written in black marker.

Her first class only lasted an hour. Since she had turned the report in early, she didn't need to report to the lab. Professor Barfield would study and analyze her findings, compare it to his own, and then see if she needed to change anything. The intern s were assigned to building the display for the presentation, so there was really nothing for her to do.

After her first class, Madison took the bus to an elaborate estate in the Historic Boston Edison District. During the travel time, she had a lot to think about. Cyrus, Hazel, Joshua, Mercy and Jamar. All these people had an effect on her past, present and future, and she needed to figure out her own life before she could figure out what to do about each and every one of them.

The house looked like it was under construction – a mini-mansion, with three stories. Most likely it was about five bathrooms with two-and-a-half baths. Those specifications didn't include a breakfast nook, a five-star kitchen, library, and a full basement.

Madison knew a lot of money was being put into this property to renovate and upgrade. There were no construction workers at the home that day, and no one answered the door. Going around the wraparound porch, she could see in the backyard, and gasped at the large glass greenhouse. Proceeding down the porch back steps, Madison came to a gate.

There was a box on the gate that looked like the kind on a hotel room door, for which she figured she needed the key card. Sliding the card through, her heart raced as the gate popped open.

Why did it feel as if she were starting a new chapter in life?

CHAPTER 18

GOING AROUND THE CORNER of the house and entering the backyard, Madison gasped at the most beautiful greenhouse she could've imagined. Nine feet wide and about twenty-five feet in length, with a ten foot ceiling, there were two glass windows on each side and a sliding door in the front. Weeds grew out of everywhere, but that diminish the place's potential for beauty.

The idea of growing something, creating something, thrilled her to the bone. She couldn't wait to get started.

She saw a shed in the yard, and with the key card she was able to open it. Inside were cleaning supplies and gloves, overalls and large boots that happened to be her shoe size. Had Jamar prepared this shed for her?

She didn't question anything else as she changed clothes, using the shed for privacy, and returned to the greenhouse.

The work of cleaning, organizing and readying the place for planting was peaceful. Madison had always loved gardening, just like her mother had. Feeling the dirt and determining the soil for planting made her feel powerful.

In a garden, she had control over life and death. She had control over something when her own life was so chaotic. The plants needed her, and she could nurture them and create whatever she wanted.

Before leaving, she left a note by the door with a list of additional items she would need. At the last minute, she wrote down a request for a self-watering system. With one of those, she could use rain water through PVC piping in order to self-irrigate the greenhouse. She had seen it done, but had never built it herself.

Madison loved to make plants self-sufficient, and she believed this would dramatically improve the greenhouse, plus make it unique for a man who didn't seem to really know much about plants and was just trying to impress someone.

Just in case the woman wasn't impressed, and this Jason was left with a greenhouse, she thought she should make the system independent.

Catching the bus home, she used her journal to log her hours.

By the time she crawled into bed, blisters had formed on her skin. She only kissed them, loving that she now had a job and she could create self-reliant plant systems.

She didn't kill herself trying to get to the bus stop the next morning, but Jamar was there, and this time he was standing outside of the car, leaning up against the front of the hood with his arms crossed over his chest.

Madison stopped a few feet away from him, realizing for the first time how tall and even more damn handsome he was.

"Hi," he said, looking at her intently from head to toe… slowly.

"Hi," she responded quietly.

Jamar reached through the open car window and pulled out a yellow rose from the dashboard. "This is for you."

"Why?" she asked.

"I was missing in action yesterday, and I'm apologizing. Your friendship means a lot to me. I didn't want you to think I took you for granted."

"You sure it's not just because of my mouth?"

Jamar walked up to her, and she was overwhelmed by how forbidden he looked and how overwhelmed she felt. The smell of soap and maple syrup hit her nose as he came closer. She raised her head up to see him.

He had to be about six feet tall, but he was large, larger than in the car. Why hadn't she noticed how big he was, how tall he was, and how physically magnificent he was before?

His thick arms circled her body and he pulled her against him. "Your mouth is just as beautiful as you." Dipping down, he captured her lips and gave her a worshipful kiss that made her toes curl. "Never doubt me," he whispered with passion.

She blushed, then groaned as her bus pulled up.

He stole another quick kiss, making her heart race more. "Call me later, if you're planning on working today."

She nodded and, yellow rose in hand, jumped on the bus. All day long, she smelled the rose and barely paid attention to anyone else. When she was done with her academic lab work, she found Jamar's number and called from a payphone in the hallway outside of the lab. In her periphery, she could see Joshua looking her way from the open lab door.

He seemed curious about her distant nature that day, but it wasn't something she wanted to share with him. She didn't even want to share Jamar with Nikki. No doubt her best friend would think what Madison was doing was dangerous and stupid.

"Joe here," Jamar answered, businesslike.

"This is Madison," she said shyly.

"You're calling from a payphone?"

"Yes. Are you busy?"

"Probably, but where should I pick you up at?"

Feeling uncomfortable," she said. "If you're busy—"

He cut her off. "Directions, please, and we'll talk about how I not only think you're beautiful, but how important you are to me."

Why did that sound like another kissable punishment?

She rattled off directions and listened as he confirmed a wait time of twenty minutes. It would've taken an hour for her to the bus ride, so this was perfect for her.

When he arrived, he jumped out of the car and opened up the passenger side. "Your chariot awaits, milady."

"I wasn't taking you away from work, was I?" she worried.

"Woman, if you ask me one more time, I'm going to put you over my knee."

She winced, remembering that recent night with her father. "Not funny, Jamar." Yet, why did it sound so appealing when *he* said it? The idea of Jamar putting her over her knee, pulling her panties down, and striking her fanny seemed arousing.

Her knees went weak at the thought of the painful but pleasurable sensation.

But Madison pretended to abhor the idea. "You wouldn't dare."

"As nice as your ass is? You don't think I will pass up a chance to rub against it at any cost."

She blushed profusely, getting in the car. He quickly came over on the driver's side and started driving toward the Grosse Pointe address.

"How was your day?" he questioned.

Starting a conversation about her day was not really on her mind, now that she was within his proximity. "How good are you at driving?" she asked, ignoring his question and popping her seatbelt.

"Pretty...damn?"

In one quick move, she pulled aside his jogging pants with his underwear and dipped her head down, while maneuvering his manhood into her mouth. She could tell he had cleaned himself up with baby wipes, because she could smell the oil on his skin, and she was touched by his consideration.

"Woman, I'm..." He sucked air in his teeth. "I'm d-driving..." He panted, but didn't stop her.

Madison had been thinking about this since the last time she had done it, and there was an uncontrollable hunger inside of her to have him in her mouth again.

Taking him orally made her feel in control, made her forget about everything else, made her feel so good at what she could do to him... made her feel beautiful.

How had he transferred this feeling to her, so deep in her soul it was irrepressible when he was around? Her urge drove her to disregard all shyness and morals.

Feeling Jamar's stiffening manhood moving down her throat, her saliva coated his shaft and she knew it made the oral manipulation even more arousing for him.

He was barely concentrating on the road, and just as they jumped off the freeway, he was cursing vehemently as he exploded in her mouth.

Insatiable in her hunger to have him, she had forgotten the cup, and he was so far down her throat, he triggered her to swallow.

Warm, sweet and thick, he pumped down her throat until there was no more.

"Fuck me... Fuck me...fuck me!" he growled, almost over the steering column, but amazingly still driving.

CHAPTER 19

JAMAR PULLED TO THE SIDE of the service drive and threw the car in park. No one was around, and with the tinted windows it was a nice shield to the illicitness going on inside.

"Damn, woman!" he hissed, still a little out of breath, but he looked at her as if she were the eighth wonder of the world. "You are learning way above the curve."

She chuckled and was about to use the back of her hand to wipe her mouth, but he stopped her and leaned over to kiss her. His other hand moved to her nape to draw her lips open, and his tongue ravished her mouth. His arm moved around her body, pulling her closer to him, and then he hooked his hand under her thigh and drew her fully beside him.

She could feel the space between her legs becoming drenched as he suckled her tongue and drew the breath from her body.

Madison moved her arms around his neck, opening herself to his onslaught of loving, how his hands couldn't seem to stay still. This was the kissing she'd dreamed of a man giving her, and she realized her past relationships had been with nothing but boys.

"You're beautiful," he whispered, breaking the kiss, and still out of breath.

She blushed, beginning to appreciate his compliments. "Thank you. I'm sorry about not getting a sample. I didn't expect you to finish so soon." Blaming her wantonness on him seemed so much better than admitting she lusted after him.

He nodded, taking the blame, while reluctantly releasing her and putting the car back into drive.

Madison used Kleenex to wipe her fingers off and found a wet wipe in her bag to finish cleaning herself off.

Out of the blue, he cleared his throat and asked again, "So, how was your day?"

The question threw her out the moment. She wasn't used to someone asking about her life sincerely, and was unsure how to respond. "It was... okay, I guess."

"Just okay?"

She nodded, unsure.

"Are you going to ask about my day?" he questioned.

"How was your day?" she inquired, shocked that he wanted to carry on a normal conversation after what she had just done to him.

The many times Madison listened to Nikki talk about guys and her exploits, never once had her best friend mentioned the guy wanted to have a sincere conversation.

Jamar spoke. "After two of my guys didn't show up yesterday morning, I found myself trying to run two sites at one time. Good thing they were across the street from each other and I could close up one site and devote myself to the other without losing a lot of money. These are our biggest clients and we couldn't afford to lose any money so close to the end of the month. When you called me yesterday, I was confirming we'd definitely have those guys this morning at the other locations, because I hate to do things at the last minute.

"One guy didn't show up this morning after I left you, and my partner was—of course-out romancing his new woman. So I had to cover that station, and then shortly after, I found out our only vendor for fresh fruit decided to close up shop in Detroit after their fifth break-in. I'm finding it difficult to find fresh fruit and vegetables at reasonable prices around the city, and I'm really trying to stick to local vendors. It looks good for the business and we get better tax breaks with the city as well."

"Really?" she asked, surprised that this was a topic right up her alley, which she could actually help him with. "I could give you a lead on a vendor who is local and could help you out. Plus, there are even grants to help you, just as long as you purchase from Michigan vendors for grocery store products."

By this time, he had pulled up in the driveway of the home and was looking at her with a shocked expression. "Are you shitting me, Madison?"

She didn't understand the slang, so she didn't know if it was a bad or good thing. Instead, she handed him a slip of paper. "His name is Roderick Price, and he's actually been doing great in terms of growing fruits and vegetables in Detroit, even in the wintertime, but also procures other vegetables around the state for distribution inside the city. I had to use his site as a thesis for urban farming in my second year, and went out occasionally to analyze his products. He has a small warehouse on the east side of Detroit. We use him all the time for our lab and seed collection."

"What the hell do you do, exactly?"

Flushing at his genuine curiosity, she was again lost for words as this man seem to look upon her as if she was the answer to his prayers. This was more than making her look beautiful; he was making her feel beautiful. "I study seed regeneration and possibilities for growth outside regular conditions."

"Explain," he ordered casually, looking interested.

"You don't need to pretend you care, Jamar," she said, testing him.

"Pretend I care? Woman, the way you make my dick feel, I can't help but care."

His crassness shook her a bit, but she liked he was direct. He didn't seem to sugarcoat anything or just say things that she wanted to hear. Jamar was an honest-to-goodness say-what-he-felt person.

"Like I said, I basically try to fool seeds into germination outside their normal environment by changing the DNA makeup."

"So you trying to grow pineapples in Detroit?" he surmised.

"Yes, that's kind of the logic. And that's a pretty good idea, because why go to Hawaii to pick a fresh pineapple when it can be possible to pull it from a plant in your own backyard? Or, why wait for cherry season to start when you want one in the middle of winter? I believe with the right manipulation, lots of the food crises around the world can be solved in our own backyards."

"But aren't people already tired of chemicals in our food?" he challenged.

"Yes, but the method I'm using starts before the seed ever germinates, so it grows naturally by itself without chemicals. It's a nature-and-nurture mixture."

"What about the people in Idaho? Won't they be upset if someone else is producing their potatoes? Or Florida will lose money if New Yorkers can grow their own oranges."

"It'll only mean those entities are going to have to step up their game, in terms of quality and production," she retorted.

"That's amazing, Madison," he said, and he seemed honestly impressed.

"Thank you," she countered modestly.

"I'm going to take a quick shower while you work, okay?" He got out of the car and came around to open the passenger door for her. "The balcony doors in the back will be unlocked. Just let me know when you're ready to go."

Madison went to the back of the home, just like the day before, where the greenhouse was. After changing into her overalls and boots in the shed, she entered the greenhouse, using the code like before.

All the items she had listed on the sheet were now lined up in the middle of the floor, and she smiled as she picked up her note that had been turned over.

Thank you. Let me know if you need anything else. Jason.

It seemed his god brother was just as nice as Jamar. In addition to the plants she could revive in the greenhouse, she found annuals and other type of plants, which she assumed Jason wanted her to cultivate.

She had taken seeds from the lab and made a corner in the greenhouse where she could test them. Not even the professor knew she produced extra seeds and stocked them in the back of the freezer just in case anything happened to the lab or their field. Earlier that day at the lab, she had taken her last samples out and decided to use them in the greenhouse, in hopes that in her report she could add that the seeds are a success in an ordinary environment instead of just the strict laboratory environment the professor demanded.

Two hours later, back hurting and hands blistered, she was ready to leave, and knocked on the balcony doors of the house. She had changed out of the overalls and boots, but was still pretty sweaty and dirty.

Jamar opened the door and invited her in.

She said, "I don't think I should. I'm pretty rank and it's not my house."

"It's not mine, either," he said with a chuckle. "But you're dirty and need to clean up before getting in my car."

"I thought of something I needed to tell you while I was out working. I live with my father and he wouldn't approve of some strange guy dropping me off at his house."

For a brief second, he looked like she had bitten him. "Then I'll drop you off a block away? You'll get home way past dark if you try to catch the bus now," he pointed out.

She agreed and entered the home. Immediately, she knew she was in the kitchen. There weren't any dishes or furniture about, and she could tell a lot of renovations were still going on. "So your partner is buying this house?"

"He's already bought it," he said, coming up close behind her.

"Where can I wash up at?"

Jamar pointed to a door off the kitchen. "There's another door in that guest bathroom that leads to a guestroom you can use too."

"I don't think it's that serious."

"You can use the shower. There're towels and soap in there for you. Use anything you want. Take as long as you want."

The idea that she wasn't timed in the shower was so appealing. At home, if she took too long, Hazel would literally come and turn the water off, even if Madison hadn't gotten all the soap off her body.

The words "take as long as you want" were like a dream come true. Heaven had smiled upon her! The temptation was too much not to take advantage of.

Going into the guest bathroom with just a toilet, sink and shower, she hurried and stripped. She was so enticed by getting to shower for as long as she wanted, she forgot to lock any of the doors.

The water was soft and flowed out like rain. She wanted to cry and giggle at the same time, feeling so happy and relaxed.

Jamar had gifted her with something better than anything in the world right now.

The best shower of her life!

CHAPTER 20

FEELING LIKE A NEW person as she stepped out of the shower, Madison took a deep breath and smiled.

There was just something about a long shower to release her thoughts and transform her thinking... for the better. She wished she had gotten a shower like that long ago. Maybe after her mother's death.

In one thirty-minute shower, she adapted a clarity about her life. There was nothing about her situation at home that she liked. She needed to change that as soon as she could.

She also thought about the report she had turned into the professor. There was additional research from working out in the greenhouse she could add to the report to give them more insight on making the experiment easy for individual processes.

And finally, her new project. She had endless ideas about what she could do with her experiments and the grants... the amazing grants she could apply for!

The prospect filled her mind, making her smile go wider.

As always, she put her stockings and garter on. She looked up at the door that led to the adjoining bedroom. With just a towel around her body, curiosity compelled her to walk into the guest bedroom connected to the bathroom.

There was a freshly-made bed, as if someone did live there, although the rest of the house – from what she had seen - looked under construction. Going to the window, she smiled, seeing the greenhouse nearby. This was a perfect view for her. She could just imagine waking up in this bedroom...

Did she hear voices in the hallway? Two male voices? Was someone else there?

She started to go to the bathroom to put some clothes on.

The bedroom door opened, and she turned to see Jamar filling the doorway.

"Hi," he said, folding his arm over his chest.

She blushed to be wearing only a towel in his presence. "Was there someone here?"

"No," he said without hesitation, and then quickly changed the subject. "How did you enjoy the shower?"

"I loved it, thank you very much."

He moved to her, leaving the door open, and leaned down to kiss her.

Madison became moist again. His hands moved down her side and cupped her rear over the towel.

Her five-foot-five, thick frame had to move on her tiptoes to respond to the sweet kisses he gave, and she circled her arms around his neck. He maneuvered her over to the bed.

"Wait!" she said nervously. "I-I... we... Jamar... I don't know." She started breathing hard, feeling like she was on the precipice of a panic attack.

"It's okay, Madison," he assured her. "I'm not going to fuck you. I only want to make you feel good; just like you do me. It's reciprocity."

She let him lay her down, and he immediately pushed the towel away from her waist, but allowing her to keep her breasts covered.

Jamar groaned as his eyes found her garters and stockings. His rough hands moved variously over her thighs and then abruptly, he dipped his head down, kissing her where his fingers had rubbed.

His partially shaven face tickled her skin, but also made her tingle all over. She gasped and nervously giggled as he moved up the inside of her thighs, kissing and licking until he came to the edges of her thighs.

His tongue traced on both sides, and then he moved over to the center of her stomach.

She moaned in frustration, and his head moved over her, manipulating her most sensitive spot until she felt a powerful eruption from her lower half, sending delicious tremors all over her body.

"N-No...ohhhh, wait...oh ...Oh... OH!" she screamed, swearing she had peed on herself, but he didn't move away in disgust.

"You're all wet, Madison," he teased.

Shamefully, she said, "I'm sorry." Her moistness had wet the sheets.

"For what?" he asked, moving up her body and resting his body against hers.

"For being so wet."

"You had an orgasm," he said, grinding his body against hers, and then kissing her.

She couldn't believe how doubly exciting his motions made her feel. His hands were still rubbing over the parts of her body that his body didn't cover, while he ground up against her sensitive spot, making those tingles come back more, and stronger... until... Madison broke the kiss and howled as more wetness flooded from her soaking her thighs.

With a few more grinds, he strained, closed his eyes, and buried his face in her neck. She knew he was coming. She thought of her specimen jars briefly, but it was way too late to get one.

Feeling his body tense over hers felt good, and she wondered how this would feel if he had no clothes on. Would it be lovemaking or fucking?

He lightly kissed her neck, then her lips. "You're so beautiful."

She was starting to believe him.

There was a sound in the hallway and she tensed. "Did you hear that?" she asked in a panic.

He kissed her again. "No. It's just the house shifting. You have nothing to be scared of here. I won't let anyone hurt you."

Yes, she believed him again. "So what happens now?"

"I clean up the mess you made me make," he teased, getting off of her. "I'll use the upstairs bathroom."

She blushed, covering herself up again with the towel while he went to the doorway.

"Get dressed and meet me near the front," he ordered, and closed the door to give her privacy.

Madison got up from the bed, but then she was positive she heard two sets of footsteps walk away from her door. But no, there couldn't possibly someone here. They would have interrupted, right?

She was just being paranoid.

CHAPTER 21

GETTING BACK IN THE big green Lincoln, Jamar took her to a small Coney Island to eat. Just talking about her world, her research, and her life to someone who really seemed to care was enjoyable.

She learned he'd grown up in Detroit and his mother was a philanthropist for various projects, while his father had worked at the auto plants. Jamar and his god brother had taken their inheritance from Jamar's father, started their business, and never looked back. She realized there were a couple of years he didn't speak about, and he seemed ashamed.

Before it was too late, he parked a block away from her father's home and kissed her fondly. Smiling broadly as she got out of the car, she started to walk away, but he called her back.

When she leaned down into the driver's side window, he passed her another envelope.

"Jason said to give you this. It's up to you to report it or not."

Madison took the envelope and stuffed it in her purse. "Thanks," she said and hurried home, knowing that he stayed at the corner to watch her the whole time.

"You're late," her father, soon as she walked in the door.

Glancing at the wall clock, Madison noticed she was only thirty minutes later than usual, which could account for a late bus or late getting out of school. There was no way her father or stepmother could know she was not on her usual schedule.

She started to explain. "I was-"

The slap across her face jarred her senses, making her fall to the ground to get her bearings.

"Didn't I say no backtalk?" he yelled angrily, and kicked her in the stomach.

Madison didn't move after curling up to protect herself from more blows to her head, stomach, back and thighs. When her father walked away, grumbling about getting cleaned up for dinner, Madison sobbed in relief and pain.

Hazel sucked her teeth at the front door. "You better be glad I don't tell him about that car I just saw you get out of," she hissed, and walked into the kitchen.

After putting her bag by the door behind the couch, Madison pressed her stomach gently to feel for internal bleeding, but found nothing; just a lot of soreness. Her hands trembled in shock and anger as she carefully eased into her chair at the dining table with her family.

"You get a job, yet?" her father barked.

Madison heard some of her half-siblings quietly giggling and whispering about her.

"Y-yes, sir," Madison sniffled, working hard to keep her voice from shaking. "I work at a private greenhouse."

"Owned by whom?" he demanded to know, before shoveling food in his mouth.

Her father wasn't sorry for anything when he looked at her. There was a coldness in his eyes and made her freeze to her bone. She could feel a ruthlessness about him when his eyes met hers, as if there was something about her he really hated.

"A person from the college," she quickly lied to save her ass.

"When do you get paid?" he asked with a mouthful of food.

"Tomorrow, I think," she lied again. "I'll know..." A pain shot through her stomach. "I'll know more tomorrow." She winced, feeling like she was about to throw up.

"Soon as you get paid, you put that check on this table, signed for me to cash. Do I make myself clear?"

Lowering her head, feeling defeated, she knew her life here was only going to get worse. The pain in her stomach, the swelling in her chest, fighting the urge not to cry, and the stinging still on her face from his earlier slap would all get worse, and she didn't know if she could take any more. "Y-Yes, sir."

Had a shower really opened her eyes, made her see and realize that no matter what she did or how she tried to be the perfect daughter, her father was never going to love her? He was always going to see her mother in her, and for that, he would hate her.

The realization made her want to cry, but she refused to show her misery at the dinner table in front of this so-called family of hers.

The rest of dinner was inane chatter, which Madison usually tried to pay little attention to, but the pain in her stomach and desolation in her heart just made her feel horrible that she couldn't hear anything at all.

After they ate, everyone was supposed to pile in the car to go to bible study. She grabbed her backpack and joined her family in the car. They stayed at the church late, but at least as they came back home, one of her half-sisters did something to upset their father, and when they all walked in the door, her half-sister was dragged into her father's study, giving Madison time to get up to her room instead of volunteering to clean up the living room. Her stomach was still killing her.

For the first time, Madison noted a smirk on her half-sister's face as she was taken into the room, leaving Madison disgusted. Did her sister enjoy the torture of being put over their father's knee?

Madison had too much other stuff on her brain to be consumed by what her half-sister and father were doing.

She crawled up the second set of stairs because she used too much of her stomach muscles.

Taking off her clothes completely, she looked in the mirror and gasped at her stomach. Despite the solid brown tone of her skin, she could clearly see her father's shoe imprint on her stomach in a black and blue outline.

After getting her formula from her secret compartment, she went to her private bathroom to wash her face. Despite the fact that she wanted to lie down and go to sleep, she wanted to make sure her research wasn't messed up just because her personal life was going wrong.

For her study, she took a picture of her face with the cell phone. When she looked at the picture she just took it saddened her even further to see the despair in her eyes. She took the first jar and washed one side of her face, and then took the other jar. Both of the formulas smelled delicious, but she'd have to figure out the refrigeration process. She loved knowing the source of her specimen, and that actually lightened her mood. Smelling the serum made her feel even better.

She took her time rubbing the second half of her face, enjoying her massage.

When she was done, Madison dipped her finger into the mixture and closed her eyes. Remembering the taste of Jamar from earlier that day, she smiled despite her face feeling sore. Her train of thought was taking a sinful direction, but she *did* make the mixture from food byproducts and his specimen was just as edible.

After she cleaned her face, she used a homemade tea tree mixture, and then went on to bed, deep in her thought.

With two more months until the research presentation for her school's grant, Madison hoped her mixture would work well enough for her to look nice.

The next morning, when she got to the bathroom, she gasped in horror.

One side of her face was completely swollen!

CHAPTER 22

SHE COULDN'T BELIEVE THE deep purple mark from her eye to her cheek. At first, she really thought it had been her formula, but seeing her father's handprint through the black and blue marks relieved her senses, as she realized the swelling was from the hit, and maybe the over-extensive massaging she'd done.

Jamar could NOT see her like this!

Gathering everything she needed, she caught another bus route that took her all the way downtown, and then over to her school. She missed her class, but made it to her labs with enormous sunglasses on her face.

To her relief, the professor had left a note stating he would be out of the office, but gave her instructions about what needed to be done.

"You okay?" Joshua asked.

She snapped, "Do I look okay?"

He looked apologetic and walked away.

Immediately, she felt bad for turning her anger on him, but was too frustrated to apologize. She would do so later, but not now; not when she was so angry she'd allowed herself to endure that kind of treatment at home.

She called Nikki, but her supposedly best friend pushed her to voicemail.

Quickly, Madison completed the tasks, assigned all the interns to work something, and then started research on her natural face cream. Hours passed and time was forgotten as she also created an all day long cream, an ointment for swelling around the eyes and even a sugar scrub with her formula included. All the ingredients were natural, including her secret ingredient, which she realized she'd need a lot more of.

Instead of taking her usual route home, she took the long way and ended up getting home late again.

So late, her father had already left for Bible study and changed the locks on the doors, so she had to wait outside.

She trembled knowing that, when her father came home, he would most likely beat her worse than the day before.

Instead of waiting at the front of the house, she went to the back. She knew a couple of times her sister had snuck out of the house at night, but she'd never seen how her sister had accomplished the task.

Getting to the back of the house, Madison saw there was a clearing of weeds by one of the basement windows.

She knew all the bedroom windows would be locked, but this window was to the back of the house, where her father kept a room that was always locked. His study was never to be bothered, and this basement room was off limits too. Yet, the window to the room looked to be tampered with. Upon closer examination, Madison saw the window had a security latch that could only be accessed from the outside to unlock all the other windows.

When she unhooked the latch, the window popped right open.

Madison crawled through quickly. Immediately she fell down on a hard table, but it was very dark. She could see there were tools on the table, but she could barely make them out. The smell of bleach almost made her eyes water and she had to cover her nose just to get through the room without passing out.

Hesitating, she was almost tempted really look around the room her father always forbade anyone to go into, but the fear her father constantly made her feel overwhelmed her. She didn't know how much time she really had and needed all she could to get everything she could out of her room.

Hurriedly, she went up to the security panel on the first floor to deactivate the alarm. Lucky for Madison, her father had not changed the code.

Hurriedly, she went up to her room, packed her experiments and clothes. She always kept her most important papers in her purse, yet there were things she couldn't carry with her, including her mother's keepsakes.

After turning back on the security, she left through the front door too terrified to go back through her father's private room. She went back in the rear of the home again to re-latch the back window. If her father returned home and found her there, the punishment could be worse than ever. Her face and body were still sore from the day before.

Just as Madison pushed the latch into the locked position, she heard the leaves crunch behind her, and someone grabbed her arm, yanking her up.

Panicked, and unable to see well in the dark due to her sunglasses, she screamed.

Jamar shook her. "Where the hell were you this morning?" he demanded to know.

Madison calmed down a little. "You scared the crap out of me, Jamar!"

"What happened to your face? Why is it so swollen?"

She tensed up again. "Nothing," she answered roughly, pushing away from him and hurrying off the property. She started walking down the street.

"Wait!" he ordered, following her.

She only continued.

"Wait, please, Madison," he begged, still following her, but not trying to physically stop her.

She stopped turning to face him. They were far enough away, just in case someone came home. "I can't talk right now; not right here, Jamar."

"Then get in the car and I'll take you somewhere we can talk. Away from here."

Wanting to get as far away from the house before her father and his family returned, but with no place in mind to go, she handed him some of her bags and followed him to the Lincoln parked at the end of the block. He opened the trunk so she could put the rest of her bags inside and then she sat in the front seat with him.

Jamar didn't ask her any more questions right then, although she could feel his eyes coming back to her face a lot. The swelling probably looked worse than what she felt right now. Albeit her brown skin didn't show the real damage, but she was sure the swelling in her cheek, under her eye and even her ear looked terrible.

"It doesn't hurt as much, anymore," she assured him.

"Please tell me what happened. What or who hit you?"

He gave her a moment to collect herself. Now that she was getting away from the only home or people she really ever knew, the severity of having no parental figure in her life ever again really started to hit her.

Maybe if she had been a better daughter?

Maybe if she had never met Jamar?

Maybe if she had just shut her mouth and not grown a backbone?

Taking a deep breath, remembering the cold look in her father's eyes as he kicked her, Madison knew she would she would never be the daughter her father wanted. She was a constant reminder of her mother, and for that, he couldn't see her as anything else.

Yet, she had to wonder what her mother had done to make Cyrus hate her so much.

"My father was upset at me for coming home late last night."

"Don't make excuses for him. There's never an excuse for a man to hit a woman."

"I'm not. I realize now, he'd just find some other excuse to hit me and it'd just get worse."

Gripping the steering column angrily, Jamar asked, "So are you leaving?"

"Well, I spent all day avoiding you and came home late, and I just knew he was going to beat me again. I couldn't take another beating like that. Not anymore, Jamar."

He agreed. "As well you shouldn't, but why were you trying to avoid me?"

Ashamed she took off her sunglasses and looked away. "I knew you'd be upset about my face. I didn't want to involve you."

"I'm involved now." He pulled up to a hotel on the Boulevard. "You're staying here for now, since it's on your bus route to school. You're not too far from the Boston Edison District either."

Touched he had thought of her transportation problem, Madison watched as he jumped out and went into the lobby to obtain a room. Was he going to share the room with her? Was she ready to get a hotel room with this man? They hadn't even had real sex yet...

Jamar returned and drove around to the back, closer to where her room was.

"You can stay here for a couple of weeks," he explained, helping her out and walking her to her room. "Until you figure things out."

Feeling like she could trust him, Madison nodded as he opened up the hotel room. He handed her the key card and she walked in while he went to get her bags out of the trunk.

There was a queen-size bed, small bedside table with two drawers, a lamp, a square table and chair, and a small love seat. The room had a closet and a bathroom with just a shower, toilet and sink. The hotel room was clean enough, and sadly bigger than the attic space she occupied.

Jamar put her bags just inside the door, but didn't step in. "I can stop in tomorrow to check on you and bring you a minute phone. It might be a little late; the business is really taking off. This isn't the best neighborhood, so be careful and make sure you keep the door and windows locked."

"Aren't you coming in?" she asked, surprised at how suddenly he was acting like a gentleman.

He looked over at the bed, seeming tempted, and licked his lips as if he were internally fighting his will. "I would, but you didn't invite me."

"What are you? A vampire?" she giggled.

Chuckling, Jamar said, "No, but I'm going to treat you like a friend despite the sexual relationship we have, Madison. A friend wouldn't take advantage of your situation."

The gesture was sweet and thoughtful. "Can I invite you in now?"

"You may, after I come back." He checked his watch. "I still have some work to do. I'll bring dinner." He kissed her forehead. "Use the phone to call me if you need anything else."

She watched him leave, then closed the hotel room door. Leaning on the back of it, she took a deep breath in, then slowly out. Her life was changing – fast.

After a finding a corner in the closet to set up her experiment, she took a long shower and put on a T-shirt and some shorts.

This was her usual garb around the attic, because her father preferred she be fully dressed around the house at all times.

Madison lay down on the queen-size bed for a moment to get her thoughts together. She reached for the phone and dialed Mercy's number. Just like she had been instructed, Madison had memorized the number by heart.

Had Mercy known Madison would need to know the number in emergency?

The cousin was strange. Madison wasn't sure she would get the answers she wanted.

"Mercy speaking," her cousin's voice said over the phone.

In the background, Madison could hear gospel music playing, far off. "Are you busy? It's Madison."

"Hold on," Mercy said, and in few seconds, Madison couldn't hear the church music anymore, but outside noises. "My sister is feeling weird today. Matter of fact, Grace has been acting weird all week long. It could be the full moon, huh?"

"I wouldn't know," Madison said. "I've never met Grace."

"So, what do I owe the honor of this call, Madison?" Mercy questioned sarcastically, as if Madison was wasting her time.

"My father… I left. He hit me and I left."

"I was wondering when Cyrus would get tired of your face."

Madison frowned, because that was what she wanted to speak to Mercy about. "What do you mean, my face?"

"You look just like your mother, Madison Oliver. You're a constant reminder of the woman who changed him for the good for once in his life and when he really was in love. I mean, from what I heard, Cyrus was a philandering woman beater, and it was like he took one look at your mother and just decided to change his whole life around. Got in the church and just became this awesome guy everyone loved. But our grandparents didn't think he really changed his ways. My mother said he did seem like he wanted to be a better person, and Aunt Mattie brought it out in him."

"So what happened?"

"Well, Aunt Mattie found out the truth that Cyrus thought no one would find out. Well, she didn't find out, that evil ass Hazel rubbed it in her face."

"What?"

"Cyrus had a son. An older son, but that wasn't the bad thing. He'd been having sex with Hazel since she was twelve years old."

Madison felt sick to her stomach.

"Hazel was determined to get Cyrus back, and had been using blackmail to keep him coming back to her. And when that stopped working, she made the secret come to light. Aunt Mattie was devastated more about Cyrus keeping secrets. It's a mistake he would always regret."

"I have an older brother?"

"You *had*. The night Aunt Mattie kicked Cyrus out of the house, he went over to Hazel to confront her. Somehow, your brother died. They said it was an accidental drowning in the tub. He'd been playing in the bathroom, hit his head on the sink, and then fell in the full of water. He was about four or five, I think. According to the police report and the news articles I saw, Hazel and Cyrus fought for hours before they realized their son was dead."

Gasping in horror, Madison couldn't believe what she was hearing.

"Cyrus lost the love of his life and his only son in one night," Mercy said. "It changed him – for the worse."

"And that's why, when he sees my face, he's reminded of his past sins," Madison realized.

"My mother said Aunt Mattie was so angry at Cyrus, she wouldn't allow him to look at her face. She wore this black veil whenever he was around. It was like punishment for him."

Madison remembered her mother doing that a lot whenever Mattie would drop her off with her father, but she just figured her mother was being dramatic because he'd moved in with Hazel. Madison had never known…

Missing her mom even more, and wishing Mattie was there to explain everything, she said, "He'll never love me, right, Mercy?"

"I'm sorry you had to come to the painful realization this way, Cousin. My mother told Mattie a million times she should tell you what a horrible man your father was, but I think Mattie just hoped you could love Cyrus and not hate him for what he did to her. Your mother was a hoper too, like you are. I didn't want to ruin what Aunt Mattie wanted for you. I mean, in a way, I thought things would get better for you, but I guess if you're calling me and telling me this, it's not."

Madison took a deep breath again and slowly released it. "I'll talk to you later, Mercy. Thanks."

"No problem. Call me whenever, and don't worry. You still have family."

Hanging up the phone, she lay back down.

Mercy was right because deep down inside, she hoped Cyrus could just love her. Maybe if she went home the next day, after her father cooled down, it wouldn't be so bad?

Her stomach muscles twitched, remembering the kick.

Yet, if she stayed away longer, her father would never want her back.

Never seeing Cyrus again felt better physically and emotionally, but there was a deep-seated conscience within her that felt bothered by the fact she wouldn't have any communication with her own father at all.

Albeit, just like Jamar stated, where she stayed was actually near one of the better bus routes to her school, and two good running bus routes to where she worked. Since it was off a main street in Detroit, she could pretty much get to anywhere she needed without a problem.

Getting her keys to Cyrus's home off her keyring, she stared at it for a long while before she dropped the key into the garbage bin.

She was tired of hoping her father would love her like the perfect daughter she fought to be. From now on, she would be her own woman, make her own decisions and do what she wanted to do to be happy.

From now on, her life was going to change… for the better for Madison Oliver.

CHAPTER 23

THREE HOURS LATER, there was a knock on her door. She open it to see Jamar standing there with a large bag from a restaurant and some grocery bags as well. He leaned over before saying anything, and kissed her.

Still dressed in his work clothes, he placed the bags on the small table and then went back out to the car.

His second trip in, he brought in a cooler with ice inside, a small tray and a microwave.

Inside the bags were items to make sandwiches and cereal. The cooler was for the milk he brought.

"You can get more ice down the hall at the ice machine. There's one on every level. Just go during the day and not in the middle of the night," he warned.

"I promise to be safe," Madison promised, touched by his concern. "But I can't pay you back for all of this."

"It's fine," he said, as if it were no big deal. "Friends wouldn't ask for anything in return."

"Can I ask you a question, Jamar?"

"Anything, Madison."

"How… well, why were you at the back of my father's house today?"

Without hesitation, he answered, "I got worried when you didn't show up at the bus stop this morning, and when I got off of work, I decided to go to my brother's house to wait for you. When you didn't show up there either, I sat at your corner. I saw your father leave, and then I saw you arrive, but you didn't go the house the normal way, I walked down there to see if it were okay. I heard you behind the house and followed you back there."

She accepted that answer because there was nothing else to believe. He'd been honest with her up to that point, and she trusted him.

"Mind if I take a shower?" he asked.

"Go ahead. You don't need to ask."

Jamar stole another kiss from her, and she watched as he went into the bathroom. He didn't bother to shut the door, nor did he seem to mind when she sat on the bed and watched him. His lean, muscular body was flawless, and her hands itched to touch him.

Remembering what she was supposed to be doing with him, she went to her bag and put specimen cups on the bedside table.

Jamar stripped down to his birthday suit and turned on the shower.

She still didn't stop watching him, mesmerized, as he lathered soap all over his body from head to toe. His short-cut groomed head even got a scrubbing before he got out of the shower.

The towel barely went around his waist.

"I'll bring more towels tomorrow," he promised, coming out of the bathroom.

"Do you work out?" she blurted out, visually caressing his body.

He flushed. "I pick up a lot of boxes and heavy items. I make sure I lift with my knees. Once I don't have to work so hard at the job, I might join a gym."

He'd brought a gym bag from his car on his first trip up, and dropped it by the table where he'd left the bag of hot food. The towel dropped, and so did Madison's mouth. She had to force herself to look away as he grabbed a T-shirt and some shorts to wear.

"I-I could turn up the heat," she offered, but from what she saw between his legs, he looked far from cold.

"I'm good, Madison," he said casually.

Embarrassed that she was acting like a teenager, she stated, "You shouldn't have done all this for me, Jamar."

"Why?" he asked, stepping into his clothes.

He began took out the warm food from the bag and was setting it out so they could eat.

She went over to the table to give herself some distance from him, and emptied out the other food bags.

Along with the milk, there was bread, apples, sandwich products, cans of soups and gumbo, plus small dinners she could put in the microwave. He had even bought plastic cutlery, paper bowls, cups and plates, along with an extra milk jug and a gallon of apple juice.

Continuing to voice her complaint, she said, "Because I don't know how long I'm staying here... with you. Remember, this is just an arrangement."

Tightly, he asked, "You aren't planning on going back to those people you call family?"

"He's my father," she defended, out of instinct.

"I don't care if that man was Jesus. He treated you badly. He hurt you," Jamar protested. "I need to be dragging you down to the precinct to file charges against him."

The embarrassment her father would suffer would be horrendous.

"I couldn't," she said. "But I can't afford to live here."

"You make enough a week from my brother to stay here and handle any expenses. I know the owner of this hotel. I've got you a monthly deal as long as you leave the place as you found it when you decide not to come back. I'll help you however I can, and you'll be fine. I said I'm your friend, Madison. Not just some 'specimen'. I can't let you go back to be beaten half to death."

A chill ran through her body because Jamar seemed to know her father too well.

His hand caressed her cheek softly. "I know mean people," he explained as if reading her thoughts. "I've looked evil in the eyes and no matter what you do, Madison, evil will never love you back, even if they are blood." He leaned over to kiss her.

The impact of his words and kiss vibrated her soul.

This time, this kiss was longer and nicer. She moved her arms around his neck to deepen the connection. He moved their bodies towards the bed, until the back of her knees touched the edge.

Jamar laid down on top of her, exploring her mouth like he wanted to taste every drop of her.

This was it, she said to herself. This was where she was going all the way...

His hands moved under her shirt, and both of them moaned as he palmed her breasts. Her nipples were hard as rocks and overly sensitive, but he was amazingly gentle as he massaged them, all the while continuing his exploratory kiss that was blowing her mind.

His other hand took her hand and moved her palm down to his shorts. He wasn't firmly hard, although it felt like he was getting excited.

It wasn't until she gripped him that his stiffness grew completely. Her confidence took over and she knew what it took to excite him.

His mouth left hers and descended down to her breasts.

Her vision blurred, her body buckled, and her skin tingled hard as his mouth manipulated her nipples, going from one to another, to give them equal attention. She could barely concentrate on exciting him as he took her body to another level of pleasure. If he could do this without even gaining entry, she knew she would explode once they got down to the real deal.

And Madison wanted the real deal. She wanted him to be the man she found real pleasure with and not some inexperience boy fiddling around her hitting and missing as had been the case in the past. Jamar's mouth continued to titillate her as she progressed, manipulating him to become harder.

His hands ventured down into her shorts and moved between her legs.

The double bliss from his hands and mouth brought her senses to a level she never thought possible.

"Damn, woman, you're so wet," he whispered. "Gawd, you're fucking coming on my finger, Madison, just like he said..." He didn't finish that sentence as he finished her off.

Just like who said? She wanted to stick with that thought, but she was coming. Her juices were running down the crevice of her butt cheeks, vibrating under him and holding him close, never wanting to let him go.

Wetness exploded from her. She was embarrassed and happy at the same time.

Blushing, she pushed his shoulders down on the bed until she was moving over him. He put his fingers, coated in her wetness down his throat and sucked her juices clean from his fingers. Damn if that didn't turn her on more.

He helped her get rid of his shorts as she maneuvered over him until she was fully able to taste him, and turning her body so he could taste her. Her tongue ventured everywhere on his lower body freely. He laid back and let her take her time. The male anatomy was not alien to her eyes, but the fact he allowed her to explore him made her grateful for the opportunity.

His moans and groans told her she was answering his sexual prayers. Soon, his hands and mouth started to explore her too, pushing off her shorts and pulling her thighs into his face.

Trying to concentrate on him while he orally pleased her was difficult, but Madison was determined to give as good as he gave. Slipping him deep down her throat, she blew out a breath through her nose so she wouldn't choke, and continuously repeated her actions, loving the feel of his shaft in her mouth.

His hips bucked, helping her take more of him, and she sensed he was close to coming. She was getting ready to come again as well. His whole face was buried between her legs, and his mouth was dripping, trying to catch her juices.

The look of euphoria was all over his face. "Uh… Mad... Wait… I'm…"

She reached over quickly and grabbed a cup, just as he exploded. She captured all of him and smiled happily, seeing how he almost filled the entire cup.

"Oooooohhhhhhhh...uuuuggggghhh," he mumbled, lost in ecstasy.

Madison licked her lips, then kissed the tip of him in appreciation when he was done. She put the cup back on the nightstand as he recovered. He now seemed determined to finish her off as he returned to bury his face between her legs. His mouth was everywhere and his fingers were also included, pushing deep behind her and at the same time titillating her clitoris, while his other fingers quivered inside her vagina. The double sensation made her eyes feel like they were about to pop out of her head. At the same time, she thought her chest and heart were about to explode.

Before the orgasm finished, he was pushing her back on the bed, pulling her shirt off her body. The rest of his clothes had long disappeared.

Jamar eyed between her legs like he hadn't eaten in years, and she knew he was not through orally pleasing her body.

She shivered in fear and pleasure at the same time. She wanted this. She wanted him.

CHAPTER 24

LAYING BACK ON THE bed, feeling his eyes on her naked body everywhere, Madison felt confident and at peace. Being with him, she was not worried, or overthinking; she was just Madison.

Jamar looked like he was about to go back to work on her body with pleasure in his eyes, as he knelt back down between her thighs to start voraciously licking her all over – ALL OVER.

She was shocked and stunned by his eagerness, but damn if her hips didn't have a mind of their own, grinding against his mouth. If she hadn't been so wet, she swore she would have started a fire. The blood in her veins felt like lava flowing under her skin.

Madison was in an unknown bliss she couldn't describe. When Jamar rose up and tore off a condom, she was barely cognizant.

He made her feel like her body was one of a kind.

Madison fully understood there was a lot more to come.

Moving over her body, he said, "Are you ready for this?"

It was the first unsure thing he'd said, but she didn't dwell on the alarms going off in her head.

"Yes," she panted, opening her legs and bracing her body to receive him.

All the times she had been with a man, she had been terrified of this moment, but tonight she was wanton for everything he could give her.

Jamar grunted and strained as he pressed against her. "Damn, Mad… so fucking tight."

She forced herself to relax, shifting her hips and opening her legs wider. The pressure… so much pressure, but then… a delirium of pleasure erupted all over her, trembling her body under his.

Jamar pressed his whole weight into her and gasped. "Fuck… your pussy… fuck…Mad."

His voice was reverential and he delivered more cursed praises as he began deep long strokes into her. She thought his fingers had been magical, but now she truly began to understand what sex was and why it could be addicting.

Exultant tremors enveloped her from head to toe, and she cried out jovially, drowning in the overwhelming beautiful sensations he evoked.

"Damn... you're so beautiful. Damn... Mad... Mad..." His body bucked hard against hers and she smiled, receiving his orgasm, loving the feeling of satisfaction she gave him and accepted.

He collapsed atop her body, panting and looking grateful. "No man's ever fucked you like that?" he questioned.

A tear ran down her cheek. "No, not like that."

He rolled on his side, yet left his thigh over her legs to hold her down. "I didn't do all this for just sex, Madison, or for you. I did this for me, too. I needed to know if I could make real love to you."

She didn't really understand. "Thank you for giving me what you gave."

Jamar actually blushed, and kissed her passionately.

Now she was hungry, but she was suddenly sleepy too, and her eyes slowly closed. She knew Jamar was getting out of bed and she thought she heard the hotel door open, but she was too exhausted from the whole day to look and see. Maybe he needed to go out to his car. Maybe he had somewhere to go.

Either way, she wanted to trust him.

***

Madison woke some hours later with Jamar's large naked body on his back beside her. She snuck out of bed to work on her project, glad she had been able to take all her items from the house.

At that point, she knew she couldn't go back to her father's house and would have to make a way for herself without disturbing her education. This dilemma weighed heavily on her mind, but she also wanted to do more work on her other research as well.

The various creams she had made were looking good and she was proud of the results.

Looking at the bed, she smirked greedily. She would need some more samples.

She went over to Jamar, who slept peacefully. He didn't wake as she pulled the covers away and crawled into bed. She didn't need his instruction anymore as she lowered her head to his sex and began to orally manipulate him to hardness.

Jamar moaned in his sleep, but far from pain. His hips encouraged her to continue and directed her to give him the strokes he needed to take him over the edge.

Jamar awoke, groaning as he came. She moved the specimen cup in place just in time, and smiled wickedly at her accomplishment.

"Damn!" he said, weakened and content, but far from upset. "I like that shit."

She giggled as he pulled her in his arms and kissed her deeply.

"When can I get some more?" she asked wantonly with a blush.

He chuckled. "You're going to kill me, beautiful. Give me an update all about your experiments so I can understand it more."

After putting the specimen on ice, she gladly told him what she was trying to accomplish. The odd part was that Jamar actually looked interested and didn't tell her how boring she sounded. They ate cold food together as she continued to tell him all about what she would like to happen for her new project.

By morning, she was back to sleep in his arms, content and happy.

He gently awoke her and urged her to get up. "I'll drop you off at school today since I'm leaving too."

Madison sleepily showered and dressed for school.

Just before coming out of the bathroom, she could hear him on the phone trying to speak quietly. "Yeah... it went good. I can't believe what you told me worked... I thought about it. I heard you outside the door, but I think it's too early."

She hesitated before opening the door. She wanted to believe he was out for her well-being. What could he want from her? He didn't know anything about her or anyone she knew, so he couldn't be in some crazy mass conspiracy. Maybe he had his own secrets about his life she wouldn't like. Everyone had vices and secrets, and maybe Jamar's were something bad that he didn't want known.

There was the two years he was ashamed of, and then the strange thing he'd said during sex. Now this? Madison would keep her observation to herself. Right now, Jamar was really all she had until she could get in touch with her cousin again and see if Mercy could help her.

When they were in the car, Jamar said, "Keep that money you just got from my brother for your living expenses and transportation. Like I said, the room's been booked for a month, and after that, you'll get a deal." He handed her a burner phone. "This is yours. I programmed my number on speed dial and even my brother's number as well, in case you can't reach me. I want to be able to reach you and I want you to always be able to reach me."

"Thanks, Jamar." Madison was touched by his concern for her well-being, but she still kept her skepticism to herself. Jamar had secrets, and she wasn't sure if she wanted to know them. Perhaps she wanted to just go about blindly while taking what she needed from him, until she had enough for her experiments.

He smiled easily. "That's what friends are for."

Right before she got out of the car, she leaned over to him and asked, "Do you think I can get more tonight?"

It was his turn to blush. "You're just hungry, aren't you, beautiful?"

She liked his new nickname for her much better than baby girl. With Jamar, Madison did feel beautiful, and not just because of the sex. He seemed to give her power and confidence. It was as if she had been on training wheels all her life and now she as taking them off, chucking them aside, and doing just fine on her own.

It was the reason she didn't want to know his secrets yet. She needed him, for more than just a specimen, but as a friend.

"I'll get you some more," he promised. "I'll get you all you want. It will be better than last night."

Madison kissed him with a smile of appreciation before going to class.

***

All day long, Madison thought about the previous night and wondered what did he have that could top last night?

Joshua seemed inquisitive. She assumed it was because they were wrapping up most of the labs and he wanted to get close to her and her work.

"Once this is approved, are you working on anything else?" he inquired.

"I'm always working on something, Josh," she said evasively. Although she loved telling Jamar about her new project, she didn't want to talk to Joshua about it.

She went to the greenhouse after doing labs. Just inside of the door she spotted an envelope with her name on the front. Money was inside with a small note of thank you signed by Jason. Smiling with security, she put this envelope in her bag and got to work.

Since the soil had been cultivated properly, Madison started planting. There was even a small space where she could start her own crop she'd created in the lab.

Her life at that moment was perfect. When she returned to her hotel room, she worked a little on her own research, washed her face, and documented her regime and progress after taking another shower.

When she was done, Madison organized her room using the second closet by the front door as a sort of kitchen and pantry. With milk crates and boxes found by the hotel's trash bin, she had her room looking presentable.

Too excited to sleep, she decided to work on her budget to prepare for everything else she needed.

As she logged in her hours, she also called Mercy but was pushed to voicemail. "Good evening, cousin. I know it's late, but I thought I should call you with my new number." She didn't want to leave what she really wanted from Mercy in a message. "Call me back, please."

She reached in her backpack and found the latest envelope received. Slowly, she opened it and gasped. How much were they paying her? Five hundred dollars?

A justifiable amount for a professional gardener, but she hadn't expected something justifiable; just enough change to put in her pocket.

Her phone chimed.

Opening the screen, she saw it was Jamar.

"*You at the hotel?*" he texted.

She replied, "*Yes.*"

"*You nice, clean and ready?*"

All she wore was a nightgown with her hair in braids. Replying back, she texted, "*Yes.*" Already, she could feel her juices running in expectation of what he was going to do to her body.

"*Unlock the door, turn off all the lights, lay on the bed and close your eyes, beautiful.*"

She was damn near about to burst in anticipation. What did he have in store for her tonight?

Obeying, she closed her eyes and waited.

The door to her room opened and she heard footsteps approaching her. She could barely breathe calmly as she felt him move above her head.

Madison just knew deep in her gut that night was definitely going to be a night she would never forget.

CHAPTER 25

H IS HANDS TOUCHED HER hips, moved over her stomach and up to massage her breasts as if he'd never touched them before. His movements were slow and deliberate, inciting arousal in her, and then moved down to pull her nightgown off.

She heard a tearing noise and gasped.

"I'll buy you a new one," he promised, but his voice sounded more in front of her, by her legs, not over her head.

Suddenly, a blindfold was placed over her eyes.

"What's going on?" she asked warily.

"Trust me," he whispered, yet again, this sounded far away. At the same time, his hands circumnavigated her breasts again, massaging them until the tips had hardened, beckoning for more attention.

He moved around the bed between her knees. His hands went down her sides to her thighs and then moved to her feet before coming back up between her legs.

She was so wet she could feel her essence starting to run down her legs.

He guided her to lie on her stomach, then started the process all over again. Touching every inch of her as if it was his first time, but also with tender and loving strokes that further aroused her. He was masterful at what he was doing to her.

By the time he'd guided her to lie on her back again, she was panting and wanton, craving sex beyond belief. How had he done this without sex was a mystery to her, but she was enthralled and fully taken almost to the point of coming, just by his touch.

He pressed a thick finger inside her to see how wet she was. She was ready for him, but then he moved away.

"Jamar?" she asked doubtfully, trying to find him in her darkness.

There was a noise, as if someone was sitting in the corner, but at the same time, in front of her there was the sound of the tearing of a condom.

"The spermicide," she warned.

"I know," Jamar whispered in front of her, guiding her to her knees and gently pressing another finger in front of her to test her wetness. He didn't waste any more time to get into position and press deep within her on the first stroke. Tonight, he seemed stronger, more confident, and definitely somehow thicker.

She sobbed in joyous bliss as he repeatedly drove into her and then moved his hand around to the front and massaged her most sensitive area, sending her senses skyrocketing to the moon. He didn't stop or slow down, and she thought for sure he was past the point of coming.

Had he come? Damn the condoms.

He nudged her more on the bed, then guided her to move on her side, while he still was inside of her, staying behind her. Did he feel bigger, or was it only because of the new position they were in? He didn't miss a stroke as he pumped inside of her, while his hand was free to explore her whole body.

He flicked his fingers over her nipples, suckled on her neck, and titillated areas of her body, keeping her heavily aroused until she was coming again, sobbing thickly in passion and pleasure.

Yet, when she tried to touch him, he moved her arms away and seemed to stroke her harder.

In that moment, she loved how all the pleasure was focused on her, until she found herself so incoherent and incapable of thinking of anything else.

In that moment, her world was quiet, and she caved into herself feeling like the most beautiful creature on earth.

His hand seemed all over her body, almost abnormally increasing her pleasure, and he was stoked into her, keeping her from thinking straight, her body burning in flames of bliss.

She whimpered her delight as her body received his pulsing to further drive her orgasm stronger.

"Grrrr...." He growled, and she could feel spittle on her back from him. He was fighting his orgasm. This was the longest he had ever gone without coming, but the more he held off, the more pleasure her body took in, until finally, he shoved her on her stomach, removed himself from her and she could hear the wet condom being removed.

He dipped another finger in her and then used her essence to masturbate him into orgasm...right on her back.

She gasped, feeling the warm liquid fill her back, and didn't move. He didn't move either, yet she heard movement around her... off the bed.

"Jamar?" she called out.

"Shhhh..." he eased her as she felt the specimen cup up against her back.

How had he gotten to the cups in the side-drawer by the bed? She had not put them out, nor had he moved.

Reaching out in front of her, she gasped, feeling someone was there. This was a thigh, thicker, longer, more...

Yanking the blindfold off, standing in front of Madison was a large man who then immediately knelt down to her. He had large liquid pools of peanut butter brown eyes, with a naturally humorous look, and a dark brown beard, with highlights of organic light brown strands here and there.

Scrambling to the headboard, she pulled the covers around her, ashamed. Desperately, she looked over at Jamar, who was putting his clothes back on. He sat on the edge of the bed, closest to her. The other man, younger than Jamar, didn't move from where he was, but he didn't stop looking at her.

"It's okay," Jamar assured her.

"What?! Who?..." She sobbed, mortified. "Why did you do this?"

"Meet Jason Knight, my partner and brother I've been telling you about."

"But why'd you fool me? Deceive me? Bring him here, like this?" she asked, appalled.

"Because I wanted to give you more," he reasoned, pointing to the bed table.

She followed the direction his finger was pointing and saw the three cups of specimen.

"I told my godbrother what you were trying to do, and he said I should masturbate before seeing you so I would last longer, and give you a larger load."

Jason sat on the end of the bed, and she squeezed her body more against the headboard, still feeling humiliated.

"I didn't mean more like *this*, Jamar," she said, angry.

Jamar eased closer and slowly pulled her reluctant body in his arms. "It means nothing less between you and me, beautiful." He kissed her brow. "I'm going to give you just as much loving as before, but more with Jason's help."

Warily, she snuck a glance over at Jason, who only gave her a wink.

Quickly, she looked away, still embarrassed, but noting how handsome he was too. Suddenly she realized who he was and gasped. "You're the one with another woman?"

Jason blushed. "You been talking about me, bro?"

"I had to let her know why you needed that greenhouse. It's true. You're trying to impress a girl to get her to hurry up and marry you," Jamar said with indignation.

"You're going to be married? You shouldn't be here," she reprimanded Jason.

"I'm not engaged yet. I'm trying to marry her," Jason corrected. "I'm trying to get my life together, just like Jamar. I haven't asked her, yet."

"And spending all this money, trying to impress some girl who wouldn't normally give him the time of day," Jamar grunted. "But until she commits, he can help you with your experiment. He's clean. I swear by him."

"You should tell her everything, Jamar," Jason urged. "It's why you brought me here, too. She needs to know the truth if she's really going to accept me here with you."

"What truth?" Madison demanded to know.

What truth could Jamar possibly tell her that would make her just accept Jason into their tryst?

CHAPTER 26

J AMAR SEEMED HESITANT ALL of a sudden, and looked away in shame. She cupped his face and guided him to look at her.

"Please, Jamar, tell me. It can't be as bad as what I feel about myself or what's happened to me."

He looked deep in her eyes, and she could feel him holding her tighter. He looked almost scared.

"I have…had a problem, sexually, Madison. You know, I used to be addicted to immediate sexual pleasure."

Jason snorted. "My brother is trying to say he was addicted to blow jobs. To the point of morning, noon or night, he was finding ways to get himself off."

She looked at Jamar, confused, and a look of shame filled his eyes. "I don't understand."

"First it was the masturbation, like I said," Jamar said evasively. "And then it was oral pleasure. It was so bad, I lost most of my inheritance trying to pay for my addiction, and then the charges were brought up. Jason made me go to therapy, but that only made me stop trying to get it all the time. It didn't help with the need."

Jason continued to answer, "Blame it on my demented Auntie; made him masturbate when she was in a good mood, bad mood, or just to make him suffer."

"Your hang-up," she remembered Jamar telling her and then looked at Jason. "You called his mother your aunt?"

"It was too strange calling that woman Mother," Jason said in distaste. "Not after what she made me do to her. I got away with calling her Auntie. That's it." He looked at Madison proudly. "Thank you for helping, Jamar. He hasn't had the capability to have sex with a woman properly in a long time. When he told me about you, I knew you were special to him." He moved to her side of the bed, closer to his brother, and knelt down.

She pulled the covers protectively around to cover her body. "Why did you need to be here?" she demanded to know.

"Because I needed his instruction," Jamar explained. "Like he said, I hadn't been with a woman... properly. I needed his help. I needed him to show me. I want to be with you like a man is supposed to, Madison. And I can only ask Jason to show me."

"There are books, videos, porn," she pointed out.

"Porn and videos are not the most conducive for my big brother," Jason said. "And he's not very book smart. Jamar learns better by hands-on instruction and watching. Do you understand, Madison?"

She looked at Jamar. "I understand, but...he's your brother, Jamar. You won't like me any less if...?" Madison didn't know how to say what she wanted to say.

Jamar kissed her. "I'd like it more if you did, beautiful. I need to be shown what it takes to please you. Jason's the only one I can ask, before he ties himself down."

Madison let him kiss her again, loving how his mouth made her feel. Had Jason taught him that?

Her nervousness seemed to wane.

"Didn't I tell you, Jason, that she was beautiful?" Jamar said before capturing her lips again, teasing her tongue to wrap around his, turning her on yet again.

That word, "beautiful," seemed to be the key to her feelings, her soul. She felt open to receiving whatever these two men were going to give her.

Jason stood up and walked to the other side of the bed.

Jamar enraptured her in wondrous kisses, pulling the sheet from between their bodies and exposing her flesh for his brother's eyes.

She heard Jason getting on the bed with them and she was nervous, but the things Jamar was doing to her body... she couldn't think straight. His hands felt her all over.

And then she felt extra hands on her back – Jason's hands. He moved them from her neck, down her backside, and then up again, repeating the motion until she relaxed.

Jamar moved around her, planting kisses on her face, neck and shoulder. Moving to her side, he caressed her breasts, continuing to plant kisses.

Jason's large body was very near and his eyes met hers again. She was naked completely. There was a hungry look in his light brown eyes that made her shiver.

His eyes caressed every inch of her exposed skin.

She tilted her face to one side and he tilted his face the other way, while moving to capture her receptive lips.

His kisses were more demanding, Madison could almost feel her soul leave her body, yet seem to fill her with a lust so deep, and it made her spirit curl.

Jason made everything feel so right, as if he was going to take care of everything. He pulled her body underneath his, roughly, and licked down her neck and chest.

His virility seemed to pull her over the edge, yet he was controlled. His touches were deliberate. He was really showing Jamar... he was really showing Jamar how to arouse her for lovemaking.

Were they the real deal? Could she trust them?... Both?

CHAPTER 27

SHE ENJOYED THE TWO magnificent men who gazed upon her as if she were the most beautiful woman in the world. Madison was in deep lust.

Jason's mouth and hands moved down her body, over her breasts, to her stomach, down her thighs, and to the sides of her calves. He left no inch of skin untouched, and when he reached her ankles, Jason started up her body, finding different spaces to kiss her. His lips and tongue kissed and suckled, keeping her properly occupied and pushing her nervousness aside as Jamar climbed on the bed naked, towards her face.

Jamar held his semi-hard manhood strong, and all she had to do was raise up a little to engulf him in her mouth.

"Slow down, beautiful," he encouraged her. "You got me all night."

Madison heeded his instructions, and even when she gagged, he told her how to overcome. Soon, she was deep-throating with expertise as Jason's mouth titillated her body, without hesitation.

Jason plunged his mouth between her legs and licked voraciously around her clit. He kissed her lower lips just as intensely as he had kissed her upper lips.

Jamar touched her neck, breasts and stomach, verbally encouraging her, breathing hard, gasping and sometimes lolling his head back as he enjoyed her oral ministrations. Just one hand massaged her breasts and soon, she also felt Jason's hand on her other breast. His mouth moved down, circling her perineum, and then moving even deeper in places she didn't know were so sensitive.

Madison almost choked, at the same time crying in pleasure as she fully continued to deep-throat Jamar with long, oral wet strokes, utilizing her tongue profusely over the tip of his thickened shaft. She knew him well enough to know he was near climax yet again.

"Fuck," he cursed. "Damn, your mouth is beautiful... oh, damn."

She sucked him hard, loving how rigid he was becoming.

"Man, let's switch," Jason urged his brother. "It looks like you've taught her real well."

Jason moved up to the other side of her, while Jamar moved down to straddle her right after he put on another condom quickly.

She gasped, "What about-"

Jamar cut her off. "I'll take it off before…" He nodded to the table where there was a fresh sample cup waiting.

Madison smiled wickedly, licking her lips, turned her head to the other side, and didn't miss a beat, taking Jason down her throat.

He was much rougher than Jamar, but she was getting used to that from him. Their shafts were almost the same lengths, but Jason's was slightly thicker.

She loved seeing her spit make Jason's light brown shaft sparkle as he gripped the side of her head with his hands, driving his manhood deep down her throat.

Jamar was past the point of controlling his own passion as he pressed himself all the way until their middles met, griping the sides of her posterior. She could slightly see him, and she delighted in the way he threw his head back in the throes of ecstasy.

"Arrgggh," he growled.

She could feel his powerful pulsing, and then braced herself. Jamar pumped so hard inside of her, her mouth abruptly dislodged off Jason's shaft until Jamar erupted inside of her.

Not at all disappointed she wouldn't be able to get a sample, all she could do was brace and hold on as the insane tremors to her body pulsed all over her. Jamar was soaked in sweat as he dislodged from Madison, who was still amazingly wet.

Moaning, she said, "You forgot the cup, Jamar."

"Damn, woman!" he growled. "I'll make it up. I promise." He took off the condom and said to his brother, "She's so damn perfect, isn't she, Jason?"

Jason returned her mouth to his manhood so she could finish him, only grunting in pleasure as she proceeded where she had left off. Speech, logic and anything coherent was gone as he thrilled in her mouth. Madison pulled out all her knowledge of oral skills she had learned from Jamar in the past few days to impress Jason.

He looked ready to pass out, and his shaft had thickened so much, she could barely grip her lips around him anymore.

Now she understood why Jamar had brought Jason. He was a perfect specimen. She could taste the virility on her tongue. She salivated more, knowing what was going to come from him.

Seconds later, Jason was giving her more specimen in the ready cup. He didn't seem to mind that she pulled away just as she tasted his thickened syrupiness and directed the stream in the specimen cup.

Jason practically roared his orgasm to fruition, and Madison smiled proudly, hoping neighbors wouldn't call the police, thinking someone was hurting her.

She smacked her lips together, putting the lid on the cup and placing it on the bedside table.

Madison giggled in glee and satisfaction.

Panting, Jason said, "You're right, brother. Her mouth is beautiful too."

Jamar moved up slightly to look down at her with a proud look in his eyes. "I love seeing you happy, Madison."

She smiled because having sex and being pleased by two gorgeous, magnificent men was unbelievably amazing. A year ago, she would have never thought she could do something like this.

Yet, that night she would have never wanted to do anything different.

Jamar knelt down and tenderly kissed her with more feeling than he'd ever done, bringing tears to her eyes. "I want to always make you happy, Madison."

"Thank you," she said with appreciation.

He stood up from the bed, gathered all her specimens and went over to the cooler. She was glad he cared just as much about her project as she did, and put the specimens on ice until she could work on her project later.

"I'm going to get you more ice and then take a shower," he said, put on his pants and shoes, then walked out, leaving her alone naked with his bigger, but younger brother… who was also naked.

"Come here," Jason ordered gently as he lay on the bed, resting his head on the pillow.

His manhood was flaccid, so she was confused as to what he could want from her, since he wasn't aroused anymore.

Still, she obeyed and scooted over to him. He guided her to straddle his hips like a pony. Her wetness rested on his shaft, and this position left her body fully open to him, physically and visually.

Jason tweaked her nipples before starting to massage her breasts.

"Jamar says you're smart, but he didn't go into detail about that," Jason said, nodding to the cooler with the specimens. "Why do you need our essence?"

Spoken eloquently, it was a valid question.

"For an experiment," she explained with a blush.

"What kind?" he inquired.

She really didn't want to tell him, and just shrugged.

Jason looked as if he was going to settle with that answer from her. His hands moved down to her hips and he grinded her hips against him. Her wetness helped him gain enough hardness to rub against her clit, while he leaned her body down, curving his body upwards.

His mouth attacked a nipple, sending her senses swirling.

"I-I need cum..." she breathed heavily, as he teased his shaft up and down her cavern.

"Why?" he whispered curiously, briefly taking his mouth from one nipple to another.

"T-to be…" she gasped as he changed the grinding to a circular motion. "To be beautiful," she whimpered. "My… research… I need …you…"

Abruptly, he swiveled his hips, making her dive on the bed sideways, but her leg was still over his thigh. He guided her hands down to his manhood, which had started to get hard again.

He smiled wickedly. "You're already beautiful, especially when you're aroused, Madison."

She watched in amazement as his body responded to her hand manipulation.

"You like what you can do to our bodies, also, don't you?" he questioned.

Wickedly, she smiled, admitting, "Yes."

"Gawd, I see why he loves you," Jason said, amazed. "He's taught you too well." He captured her mouth to try to dissipate some of the passion what was overwhelming him. His demanding kisses were so damn delicious.

"You need to know more about helping Jamar," Jason said.

"Teach me," she insisted, wanting very much to please Jamar.

"Lick my nipples," he ordered. "Just like I licked yours."

She didn't hesitate and leaned over to kiss his body. Jason had a lot more hair on his body than Jamar, but none of it got in her way as she licked and suckled his chest. With her dual manipulation to his manhood, she could feel him becoming excited.

His breathing became rapid. He rocked his hips back and forth, telling her exactly the kind of strokes he liked.

"You thought about direct insertion?" he suggested. "To be beautiful?"

"Direct?" she asked curious.

"Injection. To hurry your process."

The idea seemed scientifically smart, but the moral and health implications were unpredictable.

"I'm clean," Jason swore. "Jamar made me go test today. He said you were innocent and he wasn't messing up a good thing like you."

Biting her lip, she tried to make up her mind. He moved his hand down between her legs, tweaking her clit, and then inserted a thick finger into her.

Leaning over to whisper in her ear, he promised, "It will feel beautiful. And we'll get you the morning-after pill."

Damn, Jason was worse than his brother. He made sin sound so easy.

CHAPTER 28

JASON MOVED HIS HAND down between her legs, flicked her clit several more times, and then drove his finger deeper into her repeatedly. She gasped at how sensitive she was, and further turned as he kissed her, full on her lips, entwining their tongues together.

Madison was past the point of sensible thinking and guided him into her. The feeling of Jason's raw thickness filling and stretching her brought moans deep within the recess of her chest, almost vibrating the windows of the room with her intensity.

"S-so ... tight," Jason strained, as a layer of sweat broke out all over him.

Their bodies grinded together. Jason stroked slow, stoking a sensual burn all over her. He moved his hands to squeeze her, then plunged his finger into her rear. She howled as her body literally trembled from her toes to her head.

Jason followed closely behind her, sending her over a blissful edge again.

"What the fuck?" Jamar hissed at the end of the bed, wearing only a towel, just as they were recovering. "Jay, what the hell have you done?"

So consumed in their hunger, they had both forgotten Jamar was there. What had she been thinking? Or not thinking? Damn Jason for seducing her. She was acting like Nikki, jumping from man to man. While Madison felt there was something different about this situation than Nikki's frivolous affairs, she didn't want to be the cause of the brothers breaking up.

Jason looked guilty as he disengaged and got out of the bed. "I wasn't thinking, Jam."

"It's my fault," Madison said, yanking the covers over herself in guilt, cursing her wanton behavior. "I put him inside of me, Jamar."

Jamar didn't listen to her as he turned to his brother and railed, "She could get pregnant, Jay. We're not supposed to lose it!"

She moved to the end of the bed, not liking how angry Jamar was becoming. "Don't be mad at him, Jamar."

"Fuck, Jam, I'm sorry," Jason said apologetically. "I was into her… into the moment. You're right, she's beautiful, but we'll use the day-after pill."

Jamar turned to her, not looking angry or disgusted. He actually looked concerned. "Are you okay, Madison?" he asked.

His anxiety touched her as she moved into his receiving arms, holding him close. His body was still moist from the shower.

"I'm fine," she assured him. "But I'm just as guilty as Jason, Jamar. It did feel good." She reached down, pushing his towel down his body, gripping his manhood. "I want to feel how you feel in me." Looking up at him, she asked in her most innocent voice, "Can I have some of you?"

The shock and lust in his eyes was evident. "Fuck, woman, you're even more beautiful when you're horny," Jamar said in disbelief.

"He's right, everything will be okay," she said. She ran her hand up and down his shaft. "Please, Jamar, while the night is young."

Jason encouraged Jamar, "I'll go get that in the morning, Joe. I know exactly where to go."

Jamar looked conflicted now. "I don't want to hurt you, Madison."

"Please," she begged. "And then I can go get birth control. I promise. I want you to, Jamar. I want you inside of me."

He growled, lifting her and carrying her back to bed. She giggled, but kissed him just as voraciously, in delight knowing he had given in to her seduction.

"I'm going to play with you for a long while," he warned, laying over her. "I'm not like Jason. I'm going to make your body scream for me."

The sound of those words did not deter her. Madison wanted what he promised. They'd figure out the bad stuff in the morning. For now, she wanted all good stuff and Jamar didn't let her down.

A couple of hours later, she was still screaming for dear life as Jamar exploded deep within her. Jason had watched them the whole time, and had become aroused again. When Jamar moved from her, Jason replaced him immediately on the bed, moving her torso to twist her lower body to the side. This created a tighter entry for his thickness.

Groaning, panting and sweating, Jason took long, quick strokes, deep into her, rocking her body so hard, they shook the bed.

She had to hold onto the bedframe moments later as he released inside of her, knowing they probably woke the neighboring room with all the pounding.

Jamar laid on the other side of her, kissing her neck and cheek.

Madison cried her ecstasy, loving how these two men had changed her world.

Exhausted and overwhelmed, her eyes closed in sleep. She felt Jason dislodge from her to turn off the lamp by the bed, then wrapped his big body behind her as she snuggled closer to Jamar.

Never in her life had she ever fallen asleep without covers on her body. Yet, both men produced enough body heat to keep her nice and warm.

No, her lovers were enough. Just right… perfect.

Madison really did feel beautiful… inside and out.

***

A chill swept her to reality and she instantly knew Jason wasn't behind her anymore. Jamar was just getting out of bed, still naked.

"Good morning," he said as he found his towel and wrapped it around his waist.

She stretched like a lazy cat as he returned to sit on the bed near her.

Jamar was still as handsome as ever, and after the night they'd had, she would be crazy to be angry at him or herself.

"Jason left to wait for the pharmacy to open and to get breakfast for us. It's early." He rubbed her body and also kissed her forehead.

She only nodded and smiled.

"Are you mad at me?" Jamar asked.

Madison cupped his face and shook her head. "I should be asking you that."

Jamar kissed her forehead again. "Want to shower first? If Jason returns with you in bed, he might think it's round two."

She snorted. "You mean round five." Rubbing her nose with Jamar's, she said, "Thank you for last night."

"No, thank you, Madison," he said in deep appreciation. "Are you tired?"

"Very sated," she said.

He helped her out of bed and guided her to the bathroom. As he warmed the shower up, he ran his hands over her body. There was a hunger in his eyes Madison was starting to associate with his arousal. By the time he took her in the shower with him, they were kissing deeply and rubbing each other's bodies.

He pressed her back against the wall, rose up her thigh, and entered her.

Surprisingly, she had snapped back in place and could feel every millimeter of his shaft as he pulsed and pumped into her.

137

All she could do was dig her fingers into his shoulders and hold on for dear life.

Being with Jamar was so different than Jason. She could tell he cared for her, cherished her and worshipped her. There was an innocence of inexperience to him where he could take her orgasm and prolong her body's pleasure to culminate with his. Jamar could give as well as Jason, but when he did give, her senses and soul were rocked.

He came to his mental equilibrium before her and proceeded to wash her from head to toe. By the time he was done, she was aroused again, but knew playtime was over because Jason had returned. Jamar even made her stay in the bathroom while he went to choose some clothes for her to wear.

Madison dressed quickly, then joined both men at the table in the hotel room. Jamar had Jason get her extra ice to keep her "specimens" fresh until she returned later.

The men had set out breakfast and Jason had the pills from the pharmacy. "You take two now, and then in twelve hours, you take the other two," Jason instructed.

She remembered her friend Nikki doing the same once, and swallowed the first two pills.

Jason rewarded her with a kiss.

As they ate, the men regaled her with stories of their childhood adventures – before things had gone bad. They weren't related, but they were very close to each other like real siblings. Jamar was an unplanned late birth, and his parents had been semi-wealthy, but tended to leave their son to his own devices prior to Jamar's father dying in the accident.

"Jamar used to come over before my parents died and fell in love with my mother's turkey sandwiches," Jason said. "She used to put potato salad, honey baked ham, and mustard on rye bread."

Jamar moaned, remembering the taste.

Madison giggled.

"I loved those sandwiches," Jamar confessed guiltily. "I could eat five in one sitting if she let me."

All three of them burst out in laughter.

"Jamar is like a brother to me," Jason said. "He keeps me on track. I'd be a royal fuck-up if I didn't heed him. I leap without looking at lot of times. I've learned this about myself."

"Really?" Jamar growled. "Cause all the growling I'm doing about the spoiled rotten skank ain't doing one damn good to change your mind about her."

Madison knew that whoever this woman was in Jason's life was a sore subject to Jamar.

She intervened. "Not fair discussing other women while you're with me, Jamar," she pouted.

Jamar looked sorry. "I know. And I have to thank Jason for bringing me back from the darkness. His level head about money helped our company." He nearly lifted her out of her chair and set her in his lap. He cupped her face and kissed her.

"Damn!" Jason said, envious. "I can smell her heat all the way over here, Jam." He rubbed his well-endowed crotch, adjusting his shaft.

Madison blushed because Jamar's kisses always got her going. The man had a way of stirring up her body to want sex.

"We're playing it safe from now on," Jamar declared. "The cup or a condom, okay?"

"Yes," she agreed.

"Oh, fuck," Jason said, with clear disappointment. "How soon can you get on birth control, Mad?"

No one had ever shortened her name that much and she loved it. "I don't know."

"Can you see?" Jamar asked her. "If nothing takes long, I'd sure as hell like to go another round like last night."

She nodded eagerly. "I'll call today, but you guys don't mind sharing me? And wouldn't mind continuing to share me?"

Both men looked at each other and then at her. "No," Jason said. "I thought I'd have an aversion when Jamar suggested to show him how to please you, but then I didn't realize how beautiful you would be and how damned aroused I'd be when I'm around you. We're game if you're game, Mad."

"What about your girl?" Jamar asked bitterly.

Jason shrugged. "Like you said, bro, she's not good for me anyways."

"Then yeah," Jamar agreed. "We don't mind."

She looked from one to another and smiled. "Alright, we'll try again, soon," she promised.

CHAPTER 29

MADISON ALLOWED JASON to drive her to school. On the way, she pleasured him with her mouth. Jason wasn't as experienced as Jamar in receiving that type of pleasure, almost driving off the road in his excitement.

Showing Jason something after he gave her so much pleasure the night before made her proud of herself as she filled her cup.

"Will we get to see you tonight?" he asked as he recovered.

She rubbed her finger on the side of her mouth to get the excess saliva off. "Yes, you will."

Jason kissed her in a soul-sucking dance of their lips.

Damn, he could get her going too.

Arriving at the lab that afternoon, with two weeks until their presentation, the professor was in an absent-minded tizzy. Meanwhile, Madison was on cloud nine mentally.

"You're glowing," Joshua noticed as she set her bag down by his work area.

"I'm happy this is almost over," she said, telling a partial lie.

"That's good, because the professor is stressing everyone out about everything." He looked at her open bag and frowned.

She followed his gaze and saw the box for the morning-after pill in the side. Closing her bag and putting it on the shelf on the other side of Joshua's desk, she said, "I'll be in the clean room. Let everyone know."

She grabbed her backpack which contained the specimens she'd collected over night from the brothers.

Going into the clean room meant she didn't want to be disturbed. It was a small lab in the center that was made of mostly glass, used to extract the DNA from various plants so they could grow what they wanted to grow. The room helped so much, but she had to do what she wanted with great care.

She was able to sneak and prepare her personal "specimens" along with sneaking a few more seeds for her greenhouse project.

She noticed Joshua seemed to be watching her extra closely, and she had to be more discreet under his hard glare than under the professor's. Had she pissed him off by spurning him?

Deep down inside, she had a notion Joshua might like more than her mind, but she had never gotten involved with an intern, and Joshua was just not her type. There was just something about him that made a bad taste surface in the back of her throat.

When she was leaving the lab to get on the bus to go to the greenhouse, her phone rang.

"Are you okay?" Jamar asked.

His concern for no reason touched her.

"I'm fine," she responded.

"It's almost time for you to take your next pills," he reminded her.

A little disappointed, she had a feeling that was most likely his main concern. "Yeah, umm, I'll take them as soon as I get off the bus by the Boston Edison. I didn't bring anything to drink but the bus stop is right by a party store. I need a bottle of water."

"Next time, just call me and I'll take you over there," he said. "I can wait around a couple of hours. I don't mind."

"You don't have to take care of me all the time," Madison insisted.

"Beautiful, just seeing you brightens my day. It's more about friendship than anything," Jamar said.

Determined not to let her emotions get involved, Madison didn't respond. Instead, she said, "I promise to take the pills as soon as I get off the bus, Jamar."

When they disconnected, Madison looked in her bag where she would have tucked the pills.

To her dismay, the box was there, but the pills weren't inside. Had she left them at the hotel room – taken them out when she took out the initial ones?

She emptied out her whole field bag and purse when she arrived at the greenhouse, but to no avail.

The pills were nowhere in sight.

Madison worried the whole time she was at the greenhouse. As she was about to leave, Jamar pulled up and patted the passenger seat.

Getting in the car with him, she was happy to see him.

"How was your day?" she questioned.

"It was good. Did you take your pills?"

She smiled and nodded, avoiding eye contact. If anything, the pills had most likely fallen out of her bag at the hotel room or at the lab. So in essence, it wouldn't be a lie when she found them and took them, especially since he was dropping her off at her room.

Once they arrived, Jamar turned to her and said, "I've had a long day, Beautiful. I'm exhausted."

Understanding, she kissed his cheek. "Thank you, Jamar. I appreciate your friendship."

"It means a lot to me when you say that," he said. "You mean a lot to me. If you need anything, just let me know. Always."

After an appreciative kiss, Madison ran up to her room. Oddly, her key card wasn't in her bag where she usually kept them. They were in a front pouch where she would usually never have put them, but Madison figured she could have put them in there in her own excitement from that morning.

Her life was turning in circles, and not in the usual way. Of course, she would put her key card in a place she had never done before. Desperately, she searched the room, and just as she predicted, the pills were under the table.

Most likely the packaging had fallen out of her purse, she assumed.

The packaging looked torn, but she figured maybe one of the guys had stepped on it. Without another glance, she quickly took the pills, hoping an extra four hours wouldn't make a difference.

The next morning, she felt just a little sore, but otherwise she felt fine.

By the middle of the day, she felt perfect and decided when she got to the lab to call Nikki from a landline at lunch. Madison didn't want to give out the cell phone number to Nikki, since Jamar had given it to her.

"Oh, my lawd, girl, where are you?" Nikki demanded. "I went over to your dad's and he said you ran away and no one has heard from you. I went by your lab early yesterday and they said you hadn't come in yet, but I know you're always early."

"Wait, you were at the lab early? No one said anything!"

"Really? I spoke with one of your creepy interns. Some Josh?" Nikki kept talking. "Anyway, your father has been blowing my phone up since you left asking if I've heard from you. I was about to put out a missing person's report."

Madison seriously doubted Nikki would go so far, but it was the thought that counted. "Was everyone else so concerned, really?" she questioned in disbelief.

"Actually, no. I made the last part up about your dad. He said he couldn't care less, but I really care, Maddie. Really," Nikki implored her.

Madison had to wonder how much Nikki made up. Pushing the anger away that her father or any other family member didn't care about her, she said, "I'm fine. I got a hotel room with the little money I made from a job."

"You really got an extra job, despite all you do?" Nikki asked amazed. "Where?"

"It's nothing big and it's legit. I'm cool. I'll get a real apartment soon," she said evasively, not wanting to tell Nikki any details.

"Can I come to you? Pick you up from school?"

"No, but really I'm fine, Nikki," Madison insisted. "Don't worry about me. I'm my mother's daughter."

"How is your research going?" Nikki inquired.

"It's good. I'm ready for the presentation, but the professor is a nervous wreck. I'd like to expand, but the professor insists we go with what we have – it's enough. He said to wait until afterward to see how everything goes."

"Any time you want me to look at it with a fresh eye, to see another angle, just let me know, Maddie."

That uncomfortable suspicion crept in Madison's gut, but she didn't want to pursue any undue accusations. "That's okay, Nikki, I'll handle everything just fine."

"So where are you now? Where are you living?" Nikki pressed. "I thought you didn't know anyone and would be struggling on the street."

Evasively, she admitted, "I met this guy. He knew someone who set me up at a motel; just temporarily, until I get on my feet, and then I'll get an apartment."

"Really?" Nikki sounded shocked. "Wait. Is it that hot weirdo you were talking about with the green Cadi?"

Madison didn't remember telling Nikki about his car, but so much had happened since they'd last spoke, she couldn't be sure. "It's a Lincoln," she corrected. "He turned out to be alright."

"Who is he? What was his name again?" Nikki demanded to know.

"Don't worry," Madison assured her. "Like I said, when I get on my feet, I'll invite you over. Right now, I'm not settled and I don't feel comfortable just inviting you over to this side of town, Nikki. Trust me, it's far away from Grosse Pointe and what you're used to. Don't worry about me. I always come out okay."

Nikki dropped the pressure and started talking about herself. Her parents were on her back about actually doing something, and the scholarship committee was pressuring her about her own research. Madison had no idea Nikki was working on anything.

Madison didn't bother to offer help like Nikki had. "You haven't spoken about any research projects you've been doing."

Nikki huffed in exasperation. "I just found out a month ago, the scholarship I was granted had some fine print."

"That sounds like a big deal. You didn't read the requirements of the scholarship?"

"Who does?!" Nikki snarled.

"I do. A lot of people read the fine print, especially when you're accepting money like that," Madison reprimanded. "What is this scholarship detail?"

"I have a deadline to turn in a project. You know, like some high school science project." Nikki was trying not to make it into a big deal, but Madison could hear the worry in her voice. "On top of that," she continued, "the university wants payback for a silly grant they gave me for school. My dad's pissed because he says I shouldn't have taken the money and pissed away the college savings he had for me, but how else was I supposed to live? I see you working like a dog to make extra meat and still getting nothing. I don't want that life. I'm not like you Madison."

Feeling slighted, Madison said stiffly, "How much did he have for you, Nikki?"

"What?" Nikki asked, as if she hadn't heard her.

Through gritted teeth, Madison repeated the question. "How much?"

"Only two hundred and fifty thousand dollars. Why are you sounding like that? It wasn't your money. It was mine."

Madison couldn't believe she was hearing this, and how greedy Nikki really was. "What did you waste it on, Nikki?"

"I had to live," Nikki said, as if the answer was obvious.

Feeling sick to her stomach, remembering all the times she'd gone shopping for hours with Nikki, watching her friend spend so much money on items worn only once and then tossed out like garbage. "You spent all of that?"

"It goes really fast when you're a party girl like I am," Nikki said proudly. "I had a reputation. A couple of tabs at the casino, credit cards, trips... you know. How can he expect me not to have some fun while I'm in college?"

Nikki had selfishly pissed a quarter of million away. Madison was becoming more nauseated by the second.

"Anyway, if I don't produce something soon, I'm shit out of luck."

Swallowing the bile coming up from her stomach, Madison pushed away the cold feeling. Nikki had been there a long time. She had been by Madison's side when her mother died. Even before that, Nikki had been the only ear to hear Madison whine about how miserable her mother's boyfriend made her feel, and after her mother death, Nikki had listened to how miserable Cyrus made her.

"H-How can I help you, Nikki?"

CHAPTER 30

"**Y**OU'RE ALWAYS DOING extra experiments, Maddie. Isn't there something you can hand off to me?"

Madison was now doubly sickened, but more at herself. All their lives, Madison had never minded Nikki cheating off of her. Test and projects over the years, Madison would say Nikki hitched off her back all the way through high school.

Now Nikki didn't have Madison around all the time, and college was probably kicking her friend's butt.

"Nothing that's going to be significant enough for you, Nikki," she fibbed. "I've been so busy on my main project with the professor. But I'm sure there are some high school projects you could dig up and we could flesh them out. What about that environmental makeup idea? Remember in eleventh grade—?"

Nikki cut her off, sounding disappointed. "That was a stupid idea then and it's a stupid idea now. Maybe I'll just come by the lab and watch you work, and inspiration could hit me. I really liked doing that in high school. Remember those days?"

Lying was becoming easier for Madison, and that scared her. "The professor is paranoid someone will try to steal the seeds we've genetically altered."

"How many have you done?"

"Well, it's only four plants we've perfected. Watermelon, potatoes, pineapples and mangoes. I'm working now on bananas." She knew she was bragging, but Nikki deserved this.

"Wow," Nikki said, genuinely impressed. "Well, I gotta go."

"Yeah, me too. I'll keep thinking of something for you to do. We'll figure something out. We always have." She was about to say "I" instead of "we," because that's what usually happened.

After hanging up the phone, Madison changed for field research and was glad to realize she was not enabling Nikki anymore. She was going to forget about promising to help Nikki. She was going to start taking care of herself!

Bragging had been wrong, but it had made Madison feel good.

Madison finished her field work fairly early. So many thoughts flurried about her head, but she was so focused on working, she really became more efficient. Joshua tried to start a lot of conversations with her, but if he wasn't speaking about the presentation, Madison swayed the conversation back to the work they were doing.

He seemed frustrated.

She kept her thoughts away from Nikki, because otherwise she would become sick with angry. For years her friend had gotten away with using her and Madison had weakly allowed Nikki to do so.

If she thought about the next day, which she was going to spend with Jamar and Jason again, she was going to become flustered. If she thought about her current situation she was living in, she became despondent.

So she focused instead on the task at hand. Because, even with all her smarts, she had no clear ability to picture what she needed to do: with Nikki, with the brothers, or even with her life.

When she was on her way to the hotel on the bus from field work, she made a budget for herself. If she was going to try to live off what she was paid, then she ought to be able to maintain a stable life, plus save up for an apartment.

When she opened her door, she spotted another envelope on the floor that had been pushed under her door.

It was fifteen hundred dollars, and she knew it was from Jason. She put that money with the rest, which she'd taped under her hotplate. Beside her small cooler and hotplate, she kept her experiment, and she noticed things had been shifted around.

Frowning, she wondered whether Jamar or Jason had been touching her stuff.

Why would they when they couldn't understand what she was doing?

No, her items had been moved around as if someone was looking for something, as if they understood what she was doing.

Stepping away from the closet, she looked around.

Nothing else seemed touched or taken.

Her phone chirped to indicate someone had sent her a message.

"This is Jamar," the message read. *"Are you home yet?"*

She responded. *"Yes. Why is Jason paying me so much?"*

"You're a professional," he texted back. *"You should get paid for what you are worth and more! You've done a wonderful job in such a short time on his project."*

Madison wondered what exactly he meant by the *"professional"* comment, but didn't want to indulge in asking for details. She was acting sensitive for some reason, which usually wasn't her way at all.

After a moment, he texted, *"Can we see you tonight? I'm all rested."*

She sat on the bed and asked, *"You really want to see me again? Both of you?"* Her heart rate started increasing.

Jamar simply replied *"Yes, Beautiful."*

For some reason, she turned around and looked at her bed, then looked down at Jamar's reply.

The company of two deliciously gorgeous men again, making love to her and making her feel beautiful… What more could a woman ask for?

She was young. When would she ever have the opportunity to experience anything like this again, once she graduated? Now and in the present, she wasn't tied down emotionally to anyone, so why shouldn't she enjoy the lovemaking of two men who wanted to give her unbridled special attention?

"Yes, come," she responded back, and took a deep, nervous breath.

***

Jason arrived first with a small burlap bag. He looked as if he had been dragged around in the dirt all day.

"What happened to you?" she asked worriedly, taking the burlap bag and letting his big sweaty body in the room.

"They're rare flower seeds. Someone at the fruit market gave them to me. I told them I knew a pretty gardener and I needed a special gift for her. Jamar said you're very special to us, and special people deserve specialness." He winked with a silly grin.

She inspected the seeds in the burlap as he went to the bathroom to take a shower.

Excited about the seeds, Madison was almost inclined to get her books from her closet and research exactly what kind of flowers they were.

Yet, there was another knock at the door to distract her.

Jamar entered and immediately drew her in his arms with a deep kiss. Her heart raced as she was swept up in his passion.

"I take it Jason's arrived?" he asked.

Breathlessly, she answered, "Yes, with gifts." She showed him the burlap bag.

He narrowed his eyes briefly at her, but didn't comment. Instead, he began peeling her clothes off of her. He seemed to want to touch her everywhere and his appetite was infectious. Laying her on the bed, his hands and mouth touched, tasted and teased her mercilessly, until she was more than ready for him. He tore open a condom and jammed it over his thick shaft before entering her, deliberately rubbing his body hard against her between each stroke.

Madison could only hold onto his shoulders and enjoy the ride as he brought her to multiple orgasms. She screamed her joy at the top of her lungs.

Above her head, Madison felt the bed dent and looked up to see Jason's long, immensely thick shaft above her head. Grabbing him confidently, she swallowed him and stroked him with her mouth, loving how he felt so powerful against her tongue.

She knew from last time that Jason could give her more than enough specimen, so when his first orgasm released deep down her throat, she swallowed every drop.

"Fuck," Jason gasped, before kissing her in reward at the same time Jamar was coming.

She knew it was going to be a long, enjoyable night, and she was prepared to love every second of her gorgeous lovers.

Since she didn't get any specimens the first time, Madison would keep trying to get more from them until she was satisfied.

Jamar and Jason looked willing and ready to give her anything she wanted.

CHAPTER 31

SOMEHOW, THEY'D ALL fallen asleep together with her conveniently sandwiched between them. The only reason she woke because Jason was famished at three in the morning and was going to make a twenty-four hour Coney Island restaurant run. Jamar sleepily gave him an order and she requested a chicken salad.

Jason hungrily stole a kiss from her as if he was never going to see her again before bounding out the door.

"Are you two like this all the time?" she sleepily questioned Jamar.

"Like what?" Jamar asked without opening his eyes, pulling her naked body in his arms and curling his large body behind hers. He snuggled his face in the crook of her neck. "What do you mean?"

"I mean, do you often find women to do this with?"

"No," he responded sleepily. "Not many females would allow something so taboo. Not many would accept my brother showing me how to pleasure a woman."

She wasn't that innocent not to understand others would perceive this as wrong. "But you two seem like you enjoy sharing. Why?"

"It's just what we're used. We've shared since we were younger. He's always taught me how to do things right. Jason was the fast learner and I was the slower one. My mother looked more highly on him than on me, but Jason never gave up on me. As we got older, I wanted Jason's life and his toys and he's admired me as a bigger brother. Just feels so right when we're together like this, with a woman, even though we know it's wrong."

Madison wanted to understand more. "But do you have a lot of women who will go along with this?"

"No. Maybe for the first time, but this is actually the first time we have done it again with the same woman."

The confession made her feel special. "And?"

Jamar kissed her neck and chuckled. "We like being with you together a second time, beautiful. You feel like home, where I want to stay forever." He nuzzled her neck more tenderly, then moved her body to maneuver her thigh over his, so he could press into her. "You make it alright." He kissed her brow as he entered her.

She knew he wasn't covered, and there were no cups around to "catch" anything except her warm creamy center, where he felt so deliciously wonderful slowly pounding into her, titillating every nerve ending in her body.

"Fuck, you feel so damn good, Madison," he strained, pumping deep in her, digging his fingers into her rear cheeks.

Madison loved how he got lost in her body and how his sweat mingled with hers as he held her so close, their bodies seem to meld together.

Tears of ecstasy welled in her eyes and soon came pouring out as she was flooded with a sense of belonging, loving, and most of all, beauty.

Yes, at that moment in time, Jamar told her without words how truly beautiful she was. His kisses, his touches, and his body relayed to her how exquisite she was, with or without a man.

Madison held him close and didn't care about the repercussions.

Jamar was past the point of no return. She could feel the familiar pulsing, the moans of pleasurable despair as he gave in to her body, sucking and clenching him tightly until…

So much… Jamar gulfed, gargled and groaned his release.

They were both breathless, sated in their passion together and continuing to hold each other close.

He cursed bringing her to realization early.

Yet, Jamar wasn't finished. He was still incredibly hard and wasn't done. Far from done as he started stroking in her again. Her body didn't take long to rise again to the occasion, despite the sloppy mess they were making.

Jason had come in on them quietly. She spotted him from the mirror on the wall, where he was practically ripping off his clothes and throwing the food down at the same time. He joined them on the bed, pressing from behind, rubbing and touching all the places Jamar didn't touch.

The double attention was excitingly overwhelming as Madison felt Jamar kissing her breasts, while Jason kissed her neck and back.

Jason's hand massaged her thighs and between her lower cheeks. His finger dipped near where Jamar was stroking inside of her, and she felt Jason rub that wetness around her rear before pressing a slick finger inside. With the area being virgin territory, but wet as hell from Jamar and Madison's lovemaking, Madison only gasped at the new sensation, but the eroticism excited her.

Jamar kept her senses enraptured in pleasure until she realized Jason had pressed something thicker than his finger inside of her.

She dug her fingernails into Jamar's shoulder and he didn't protest, but kissed her voraciously.

Jason hummed, grunted and whimpered as he moved even deeper into her plump rear.

The wetness Jamar had produced ran back, helping Jason's entry until he countered Jamar's stroke in a rhythm that made her entire body reel in hot bliss.

Multiple orgasms racked every millimeter of her body as she felt their culmination combine with one of her torrential, earth-shaking quakes.

Jamar barely dislodged before he shot over her stomach, but Jason stayed inside, rocking her inner sanctum, sending even more pulses hard through her body. She swore she could feel the younger brother's heartbeat inside of chest.

The sensation was too thrilling, and Madison knew she wanted to do that again!

"Is that wicked I enjoyed that?" Madison asked them breathlessly as they both still held her tightly, despite the wet mess she was.

"Never," both men said simultaneously.

Madison didn't feel one ounce of guilt. Jamar guided her from the bed and into the shower. They washed up together, but of course, he also showered her with kisses and touches between everything else.

When they were done, they ate the food Jason had brought, dressed in towels, while Jason cleaned up. He'd already eaten while they were in the shower.

"Do you miss your family?" Jamar asked.

"No," she said without hesitation. "And I know they don't miss me."

"Do you think we're bad for you?"

She wondered where these questions were coming from, but answered him. "You can't do to me anything I don't want done to me.." She chewed her food before continuing. "I learned that lesson from my father. His bad treatment was only allowed because I allowed myself to be treated that way. I didn't feel my worth then, but I understand it now."

"You're worth more than a universe, Madison" he said.

She smiled, blushing. "Thank you, Jamar." His compliment meant more to her than everything.

When they were done, he guided her back to the bed to lie back down. It was still early morning, and they all could get some more sleep.

Jason joined them soon, lying behind her, enveloping her in his heat, keeping her warm all night as she fell asleep.

When Madison awoke hours later, alone in bed, the rest of her salad was still on the table and someone was in the bathroom shaving.

She was famished again and ate until the bathroom door opened. She had rewrapped the towel around her body and smiled sheepishly, pleased to see Jamar.

"Jason's gone to get coffee. I'm going to take you to school," Jamar explained, kissing her forehead.

"You shouldn't spoil me," she warned.

"Shouldn't we?"

"No," she said obviously. "I'll get used to it and become spoiled."

"Maybe that's what we want to do?"

Being realistic, she said, "Really, Jamar? We haven't known each other that long and Jason is still trying to go after some woman you don't like." She patted his leg to let him know it was okay. "I'm a pragmatist, Jamar. I know I can't get emotional about all of this. I can only have fun while it lasts, right?"

He looked hurt for a second and shrugged. "I'd like to make you happy, Madison. I'd like to make you mine."

"Let's be honest with each other, Jamar, please."

Jamar looked like he wanted to say more, but she knew the conversation could get too deep and decided not to ruin a wonderful night with a serious discussion. She kissed his forehead, using the same calming technique he used on her. Gathering her clothes for school, Madison went to get dressed in the bathroom.

As soon as she closed the door and turned on the bathroom faucet, she heard Jason returning. She looked at herself in the mirror and noticed her acne wasn't as prevalent.

Had their sperm really started to work on her?

No! It wasn't that powerful, but there was a strange glow about her face.

CHAPTER 32

"WHY'D YOU GIVE HER those seeds?" Jamar asked angrily, trying to keep his voice down.

Madison eavesdropped on their conversation because she had never heard Jamar this upset.

"Because I wanted to give her something special," Jason answered obviously.

"After that silly girlfriend refused those expensive seeds?"

"Well, I knew Madison would appreciate them."

"You hope she would, just like you hope that gold-digging whore will appreciate anything you do for her," Jamar sneered.

"Why are you on my back, Jam? Madison won't know."

"But I do, and while you're pursuing some asinine chit that don't appreciate you, you could be messing up the best thing that could have ever happen to us."

"This is only temporary, you said it yourself. That's what she believes. Plus, these things don't last for long, Jam. We're lucky to have a go again at her, but we have to know this all can't work out," Jason said disappointedly. "They always end and they leave us empty, tired and frustrated. I'm just preparing for the evitable. I'm trying to be normal."

"You're trying to be what *she* expects you to be, just like always. I'm not the only one suffering from her abuse, Jason. Don't act like I'm the odd one here."

Madison figured they were speaking about Jamar's mother now.

Jamar continued. "It's not what I want and it's not what you want."

Jason sighed. "I'm young, Jam. You can hope, but I'm just scared and impatient. I've seen it go away too many times to know it's not going to work. Yes, Madison's perfect, but all I can go is by past experiences in this situation."

"Let's just give it a chance, Jason. One more chance and she's it. I promise, but I got a feeling she's the one," Jamar implored. "Now go in there and make her feel it."

Madison moved away from the door and pretended to be enraptured in brushing her teeth.

Seconds later, Jason's gorgeous topless body entered the bathroom. Despite what she'd overheard, nothing changed her opinion. She was still going to be sexually attracted to both of them.

After spitting out her toothpaste, she dropped to her knees, opened his pants and gave him the best head of his life, taking her time and deliberately holding off his climax as she touched him orally and gently pulled on his scrotum.

By the time he was coming in her mouth, the man was crying.

Madison smiled, pleased at her effect on Jason. Whoever this other woman was, she certainly didn't appreciate Jason like Madison did.

He pulled her to her feet and kissed her. Jason's hands were playful all over her body, arousing her. He pulled out a condom, quickly placed it on, and turned her around as her towel fell to the ground.

This was becoming her favorite position, and she was in heaven as he stroked deep inside of her, hitting the hilt, filling her. She held onto his thighs, receiving every thud he made to her ass.

"Ugh… uhhh…," she gasped breathlessly. "F-fuck… yes, Jason… yes."

He gripped her hips, until… yes, Jason was a very virile man, and she enjoyed receiving pleasure from him from the inside out. This time he bit down on her shoulder, sending ripples of pain and pleasure pounding through her body.

She should've been sore, but she wasn't.

"Damn, woman, you bring out a horniness in me I've never experienced," he admitted, panting on her back.

"That's a good thing," she teased.

He withdrew from her and she straightened up. Keeping her voice low, she said, "I heard what Jamar said."

Jason looked guilty. "It's nothing."

"You're right, it isn't. This might not last, but I'm going to enjoy it while it does."

He kissed her tenderly. "Thank you, Madison." His smile was infectious.

"I'm sensible, Jason." She placed a hand on his chest. "I think we both are."

He nodded, kissed her again, and left her to get ready for school.

Jamar helped her pack up her field bag after she secured her samples.

"What happens when you don't need our samples anymore?" Jamar questioned.

"I think I like having sex with you, Jamar. You and Jason," she admitted. "Maybe someone will like my project and I won't ever need to give you two up." She playfully winked.

He seemed to relax a little and walked her to his old Lincoln. When he was on his way, driving to her school, she asked, "What happens when you two get tired of me?"

"Never," he said without hesitation.

"What do you two do, exactly? I know you said you're starting a type of grocery food business together, but I'm cloudy on the details. Plus, I'm dying to know how Jason could get his hands on those expensive seeds."

"We run a mobile grocer. We've gotten fourteen clients. I'm in charge of set-up. Jason is in charge of products. Your lead on that distributor was awesome, by the way. You're really too good to be true." He smiled gratefully, squeezing her thigh.

If he kept up all his compliments, she knew her heart would get involved, and that was the last thing she needed now. Coming from trying to please the cruel Cyrus and losing her mother, she wasn't ready to commit her heart to a new relationship. "Let's please keep this realistic, Jamar," she said as he pulled up to her school. "We'll take this thing as far as we can. No strings, no expectations, and most of all, honesty. Okay?"

Tenderly, he kissed her. "That's the best advice. I'll tell, Jason."

She was glad that Jason had already agreed with her. He would most likely act like he was hearing it for the first time when Jamar discussed it with him.

Getting through her first class, she was still feeling high from the night before, until she rounded the corner to her lab and saw Cyrus standing in the doorway.

Internally, she groaned and the good feelings immediately left her. Cyrus was dressed in his Sunday best, even though it was the middle of the week.

He spotted her. Striding up to her angrily, he looked like he wanted to choke her. The hallways were pretty much empty, giving them privacy.

"What are you doing here?" she asked warily.

"You have nerve after you broke into my house and stole stuff," he accused her.

Shocked at his accusation, she defended, "I only took what was mine."

"And you looked through my stuff, didn't you? You went in my study."

"No, I didn't touch your stuff. I only took my stuff. Things I'd brought in. My mother's stuff."

"So, how'd you find out about me? Sister Onetta?" he guessed.

It took her a moment to remember the woman. "I met her getting off the bus. She recognized me, said I looked just like my mother."

"You're lying. You went in my study. I know you did. It's the only way she could find me and brag about how she was making up for what I did wrong."

"What are you talking about?" She played innocent. "What did you do wrong?"

He cut his eyes at her. "Don't play dumb, Madison. What are you keeping from me? You think I wouldn't find out?"

Her father would never confess to his sins, not to her, and she knew at that point she would never hear the truth from his mouth. Tired of trying, she decided she wasn't going to take his treatment anymore, but leave him with the truth, which she had always done.

Firmly, she said, "I did go in your office, Cyrus, but I didn't take or touch anything. After I met Sister Onetta on the bus, she directed my cousin to me. When I spoke to my cousin, whom I never knew I had, she dropped me off at your house. She must've told Sister Onetta about where I stay. That's what I'm guessing." Taking a deep breath, trying to remember she had to respect this man only because he was her parent, she kept her cool. "Please leave. Just go. I never want to see you again."

Cyrus looked defeated for a moment. Suddenly, he grabbed her arm and shoved her back, hard against the wall, knocking the breath out of her. His other hand came up and grabbed her around the neck, squeezing hard to keep her there, but also making it difficult for her to breathe.

Cruelly, he sneered, "You think it's that easy? What did that cousin bitch promise you? Money? More money? If you stay away from me, right? That's what she made you do?"

She was still reeling from the fact her father was trying to kill her. Choke her!

"Just like your bitch mother's family to offer you a way to get away from me. Keeping the money they should've given your mother. The money I needed." Cyrus continued, "That's why you're acting like this. That's why you ran away. To get the money that's supposed to be mine."

Air was becoming a necessity for her, and a fighting instinct surged in her gut. Madison wrestled to wrench away from him, going so far as to claw at his face.

He released her, roaring in pain, holding the side of his face with one hand, but trying to grab at her again with the other. She swung her backpack with her laptop, hitting him in the head. He fell to the ground and she ran into the lab, locking the door behind her.

She ran to the phone, called security and then crouched down on the ground, listening to Cyrus pound on the lab door, demanding her to open it. Closing her hands around her ears, she prayed security would come soon.

Looking over at her backpack, she could see a lot of blood. What had she done?

How had the best night of her life been followed by the worst day of her life?

CHAPTER 33

T HE DETROIT POLICE questioned her about the incident, and ruled she was only protecting herself.

Witnesses had seen Cyrus attack her and gave statements as well.

Cyrus wasn't dead, and in a way, she was glad about that. But he was severely injured with a laceration to the side of his face. After being transported to the hospital, he was going to be arrested.

She filed charges against her father. Feeling awful about having to do so, but also knowing he would probably come back at her again if she didn't, she knew she had to do what she had to, in order for him never to bother her again.

Sitting down on a bench in the hallway by the lab, she felt horrible.

"Madison," Mercy said, sitting beside her.

Looking over to see her mother's eyes on her cousin's concerned face, Madison finally broke down and cried.

Mercy pulled her in her arms and hugged her, comforted her, and assured her everything was going to be alright.

"He kept asking me about money, Mercy. He was going to kill me if I didn't tell him about the money."

Mercy shook her head. "He still thinks there's money left. That our grandparents left money for your mother." Shaking her head in disappointment, she said, "There isn't. The will was changed to cut your mother out. There's only a trust for me and my sister, but even we can't get to the brunt of it until we marry, respectively." She rolled her eyes. "As if that's ever going to happen to me. Maybe Grace, but not to me. I'm doomed." She sighed dejectedly. "If it's money you need, I can help a little. We only get so much of a stipend a month."

Shaking her head, Madison said, "No, I'm fine, Mercy. It's Cyrus who wants money, not me. I have a job. I'm taking care of myself just fine."

"Let's go, Madison. Let's get out of here," Mercy suggested. "You need a break."

"No," she said, shaking her head again and looking at the lab door. The interns were in there, looking as though they were trying not to seem nosy. The professor stood at the window, staring shamelessly. Oddly, Joshua kept towards the back. "I-I have... I have work to do."

Mercy looked towards the lab and frowned. "That guy back there, the white guy with the dark hair. Who is he?"

"That's an intern, Joshua."

Narrowing her eyes, Mercy said, "He looks familiar."

"You saw him before, when you were last here."

"No, somewhere else, I think." Mercy then appeared to shrug this off. "You have my number, Madison. Don't hesitate to call me for anything. I mean, I have my own problems, but you're family. I'll do what I can to help. Okay?"

They hugged again.

"And don't worry," Mercy added. "You didn't kill him. Karma's going to kick his ass. And if it doesn't, I'll personally take out a loan to pay someone to kick his ass."

Madison needed her cousin's wit.

The professor came over to check on her. "Listen, why don't you go home, Madison?"

She shook her head. "No, the project is coming up, Professor. I want to make sure everything is perfect." She looked at Mercy, who was peering into the lab at Joshua again, narrowing her eyes as if still trying to remember how she recognized him. "I'll work. It'll keep my mind off of everything. Busy work is good for me."

The professor nodded with appreciation and returned to the lab.

"Are you sure?" Mercy asked her.

"Yes, I'm sure. We'll talk later, okay? And I promise I won't just call you when it's bad."

Mercy hugged Madison and genuinely smiled. "I do want to know what's up with Cyrus, though, and if he gives you any more trouble."

"I will definitely keep you updated."

When her cousin left, she went into the lab to work next to Joshua. "That was my cousin, Mercy," Madison said, matter-of-fact.

"Really?" he asked innocently.

"Yeah. She said she recognized you."

He stopped what he was doing. "Really? From where?"

Madison shrugged. "She just said you looked familiar."

Joshua chuckled. "You know what they say about white guys."

"What?"

"We all look alike."

Knowing he was joking, Madison chuckled and let Mercy's suspicions go. Joshua had never done anything to make her think she should be suspicious. He had always been helpful and over-inquisitive, but that wasn't anything new for overeager interns.

She relaxed and went to work. Afterwards, she caught the bus to the Boston Edison District and worked on her plants. The natural growth was amazing in that environment. On the way home, she texted Jason about working at his greenhouse.

"*You should let my brother take you there and back. Catching the bus takes a long time,*" he texted back.

"*I don't mind. Gives me time to think,*" she replied.

Getting to the hotel room, she saw another envelope had been shoved under her door. Another five-hundred dollars.

Going to the payphone in the lobby of the hotel, she called Nikki's number. Surprisingly, Nikki picked up right away.

"How's everything?" Nikki inquired.

Immediately, Madison was on alert. Nikki never asked how she was or actually cared, unless she wanted to cipher information out of Madison. "I'm great, and you?"

"I'm good."

"I wanted to let you know what happened with Cyrus," Madison said. "He came to the lab demanding money, because I was in contact with my mother's side of the family."

"You never told me this."

"I don't tell you everything, Nikki. You've been pretty busy and consumed with your own life. You haven't even offered me help, even though you knew I was homeless."

"Like you said, I've been busy, okay?"

"I'm not being hard on you Nikki," Madison said. "I'm just explaining why I haven't been forthcoming on information."

"So what happened?" Nikki asked. "With Cyrus?"

"He got violent. Real violent. I mean, scary-violent, Nikki. I had to defend myself, but I think I almost killed him. He's in the hospital."

"Oh, my gawd, Mad! Why would you hurt him?" Nikki cried accusingly forgetting every bad thing Cyrus had ever did to Madison. "He's your father."

"I don't care who he is. I told you, he was violent. I did what I had to do. I thought you'd understand, Nikki. You know he hasn't treated me right."

"Well, yes, I do," Nikki said, a bit frustrated. "But, I know you're loyal to blood and that you wouldn't do anything to hurt your own father."

Madison was tired of talking to Nikki. "Never mind, Nikki…"

"Wait," Nikki said, cutting her off. "I got something to tell you too, Madison."

Impatiently, she snapped, "What?"

"I'm pregnant."

Madison was shocked. "By whom?"

"It's a long story. Why don't you tell me the motel you're living at, and I can come by?"

Madison was exhausted and selfishly didn't want to hear all about Nikki's drama. "I'll call you tomorrow and we can meet for lunch around the campus."

Nikki didn't sound happy about that, but agreed. "Okay, but don't forget to call me. I have no way of contacting you."

Madison wasn't about to give Nikki the cell phone number Jamar had given her. Hanging up the payphone, she returned to her room.

Jamar had sent her a text while she had been taking a shower to wish her goodnight and tell her how much he missed her. She replied back the same, barely able to keep her eyes open.

"See you soon. Stay in touch and don't hesitate to let me know if you need anything," he texted.

Damn, he was wonderful, she said to herself, and texted, *"Thank you. Will do."*

Lying down finally, she started to close her eyes, but just as sleep was about to hit her, she sat up in bed abruptly.

She'd never told Nikki she was staying at a motel. This bothered her all night.

CHAPTER 34

MADISON DIDN'T CONTACt Nikki back. Waking up the next morning, she somehow remembered the hundreds of times Nikki had never called her back, despite how desperate she was to hear from her.

It really wasn't about payback, or getting Nikki to understand she needed to reap what she had sown in their friendship. Madison was starting to gain perspective on what was important to her.

She also woke up feeling like she should share more of her life with Jamar and Jason, but their relationship was so new, and she didn't want to overwhelm them with her personal problems.

A couple of days passed, and she was in constant contact with Jamar and Jason. Jamar was always concerned with her safety, and called at the end of the day, just to hear about her day. Jason sent her funny pictures, links and texts. He would call in the morning to wake her up.

Jamar started picking her up from school and took her out to lunch, and then over to the greenhouse.

After she'd started working about four days after her father's incident, she called the police station to talk to the detective in charge of the assault case and to check on Cyrus's condition. Sergeant Tobias Avery took her call and answered her concerns.

"There's nothing we can say over the phone, Ms. Oliver," he answered. "Especially since he said he's filing charges against you."

"I'm filing charges against him! He attacked me first," she said angrily.

"I've seen the tape. I know the truth. I don't think he knows he was being taped. Your professor said he'd installed a security camera in the hallway outside of the laboratory as an extra precaution against theft and tampering with his equipment and research. . He provided the footage to us.

"Once he recovers, your father is not going to leave police custody," the sergeant went on. "After I saw the tape, I ran his prints. We believe he's in connection to an older woman we found strangled outside of her church the night before he attacked you."

Dread filled her gut. "What woman?"

"A woman by the name of Onetta Nate. Do you know her? Because Cyrus said he knows nothing about her."

Gasping, she said, "Y-Yes, I do. She… she knew my parents when I was little, went to church with them. I met her riding the bus recently, and she said Cyrus was one of his previous lovers. She connected me to my cousins. She's really dead?"

"Yes, and your father's fingerprints are all over her murder."

Madison gasped again.

"It appears he choked her, but she was also stabbed, and we don't recognize the prints on the weapon at the scene. Hopefully, we'll be able to get him to testify against his accomplice."

Getting off the phone, Madison took a deep breath and then texted Mercy. The number she had didn't go through, as if Mercy's number was disconnected. Dialing the number, she received the message, "This number is no longer in service."

Not wanting to take away her energy away from work, she pushed everything aside and resumed her responsibilities around the greenhouse.

She checked on her plants, and had planted a couple of the special seeds there as well, along with the plants Jason had specified. In her research, she found out the seeds were rare hyacinths that only grew in the rain forest in Cuba, and were actually endangered.

Changing part of the environment in the greenhouse so that she could nurture the plants to grow was a challenge for her, but she managed the task beautifully.

Madison had not used all the seeds, and had even used some DNA splicing methods to manufacture her own hyacinths that were unique with the colors from the same plant. During her research, she found out the oils from the flower could make a person's skin softer and, producing her type of plant, she wanted to see if she could grow the same oils on her own.

She couldn't wait to germinate and dissect the flowers once they were full-term, but knew patience was her greatest strength.

Many times, Nikki had failed in her research and experiments because she tried to rush everything. Madison had learned patience was a virtue and the key when trying to work with nature, and her projects always paid off because of that.

After waiting at the greenhouse for her to get finished, Jamar took her to dinner at a small Mexican restaurant. Being with Jamar helped her with her anxiety about Onetta Nate, but she didn't discuss what was bothering her.

Jason met them, looking a little put out.

Jamar was in too good of spirits, and explained Jason's mood. "His new girl has given him the flux. She wants this and that, and Jason's not able to keep up with her. Sexually, he could rock her world, but out of bed, he's frustrated."

Hearing about another woman in Jason's life peeved Madison just a bit, but she tried not to show she was becoming emotionally attached to the brothers.

After sharing a dessert, Jason took her home. On the way, he tried to make small-talk, but her usual quietness was probably a tell for him.

Jason kissed her knuckles. "Aww, Madison don't be mad at me."

"I'm not. I understand the relationship we have," she said, cutting Jamar a warning look. "And you were chasing her long before meeting me. I'm not going to ask you to choose. I like our arrangement, but just be safe."

"Well, honestly, I'm not having sex with her," Jason admitted. "Initially, she insisted we not do anything, and now I haven't pressed it, now that I'm with you. I really do like you, Madison. You're cool. And beautiful. Plus, you're smart. I can't believe you like the both of us. You've done a lot for both of us and though I rarely admit it, I know Jamar and I need you in our lives."

It was she that should be honored, but Jason made her feel like he was so blessed to be able to be with her.

Squeezing his hand, she leaned over and kissed his cheek. "Thanks, Jason," she said before getting out.

When he drove away, Madison felt a sharp pain in her stomach she'd never felt before.

At the same time, her phone beeped. It was Jamar.

"I hope your presentation goes well tomorrow. I wish I could be there and see you win the grant."

Madison relaxed, disregarding her stomach pain as her nervousness seemed to overshadow the sudden nausea and mild body ache.

The presentation meant a lot to her and the professor--but especially the professor. He had the whole lab riding on receiving this specific grant.

"Thank you, Jamar. I'll call you after everything."

"You mean after you get the grant," he corrected her happily.

She needed that. She really needed someone to tell her that, and she smiled to herself with hope. "Right," she agreed. "After I get the grant, Jamar."

Sleeping was a little better after speaking with Jamar and Jason. Madison could feel herself swelling with pride from all her accomplishments, and after tomorrow... after the presentation, life would get easier, she just knew it.

Madison figured the pain in her side and sudden sickness was most likely all the stress she was feeling about everything with her father.

Not being able to contact Mercy, Onetta being killed, and Cyrus a part of a murder with an unknown suspect...possibly Hazel?

Tomorrow was a new day, Madison proclaimed to herself. Tomorrow was going to change her life... forever.

CHAPTER 35

T HE PROFESSOR CAME TO her hotel room. She had given him her address, because he wanted to be able to pick her up in case there were any last-minute changes.

"I've been up since four A.M. getting everything together," he chatted. "The interns are still there from last night, monitoring the other presentations and making sure our display is ready to go." He handed her the flash drive to her PowerPoint presentation.

"The interns are incompetent and I'm frazzled trying to set everything up since last night." He gave her a sharp look. "I know you've been going through a lot, but I really need you to bring everything you have this morning, Madison. I'm already so nervous."

She put a reassuring hand on his arm. "We're going to be fine, Professor Barfield. We've taken extra measures to make sure our project is safe." Holding up the flash drive he'd just given her, she continued. "We're going to blow their minds, and with the extra steps I've taken to not have all our research at the lab, I think we're pretty much going to give everyone, including the interns, a surprise."

The professor still chattered out of nervousness the whole way to the conference center where the presentations were held, but she was feeling confident about the project, and wanted to get in front of the crowd to voice her ideas.

Soon as the car was parked, Joshua came hurrying up to the vehicle, looking frazzled. "Professor, we have a problem."

The professor looked ready to pass out. "What now? What happened? I don't think I can take another thing going wrong today."

"Western University is here and I just snuck in to see their presentation." He didn't look well either, but she did notice he avoided eye contact with her.

Madison also knew Nikki went to Western.

"What? Why? How?" the professor said in disbelief.

"It should be fine, professor," Madison said confidently. "Our presentation will rock."

Professor still looked worried. "They weren't scheduled to appear. What did they present on?" he demanded to know.

Joshua took out his phone. "I snuck some photos, sir. It looks just like our research. I swear."

The bottom seemed to drop from her stomach as Madison looked down at Joshua's phone screen. Gasping, she saw Nikki standing next to what looked just like Madison's research from the flash drive she had left in Nikki's vehicle.

The professor grabbed the phone and searched through the various pictures, looking horrified.

There was a gallon of sweat dripping off his brow. "Joshua, Get Madison to the platform now!" he ordered Joshua. "I'll be along shortly. I need to make some calls."

Joshua took her arm and dragged her to where Western was giving their presentation.

Whatever high she had been on from the night before had completely dissipated as she listened to her best friend presenting the same research Madison had painstakingly conducted and intended to present.

Her eyes went wide as saucers as she listened to Nikki standing on stage and repeating Madison's hard-earned research, word for word.

The bitch didn't even try to change anything.

Joshua's phone rang, and he walked away for a second to answer the call.

"What the hell did you do?" the professor accused Madison frantically, coming up behind them.

His eyes were bugged out and he even shook her, making her find her voice from the shock she was in.

"I didn't—"

The professor shook her some more, cutting her off. "They have all our research, Madison! Everything! How?!"

"I didn't do anything," she said. , She was having a hard time breathing, but even she didn't believe the words coming out of her mouth, because she was just remembering how she had trusted Nikki, and didn't think her so-called friend would take away the only opportunity Madison had going for herself. "I wouldn't... didn't..." Her voice drifted as she clearly remembered Nikki taking the flash drives. In that short time, her supposedly best friend could have made copies. But opening the encrypted files should have been extremely complicated, and how could the school reproduce the seeds splicing in so short of time?

"I really didn't," she pleaded.

Joshua shook his head in pity, hanging up his cell, and rubbed the professor's back in remorse. "He knows you couldn't have, Madison. He called the school."

Professor Barfield looked sicker to his stomach, but couldn't explain.

She looked at Joshua for an explanation.

"The lab was just tampered with while we were driving down here," Joshua explained grimly. "I got a call from one of the interns still on campus earlier, saying he saw someone in the lab he'd never seen before. That's what made me go check out the competition. Security at the school confirmed all the research was destroyed. Someone's set fire to the lab."

Professor Barfield cursed and began to pace.

Madison was at a loss. She shouldn't have bragged to Nikki about her research. Damn her pride. Sinking internally into despair, the only thing she wanted to do was physical damage to Nikki's face.

"What can we do, Professor Barfield? We can't present the same exact presentation."

"Fuck it!" The professor said, giving up. "We should just leave. We just won't do anything. We ought to give up. It's over. Everything."

"But sir, this is my life! I have nothing after this!" Madison cried in panic. "If we gave up, I would never be able to recover!"

She was determined not to be knocked down. She knew she was smart and beautiful! Dammit, Jamar and Jason believed in her. She needed to believe in herself!

"Wait!" she exclaimed, as the professor began to walk down the hall.

"Just let it go," he demanded, looking as if he was about to have his own nervous breakdown.

"NO, we can't," she insisted. "Can you stall for about thirty minutes?"

"What do you have planned?" Joshua asked hopefully.

For once, she was grateful the student intern liked her and wasn't ready to give up either, believing in her.

"How fast can you drive me over to Boston Edison?" she asked Joshua.

He took out his keys. "Let's go!"

* * *

Joshua should've signed up for the Indy 500 as he expertly weaved in and out of the Detroit morning traffic.

They returned to her motel room to gather her skin experiment and returned. On the way back, she explained all he needed to do once they arrived. Joshua was able to set everything up, just like she told him.

Their school display already had natural fruits and vegetables for show. Madison sent another intern to the grocery store for the other ingredients, and gave a third intern her personal flash drive to download the pictures she had taken of herself.

Once it was their school's turn, with the plants already on display, she was easily able to wing a presentation, combining everything she had prepared about natural skin rejuvenation.

All but the research was complete, yet with her pictures and just the partial chemical makeup of her "secret ingredient," she was able to sway some of the judges to keep their school in the contest.

As she was getting off the stage, she was met with a supporting hug from Joshua. The professor looked skeptical, but nodded at her in approval.

Nikki moved past both men with the nerve to stand in front of Madison after what she had done.

Surprisingly, Nikki looked angry. "You said you didn't have anything, and that was pretty damn good for nothing, Madison. Almost too perfect for a last-minute ditch." She then brazenly added, "But you know my school is going to win."

With all her might, Madison hit Nikki with an open palm, right across on the nose.

Nikki screamed in horror and covered her face as blood shot out.

Joshua came to Madison's side, but only to hold Madison from doing any further damage, which she really wanted to do.

"You bitch," Nikki screamed. "You broke my nose!"

"You stole my research!" Madison shot back as Joshua still tried to hold her back.

"You can't prove that," Nikki sneered, still holding her bloody nose.

Pushing Joshua out of the way, Madison got another hand across the girl's face, knowing this time she had loosened some teeth.

Nikki fell to the ground again, screaming as if she were dying.

Only a little regret surfaced in Madison as she remembered her now ex-friend was pregnant. This was the only thing that seem to calm Madison a little from killing Nikki.

Professor Barfield was completely stunned, while Joshua tried in earnest to continue holding Madison from jumping on Nikki again. Although, Nikki could have been lying about that as well.

"You're supposed to be my friend, you bitch!" Madison screamed hysterically. "You were supposed to have my back!"

Suddenly, a huge figure pushed past them to help Nikki up.

Madison instantly stopped trying to attack Nikki as she recognized the person helping her now ex-best friend.

"Nikki, are you okay?" Jason asked, concerned.

"No!" Nikki hissed. "My nose is broken!"

"Jason?" Madison exclaimed.

He turned around, shocked to hear Madison's voice. "Madison? I didn't even recognize you from behind and screaming like that."

"You know her?" Nikki asked suspiciously.

"Cut the fake, Nikki!" A sob almost choked Madison. "So, this is how you stole from me?!" she shrieked to Jason.

Jason was still confused. "I just got here, Mad. I don't know what you're talking about."

Her trust in them was gone and she couldn't' believe a word he said. "This was all planned between you and Jamar?" She suddenly felt faint as everything starting to spin. Gripping Joshua's arm to stay steady, she saw Jason was about to help her, but she stepped away in disgust, pressing herself against Joshua.

"Don't you ever touch me!" she cried to Jason. "I never want to see you or Jamar, ever again."

"Good riddance," Nikki snarled, pressing up against Jason, who looked lost.

"I hope it was worth it. I hope it was worth every ounce of hate I'll have for you both." She turned to Joshua. "Please take me out of here. Take me away from here, Joshua." Madison was sick to her stomach, but didn't want to throw up in front of anyone.

Joshua looked at Nikki and Jason. "Stay away from her," he proclaimed, helping Madison away.

"Madison!" Jason called out, still sounding confused. "Madison, please come back."

Those words hurt more than anything. He had nerve! They were nothing but deceivers! All of them and she never wanted to set eyes on Jamar and Jason again.

Madison didn't turn around, and held everything together until she was in the parking lot. She threw up what was in her stomach and anything else, and then got in the passenger side of Joshua's car to start sobbing.

Joshua tried to comfort her, but she knew nothing could help her.

"I'll get the project and bring it to you, okay?" he assured her. "I'll make sure no one ever steals from you ever again."

His comfort still wasn't helping.

Her mind was already trying to break down what to do. She knew if she went back to the motel, Jason and Jamar would eventually come to her and try to explain themselves. She didn't want an explanation. She just never wanted to see them again.

Joshua left her to go back into the conference center to gather everything from her project and presentation. When he returned and put her project in his trunk, he updated her as they took off.

"Professor Barfield is still in a daze."

Only partially worried, Madison questioned, "Did Nikki call the police on me?"

Joshua shook his head. "But that big guy called his brother and they were demanding to know where you'd gone. I told them you took an Uber and left."

"Can I ask a favor, Joshua?" she asked him.

"Sure," he said easily. "Anything for you."

"Can you help me pack my things at the motel? I need to move somewhere fast."

"Oh, yeah. I'll help. My car can fit all your stuff."

That was truly sad, that her whole life was nothing but a carful. Madison pushed the hurt away, promising she wouldn't regret anything.

She was young. She was allowed to make mistakes, and she had made the biggest mistake of her life, becoming involved with Jamar and Jason. Never again would she trust her work, her life or her heart to another man. Never again!

CHAPTER 36

PEOPLE SAY TIME HEALS all wounds. Madison wasn't so sure about that. She'd thought about conducting research on the saying, but people would just laugh at her.

Already a recluse, she knew she overthought too much, anyway.

Time was supposed to be able to at least close the wounds, and she was at least sure she wasn't bleeding from her heart as much anymore after a few years. Yet, why couldn't time heal as much in the passing of the minutes? Why wasn't there a scientific configuration on lessening the pain?

In her reality, time hadn't healed a damn thing. Time had only made her bitter. But Madison was glad she still had something to research.

After Nikki's college won the main grant, Madison's university had come in second place. The grant was just enough to rebuild the lab after the mysterious arson, but not enough to keep their previous research open, or start new research.

The professor's budget was shot and his contacts stopped answering his phone calls. A few months after the horrible day, he was no longer mentally able to stay at the school for any new projects or research. Professor Barfield moved out-of-state, changed his contact numbers and never answered any of her letters or emails.

After the embarrassment of having her research stolen, but not being able to prove anything, the university gave her leave. At least they allowed her to graduate and only supplemented her research because even they couldn't explain how security tapes were either destroyed, deleted or just missing.

Madison was allowed to have one assistant and, of course, she chose Joshua, whom she believed would have worked for her for free, just because he admired her work so much.

"I believe you're meant for greatness, Madison. You're the smartest woman I know."

Joshua had become a true platonic friend. Instead of driving her to another motel, he took her to his father's house in west Detroit, who had a space above their garage for her to stay in. With the extra money she had been saving under the hotplate, she was insistent on paying rent. Joshua had also found cost-of-living-expense grants to help sustain her. He took over managing the lab too, so all her free time could be spent perfecting her organic acne cream and skincare line.

With the new strain hyacinths she had designed along with her "special recipe" she cornered the market quickly with a low cost effective face clearing, skin moisturizing products.

Joshua was amazing at finding money to assist her, and he kept her focused on her goals. After college, she was able to make her patent research and open her own company. Joshua didn't hesitate to assist with setting up the company and managing the administration, while she continued to work in her lab.

Soon, Madison was recognized and awarded for her efforts to help women who couldn't afford expensive skin treatment in order to get rid of acne. Madison had set up a nonprofit with Joshua's help, to grant skin kits. Joshua even came up with the genius idea to start subscription services for customers. With the subscription model in place, Olive Skin Care Line's customer base grew, and a steady stream of guaranteed income assured the company could stand on its own two feet by the third year.

Now it was five years later, almost to the day, and Madison spent her days in the lab and her nights at home. Joshua continued to take care of administration and marketing, while she just concentrated on developing new products.

This year would be when she introduced the new product line that she was keeping a secret, even from Joshua.

"You know, you should learn to trust someone," Joshua said, but he wasn't pressuring her.

They were at their usual Monday standing appointment at Gaston's Restaurant, a bistro internationally known for its delicious desserts, called Gaston's Delight.

She pulled down the edge of her turtleneck, feeling uncomfortable. As a way to remind her of her past, she did everything in her power never to show skin.

As was her usual attire for the last half-decade, Madison was dressed in dark clothing from head to toe, complete with a turtleneck, plus scarf. Her hair was pulled back in a tight ponytail and her face scrubbed so clean, one could eat off of her skin morning, noon or night.

Amazingly, the acne that had riddled her face was completely gone. A great skin regimen and a healthy diet had taken care of everything. Using the same products and methods she manufactured (but refused to be the face of the company), she relied on Joshua to find models and customers who swore by the products.

Shooting a sharp glance at Joshua, Madison didn't dispute his statement knowing she had trust issue. "You know full well why I don't trust anyone, Josh and it'll never change."

"I know, but the investors are getting anxious," he stated.

"Tell them it's worth the wait," she promised. "I've been keeping the new product line under wraps on purpose. When we premiere, I swear to you, everyone who is even thinking about investing will be throwing checks so large at our IPO, you won' know what to do with yourself."

In the beginning, Joshua tried to flirt with her, but she never took up his advances, even up to a year after her ordeal. He could never understand the complexity of the pain she had suffered, and she had never told anyone about the ordeal she had gone through.

She had been overwhelmed with life, and still wallowing in her own misery. Cyrus and Hazel's murder of Onetta Nate hadn't helped. Once the long trial was over, Madison tried to get on with her life. Yet, knowing her father would be locked up for murder for the rest of his life really depressed her in a way. The man whose approval she had tried all her life to win, for whom she'd tried to be perfect, had committed the worst deed ever.

And, though he had killed someone, he *still* looked at her as if he were better than her during the trial; as if she were no better than ground he walked on. That's when Madison's health began to fail her.

Mercy moved in with her during this time, and helped Madison through her medical condition, which Madison initially believed it was from all the stress. By this time, Madison had her own place and having someone at the apartment was nice.

Joshua had tried to change their relationship to a more serious one, but after a while, even he stopped trying to change their relationship, and married another woman. Being with anyone else was hard on Madison. She had constant reminders about what had happened, and though she had not regretted her decision to involve herself with two men, she was still angry about their betrayal.

When Joshua had announced his engagement, Madison was happy for him and put away the possibility that he even liked her in that kind of way anymore.

"When the debut of our new product line is finally showcased, you aren't going to forget your promise, right?" Joshua reminded her.

She rolled her eyes at his constant reminder for her to take a break. Her hard work and dedication to the company should be well-deserved, but she never felt she worked hard enough or that anything really was good enough. So, she worked harder and refined the product.

"So, now that I'm updated on everything, is there anything else? I'd like to get back to work," she said, but in truth, she just wanted to get away from him to wallow in her own feelings.

He responded, "The Goldengate foundation would like to award you with their highest honor this year for humanitarian honoree. You ought to go."

"Why me? Can't someone from the company be a proxy?"

Joshua sighed. "They aren't honoring the company. They are honoring you, and I promised them you'd go."

"Is this for more grant money, Josh? Because I think we're doing fine without it."

"Dammit, Madison, please let someone do something nice for you for once." He seemed agitated. "The foundation is putting you up at the Westin Book Cadillac Hotel for the three-day conference. That's a five star hotel! You'll be the guest of honor at their banquet Friday night, and a judge for their youth science project on Saturday morning. Saturday night is the ball, and then on Sunday, you'll be the keynote as you accept their prestigious humanitarian award."

"I still don't understand, why me?"

"Because you're amazing. I've been saying that for years and it's time the world recognizes you and you accept the truth. You are beautiful, inside and out."

She stiffened because she had heard those words before, and she didn't want to hear them ever again.

He continued to speak. "The board picked you above hundreds of nominees, Madison."

"No one nominated me," she pouted.

"I submitted your name. Besides, in the early days of our company, the Goldengate Foundation provided so many grants that kept you stuck in that lab, you should at least thank them," he replied.

"Are you sure I can't send someone?" she balked.

"Face to face. The humanitarian award is like receiving the Nobel Prize in medicine. It's internationally recognized."

"We've been recognized enough.".

Joshua agreed. "Yes, the company has won many awards, accreditations and wonderful certificates, but you need to be recognized for what you've accomplished so you can see the beauty you have done in this world, Madison. I wish you'd read the letters we get and the gifts we receive for what you've done, the people you've helped. I may be the face, but you are the company, and without your hard work, all of this would be nothing."

Madison didn't want people looking at her.

Joshua continued, "The limousine will pick you up Thursday afternoon. I've already made arrangements for everything, including with Mercy."

"What about-?"

He cut her off. "I've thought of everything. You won't worry about work or home while you are enjoying yourself. Monday is the big announcement of the IPO and our new product line, and I need you well-rested." Joshua handed her the agenda for the weekend. "Don't even pack. I've arranged all your outfits and a personal stylist for every event."

"This really is unnecessary, Joshua," she protested.

He stood up, straightening his jacket, and took the bill. "It's way necessary. I'm only doing this for you. Please, relax. Get ready for this weekend and the product release to come."

Madison couldn't think of another excuse, and she was left to stare at the agenda.

What a waste. She lived on the eastside and could very well drive herself to those events. She had perfectly acceptable clothes at home. Why was this so important to Josh?

Gathering herself, Madison headed home. It wasn't as if she had much of a personal life, she supposed.

The agenda looked nice, too. And rest was so needed.

Madison literally had not had a real vacation, ever.

So many shameful and illicit thoughts about Jamar and Jason crossed her mind, and when she worked, there was still a hollowness inside of her she couldn't fill.

Nothing she did filled the void, the moments in time she tried every day of her life to forget. No other man had ever touched her again. Nothing could give her the equal pleasure or satisfaction she had once felt, so she kept to herself, kept her life simple and secure. She told herself repeatedly she never needed anything, or anyone, to make her feel special or, especially, beautiful.

Maybe after Monday, Madison really would take a much-needed vacation. That weekend, she would spend that time actually thinking of where she wanted to go.

CHAPTER 37

THURSDAY SEEMED TO COME faster than expected. As the agenda stated, the limousine picked Madison up in front of her home exactly at 9 A.M.

Mercy and Pheare were there, looking distrustfully out the curtains at the dark, long vehicle.

"Are you sure this is a good idea?" Pheare questioned.

"I don't know," Madison answered, handing her purse and small bag to the driver. After telling him she'd be out in a moment, she closed the door, waiting for the two to go at her with something negative.

Pheare was paranoid because that's how she grew up with her twin sister, Phoenix RayneTree. They were African-American mixed with Sioux and had spent most of their lives on a reservation.

Coming to Detroit had been Phoenix's idea because they found out their parents weren't their parents. The people who had raised them had only been a relative of their father, who'd died of alcohol poisoning, while their mother lived in Detroit.

Unfortunately, their mother turned out not to be a very nice person, and Pheare stayed as far away from her as possible.

Surprisingly, Mercy defended Madison when she usually sided with her friend. "She needs to get away. She's actually driving me crazy around the house."

Pouting, Madison said, "I'm mostly at the lab, Mercy."

"But when you aren't, all you do is mope," Mercy complained.

"I don't mope," she denied.

"You really do mope a lot. More than my sister, and she's a professional moper."

The two women seem to get a kick out of egging, so Madison decided to just leave.

"Goodbye," she said harshly and started out of the door, but then paused and looked up the stairs.

"You've said your goodbyes, enough," Mercy warned.

Looking back at Mercy, she mouthed a grateful thank you.

Mercy just nodded.

Bounding out of the door, Madison now felt the urge to just stay at home, but she knew she needed this vacation. And she had promised Joshua, right?

Despite Joshua's warning to not take any work with her, she smuggled her electronic Notebook and phone in her purse, just in case.

Madison was now so paranoid, she changed her passwords on all her devices every thirty days. Every year, she ordered new devices and had the previous ones destroyed in front of her. After personally wiping all her hard drives clean, Madison kept constant secure backups in a lockbox at a bank, which only she could access. Furthermore, no one was allowed in her home office, which she kept under triple lock and key.

On every electronic device she worked on, there was an installed app to wipe the device if three attempts of the password failed.

Joshua thought her security provisions were overzealous, but respected her demands. All employees and interns were given thorough background checks, and her security was almost better than the Pentagon. Government agencies had even contacted her to discuss her security protocols for their own departments.

She was the only one that could grant a security overview because Madison was the only one that really knew every single security protocol.

The limousine driver nodded with a happy good morning in the rearview mirror. She only gave him a wary eye as they got closer to her destination.

Nervousness took over her stomach because she hadn't been personable with strangers in years. Madison had been big on keeping to herself.

The driver took her to downtown Detroit where the prestigious Book Cadillac Westin Hotel four-star hotel sat on the corner. The architecture of the building was colossal and the inside simply beautiful.

She was escorted inside to the lobby where a perky Asian woman with honey blonde highlights in her pitch-black hair greeted her.

Extending her hand, the young lady said, "Hi, my name is Heidi Chon. I'm assistant to the Director at Goldengate and I'd like to personally thank you for attending this weekend."

Madison shook her hand warily. "Such extravagance, really? I don't need all this."

"Oh, Mr. Golden clearly expressed nothing but the best for his special guest. This weekend is one of our biggest events of the year, where even our largest sponsors and benefactors come together to donate more to research like yours. They care about who we give our grants to. We want them to know we put their contributions to good use, and they want to know their contributions have made a difference in the world."

Put like that, Madison couldn't help but feel grateful to the Goldengate Foundation helping her out, and for the honor they were presenting her with.

"Why me?" Madison inquired as they got on the elevator.

"Mr. Golden, our director and CEO, has always wanted to honor our successful grantees for a long time, but had to wait until he could do so without the board's interference. This year, the Gates family gave Mr. Golden full authority over the foundation."

"Was there trouble with the foundation?" Madison questioned.

Heidi explained as they got off the elevator and headed to Madison's room, "It was a personal matter. Nothing for our grantees or contributors to be concerned about."

The perfect response for a company's PR rep.

So, you're Mr. Golden's personal assistant?" Madison questioned.

"Yes," the woman proudly responded. "Although, during events, I'm given the honor of taking care of special guests."

Madison didn't think too much of this woman's enthusiasm as they entered her hotel room.

"This weekend, I'm assigned to be your PA as well," Heidi said, handing her a business card. "My cell number is on the back."

The suspicious and distrustful look on Madison face must've encouraged the assistant to explain more.

"Mr. Golden knows I take my job seriously."

Madison turned away to peruse the opulent hotel room, and the young lady gave her the card key to the room.

Heidi explained, "I'm a floor down. Here's your itinerary and more information about the hotel. Call guest services for food and anything you may need. Your bill is already covered by the foundation."

Protesting, Madison said, "I can cover my own bill."

Heidi smiled. "Your VP said you would balk at being taken care of. I'm to let you know you are on a mini -vacation and we are here to make your life easier."

Madison bit her lip, trying not to protest at all this "babying".

"I can take care of anything else you require. I insist you use me, Ms. Oliver," the assistant said. "Did you need unpacking services?"

"No, thank you," Madison said, glad she could draw the line at something.

"Tonight is a private dinner with our contributors and investors. Mr. Golden won't be back in town until tomorrow morning, and he's requested a private breakfast with you in his suite before any of the activities start for the day."

Madison nodded her acquiescence to meet this Mr. Golden. If she could get through the night with all the wealthy contributors, she could certainly breeze through a single person at breakfast.

"I'll return to escort you for dinner tonight."

"Thank you, Heidi," Madison said. "I'm sorry for being so difficult. I'm just nervous."

"It's not a problem. By the way, your wardrobe is in the closet and a stylist will be here in an hour for hair and makeup."

When Madison was alone, she pressed the firm queen-size mattress down and smiled at the luxury. She remembered lying on the pullout couch at Joshua's father's house and the pain of her back hurting for so long until she could afford a nicer mattress.

She had been insistent on taking care of herself and, with Mercy's help, Madison had been able to distance herself from handouts and dependencies. Plus, it was nice having family around, even though Mercy had her own secrets, which the cousin chose to keep to herself.

Turning around in the hotel room, Madison fell back on the bed and giggled her approval. All the hard, cheap beds Madison had ever slept in, she always tried to convince herself she didn't need more…

She had always been determined to keep her life simple and herself unnoticeable.

Her cell phone rang and already she knew it was Mercy. Her cousin had a strange way of calling whenever Madison thought about her.

"How's everything at home?" Madison questioned.

"Perfect as usual, but your lawyer just called to inform us about the case. He thought you'd like to know, but he knows how you get upset speaking about it, so he called me."

Dreading what she was going to hear, Madison braced herself. "What did he tell you?"

"Hazel will be serving time for the rest of her life. She didn't even fight the charges."

"All of sudden, no fight?"

"Maybe someone visited her and told her if she didn't, they'd make sure to find each and every one of her bastard children to make their lives a living hell. And that certain someone went down the list of how they would do so."

"Mercy, you didn't!"

"No, but Phoenix and Pheare certainly didn't mind."

"And this made her agree to a prison sentence? She's been denying any involvement in the murder with my father for years."

Mercy said, "Pheare felt we needed to help Hazel make the right decision. I know Pheare doesn't speak a lot to you about how's she's feeling but she highly respects you and really wants nothing but good for you. She told me you deserve something good out of all the good you do for others."

"Did you have a hand at getting Hazel to agree too?"

"I push and agreed with what they wanted to do because I feel the same way, Madison."

Madison couldn't be upset with what her cousin had done. Hazel's trial had dragged on for much too long, and now Madison could go on with her life and leave the past behind in regards to her father's deed.

That part of her life was over, and if she could just forget the other part that had to do with Jamar and Jason that would be over too.

Sighing, Madison knew, despite how she'd work so hard to get the attention of her father's love, her heart was still weak for those brothers, and she would have to work harder at not thinking about them again... a lot harder!

CHAPTER 38

G OING INTO THE SHOWER, Madison saw a note in Joshua's writing on top of a bath kit. "Please relax this weekend and know that everything's taken care of; you deserve this."

She smiled and took his advice, drawing herself a bath. She sunk deep into the tub and sighed. Right before the water got cold, Madison rushed to wash up and pamper herself with the wonderful lotion and skincare products from her own company.

Joshua was too thoughtful, and after the glorious self-pampering session, she decided that whatever raise he wanted that year, she'd give it. Although, she never disagreed on anything Joshua decided for the company.

There came a knock on the door, and a muscular black woman entered with the most unique amber eyes.

"I'm Phylis," she introduced herself with a deep voice, and immediately Madison knew this was a transgender person. "I'm here to do your hair and makeup."

Her own makeup was flawless. Leading Phylis over to the vanity in the bedroom suite, Madison let Phylis get to work.

An hour later, Madison was beautifully dressed in a royal purple silk maxi dress with matching, open-toe sandals. Joshua must have let them know about her aversion to heels.

Phylis had put in a purple comb around her natural curls with a feather and encrusted diamonds around the tip, which also perfectly matched the shoes she wore.

Phylis looked pleased, then said her goodbyes after finishing Madison's makeup. The woman was an artist with a brush and had not given Madison too much makeup, but just enough to highlight her best features.

Heidi returned as Phylis was leaving. The assistant had changed into a shorter, after-five black dress with her hair down with a slight bend on the ends, accentuating her blonde highlights.

Heidi escorted her down to the dinner on the first floor, near the hotel's patio. A great buffet was set out, and Madison was led to the podium.

All night, she was greeted by sincere and wealthy people who had supported her grants throughout the years. Heidi was a great assist in making sure Madison knew who each person was, their level of donations to the Goldengate foundation, and even their level of admiration for Madison's company.

Many supporters and donators had grown to know her since Madison had first started, and they supported her research almost as passionately as she had worked on her project. Others had known the people whom her products and research had positively affected.

The night kept her on a grateful high, and for the first time in her life, she really saw the impact of her work.

Joshua joined her later that night, and she thanked him with a hug. "I appreciate you forcing me to do this, Josh."

"I'm glad you're enjoying yourself. I was worried you wouldn't. I know how you over worry about your household and the lab. I assure you, I have everything under control." He blushed a little. "Well, Mercy and I have everything under control."

Madison chuckled, completely relaxed knowing that, if Mercy were there, she would demand recognition of some type for any work she had done. "I really needed this night, Joshua. I'll never complain again at attending one of these."

He escorted her back to her room once the function was ending. Before they left, Heidi whispered something to Joshua, but he only shook his head adamantly.

Madison noted Heidi looked disappointed by Joshua's reply, but she walked away, immediately making a phone call.

As they were on the elevator, Madison questioned, "What was that about?"

"Mr. Golden is arriving in town in a couple of hours and wanted to request a late-night drink with you," he said without hesitation.

"I'll still be up. I wouldn't have-"

Joshua cut her off abruptly. "Just because he's head of the company doesn't mean he gets any special privileges. He can wait to speak to you."

In those moments, she felt Joshua's attraction for her was still just as strong, but dormant, as if he were waiting for the perfect opportunity for her to fall in love with him, despite her telling him she'd never want to be with another man again.

Plus, he was married. But when he did overprotective things like this, she was worried his heart was still pining after her.

Joshua continued, "I want you to stick to the schedule. This is going to be a busy weekend already. Just take it easy."

They walked into her room. Maybe she was just being silly. After all those years, Joshua would be a fool to still have romantic feelings for her.

"Go on the balcony," Joshua said, kissing her cheek. "I'll make us drink."

Madison was surprised by the kiss—and the gesture. "You're staying?"

"Just for a while. Don't worry; my wife is waiting up for me, so I won't stay long. I just want to make sure you're settled."

She wasn't worried that Joshua would try anything. He had never tried anything in the past; Not like Jamar and Jason. No man had ever touched her like them.

Taking a deep breath, she walked out to the balcony to embrace the warm, beautiful night Detroit was offering. There was a longing in her soul, and she wished she had someone of her own to share the moment with. Someone who would give her a shoulder-neck kiss, put their arms around her waist and hold her close. Someone who would make her feel…

Joshua interrupted her deep thoughts. "Let's not play games, missy. I can see it in your eyes. I know when you're thinking of them. Which one this time?"

She blinked innocently, unable to lie quickly.

"Don't do that," Joshua said, handing her a small shot of cognac on the rocks.

Madison took a little sip, knowing full well what alcohol would do to her. "What am I doing, Josh? " she asked, knowing he was reading her like book. She had admitted to Joshua a little bit about the deceit, just not the full extent. She had admitted to sleeping with both men, but never told Joshua it had been at the same time.

"It's all really a blur," she lied feebly.

"Yet, you can't let them go," he determined. "You won't allow yourself to be happy because of them, Madison."

"I AM happy," she lied again, forcing herself to smile.

"I've been your friend too long to know when you're lying to me, Madison. Why can't you let go? You've accomplished so much without them.

You've done incredible things as a woman on your own. They haven't even tried to contact you. They haven't even tried to apologize for what they've done."

Weakly, she admitted, after taking another sip of alcohol, "It doesn't matter. I know I'll never feel like that with another man."

"Both of them? You felt that about both of them?" he asked, confused.

"You wouldn't understand," she said. "It's complicated, Joshua."

"Have you even tried another man, Madison?"

"I've tried to go on. I went on dates, but the moment I think about going any farther..." She sighed pathetically. "In the back of my mind I say why bother when I'm not going to feel the way tey made me feel or any better."

Sourly, he questioned, "Even the ones Mercy finds for you?"

Madison ignored the question. Mercy never gave Joshua the time of day. Matter of fact, Mercy did her best to show Joshua he didn't exist by not saying one word about or to him as much as possible. "None of them could understand me or give me what I needed to feel."

Joshua downed his drink with a cruel, cold look in his eyes and kissed her forehead. "I got a suspicion a month ago about some things. I wanted to come here tonight and share them with you."

"About what? The company?"

"It has nothing to do with the company." He sounded hurt, but then shook his head as if it wasn't a big thing. "You never see anything past the company or yourself, you know that? No one is trying to hurt you anymore, but you can't see anything else. Not until you get Jamar and Jason out of your system."

She knew whatever she said or had done had hurt Joshua. Laying an apologetic hand on his arm, she said, "I'm sorry, Josh. It's just going to take a lot more time for me to get over them; Especially when..." She couldn't say what she wanted to say, because he knew of the constant reminders in her life.

"It's fine." He kissed her forehead again. "Goodnight, Madison."

When he was gone, she finished her drink and went to take a shower.

CHAPTER 39

MADISON REALLY TRIED NOT to think of the past, but at moments like those, when she wasn't in the lab or at home, she couldn't help but remember Jamar and Jason making love to her, pressing their bodies to her, kissing her all over, and filling her up until she ran over.

These thoughts and desires were so wrong, yet she couldn't help thinking of them, wishing for one more time, one more moment… hell, at that point, one more kiss.

Lying in bed, she closed her eyes and allowed herself to think deeply about them, damning the consequences to her emotional state. Their bodies entwined, everywhere she turned, and Madison could kiss someone, suckle a warm body part, and hold someone close.

Jamar's body confidently stroked inside of her, while Jason's curiosity prompted him to vary his strokes in her rear, giving her the best he had to offer.

Their bodies had been so warm, masculine, and virile, until finally…

In the bed alone, Madison buckled her hips, clasped her thighs tight and came.

After she regained her senses, she turned to her stomach, still unable to sleep. Usually playing with herself put her right to sleep when sleep wouldn't come. But with no lab or home, she was just feeling foreign.

Maybe she should go home?

No one would know if she left and came back before Heidi returned for her in the morning for breakfast.

Speaking of Heidi, she could hear the assistant in the hallway.

Getting out of bed, Madison looked out the room's peephole to see Heidi pacing in front of the door across the hall, looking nervous.

"He's here?" Heidi asked, suddenly stopping with her cell phone. "Okay, take him around the rear and bring him up the service elevator. I'll meet him at that end of the hall. Thanks, Luke."

Madison watched the assistant walk away, and curiosity was killing her. She wondered what Mr. Golden looked like.

You do remember what happened the last time you'd gotten curious? She reprimanded herself.

Moving around the hotel room, Madison couldn't find any literature on Mr. Golden. Going on the internet, there were no pictures of him. She read on a newspaper website how the foundation had been going through personal family troubles. The powerful matriarch passed, and the family had to decide who was left in charge of the foundation.

As the Gates's were another family that also was part of founding the organization, according to the report, with the Golden family divided, the Gates's has had to pick sides.

GarettMarick J. Golden.

She twisted her nose at the name, but read how he was named for his father, who'd died in an accident.

GarettMarick J. Golden wasn't married and had been running the foundation as Director since the matriarch died. Just the previous year, he'd been given the title of CEO, once the personal family dispute was settled. A fun fact she found out was that the *J* in the middle stood for absolutely nothing. His mother just forgot to finish filling out the birth certificate, so the *J* had just stuck with him.

In that day and age, Madison found it hard to believe GarettMarick J. Golden didn't have any pictures on the Internet. They believed the foundation's spotlight should be more on the people the foundation benefited, and not on who was behind it all.

Madison picked up the receiver to call the front desk, and almost changed her mind until the male receptionist answered.

"Front desk, how may I help you?"

"Is Mr. Golden in?"

"Who?" the receptionist questioned.

"I don't know his room number, but his first name is GarettMarick. I know he's supposed to be checking in now across the hall from me," she explained.

"Oh, Mr. Golden," the guy said. "But you should know, it's pronounced *Jar-rett-Mah-rick*. He already hates the name, ma'am. Careful not to further annoy him by saying it wrong." He said this jokingly, but also as if he was doing her a favor.

Stiffly, she said, "Thank you," and waited for her information.

"He's just checked in and is headed for the twelfth floor. Would you like me to transfer you to his room?"

"No!" Madison snapped in panic and hung up the phone, completely losing her nerve. She was on the twelfth floor. Anxiety raced through her as she went over to the hotel room door to hear voices coming down the hall.

Curiosity was eating her up, and she cracked her door just a little to see if she could catch a glimpse of him. Leaving all the lights out in her front room, Madison could see the hallway perfectly.

Heidi and a valet suddenly appeared at the door across the hall, and the perfect assistant was instructing the valet to leave a bag by the door. "Mr. Golden can carry all these in."

"Will he require turndown service?" the valet questioned.

"I don't know. He should, after walking up twelve flights of stairs instead of taking the elevator," she said, rolling her eyes. "But when he's stressed, he doesn't want to be bothered. He'll come out when he wants and bring his own bags inside. Follow me downstairs to my car, please."

And they left to get on the elevator.

Madison heard the ding and the metal doors opening.

Looking down at the bags, she wondered what kind of clothes this Mr. Golden wore. Stepping into the hallway, she looked around. No one was in sight. The hallway was completely empty and everything was quiet.

Tip-toeing over to the door across the hall from hers, Madison pressed her ear hard against the thick wood, but was disappointed to hear nothing.

"Spying is not sexy at all, Madison Oliver," a deep, familiar voice said behind her.

Slowly, with guilt, she turned around as her brain took in the large figure. Calm, auburn eyes caressed her face, warm and welcoming and not filled with one bit of apology. After all these years, Jamar Ross had the nerve to look like nothing had been done.

The bastard! WHAT WAS HE DOING HERE?!

"Fuck you, Jamar!" Madison seethed, and started to go to her room, but he was in her way. When she tried to step around him, he moved more in her way.

"Madison, wait!" he implored. *"Ow!"*

She had used all her weight to stomp on his toes. He moved out of her way, and she ran to her door, but only slammed against it, as it had automatically closed.

Her keycard was inside, along with all her decent clothes.

Slowly turning around to glare at him, fully realizing she was only wearing a long, pink nightgown, she was forced to face her anger from so long ago.

Everything inside of her wanted to punch his face, but she noticed that he was bigger, even more muscular than she remembered, and if she tried to assault him, she would most likely hurt herself more than him.

He apprehensively approached her with his hands at his sides, making no attempt to come any closer than a foot away.

He was making her sick to her stomach with the glad-to-see-her grin, and the revealing nightgown was no help either. If he looked hard enough, he could probably see everything she'd never shown a man since he'd last laid eyes on her. Would he see the scars?

Feeling exposed, Madison folded her arms over her chest and tried her best not to look at him.

"My room is open. You could use my phone to have someone bring a key," Jamar suggested.

Why the hell did he have to sound the same? And evoke the same warm feelings deep between her legs? No, she was not still attracted to him. He was the enemy.

Madison had deliberately never made an effort to never see what Jamar and Jason had been up to, or to make an attempt to find them, not even secretly, because she was terrified of what she would feel.

The sexual attraction was still strong. It took all her concentrated effort to fight from looking directly at him.

"I never want you to help me out for the rest of my life, Jamar Ross. I want you to stay the hell away from me."

"I knew you'd say that the moment you saw me." He actually sounded hurt. "Madison, I know there is a lot of explaining to do. You just don't know how many times I've thought of what to say, given the chance to see you, but..." Jamar sighed, defeated. "There were circumstances that you wouldn't understand."

Glaring at him, she seethed. "No, I couldn't understand the stabbing in my back."

He looked down at his feet. "You're right. Things should have been clearly understood before Jason and I involved you."

"Understood?!" She cried, and choked back the sob that wanted to burst forth. "No. NO! I don't want to understand. I just want you to go away again, Jamar. Go away and never set eyes on me again."

Someone came out of their hotel room, glared down the hall at them, and then slammed the door.

She was now triple embarrassed to have disturbed the other patrons, and turned her back to the hotel door she was supposed to be on the other side of.

Damn her. Her penchant to be curious when it came to men always seemed to get her in trouble.

Jamar opened his hotel door. "Please come in, and I'll call someone to bring up another key for your room."

Slowly turning around, she looked at the door he had opened in shock. Madison looked down at the bags Heidi had left for Mr. Golden at the doorway, and then looked at Jamar. "You know Mr. Golden?"

He smiled. "I am Mr. Golden. I'm the director and CEO of the Goldengate Foundation, Madison."

The hallway began to spin, and Madison couldn't help herself as she gave in to the blackness that surrounded her.

***

Next time she wanted to be curious, she needed to do so when she was fully dressed.

The door to the bedroom opened and Madison immediately feigned sleep, breathing as deeply and calmly as possible.

"You're not asleep, Madison," Jamar called her bluff.

Opening her eyes, flashing him anger, she slowly sat up, but there was still some dizziness.

He walked over to the bed and placed a keycard beside her on the table. "I had the front desk bring you a keycard for your room. And there's a robe at the end of the bed so you can leave out of my room appropriately dressed, if anyone is in the hallway."

Madison pushed the covers off herself, moving slowly so the dizziness wouldn't get to her again. Getting away from Jamar as fast as she could without passing out again was extremely important right now for her sanity.

He stood away from the bed.

Tears wanted to well up in her eyes because she was having a mental, emotional and physical conflict with herself.

Under no circumstances did she want him to know what was going on inside of her.

Jamar still looked good, even better than she remembered.

Forcing herself to look away, she put the robe on. He started to assist her, but she put up a hand to stop him.

He took a chair from the work desk and moved to the end of the bed. His hands were folded on his lap, but otherwise his body language spoke clearly that he was still happy to see her.

"I hate you," she seethed.

"You have every right to. After the smoke cleared and I understood the enormity of our foolishness, I respected you needed your space. I didn't think it would be over four years before we got the chance to see you again, but I guess that's what I get for making a deal with the devil."

"You and Jason betrayed me, Jamar, and there's nothing you can say or do to make me forgive you." She put her feet to the floor, hoping the dizziness wouldn't return. She wanted to get away from him, the hotel, and the scenario before she forgot how angry she was at him.

"You shouldn't forgive me. All I can do is say is how deeply sorry I am. I'm sorry I allowed lust to get in my way. I'm sorry I let my love for you allow me to ignore the warnings. I'm ashamed of what happened, because if I had not been so wrapped up in being happy, then I would have seen what was coming, but I thought... I really thought Jason was going to get rid of that evil woman. I mean, back then I didn't know everything. I couldn't believe she would do something like that. But I guess when money is involved, people get selfish and stupid."

He leaned forward in the chair. "Madison," he said in a deep, compassionate voice. "I want to do whatever I can to make up for the horrible deeds I've done, how I've made you feel, and how I've possibly ruined the beautiful and intelligent woman I've always thought you to be. I cannot say sorry enough, but I'm willing to do whatever I have to do, in order to make things right for you, even if it means I'll never have you in my life. I want to do whatever it takes to make you happy, Madison. No strings attached."

"You think using your foundation to give my company money is supposed to make me forget what you did to me, Jamar?!"

"No. Actually, Joshua came to us with your project... well, he came to the foundation. Now, please don't be angry with him. I think initially, he didn't know this was my mother's foundation or that we were in charge after she died. It was an offside endeavor started by my father and when he died, fell in her lap and when she passed away, came to Jason and I. By then, the foundation was already funding you. I didn't find out until the second year that the board had approved your initial research. But after I found that out, I did everything in my power to make sure we could continue to support all your research and endeavors. Not out of guilt, but because I've always felt you were the most intelligent woman I've ever known and the work you have done has been phenomenal, and the world needs to know that."

Her legs were steady enough for her to stand.

He stood too, but didn't move the chair out of her way. She knew it would be ridiculous to try to make a run for the door. Thick as a concrete wall, Jamar looked like he was in peak physical condition.

Closing her robe, straightening her spine, she hissed, "You can take your recognition and shove it where the sun don't shine, Jamar Ross or whatever your name is!"

CHAPTER 40

MADISON GRABBED HER keycard and strode out of the room. She could feel him following her and knew the man could probably see every curve of her body. The heat of his eyes was on her, but she refused to acknowledge any of his attraction, and especially not hers.

"Please, Madison, please," Jamar begged as she got to her door.

She put her keycard in the lock and watched it turn green.

"Please," he beseeched again.

Why did his voice wrench at her heart? He sounded just like…

The light on her door turned red because she had taken so long to open the door. Looking back at him, she saw he was staying a foot away and forcing himself to keep his hands to his side, but she had a feeling he itched to touch her.

"What could you say to make me want to trust you again? Be with you right now, Jamar?"

"Nothing. All I can do is answer your questions as best as I can. As honestly as possible," he said with a promise of so much in his beautiful amber eyes.

Damn her curiosity. She turned around slowly to face him. "Why did you give my research to Nikki?"

"I swear on everything holy, we didn't give anything to Nikki. We'd just realized you knew Nikki that day, and I hated Jason for a while because of his lust to have his cake and eat it too. If he had just…" He stopped talking. "Jason and I didn't even know how deep the seed research was. You never really spoke about it to us. I knew of the other research we helped you with, but not much about the research Nikki stole."

"She took everything from me."

"And you have every right to believe we were a part of that, but I swear, Madison, we had no idea. Why didn't you fight for what was yours? You knew she was selling the idea to a company. You could have fought and won."

Feeling upset just talking about what Nikki had done, she snarled, "Because what was the use? She always wins!"

He looked defeated, as if he knew that was true. "She usually always gets her way, but you do know the research was bought out by a company, right? And she has yet to prove the results she promised in the presentation."

"How do you know this?"

Jamar shrugged wickedly. "Maybe because I know the company that bought the research and I know she can't deliver."

"How do you know?" she demanded.

Reaching inside of his coat, he pulled out an old keycard. "Do you remember this?"

She took the keycard and gasped. "It's to the greenhouse."

"I bought the house from Jason two years ago. He never moved in. Nikki wanted something bigger and better in her mind."

"Wait, what?"

Regretfully, Jamar admitted, "He married her. After you left and I stopped talking to him, Nikki was able to convince him she was all he had. Of course, it was all for his money, which they ran through the first year of marriage. Nikki moved in with her parents waiting for my mother's trust to come to us and she managed to clean her parents out until they died and then the almost all the money and assets that was left in the trust my mother had left him. By this time, Nikki realized everything else had been left to me. She thought she could get Jason to fight me, reveal to the world how much my mother hated me, but in truth, my mother had to give most of everything to me, because everything she owned came from my father, who had deemed in his will that, upon her death, I would be given mostly everything."

"Your mother hated you that much until she died?"

"Pretty much," he said.

"And all these years, you've been fighting Jason? That must've been hard, considering how close you were."

"Jason and I never wanted to fight, and that's why I convinced a company to buy Nikki's research almost a year ago. If she doesn't prove by Sunday night she knows what she's talking about, then she'll have to pay all the money back."

"How much?"

"Five million dollars."

"Oh, lawd," Madison said, almost feeling bad for her former best friend.

"I know, because Jason will lose everything as well, because he's married to her. Despite all the mistakes he's made, he doesn't deserve what's to come."

Narrowing her eyes suspiciously, Madison asked, "You aren't asking me to help Jason, are you, by helping Nikki?"

"Oh, hell no!" He walked closer to her, looking as if he wanted to say something else.

"Then what?"

"Nothing. I just wanted to spend the weekend showing you how sorry we are, and hopefully receiving your forgiveness."

"I'm not taking you back, Jamar," she warned. "I want nothing to do with you."

"Of course. I'm not asking for that." He stepped even closer. "But I should let you know, your body says differently."

"What?" she asked, flushed.

"Madison, I can smell your heat from here."

Pulling the robe tighter and stepping back until her back was against the door, she said, "I don't know what you're talking about. I'm not... I'm not heated... I mean, I'm angry."

He put a hand on the door, right by her head, and leaned down. Their eyes were locked and she couldn't look away to save her life.

It was like she was transported back into that Lincoln, looking into his eyes and knowing what his mouth could do to her body.

Yes, she kissed him, and Jamar didn't hesitate to respond. Locking lips, feeling his warmth, tasting the familiar man of Jamar was like heaven on earth. His lips pressed harder and she felt her resistance melt as tears came to her eyes.

Her arms circled his neck, while his hands moved into her robe and his arms moved around her body to mold her against him.

The feel of him was just as she remembered, yet even more powerful as she'd missed him more than she cared to admit.

His tongue pressed between her lips and she wanted to die, circling her tongue around his mouth and then suckling, deepening the kiss as her senses flooded with arousal. The taste of him brought back so many beautiful memories, and she allowed him to deepen the kiss more.

His arms stopped gripping her body so hard and pressed her harder against the hotel door. Madison didn't care about their surroundings tightened her arms around his neck, grinding her body against his.

She was feeling pure bliss in hyper-drive as he dug his fingers in her rear cheeks under her night gown.

Jamar groaned in her mouth at the knowledge that she wore nothing underneath, and somehow, his pants became unzipped. In the back of her mind, Madison fully understood the danger of accepting him raw, but at that moment, she didn't care.

He broke the kiss and pulled her gown to expose her chest so his mouth enveloped her hardened nipple. She didn't remember his mouth being so hot, but he seemed to be scorching her skin in unbelievable pleasure. Madison roasted in arousal and gasped, clawing at his body, wanting to feel more.

He guided her back through his open hotel door, in the barely-lit room, and then to the nearby couch. Kissing her face, neck and chest, he kept all her senses occupied.

Madison didn't care. Her body wanted this more than her hatred wanted to stay away from him. She couldn't think straight, especially as his hand moved between her thighs.

Tears welled in her eyes at the adoration his hand showed her, and then he pulled his fingers away to suck all the juices from his hands.

His mouth dipped to her lips again, and the taste of her and his masculinity was a powerful aphrodisiac. If she wanted to have stopped, she couldn't have. Madison was on a mission to have lust with Jamar.

Everything was just like old times. Just once more.

The rest of their clothes somehow ended up on the couch, while their naked bodies ended up on the floor nearby. Engulfing his shaft in her mouth, Madison remembered the taste of his body, his thickness on her mouth and the smell of his essence. She loved the way his groans of pleasure seemed longer, deeper, stronger, making her ears tingle and her body long to have more of him.

He was a drug. A habit she had never really broken from, just denied. He pulled her up and kissed her hard.

"Gawd, I've missed you," he said breathlessly, his eyes welling up with tears, right before he kissed her with an abandonment she could feel in the bottom of her soul, swelling her and exploding as he plunged deep within her wetness.

Madison cried, too. She cried because she'd missed him so much. She cried because she needed this so much. She cried because, as they culminated together, she knew she was so bad, but this felt so damn good.

CHAPTER 41

REALITY WAS QUICK TO wake her to the truth. She had given into her lust and she shouldn't have. He unwound his body from hers to stand up and find his pants, but never stopped looking at her.

Madison didn't move from where she lay, but pulled a pillow from the couch to cover her middle.

"You were never ashamed of your body before," he noted with disappointment.

"I was a lot of things in the past, Jamar." It took every bit of her control not to sound snippy.

He dropped to his knees as if she had struck him with a knife. His large body over shadowed hers and she had forgotten how truly handsome he was.

"I haven't heard that name in so long. I miss you saying my name the most." He gripped his chest as if his heart hurt. "Say it again, Madison."

She pressed her lips together in resistance, not wanting to give him the satisfaction because it made her feel good not to. Madison didn't want to feel good from him anymore; not when her body was already shamefully satisfied.

Jamar sat down next to her and traced a fingertip on her bare shoulder, down her arm and then up again, repeating this action as he spoke.

"I'll never be able to right any wrongs I've done to you, Maddie."

She closed her eyes, trying not to feel those blissful pulses and wonderful tingles at the familiarity of him.

"But I don't want this night to end without you knowing how sorry I am that I could not make things right."

She didn't speak or ask questions. Madison had decided a long time ago she would never wonder what had happened to them or to her research. In order for her not to go insane or wallow in misery, Madison had put her life's work out of her mind once she knew it wasn't hers anymore.

Fighting would have been too hard on her soul and heart.

"But if we can-"

Putting her hand over his mouth to cut him off, her eyes spoke volumes, telling him not to speak another world.

Their eyes were locked, and she slowly shook her head, seeing how there was the pleading look still in his amber brown eyes. "There is no way to go forward, Jamar."

He took her hand from his mouth and kissed each fingertip before he leaned over and kissed her lips.

She let him, telling herself she could just finish enjoying him until the morning.

"So we can still have one night? This night?" he asked apprehensively.

Madison couldn't refuse. What was one night? One time in her life, she would let go and allow herself to be lusted after by Jamar.

This would be the last time, she swore to herself.

He took his time kissing every centimeter of her body, as if trying to remember the touch and taste of her skin all over again. Front to back, he built her passion and lust to an all-time high.

He finally turned her on her back to move his head between her legs. His mouth worshipped between her thighs until she glorified his name repeatedly.

When she clawed at his back, demanding to have him inside of her again, he finally granted her wish, plunging deep into her wetness and nearly whimpering from her tightness.

"Damn, Maddie, you're still so damn tight," he growled, but she knew it wasn't a complaint. His groans continued as he gave her long, slow strokes, guiding her body to orgasm as he adored her face, neck, and breasts.

Madison cried, whined and screamed her joy. Her good sense had long left her and she dug her nails into his back, suckled his neck, kissed him with abandonment and locked her thighs around his waist, never wanting him to stop.

Her body radiated a glow, loving every culmination he gifted to her. He disengaged and plunged his face back between her legs again, but this time turned his body adjacent to her. She only needed to tip her head to the side and grip the base of him to guide his thickness down her throat.

He moaned his enjoyment as his mouth ravished her succulent womanhood.

They voraciously tasted, suckled, and nibbled on each other for what seemed like hours before he rolled on his back and she moved to straddle his hips. Guiding him into her and riding him to repeated glory brought tears to her eyes.

His hands couldn't stop touching her as he pounded up into her to meet her downward motions.

She could feel him pulsing deep inside her, the thickness growing, until finally she thought he was going to climax inside of her.

In moments, he did, and all she could do was hold on for the most splendid ride of her life.

Her body, soul and mind melded with his, and for unknown moments in space and time, they were one.

This time, Madison sobbed hard. All the years of frustration, hatred and pain she had gone through seemed to be forgotten just then.

Yet, as their breathing came under control, the cool air of the room hit their warm, sweating bodies. The stillness of the night seemed to scream at them like a thunderstorm. Madison knew the euphoric moment was over, and the cold, real issues came back into place.

"Leave," she ordered him.

"But-" Jamar started to protest.

Putting her finger over his mouth, she could feel her body trembling with anger. "Not another word, Jamar or I swear I'll scream this entire hotel down in my fury."

He moved away from her and found his clothes. She pulled her robe on and refused to look his way.

The only way she knew he was by the door was that he whispered, "I'm sorry," before shutting it behind him. She curled on the couch and cried the rest of the night.

***

Madison wasn't even in her own hotel room. Jamar had been gracious to leave her alone in his room. At six in the morning, she came out and went back to hers. He was nowhere in sight.

Phylis arrived to hide the puffy eyes and ravaged lips without any questions. While Madison was getting prepared to leave, the stylist let her know she'd return later on, to prepare her for the first awards ceremony, where she was to help with awarding other's recipients of The Goldengate grants.

Madison was grateful for Phylis's help and tried to tip her, but the stylist insisted she couldn't take anything.

"All fees and tips have been taken care of," Phylis insisted.

Madison didn't press the matter.

Heidi then appeared at Madison's door, bright and early at eight in the morning, with a smile from ear to ear, clearly excited to escort her to the day's event. "My boss has been looking forward to this breakfast all night. I don't think he's slept a wink."

Madison surmised from that statement that Jamar had told Heidi absolutely nothing.

"Neither have I," Madison said sourly. "But not in excitement."

This bubbly assistant wasn't helping as Madison was trying to get a little caffeine to liven herself up.

There was a lot of free time in her schedule. After her breakfast with Mr. Golden, she was to judge the science awards. She'd have a lot of free time between the junior dinner that night, and then her schedule was free after that.

The following day was the technology fair, where she would also guest judge. The rest of her afternoon would be free if she wanted to visit the pavilion or spa, which she knew Joshua had signed her up for.

She really should be angry at Joshua. Piping hot mad, but on the other end, she felt Joshua had done things for her company, yet why had he kept it all a secret? Probably because he knew she would have been stubborn enough to refuse the money from the foundation once she knew it had anything to do with Jamar or Jason.

Her anger should be directed exactly where it should be! Jamar and Jason. Joshua was only trying to help her.

She would call Joshua to check on the lab and her home after the science fair, even though she knew she didn't have to. Joshua was good at handling things when she wasn't there, but she needed something to distract her thoughts. Mercy most likely was holding things down at home, and that was why she had not contacted Madison either.

Both felt she needed a vacation, but Madison knew this wasn't the kind of vacation they had imagined for her. Or had that been why Joshua refused her to see Jamar for a "late night drink" with the CEO?

Joshua was only trying to protect her, but why had he felt to surprise her like this?

Still she couldn't be mad at Joshua. She wouldn't be mad at him because of all he had done.

She didn't know how she could handle seeing Jamar again, and what if Jason appeared? With his wife?

Her stomach churned with stress.

Nothing seemed to come from the hotel room across from hers, where she wondered if Jamar had ever returned after she left.

"Are you ready for the day, Ms. Oliver?" Heidi questioned.

"As ready as I'll ever be," she grumbled in an attempt to sound positive.

Heidi led her out of the room, but they didn't go across the hall. They headed to the elevator.

"I thought I'd have breakfast with Mr. Golden in his room," Madison pointed out.

"He had planned that, but changed his mind, feeling it was more professional if you had breakfast downstairs. I reserved a conference room by the dining area." Heidi looked frazzled for a moment.

"How are you always so perky?" Madison questioned, amazed.

Heidi smiled graciously. "I've been up for a while, but it's an honor to help facilitate this, ma'am."

She followed the assistant from the elevator to the dining area.

Near the rear, they entered through the private door where a buffet of food was laid before her.

No one else was in the room, but a setup for two was assembled in the middle.

"He'll be down in a moment. Please fix yourself a plate," the assistant urged, before leaving.

Getting a moment alone gave her time to get her mind together. Madison was actually feeling a little better now that Heidi was out of the room and she was on her own to think.

Pushing away the fact she'd been a wanton freak the previous night, she could face Jamar and pretend nothing had happened. She'd put on the cold demeanor she had worn for so long in her life and deal with him no matter what he said or how he looked.

As long as he didn't touch her!

Deep down inside, she couldn't hate herself for meeting Jamar and Jason. Although her life's work had gone to waste, they had helped in initiating her new venture and she couldn't lie, it had been fun. They had gotten her to her new research and she'd made a very lucrative life for herself as a result.

Bad or good, she had become successful and should've been thanking them instead of hating on them.

Holding on to a wrong for so long was unhealthy just as Joshua had hinted in the past.

"Ms. Oliver," the assistant said, bursting in the room as if she was about to introduce the President of the United States. "I'd like you to meet Mr. GarettMarick J. Golden, CEO of Goldenngate City Foundation."

Madison's back straightened, and the thing about forgiveness had completely gone out of her mind as she became upset again. She forced herself not to show what she was feeling.

Jamar's wide, sexy body walked through the door with a natural swag that made her moist. She fought the urge to bite her lip and pretended to wipe her mouth, using the napkin as a shield.

He was pretending he had not tasted her body just hours ago.

Madison didn't know if she should be happy about his disregard.

Reluctantly, Madison extended her hand to him, and he shook it briskly.

"Leave us," he said harshly to the assistant. "And no interruptions please, Heidi. Have my man stay posted at the door."

Heidi was obviously used to his snippiness and excused herself.

Damn! Madison was hoping the assistant would've stayed so their conversation couldn't get personal.

"You're nothing but a lying, deceptive son of a bitch, Jamar," she hissed.

He looked ready for her verbal confrontation. "I had a lot to think about last night, Madison. I'll accept I'm the son of bitch, but I've never lied to you. I've done nothing except helped you, give you pleasure and love you, Madison."

"You've only felt pity for me. From the moment I met you. You preyed upon me. You don't own me. I don't owe you or Jason shit."

He sighed and sat down without getting anything to eat. "I can see we've both had a good night's rest."

Sarcasm dripped from his voice and, for some reason, she calmed down slightly.

"You're right, but your applications were chosen by the committee, not Jason and me. Now, the fact that I told Joshua what to put in the application to sway the committee was ethically wrong on my part…but at the time, my mother's people was running the organization. I knew her criteria and what they'd be looking for. Your application was picked in fairness without my vote."

"I'll never believe another word you say, Jamar."

He sat back and even had the nerve to look relaxed. "You don't have to believe me. Just believe what's in your heart, Madison. That doesn't lie to you."

She turned away and pretended to fill her plate with food as if she were really hungry.

To change the subject, she asked, "Why do you go by that name instead of Jamar?"

"It's more professional and it irked my mother to death. She married for money and had very little choice in her life until my father died. Once I became an adult and not under her thumb, I found I had the power to hurt her without laying a hand on her." He stood up and walked beside her. "Do you really need all those eggs?"

She'd almost made a tower on her plate in her distraction.

He purposely stood very close to her. "Jamar is a nickname I only let people I care about call me," he admitted softly.

Why the hell was she feeling warm chills down her spine?

"I need to leave," she said. "I need to go home."

He took the plate from her and then took her hand. "You can't. This weekend is about you. People want you here. Joshua assured us you would stay."

"Joshua doesn't control me."

He snorted. "I should hope not, but he was the only one I could trust to ensure you came. He said your home assistant wouldn't be so favorable toward me."

"Home assistant? Mercy isn't … she doesn't work for me. She's my cousin."

Jamar looked shocked. "I didn't know you had any family once your father was sent to jail."

Proudly, she said, "I have two cousins… Wait, how do you know about my father?"

"Just because you haven't thought about us, Madison, doesn't mean we haven't thought about you. I remained concerned about you after you left, but you kept your personal life very damn personal."

She panicked. "You've been following me?"

"No, I'm not a stalker. I followed what the media knew about you. I kept my distance, understanding you'd become a recluse and would have a hard time trusting anyone."

"I have every reason to not trust anyone, Jamar, and I still have every reason to leave you now."

"Please," he implored, and she knew deep down inside, he wasn't asking on behalf of anyone else but himself.

Damn, he was getting to her.

To see just how much he really wanted her to stay, she demanded stubbornly, "Then tell them you fucked me and I was so disgusted I wanted to leave."

"Fine," he agreed.

His acquiescence surprised her.

Dubiously, she asked, "You'll do that?"

Nodding easily, Jamar said, "I'll make an announcement to every conference attendee right now that I fucked you and disrespected you, but I'll also tell them that I'm saying sorry from the bottom of my heart. Sorry for the past, and sorry for taking advantage of your weakened state last night."

His admission shocked her.

He continued, "Jason and I honestly had no idea what Nikki was doing. We didn't know she knew you, and when Jason told me what happened that day, I was really angry at him for allowing things to get so out of hand. You'd helped us, changed us, and brought us together. But I didn't know how to convince you that we had no part in Nikki's deceit. I still don't." He paused, looking frustrated. "I felt all hope was lost for Jason and me to ever find what we had in you, and I left the country and tried not to exist. Jason stayed and married her."

"Why?" she demanded to know with disgust.

"She told him she was pregnant and at that point he didn't have anyone to rely on. After seeing how really horrible she was, Jason tracked me down and explained Nikki had blackmailed him into marrying her. My mother had died and her estate was coming into my hands, and I had to come home, or Nikki would take what was mine - again. I decided I was going to do whatever I could to help you, even if I couldn't have you. And I really missed Jason. I even tried to ..." He looked ashamed.

Her eyes went wide with horror. "You...and Jason..and Nikki?"

"The thought crossed my mind. I had even started to seduce her, but I couldn't stop throwing up when I was around her," he admitted.

"I can't imagine Nikki accepting a situation like that."

"You're right. That plan was derailed when Jason got sick, and I found out I was a match for him." He bristled. "I had to get really healthy. Being out of the country and depressed, I had let myself go a lot, but I'd do anything for him or for you."

212

For some reason, she became concerned. "A match?"

"He needed a kidney. He was going to die."

Her heart wrenched, knowing how much Jamar loved Jason. "And now?"

"The doctor said he could live a long time, as long as he isn't stressed. He's healthy." Jamar looked hurt. "But in return for the stress-free life, Nikki made me swear to stay away from him."

"She keeps you separated by using your love against you?" Madison asked, horrified, pressing her hand to her chest, almost feeling his pain in knowing how much he cared for Jason. Not being able to be near him was most likely tearing Jamar apart.

"Yes," he answered vehemently, slumping in the chair.

Sitting down at the table across from him, Madison was still angry, but a lot of understanding hit her at once. Knowing how passionate those two were together had to be difficult on them. Nikki didn't understand their closeness and their bond, but Madison did; she understood so much about these men.

A secret smile crossed her lips.

"What's so funny?" he asked almost affronted.

Blushing at being caught with wicked thoughts, she used her napkin again to cover her mouth. "I find nothing funny."

"Really?" His sarcasm returned heavily. "I've always watched you. I have always loved looking at you. And I clearly saw a smile, Mad."

The intimate way he said her nickname made her blush again. She put the napkin to her lips again.

Jamar leaned forward and pulled the napkin out of her hand.

She tried to avoid looking at him, but was aware when he knelt in front of her and cupped her face so she had to look at him. He kissed her.

Resisting was futile when her body wanted him to kiss her. She even tilted and parted her lips to deepen the kiss, surrendering to the tingling all over her body. His arms circled hers and he groaned into her throat.

Jamar had missed her.

Madison had missed Jamar.

CHAPTER 42

M ADISON COULD FEEL HIS need for her pressing against her stomach as the kiss deepened. Damn, she would have much preferred to have breakfast in his hotel room.

There was a knock at the door, and in a moment, it opened.

The moment gave them time to adjust themselves, and Jamar stood up.

His assistant stepped in to give an update. "I'm sorry to bother you, but the science fair starts in thirty, and then the brunch."

"Thank you, Heidi. Come get us when it's time for the judging to start. The moderator can handle the fair until then," Jamar ordered.

When Madison was alone with him again, she said, "It's no use starting up what happened in the past, Jamar. I'm never going to trust you again."

"I understand, but I can't help kissing you."

"She stole my life's work and I think you both knew."

He implored, "We didn't, but I'm not going to try and convince you of that. I do need to say something."

"In your defense?"

"No," he said. "I said I'm not going to try."

"What is it?" she asked stiffly.

"Her plan didn't work. After she won the grant and got all the investors, she was unable to make the experiment seed properly. The fruit died within the first month after reaching gestation."

Knowing what she knew about her project and about what she had created like the back of her hands, she knew even if the seeds weren't properly cared for they still would have lived. That was how she had designed them, which could only mean Nikki didn't have the original seeds Madison had designed. Nikki most likely just had the paperwork, and couldn't follow or understand the notes. Madison gasped. "Are you sure?"

"Positive. Our company went broke investing the largest part of her research, because we wanted to get our hands on cheaper, better fruit for neighborhoods in Detroit that couldn't get any. Jason built a whole damn farm in the city using vacant lots, thinking we could make it work, but unfortunately, we were left with no plants that survived and a lot of land we still farm on, but he can barely make taxes. If nothing happens by Sunday, the end of next week, Jason needs to file for personal bankruptcy paying all the investors back."

"You no longer own the company?"

"No, I had to choose between running that company or becoming CEO of this foundation."

"That's almost terrible what's happened to Nikki. Almost."

"Without the foundation's money and no more trust, Jason can only live off the failing business and savings. I won't give him a dime while he's married to Nikki. I know it will only line Nikki's pockets. But I found a buyer for him for the land, and I found investors who would prove that Nikki's is a fraud."

"Really? Nikki's not a fool. She wouldn't go into a contract if she knew it would prove her to be a fraud."

"I knew that, and so did others, which is why we threw enough money at her and made her pretend there were some successes to the program. If she's not able to explain the science, she won't be able to get anything and she'll have to pay back everything."

Madison looked shocked. "Does Jason know what you're doing?"

"Not everything. He's aware I planned something, and has chosen not to know everything. He doesn't even know you're here."

"You're planning everything for revenge for what she did to me?"

He shrugged slightly. "I cannot confirm or deny that, Madison."

"That's got to be some legal mumbo jumbo you're preparing for if you get caught."

Jamar only winked in response. "We made sure she was aware of the clause in the beginning, because it also links to their divorce decree. When I say she gets absolutely nothing, I mean nothing, even from him."

Madison now felt bad for Jason for having to endure Nikki.

"And my work?" She was almost afraid to ask.

"It's actually still where you left it. Remember the keycard I gave you last night?"

Her eyes went wide as saucers.

Jamar blushed. "I got a little caught up last night to fully explain everything." His fingers stroked the side of her face. "Nikki's been in the lab these past five years and has accomplished nothing, except growing better potatoes."

She was completely dumbfounded by this news. "What do you mean? My research consisted of four seedlings including pineapples, mangoes, bananas and the African Shea tree."

His eyes grew wide with shock. "No, Madison, she hasn't shown any of that to the investors."

Madison narrowed her eyes suspiciously. "Nikki could be hiding her research. She understood how important it was to me and was probably scared I could get enough money, hire people, and get my research back."

"For five years?!" Jamar exclaimed in humorous disbelief. "Knowing her household was losing money and she was losing support from her investors? It's made her ten times more of a bitch. I'm pretty sure she doesn't have the seeds you manipulated."

She almost smiled, but was still pretty sure she'd lost her life's work. "I still don't understand how she stole from me, got the work patented, and got through all the grants she's received without being found out as a fraud by now."

"I'm not a scientist. She knows how to emulate her betters and say whatever she can say in order to get what she needs at that time. I wouldn't make anything up to help Nikki. She's caused more heartache to my life than anyone else, besides maybe my mother, so when I tell you she is going to fail, I mean it. That's why this weekend was so important to have you here."

"Does Joshua know anything about this?"

"No. I've been keeping this to myself."

Madison was feeling conflicted. At one moment, she wanted to believe everything Jamar said, and the next she was terrified he was trying to drive another knife into her back.

"So you've never had any of the research from your life's work all this time?" he questioned.

"Only a flash drive she stole from me, but Joshua said since she did that presentation and patented the work, I had no rights to it anymore. I stored it in a secure location and haven't looked at it since."

"Did you investigate and see what she was doing? How far she had gotten along?"

"I closed that part of my life, Jamar, knowing you and Jason and my work were involved with Nikki. I completely ignored everything."

"So you don't know about her six-year-old son?"

"I slightly remember," she answered.

"He's not Jason's. I'm positive about that."

Her stomach did triple flip flops. "She said she was pregnant the last time we spoke before everything happened," she recalled.

"Well, once you were gone, Jason didn't think he'd ever receive your forgiveness. When I left, he was completely distraught. He married her a month later, and two months from then, she was near full-term, but he swears he never had sex with her prior to marriage."

She could see Jamar was angry. "DNA results came back that told us he was not the father."

"And he still stayed with her?" she questioned incredulously.

"Yes," he said with a lot of strain. "I think he feels it's his penance for what he did to you, even though he didn't have anything to do with your research being taken."

"So he's suffering because of me?"

"Because he knew he should have told you how he felt about you, instead of thinking things wouldn't have worked out as they never did in the past. I couldn't believe how perfect we were together and he definitely couldn't believe it either."

"Worked out?" she asked incredulously. "What we had, Jamar? That was just temporary, right? The three of us couldn't have… I mean… That's not natural." She became frustrated. "That's not normal. You know that. I know that."

"It wasn't a charade. We both cared for and loved you deeply."

"As friends."

"And you don't think we could have still been friends, still together, if everything with Nikki hadn't happened? Dammit! I love you, Madison. I have always loved you, and will do anything to see you happy, whether you want me in your life or not."

His words of love was really starting to affect her. She had to steady herself using the table.

He reached out to touch her, but she abruptly moved away to stand with the table between them.

"Madison—"

She cut him off. "No, I won't let you deceive me again. I don't trust you, Jamar. I can't."

"I won't hurt you," he promised.

The assistant popped her happy face in, and Jamar went over to Heidi to give Madison time to collect herself.

When Madison strolled across the room, hiding all the pain and conflicting emotions she was reeling in, Heidi led them out of the room.

"We're all set," she said, handing Madison a clipboard with judging slips. "You're the final judge, and once we tally your points with all the other judges, we'll be able to announce the winner at the brunch ceremony."

"Thank you," Madison acknowledged, and did her best not to look at Jamar, even though she knew he was looking intently at her.

Just before they entered, the assistant let her know, "As Mr. Golden instructed, I haven't let anyone know about our guest judge, so I'll announce you before you come in, and then show you around to each project that's reach the final round."

This gave her a few more moments with Jamar.

He still looked at her as if he wanted to rip every piece of clothing off her body and do things that could be considered illegal in several states.

"Why didn't Jason contest the child to Nikki, face to face?" she questioned Jamar.

"If you met her boy, you'd understand," Jamar answered.

Madison was glad to hear the assistant announce her, and she burst through the doors, happy to know she was well-received.

The assistant guided her around the room and her mood was lightened speaking with each youth as they showed off their project. Their insight into scientific and mathematical concepts kept her in awe and lifted her spirits.

The second to the last youth was a beautiful little boy with the largest brown eyes on his face, with a name tag of Golden. He smiled widely as she approached, and bumped his chest out widely.

"Ms. Oliver," he said, politely and articulately for a six-year-old. "It's a pleasure to make your acquaintance." He outstretched his small hand.

She shook it. "And you are?"

"Jerrell Golden. I've read all your research on skincare and natural rejuvenation."

Madison was impressed by his large vocabulary.

"So, show me your project, Jerrell," she encouraged.

Excitedly, he began to explain his hydro-solar powered system for outside rain usage for a home. Madison was in awe and marked approvingly on the clipboard.

"How old are you, Jerrell?" she marveled.

"He's going on seven," a female voice said behind her, as Madison finished filling out the judging sheet for Jerrell. "My son definitely deserves higher marks, Madison."

"Mom!" Jerrell said in embarrassment. "Please don't!"

The way his voice sounded, Nikki seemed to butt her nose into her son's business often. Jamar stepped back with a disgusted look, choosing not to speak with Nikki.

"I score fairly and by what is expected of me, not by what I feel, Nikki," she said, trying to keep the animosity from her voice. "And what I score is none of your business."

"Well, its Jerrell's first time entering this contest. With our departure from the foundation, it's made him eligible to participate."

Nikki had aged considerably. The years had not been kind to her. Crow's feet were etched beneath her eyes, and her lips were darkened by smoke lines. The effects of a lot of alcohol and nicotine had caused age spots to break out all over her forehead, on which she'd tried to use a mound of make to cover up. There had definitely been some surgery, but with constant liquor and nicotine intake, the surgeries were a waste of money. Nikki must not have known that.

She was still ungodly skinny compared to Madison's plump shape, but now as age crept on her, her small stature made her look malnourished.

"I see you're proud to have him compete?" Madison asked tightly.

"I think awards are more important than philanthropic efforts."

Nikki made their exit from the foundation seem like it was all HER idea.

The woman continued to speak imperiously, "Plus, it was a waste of our resources and time to be a part of the foundation, when we could make so much more money on my research."

"Your research," Madison hissed.

Nikki suddenly looked uncomfortable, just as Jason walked up to them. He only smiled stiffly as he met Madison's eyes. He looked like he was expecting her to say something, and at the same time, like he wanted to say something.

"Maddie," he said breathlessly. "You look wonderful. You haven't aged a day."

"Of course not," Nikki said sourly. "She uses her products."

"And her products actually work," Jamar said, coming up beside Madison.

Madison was astounded by the way her body had reacted upon seeing Jason; handsome still, and brawny. He'd kept in perfect physical condition, and the attraction to him was still powerful.

Jamar rubbed her back to reassure her and helped guide her away. "You have one more contestant, Ms. Oliver."

She could barely think straight and needed Jamar's help. Slightly appreciative of Jamar's assistance in walking away, she looked at him with a nod of thanks.

He even handed her a bottle of water to cool her inner libido, but that didn't help. She went to the last table and barely graded the contestant. Jamar assisted her, then led her out of the door to the elevators after Heidi collected the clipboard.

As the elevator moved off the floor, Madison was glad for the distance she was given away from Nikki. The urge for violence and to fight back had never been forefront in her life, but she now wanted to knock the wind out of Nikki—and not just physically.

CHAPTER 43

"I WASN'T READY FOR that," she admitted, gripping the handles on the walls of the elevator.

"I could see. I'm sorry. I wanted to warn you, but I didn't know she'd bombard you like that. I wanted you to judge Jerrell fairly. I still can't stand to be in her presence for very long without wanting to strangle her."

Madison felt his animosity towards Nikki, but wanted to change the subject. "You were right about Jerrell. I can see why Jason stays."

"We could go to my room until the judges finish tallying the scores," he suggested. "We shouldn't be bothered until it's time for the brunch."

"I hate you," she seethed.

"You should," he agreed.

"And I hate him."

"You have every right to."

She collapsed against him and cried. "You're horrible, Jamar. You have no idea how much... I was..." She sobbed. "And the pain..." She couldn't finish as another large sob caught in her throat.

Jamar's arms tightened around her.

Damn, he smelled good. Her senses reacted to his manliness, and soon her body followed. He took out his handkerchief and dabbed it at her face. Then his lips followed, kissing her tears with a gentleness she hadn't felt in years. He moaned, receiving her kisses. She could feel the smile on his lips and the relief in his body as his tongue parted her lips to deepen the kiss.

The elevator opened on their floor and he guided her to his room. Soon as they entered, Jamar wasted no time resuming the kiss and leading her to the bed. He stripped her clothes from her and she let him move her onto the bed. His mouth moved down her body, licking, kissing and laving all over until his face was between her legs.

The touch of his tongue against her clit almost made her faint. He licked just around the edges, running his tongue from her perineum back up the folds and around her love button. Madison moaned her desire as she squeezed her thighs against his head.

His mouth became rambunctious as he savored her juices, slurping and swallowing every last drop of her, and when she though nothing could get better, Jamar pressed a thick finger deep in her wetness, making her soul liquefy. His lips seemed to do double-duty kissing, manipulating her body to climax, while his finger pressed in and out; sending ripples of delight through her.

Madison screamed her praises as he pushed another finger inside of her and then slowly twisted his hand around while he circled her puckered rear with the moist tip of his thumb.

She didn't know whether she was coming or going, but she didn't care as she clawed his back to move up.

Jamar obliged her, moving up her body between her legs, capturing her mouth as he pushed deep within her.

Tasting herself all over his lips, while at the same time feeling him inside of her brought a moan from the recesses of her soul, full of joy and bliss. He cautiously stroked her as if she was going to refuse him.

"Harder!" she ordered, and Jamar obeyed, pounding into her as if his life depended on it.

She was definitely over the edge, but she needed one more thing from him.

"Come with me," she begged.

He gave into her command. His eyes rolled to the back of his head while he drilled so hard into her, she knew would be sore walking for at least a day.

When it was over, he drew her into his arms and kissed her tenderly, with gratitude.

She knew he was silently telling her she still had control over him. Deep in her heart, she knew that already too.

Yet, trusting him was so hard.

They lay there for a long moment before he insisted they shower and put their clothes back on.

"Heidi will be up any moment," he warned.

She nodded and quickly got herself back together after a shower. They were both quiet, giving each other silent looks to let the other know how much they had enjoyed each other.

The fear of talking and ruining the moment pretty much ran her thoughts at that moment, and Madison was grateful for the knock on the hotel door soon after she and Jamar were done dressing.

Cheery as ever, Heidi said, "The ballots have been counted and the participants are getting situated in the ballroom. The opening ceremony has started, Mr. Golden. Mrs. Gates and her husband have arrived."

Stiffly, he said, "Thank you, Heidi."

Madison was almost back to normal on the outside. There was soreness between her legs and she opted not to wear heels to the brunch. She could feel Jamar trying not to stay too close to her, but when she looked out in the crowd, amazingly she found Jason glaring at the both of them jealously.

Why would he be upset?

He chose to marry that woman who betrayed Madison!

Nikki looked from her husband to Madison, and there was a deep-seated jealously in her eyes as well.

Their son, Jerrell, came in fourth place, and Nikki did not look happy about that either. When Jerrell tried to accept his award, Nikki dragged her son out of the ballroom, completely embarrassing the child.

Madison, who was helping Mrs. Kimberly Gates, watched as horror as Jerrell protested and begged his mother to let him stay. But Nikki won, as usual.

To recover the audience, Kimberly said, "I guess when you have to go, you have to go," she said, touching her stomach. "As a mother, I know firsthand."

The audience chuckled.

"I want to thank Ms. Oliver for helping me present these awards." Kimberly gave her an assuring wink as Madison sat back down, still holding Jerrell's trophy.

Jason had disappeared and Madison looked at Jamar, who looked disappointed and embarrassed.

Kimberly's husband was sitting next to Jamar and whispered something in his ear.

Jamar stood up just as Kimberly was introducing him. They hugged and Jamar unfolded the speech he'd written.

The lost connection between the brothers pained Madison, and she tried not to be sympathetic, but she could almost feel them to her core.

After the brunch, Jamar was called away on business, but said he would meet her for dinner in the hotel's restaurant.

"You aren't trying to establish anything permanent between us, Jamar?" Madison questioned suspiciously.

He tried so hard to look innocent that it was comical. "Me? Trying to underhandedly seduce you?" He stole a kiss with a playful look dancing in his sexy, deep amber-brown eyes. "I'll get what I can take from you, Madison."

She pushed on him to step away so as not to be swept up in his gorgeousness. "Seriously, Jamar."

"I understand, we're only in temporary lust. This weekend at least, right?"

"Until I say no more," she said, determined.

"You have all the control, Madison." He walked away and dammit, she couldn't stop watching him until she couldn't see him anymore.

CHAPTER 44

WHY DID HER WHOLE body want to mold against his and ravage his lips? She almost ran to him, stopped him and hauled him back up to the hotel room.

"So, you're the Madison Oliver I've heard so much about," Kimberly Gates said beside her.

Madison was glad to drag her mind away from her body's lustful inclinations.

"Yes, Mrs. Gates."

"Please call me Kimberly," the dark-skinned woman insisted.

Her husband stood only a foot apart on his cell phone, deep in conversation, but often glancing at his wife.

"How did you get involved in the foundation, Mrs. Gates?" Madison asked to keep her mind off of Jamar.

"My husband's father died. He'd started the foundation with Jamar's parents. My husband wasn't feeling so philanthropic to involve himself in the foundation, but I was driving him crazy at home. With my children not being so dependent any longer, I was feeling like I needed to nurture something, so he suggested I become involved. At the same time, Jamar's mother passed away, and Jamar came to me to let me know his position with foundation. I took sides and chose my heart. I knew what Nikki had done to the family's finances, and I knew we had to choose Jamar's side if the foundation was to prevail."

Kimberly sounded like she had a good head on her shoulders.

"I think your heart chose well."

Looking down at the statue Madison still held, Kimberly said, "Too bad Jerrell couldn't choose his mother. I feel bad for the child. I've watched him be used by her for so long and I fear..." she stopped.

"What?"

"Well, she's made promises to people that I don't think she can live up to. People I don't think she should have accepted money from."

"What people?" Madison asked.

"Let's just say some people aren't into loaning money for research just to help others. Some people are looking for monetary reasons to back projects like yours. Nikki promised results by Sunday, and if by then she doesn't deliver, they will do everything in their power to make sure they get every last dime back."

Madison worried a little because Jamar had said he had "found the investors." "Who are these people?"

Kimberly shuddered. "It's none of your concern. Like I said, some people get into research only to make money from other people's ideas, not because they believe in them. I'm just glad Jamar is not associated with his family anymore. Despite how he feels about his brother, it would've been his downfall and the foundation's as well."

Nikki had done too much to hurt people and didn't care. Madison angrily gripped the statue.

"She's got until Sunday?"

Kimberly nodded. "Sunday to pretty much prove she didn't lie or make all of the science up. The patent license will become null and void. No one will own anything accept the person who really knows what they are doing."

Madison couldn't believe her ears. This was an opportunity to get her research back! Jamar must've known this, which was why he convinced Nikki to sign with a company who would hurt her financially, but didn't that mean it had to hurt Jason as well. But Jerrell would suffer too, being that this was his family, and the only home he knew.

"I'm so sorry to keep you," Kimberly apologized. "You've had a long morning. I hope to see you at the other activities, Ms. Oliver."

"Please call me Madison," she insisted.

They shook hands, and then Kimberly joined her husband.

Madison returned to her hotel room. Her first inclination was to take a long, cold shower.

Her cell phone rang before she'd even closed her door.

"Hi, Mercy," she said without looking at the screen.

"Everything's fine in case you wanted to know," Mercy said.

"I know it is good at home and at the lab. I've gotten texts from everyone almost every hour they're awake, plus I know you'd come get me if everything wasn't okay at the house. I was actually going to video call tonight."

Mercy sighed. "How'd you know it was me?"

"Because I know you're probably wondering why I haven't called and screamed your head off for convincing me I should come."

"Or, I'm wondering what the hell do you think you're doing?"

Guiltily, Madison asked, "What do you mean?"

"I'm looking at the society page from last night. Wow, and wow. You look gorgeous, but then I decided to look at the itinerary of the whole event. Joshua didn't tell me about *Jamar's* involvement."

Madison paused before answering. "He didn't tell me either."

"And? What's happened? I know you've spoken to them, Madison. I can hear the guilt in your voice. And Nikki! Oh, my gawd! She's there! I Googled all of them!"

"I've only spoken to Jamar," Madison said defensively.

"I have a good mind to come down there, Madison Oliver, and drag you home."

"I'll be fine. I've… I've gotten a lot of clarity this weekend. Not just about everything I do, but, well, Mercy, I'm good. I swear. I know you saw me through a bad place in my life mentally and emotionally and you're worried I'll go into that dark place again, but I won't. I've learned a lot about myself these couple of days and I know Monday I'll be great." After speaking with Kimberly Gates, she was confident about her statement.

"How are you so sure, Madison? I mean, I hear it in your voice, but I need to be sure. Picking you up spiritually was hell in a handbasket," Mercy said, concerned.

"I can't leave. This is important to others and has nothing to do with my past feelings toward the brothers or my current hatred towards Nikki. Despite Joshua not letting me know everything that was going to happen--including meeting Jamar, Jason and Nikki— I really needed to see this. Meet these people who've helped my research, believed in my work and supported the foundation, which has supported me."

"I'm not asking you to leave, but we could come—"

"No!" Madison said. "I need you to stay there. Don't come."

"What if I have Grace—"

Madison cut Mercy off. "Please, cousin. Mercy, I need you to stay there. I wouldn't trust the house with anyone else right now, and I really don't want to explain myself."

Mercy didn't speak for a long moment. "You'll call me later so we can talk. Really talk, Madison."

"Yes," she promised. "And don't be mad at Joshua. I really did need to come to this wonderful event, despite the people that are here."

"Call me later," Mercy reminded her.

Madison's nerves were shot to hell as she got off the phone. She did miss home and the lab, but that weekend was needed. She didn't regret giving her body to Jamar.

It wasn't as if she wasn't on birth control just to control her period, although her lack of sexual responsibility with Jamar was stupid.

She was still having powerful sexual urges. Sinking on the couch, she hiked her dress up and moved her panties aside as she imagined the arousing kisses Jamar had placed on her body. She loved how his touches stimulated all parts of her, inside and out, and then she imagined Jason joining them, pushing inside her body from the rear just as Jamar was ejaculating into her... the thought sent her over the edge and her body exploded, drenching her fingers all the way to her wrists.

Madison panted and trembled as she let the wave of lust run off of her, and then she heard a throat clear.

Blinking several times to focus herself, she looked up into Jason's warm brown eyes.

"W-what are you doing here?" she demanded to know, flustered and embarrassed, yanking her dress down and standing up.

"Do you want me to be here?" he questioned, taking her wrist.

He pressed her wet fingers to his lips and licked her fingertips. His eyes closed as he relished the smell of her.

Looking behind him to see her hotel room door still open and the key still in the slot, she sighed. "What I think doesn't matter." She tried to fight the lustful tremble and took her hand from him. "You shouldn't be here, Jason," she said, coming fully to her senses and moving to the other side of the couch to put distance between them.

"But I want to be here with you, Mad. I always wanted to be with you and only you, but my youthful ignorance blinded me."

Her heart wrenched at the sincerity of his words.

"You don't mean that."

"Yes, I do," he said, moving around the couch to face her. "I was young and too stupid to understand what I was doing."

Facing him, remembering the betrayal, which changed her life, she said with quiet anger, "And I'm just supposed to forgive you? Forget what you have done?"

"No," he said. "But if you would come with me and let me show you something, I promise to never bother you again. I know Jamar give you your old keycard back, right?"

She nodded.

"Then please come with me. Let me show you what we've done for you."

Curiosity was killing her, and she grabbed her purse and let Jason take her hand.

This was stupid, and Mercy would not have approved one bit, but she needed to know what he wanted to show her.

CHAPTER 45

THEY WEREN'T ABLE TO speak when they got into the elevator. It was packed with people, but Jason didn't let go of her hand. He confidently guided her through the lobby and out to the front where his car was waiting.

For some reason, she was hoping Nikki could see them. Payback was a bitch, and Madison wanted to be a little bitchy.

When they were in his car and headed away from the hotel, Madison questioned, "Won't your wife be upset with you?"

"I'm starting to not care so much what my wife thinks," he said tightly, with gritted teeth.

"When did you start to not care?" she wondered.

"About four years ago, when I received the DNA results."

"Do you care for Jerrell?" she asked.

"From the moment I set eyes on him. It's the only reason I have not left his mother."

She noted how he didn't specify who Jerrell's father was. Did he know? Was it a subject she wanted to pursue? "Where are we exactly going? I don't like surprises. To the house?"

"Just a few more minutes and we'll be there, Madison," he promised.

"Why can't you tell me everything now?" she argued, irritated.

Jason stopped the car in front of the property she remembered him having in the past. Bitterly, she asked, "You brought me here to show off what you wanted to give to your wife?"

"NO," he said. "She made me buy a bigger house and bought new furniture."

"Why'd you keep this?" she questioned suspiciously, wanting to hear his reasons from his mouth despite what she knew.

"I didn't. Jamar insisted I sell it to him. He never changed the locks, but only allowed access to the back of the house to people he wanted. I only sneak and come here sometimes, but I don't have the keycard because I don't want Nikki to know about this place at all. It's been a secret I've been glad to keep from her."

"So why are do you need to show me so bad? I could have come on my own at any time."

Jason didn't answer her, but got out of the car and came around to the passenger side and opened her door.

Taking his hand, Madison let him guide her out and to the side of the house. Though it was cool outside, she was dressed warmly enough for the excursion. They stopped at the back gate and he explained, "I think you needed to see this with me to really understand how much we love you Madison and how much I'm sorry for being a young stupid fool who should have trusted his heart."

Digging in her purse, she found the keycard Jamar had given her. Inserting it in the lock device was almost like old times.

The lock clicked and Jason swung the thick iron gate opened.

Behind the home, the greenhouse still stood, but additions had been added to the sides and the rear to make the structure larger. When they were close enough, Madison noticed how the plants inside were beautiful and so healthy, some of them rising to the top of the greenhouse.

She paused in her steps and asked bitterly, "Are you sure you aren't showing off what Nikki is doing with my research, Jason?"

"No," he said innocently. "I'm showing you what you gave us."

"I gave you?!" she questioned incredulously. "You helped Nikki steal my life's work!"

Confused he said, "I don't know how, but I've been sorry for my stupidity and greed. For whatever I did to hurt you, I'll be sorry for the rest of my life. But I swear, I never gave her anything you'd done."

Madison walked to the greenhouse, angry as hell, remembering all the hard labor she had put in there. The code was still was on the back of the card and she punched in the numbers. Jamar had apparently never changed her code, and the door popped open.

"I never gave her the combination or access to this place," Jason said.

Madison entered the greenhouse, prepared for whatever, but was instantly shocked at what she saw.

Her seedlings had hatched and taken over, beautifully nurtured to fruition.

All around her, Madison could see the success of her life's work, and she fell to her knees, shocked.

"Nikki doesn't know about this?" she surmised after a deep, regretful sob.

"Of course not."

Looking at him, she questioned, "You never told her anything about what I was doing with the greenhouse?"

"Not a word," he answered. "Not even back when I hired you, because I wanted it to be a surprise. And then, after you left, I didn't want her to have any part of you. To this day, I still never tell her about this. I don't understand the science, but I know it all belongs to you. Jamar made me swear never to say a word."

"But you married her!" she said, standing up.

"I found out how sick I was after you left. I found out I couldn't have kids anymore, so when she told me about the baby, I thought I had to sacrifice something, since I hadn't sacrificed anything for you. And she was going to make it difficult to see my child."

"Don't lie to me, Jason. Did you give her anything of mine or tell her what I was working on?"

"No!" he said without hesitation.

Her heart told her he was being honest, but her head told her not to believe him. "Why? It would have saved you. It would save you being devastated financially."

"I never knew exactly what your research was, Madison. You tried to explain it to me, but I didn't get anything. I was young."

"She had my work. She presented my work! You saw that."

"I came late to the presentation. She said she'd created the work in high school. I saw pictures of her in front of the research at a high school science fair. And she was presented with certificates. I saw them."

Madison remembered those pictures. "That was MY science fair project she took a picture in front of, and MY certificates she was holding, as a joke."

"She used that to take credit for your work. I'd seen her over the years and no one has tried to discredit her."

Hating her own laziness at not taking action and doing more when her work was stolen because her heart was broken, she cursed violently.

He continued, "She said she created the work. Since no one discredited her, she was able to get the grants and the patent. She convinced me to invest everything I had into her research, and then after we went through that money, we went through Jamar's mother's money."

"Did Jamar give her anything? Hold anything over her?"

"Jamar would barely talk to her, and only deals with her now because he loves me, and he loves Jerrell as well."

"So how did she get my research?"

He looked just as perplexed. "I don't know, Madison."

"Please take me back to the hotel," she ordered Jason, wanting to get away from him as fast as possible so she could think straight.

He didn't hesitate, and while they were on the way there, she texted Joshua to drop everything and get to her. *'We have to talk.'*

Jason walked her all the way back to her hotel room. "I'm sorry for fucking everything up; for being stupid and young, Mad. Do you understand I never meant to hurt you? I never meant to hurt Jamar."

Madison placed a hand on his chest in assurance, to show she was no longer so angry with him. His use of her nickname endeared him to her. "I understand. The past has a lot of unanswered questions between us."

"I really was young and stupid. I didn't understand how much you meant to me until you were gone." His arm moved around her waist and slowly drew her in to him.

The idea this was now Nikki's husband was prevalent in Madison's mind, and in a way, his affection towards her and not his wife was a turn-on, yet she felt guilty.

Pushing away from him, she said, "As much as I would… you're married, Jason. To her, no less, and you have a child. I hate what she did to me and I despise what she's doing to you. It's not fair, but it's life, and I'm not going to stoop to her level or allow you to be adulterous with me just to get back at her for all she's done to me."

He nodded with respect and kissed her forehead. "Goodnight, Madison."

She watched him return to the elevators before she walked into her own room.

Joshua was already there.

CHAPTER 46

"WERE YOU ALREADY AT the hotel?" Madison questioned, pushing the keycard down in her purse and setting her purse in the closet.

"Heidi wanted help with your bio to be read at the banquet, and she didn't want to bother you. I also thought you'd like me to approve the PowerPoint slide they'll be using when they present you. Heidi had the cleaning staff let me in to wait for you."

Madison fully believed his excuse, but still asked, "Couldn't you two just use email?"

"I could've, but then I'd miss a chance of checking on you, which was my real reason for coming." He winked at her playfully. "It's seems I was needed from the urgency of your text?"

"I just thought you'd be home with your family. It's very late."

"No rest for the weary, right? Your words."

"You're weary, Joshua? Really?"

He changed the subject. "I heard your conversation from the other side of the door, Madison."

"I should be very angry with you Joshua. You knew Jamar and Jason's involvement with the foundation and told me nothing of what I was to expect this weekend or we were accepting money from them."

"I'm sorry," he said. "But I knew you would have been stubborn and refused the money you needed and I wanted a bottom line met, I didn't care where it came from."

In a way, she had a feeling he was going to say this. Nodding to let him know she accepted his excuse, she added, "I forgive you for keeping me in the dark, Joshua."

His eyes narrowed. "I must say, I'm rather shocked after all these years, you're taking the high road when it comes to those brothers after what they did."

"You were ear-hustling?"

"Somewhat," he said, embarrassed. "I must ask why you aren't angrier with them. That's what I predicted would happen when you saw them. They helped her steal your life's work."

"I'm starting to think I might've been wrong about them, Joshua, and I'm also coming to find out, karma is a bitch. Despite the struggles I've been through because of what Nikki did, I have to say I was blessed. But when I look at her life, I see pure misery in everything she's touched. What would be the point of me trying to cheat with her husband, destroy his life and also her child's life? The poor kid's not even his son."

Joshua still looked shocked.

"Besides," Madison continued. "I don't plan on carrying on a relationship with either one of them after this weekend. I know now I can't have one without the other."

He cut her off, demanding, "What do you mean, it's not Jason's son? How do you know?"

"Jamar told me. He said the child was tested a while ago, and it was proven Jason is not the father, despite the fact Nikki put Jason's name on the birth certificate."

Joshua sat down, perplexed. "All these years, she lied?"

"You've been watching her?" Madison asked suspiciously.

"Unlike you, I wanted to know what happened to her and your research, Madison," he explained.

She answered his earlier question. "Yes, she's deceived, and didn't care she was hurting Jason, even after the truth was known."

Joshua looked almost ready to cry.

"Are you alright, Joshua?" Madison asked, concerned.

Stiffening his demeanor, he asked, "Why'd you ask me over here, Madison?"

"I wanted to share with you, I just found out Jason or Jamar never gave Nikki my research," she confessed.

Now it was his turn to look skeptical. "How do you know this for sure?"

"Because I saw my own seedlings hatch and successfully grow in an untamed environment."

"How?" he asked, amazed, as he looked at her phone from the pictures she had taken at the greenhouse. "All your seeds from the lab were burned. Where is this?" he demanded to know.

"Right now, that's neither here or there, but if they had been in cahoots with Nikki, they would have given her this information and let her claim it as her own."

"How did your seedlings get there? We saw the lab burned to the ground. Plus, the professor had so much security and everything was locked down, no one could get samples out of that lab. You could barely take air from there."

"You forget, I was with the professor all the time. I helped design the security, so I knew the loopholes. I did some smuggling way before the lab burned down, when I was given another opportunity. The professor was so busy making sure the interns didn't steal anything, he took his focus off the work he was so worried they'd steal." She sighed disappointedly. "I guess it's the reason the professor was so mad at me. He felt I'd betrayed him. He clearly thought because he had taken his eyes off the prize and trusted me, I'd allowed Nikki to steal the work. And for a while I thought I had, because I couldn't explain how she'd gotten my work. I still can't."

Joshua looked as if he wanted to provide some kind of comfort, but Madison really wasn't in the mood to be comforted.

"How sure are they about the child not being Jason's?" he questioned, changing the subject again.

She figured he was just making conversation and aloofly answered, "Jason and Jamar mentioned tests done."

"So they're sure?"

Shrugging, she said, "Unfortunately, but Jason loves him like his son."

"That angers you?"

She cut her eyes at him. "No."

"You still love them after what they did."

"I don't feel the betrayal anymore, Josh. Not after today. Things don't add up anymore for me to be upset over the past and those brothers. What I found out today, and knowing Nikki still never fine-tuned the research, I'm almost convinced the brothers had nothing to do with the theft of my research."

"So, you think you made a mistake with them? Pointed the finger at the wrong persons and all these years… what? You could have shared yourself with them? Do you really think that?" he questioned incredulously. "Whether they betrayed you or not, getting away from them and seeing their perverted ways was clearly the best thing for you, Madison."

She was still confused. "I'm going tomorrow to work at my lab at home. I'll let you know my results on the seedlings." Turning her back to him, she said, "I'm going to bed, Josh. I'll talk to you tomorrow after the award dinner."

Joshua nodded in understanding.

She wanted to be left alone, and the subject of her being with Jamar and Jason was too sensitive.

Yet, he stopped near the door, by the closet, saying remorsefully. "I know what you're thinking about, Madison. You're thinking about letting them know the truth, aren't you? I hope you remember, they're still perverts. They're just trying to get you back because you're the only one that accepted being with them like that. Promise you'll be careful with your heart. I'd hate to have to help pick up the pieces again."

Fighting back the tears of all the long nights of crying, Madison only shrugged, hoping he'd hurry and leave.

When Joshua was gone, she took her purse out of the closet and then went to take a shower to wash away the day.

Just as she was stepping out the shower, she thought she'd heard someone by the door. Going out, she saw the closet wide open, but thought she remembered closing the door after she had retrieved her purse from there before her shower…or had she?

Looking around the hotel room, she didn't see anyone or anything to indicate someone was in her hotel room.

A knock at her door startled her and she tightened the towel around her chest as she looked out the peephole.

Jason stood there looking nervous.

Why had he returned?

Slowly opening the door against all warnings in her head, she looked up into his eyes. "What are you doing here, Jason?" she demanded.

The doubt in his eyes grew, and hesitantly he held out a folder.

Skeptically, she took the folder and perused over the paperwork.

He explained, while she read, "It's the deed to the house. I had Jamar sign it over to you. I told him it meant more to you than either one of us."

Confusion set in completely. How could she have thought they had deceived her all those years when they were making such magnanimous gestures?

"Why?" she questioned, full of doubt.

"Because," he explained as if it were obvious. "We love you. We've always loved you."

Turning away from him to gather herself as she stared down at the deed, she heard him enter and close the door.

Turning around, she handed the deed back to him. "I can't accept this, Jason. Not after... I just can't accept your generosity."

"Hell, Madison, you deserve so much more. You deserve the world." He walked up to her and wiped away the tear rolling down her cheek. "If I could apologize a trillion times, I would. Whether it was my fault or anyone else's fault, you never deserved the misery you had to deal with."

He was close enough, and hesitantly moved his arms around her waist to hug her. She allowed him, and almost sobbed at how much she'd missed him. Not just the sex, but the deep connection they had come to form in such a short time.

"I've missed you, Madison," he confessed in her ear.

"I've missed you too, Jason," she admitted.

"And I understand what you meant about me being married. I know... I understand, but can I have... can I just hold you tonight, Madison? Please?"

Taking his hand, she led him to her bed.

CHAPTER 47

HE STARTED TO SPEAK, but she pressed her fingers to his lips. He nodded, understanding she didn't want to hear any rhyme or reason why they were there, but they were going to share a night together.

Her hands moved down his chest, and she remembered what it was like to be with Jason so clearly. After pushing the jacket off his broad shoulders, she removed his tie and opened his shirt.

He had a small scar on his side, most likely from his operation, and she could see there were recent needle punctures in his arm. She also noticed small bruises on his chest, waist, and some on his thighs.

"I still need treatment," he explained. "Sometimes…"

She nodded and opened his pants, which stopped him from going into more explanation.

Pushing those down to his ankles, she moved to her knees to help him step out of them, along with his shoes and socks.

He pulled her hands up, making her stand up, and began to undress her. This moment with Jason seemed magical. As if they were transported back to that old cheap motel room, just the two of them together, listening to the breaths of excitement from each other and worshiping the beauty of the other's body.

When she was only in her underwear, Jason lifted her on the bed and lay next to her. He curved behind his body and cuddled behind her, holding her close.

Her sensual oxytocin levels were unbelievable, and her mind cleared. She slept soundly, loving the warmth and comfort his proximity provided.

***

In the darkness of her dreams, she felt powerful vibrations all over her body. Suddenly, Madison realized she wasn't dreaming.

Shooting out of sleep, she gasped as Jason's fingers flicked her sensitive nub, and then pressed his finger back into her thickened warmness. He must've been warming her up in her sleep for a while, because just as she realized what he was doing, she was coming powerfully.

Digging her nails into his arm, she found herself uncontrollably grinding her hips against his. Before she could regain her equilibrium, Jason dipped down between her legs and replaced his fingers with his mouth.

She shouted. She screamed!

She didn't stop him.

Her thighs gripped his face as he licked and slurped her to fruition.

Madison's body was in a different world where the stars shot through her veins a trillion miles an hour, and her whole body was going to explode like a cataclysmic spatial burst from her brain to her toes.

Looking down, just as she came back to reality, she saw he had cried. Tears were on his face as he lavished kisses on her thighs and stomach.

Pulling him up, she kissed him too, feeling the tears roll down her cheek as well. That connection they had shared so long ago was still there, and they both knew they wanted more.

"Damn you," she whispered, cupping his face.

"I know," he accepted her curse, obviously knowing why she was agitated.

"I should have told you how much I loved you in the past," he said. "I should have realized you had my heart, and not thought I had time, Mad." He kissed her cheek as he pulled her into his arms again. "I'm not asking for a do-over. Hell, you can be angry at me for the rest of your life, but what I need is a restart for Jamar."

Pushing away from him, she sat up in bed.

In the low light, she saw the puncture marks on his arm were fresh, and there was much more to the treatment than he had told her about. She also saw bruises on his chest and lower hips.

"Isn't a restart like a do-over, Jason?" she asked, running her fingertips over the surgical scar on his side.

"Jamar never asked for this. All he wanted was to love you and for all of us to be together. I hurt you. I destroyed what could have been our future."

"What aren't you telling me, Jason?" she asked.

He sat up in bed and took a deep breath.

"If we're to restart, Jason, shouldn't we be completely honest with each other?"

Immediately, Jason looked at her with shame and sadness.

"Nikki did this?' she said, touching a bruise on his chest.

Uneasy, he said, "I never told Jamar. He'd kill her if he—"

Madison cut him off and angrily asked, "How long, Jason?"

Jason shrugged, ashamed. "For a while. The more you were a success, the angrier she became. First, it was with her hand, but when she saw this didn't affect me, she'd scratch me or use objects with socks over them to cover the damage."

"Jason," Madison said with distress. "You let her."

"I really thought it was my punishment for what I did to you and Jamar."

"You can't stay there. You can't go home to that anymore."

"I have to. Jerrell is there. If I don't go home, her anger will be directed at him. She already uses him to read and study and try to help her find ways to solve her problems. When Jerrell didn't win yesterday, it just made her angrier, and seeing you didn't help, either."

"Jerrell is not even your son," she said bitterly, incensed at what Nikki had been doing to Jason for years. "Why do you care? You could just report her to child services if she lays a hand on him?"

"I care very deeply for him. I cared for him the moment I held him in my arms." He put his head down. "I can't have children of my own, Madison."

Shocked, she asked, "Because of the kidney damage, right?"

"After Jamar left, I sunk into deep depression. The more depressed I became, the angrier Nikki was with me, until one day, she hit me with something that... well, I ended up in the hospital with over twenty-two stitches needed, but that's when they found the cancer."

A chill went through her body. "Jamar donated an organ to you. They wouldn't have given you the organ if you were dying."

"I went into remission. I was better for a while, but the chemo had damaged my organs. His donation not only brought Jamar and me back together for a time, but gave me a new lease on life and a plan to make everything better for you and him."

"But that didn't last, did it?" she assumed.

"No, it didn't. Early this year, my cancer returned with a vengeance. Hodgkin's lymphoma."

Madison wanted to scream as tears welled in her eyes and began to slide down her cheek. "How long?"

Jason cleared his throat. "Any day now."

"No," she denied, rushing into his arms and hugging him. "No, Jason. That's not fair."

Returning her hug, he comforted her, "It's alright, Maddie. I did what I set out to do. After tomorrow, Nikki will be devastated; she'll lose everything."

"But what about you? She'll take her anger out on you, Jason. She doesn't care you are sick. You know where this could lead? You know if you stay, she could eventually kill you?"

"I'm going to die anyway, Madison."

Madison sobbed into his neck, wishing he would take everything back. "Why'd you tell me? Why didn't you tell Jamar?"

Jason hugged her tighter. "Please don't tell Jamar. There's no telling what he may do to her if he found out."

"Found out what?" Jamar demanded to know from the doorway.

CHAPTER 48

GASPING, MADISON HURRIEDLY wiped the tears away. Jamar leaned casually against the doorframe, as if he were pleasantly surprised, but far from angry. Madison didn't need to look over at Jason to know he was just as shocked as she was. But she did move in front of Jason, so Jamar couldn't see his brother's open shirt, displaying the scars.

When Jamar didn't hear from either one of them, he decided to explain his surprise appearance. "I saw the door wasn't closed all the way. I was worried." He looked from Madison to Jason. "At least your personal safety is fine," he said, looking at Madison.

"I'm fine," she confirmed, and looked at Jason worriedly, who had just finished buttoning up his shirt.

"I also was concerned when Jason didn't return after telling me he was coming over to make amends for the wrong he had done to you."

"Why? Did you think Jason was going to hurt me?"

Jamar chuckled. "No, I thought you were going to hurt Jason. But I can see you've come to an agreement if he stayed the night, fully clothed."

"No… yes." Rolling her eyes, Madison groaned, cursing to herself for the weakness she had for the brothers. "I don't know."

"Please," Jason said, taking her hand and kissing her knuckles, one by one. "I only wanted to help you understand the past, Madison. I want you to accept the property and get credit for the work you deserve. No one else should get their hands on your creation."

Madison wanted to hide her face in the covers, needing a moment alone to gather what Jason was giving her, and also what he had just revealed to her.

"Are you leaving anything out, Jason?" Madison demanded to know. "I want to know the whole truth about everything, even if you think it meant absolutely nothing. If you want a reset between us all, honesty is important."

"Yes," Jamar said to Jason. "Are you leaving anything out?"

"I confessed to Nikki weeks before the presentation I'd had sex with someone else. I mean, she was having sex with someone else as well. I wanted her to know I wasn't just waiting around for her to make up her mind about me. I was acting prideful, I know, but like I said, I was young and stupid." Jason took a deep breath and continued explaining. "She demanded I take her to meet you, and I took her to the motel one day, but you weren't there the day we came. She somehow swindled a key from the main office and we entered your room. Nikki said if she was going to be in competition with someone I was attracted to, she should know all about you. The minute we got in there and she started looking around, she demanded to know your name and how I'd met you. I told her everything about you."

"She never indicated she knew me?" Madison questioned.

Jason shook his head. "She never said anything, I swear. If I had known what a diabolical disaster it was to be there, I would have never allowed her to do that to hurt you. I didn't know. I mean, I did know you were smart, but I didn't realize how incredible you were. I just wanted to brag to her that I could be with someone on your level. She was always saying I wasn't smart enough to be with her."

"She still believes that," Jamar growled under his breath.

Madison believed Jason, and she also agreed with Jamar. "Go on, Jason," she urged.

"Nikki looked at the research you had beside the bed," Jason admitted.

"What was she looking at?" Jamar demanded, which Madison was about to ask herself.

Jason answered, "Some notes on some plants, but I told her to put it back because we weren't even supposed to be in there. I think that's when alarms went off in my head, but I was too stupid to listen to them. She quizzed me to death about some seeds, but I told her I knew nothing. She said she heard someone outside. I went to check out the door, and when I turned back around, she had the refrigerator open. I didn't see her take anything, and I repeatedly demanded we leave. I swear, I didn't see her take anything."

Madison narrowed her eyes, trying to remember when she'd put the extra seeds in her refrigerator after stealing them from the lab.

Madison could barely remember, but she knew she had put leftover samples she had not used in the freezer, which had all been potatoes. This could be why Nikki was only able to produce potatoes.

Listening to everything the brothers told to her, in her heart and gut, Madison knew they were being absolutely honest. Maybe she should trust them with her secret?

"If all she took was the potatoes seeds," Madison said, "I can see why she can only get those to work. She just needs to duplicate from the original, and not allow any cross-pollination to occur. There were no other seed samples in the freezer. I planted all the other ones I'd stolen in the greenhouse by then."

"That was good, then?" Jason questioned. "Well, not so good that she was able to get to even those seeds."

"My lab work on the flash drive could only be extracted if someone knew the codes we used in the lab," Madison determined. "The research was just what we'd discovered our first year in the lab, which only had to do with the potatoes. I'd never changed that encryption, just in case the professor needed it. The rest of the research and studies were encrypted differently, and only I knew how to unlock those files. The interns only knew the process of cultivating the plants, not the splicing and extraction techniques. That was the secret."

"Who else would have known the lab's encryption codes that would be close to Nikki?" Jamar questioned.

"No one I knew," Madison said, confused.

"It had to be a guy," Jason offered. "I heard her say she had been kicking it with a young college guy who wanted to get serious too fast, but couldn't compete with her financially."

Madison could see he was still ashamed about his relationship with Nikki. Jamar tightened up about the subject.

"We didn't talk about her past relationships that deeply," Madison admitted. "I knew she was promiscuous and often used sex to get what she wanted from men. For a while, I even thought she and my father were sleeping together, because she was the only one of my friends he allowed me to still see when I stayed with him."

"Wasn't the guy white?" Jamar questioned Jason.

"Her father?" Jason asked, confused.

"No," Jamar said, rolling his eyes. "The dude Nikki was kicking it with. I remember you saying you saying you're going to kick some white guy's ass if he kept pestering Nikki."

Jason nodded, remembering. "Yeah, because she was saying how she wasn't into white meat, but he was like, mindlessly in love with her and did whatever she wanted, following her around like a puppy."

Madison's mind was going a hundred miles a minute, trying to figure out who this other guy was. She needed to be alone. "Now that you know I'm safe, you two can leave."

"Do you really mean that, Madison?" Jamar questioned, sitting on the side of the bed by her.

"What are you implying, Jamar? That you think I want to relive old times and sleep with both of you at the same time again?"

Jamar looked at Jason, and then back at her. "What's one more night?"

"I can't," Jason said. "I can't let her do something like that, even if we could convince her, Jamar. She's right. I shouldn't, because I'm married."

"Fuck Nikki," Jamar growled.

"I also can't," Madison said quickly.

"Why?" Jamar demanded to know.

Jason looked at Madison.

Madison knew Jason was scared at what he would have to confess. Leaning over, she kissed his cheek to reassure him everything was going to be alright.

"Jamar, I'm sick." Jason choked up.

"Sick of Nikki?" Jamar questioned.

"Yes, I've been sick of her…but I'm really sick with cancer."

Jamar blinked back his surprise and looked at Madison, who nodded seriously.

He looked at Jason, hurt. "What about my donation?"

"It only prolonged my life, Jamar. But didn't save it, I'm afraid."

"Why didn't you tell me?" Jamar asked, becoming upset.

"Because I didn't want you feeling sorry for me. I didn't want you to hold up your own happiness. I wanted to spend my last days helping you two." Jason put Jamar's and Madison's hands together.

"Last days?" Jamar asked painfully. "How long, Jason?"

Jason closed his eyes and held their hands tightly before bravely looking at Jamar. "Soon, I guess. I try to take one day at a time."

Jamar moved his other hand on Jason's nape and touched their foreheads together. "Damn you, Jay. Damn you!"

Madison leaned between the two of them and closed her eyes, just as sad as they were.

CHAPTER 49

———◆✕◆———

A HUGE DOSE OF GUILT hit her suddenly, and Madison needed a moment alone. She disengaged from the brothers and went into the bathroom. Leaning over the sink, she wanted to throw up, sickened at what she had done by keeping away from them all those years.

Jamar knocked on the door. "You okay, Madison?"

"I'm fine," she said, wiping the tears off of her face. "But my bladder isn't." She quickly took care of her private business and then tossed water on her face to hide the fact she had started to cry. "I do need a moment alone."

"Yeah, sure," Jason said. "We'll be across the hall. Can we have breakfast together?"

She sighed, knowing she needed to do more than have breakfast with them. They'd been open and honest with her, and she needed to come clean with them.

"Sure," she said hesitantly, and was glad to hear them leave.

Taking repeated deep breaths, she calmed herself and started to really think, putting the pieces together.

No other intern had had access to her files, yet that hadn't stopped someone from helping Nikki.

There were four interns in all. They were all paid for part-time hours, but out of them, only one worked as if he was being paid full-time.

Only one was male.

Only one was white.

Grabbing her phone, she called Mercy.

"Hey, stranger," her cousin said sarcastically. "Did you forget about me so soon?

"Whatever, Mercy. I need to come by the house this morning with Jamar and Jason."

"No!" Mercy said harshly. "You've worked too long to get rid of them."

"You know I've never gotten rid of them, and I've learned a lot these past few days. I've learned the truth, Mercy."

"How do you know they aren't just trying to manipulate you again?"

"I know they aren't, Mercy."

"I have a hard time trusting them, especially with their association to Nikki."

"There's more, Mercy. There's a lot more."

"What? What could they have said to possibly change your mind?"

She went into explanation, because she really needed Mercy to be on board.

***

An hour later, Madison was knocking on Jamar's hotel room door. Jason answered, looking relieved.

"You act as if you didn't think I was going to come," Madison said.

"You didn't sound like you wanted to through that bathroom door." He hugged her and she relished feeling him alive in her arms, cherishing the moment.

Jamar also looked relieved. "Are we ready to eat?"

She nodded. "But before we do that, I have to take you somewhere. Can I drive?"

"I'll call to have them pull my car around," Jamar said.

Jason went to request the elevator.

They had more than enough time to get around and do what they needed to before returning to the hotel to get dressed for the night's awards presentation.

"Can you give us a little hint as to where we're going?" Jason questioned.

"No," she said. "But I want you two to know, I honestly do believe you, and can forgive you for all you've done."

Jamar handed her the keys to his Jaguar that looked as if it had just been rolled off the production line that morning. Jason squeezed his big body in the back and she drove in the direction of her home.

"What made you plan this weekend, Jamar?" she inquired.

"Actually, Jason thought it over. The investors were getting anxious about Nikki's project and he thought this weekend would be perfect to show out," Jamar answered.

Jason added. "And with so little time left, I wanted to make amends with you. I needed to know you two would be okay together."

She tried not to think of the sadness she felt when he said things like that, but Jason had grown up a lot and had accepted his reality without remorse. That was so strong of him to do and she needed to be strong for him as well.

Jamar didn't look at all pleased at this realization. She could see the disgruntled look on his face.

"So she doesn't know?"

"She knows she has to present in front of the investors, but she's unaware you know anything about what she has to do. I think she plans on flubbing through it and trying to charm her way out of everything, but if you're there, you can put out the questions no one's ever thought to ask her."

"I can't be there, Jason. She's intimidating," Madison pointed out.

"She stole from you. I don't care how intimidating she is," Jamar snapped. "This ends tonight, Madison, and we'll be there for you."

With them, she felt powerful and knew she could. But first, she really needed to know if they would be there for her.

Pulling in her driveway, she honked the horn to inform Mercy she was there.

A few minutes later, Mercy came outside on the porch, looking apprehensively at the brothers. "I know I said I would be okay with this, but after I got off the phone, I don't know, Madison."

"Apprehensive about what?" Jamar asked.

Madison decided to introduce Mercy. "This is my cousin I spoke with you about, Mercy Oliver. She's helped me through these past years at home. I couldn't have done a lot of my research and run my company if it had not been for her."

"You couldn't have picked yourself off the floor if it had not been for me," Mercy snapped.

"Mercy please," Madison begged. "They need to know the truth. They've been honest with me and I need to be honest with them."

Jason and Jamar looked at Madison.

"You've always been honest with us, Madison," Jamar declared

Mercy snorted.

"No, I haven't," Madison confessed. "I mean, after the debacle with Nikki, I didn't know what to do in life. My heart was broken, my mind was in pieces, and my soul wanted to go into darkness."

"Just because he's sick doesn't mean shit," Mercy snapped heartlessly. "They never deserved you in the first place, and they still don't deserve you."

Madison shot her cousin a "shut up" glare.

"My cousin is bitter from her own sickness," Madison explained. "She's been unable to acquire a man, so she's rather bitter towards—"

"Shut UP!" Mercy snarled, and then huffed. "You're only saying that to make me go away."

"Is it working, cousin?" Madison asked, amused.

"Fine!" Mercy slammed into the house.

Jamar and Jason looked back at her. "What was that about?" Jamar asked.

Madison nodded for them to look back at the door.

"What?" Jason asked impatiently.

The door swung open, and two five-year-old boys bounded out, ecstatic to see Madison.

"MOMMY!" they screamed in unison, running down the stairs and into her arms.

She hugged them like she hadn't seen them for centuries.

"We missed you!" they cried.

She tried to give each handsome little face a million kisses, and they giggled in happiness.

"Who are they?" the boys asked her.

Madison stood up and looked at Jason and Jamar, who both appeared shocked.

"Are they...?" Jamar asked, looking at her and then back at the fraternal twins.

Her breast swelled with pride as she held the boys' hands.

"Whose are they?" Jason questioned.

"It's called *heteropaternal superfecundation*. They have two fathers. Merrick, Mason, I'd like you to meet Jamar and Jason."

Merrick, who stood on her right side pointed at Jason. "He looks like you, Mason."

Mason, who stood on her left side, pointed at Jamar. "He looks like you, Merrick."

Jason knelt down to Mason with a look like he couldn't believe it.

Jamar kissed her passionately before he knelt down to Merrick.

Both boys reached out at the same time and touched their father's faces, then smiled.

Jamar and Jason looked ready to cry.

"You did this all by yourself?" Jason asked incredulously.

Mercy cleared her throat menacingly at the doorway, holding a small little girl, the same age as the boys, who buried her face in Mercy's neck, peeking out a little with one eye.

Merrick and Mason giggled.

"I'd also like you to meet, Jamiliah." Madison went up the stairs and took her from Mercy.

The little girl clutched Madison tightly, almost trembling.

Jason almost sobbed because that was his mother's name.

"Triplets? You had triplets?" Jamar asked, choking her with his hug.

The little girl peeked at him and frowned, then she peeked at Jason and frowned harder. Looking back at her mom, she pointed at her eyes.

Madison automatically knew what the girl meant.

"Jamiliah notices you two have her eyes. Can you show them your eyes, Melah?"

The girl shook her head and buried her face hard into Madison's neck.

"Show them your funny eyes, Jami!" Merrick and Mason urged her, tugging on their little sister's legs.

Madison thought the girl was going to choke her to death. Gasping for breath, she explained, "It's nothing to be worried about. It's called *heterochromia iridis.*"

"Please," Jason begged. "Please, princess, show us."

Jamiliah looked at her mother, and then slowly looked at the two men, blinking up at them. One eye was Jason's soft, brick brown, while the other was Jamar's amber-cinnamon brown.

Jamar and Jason gasped.

"She's a chimera," Madison explained. "She's even more special than her brothers, because she has two sets of paternal DNA and one set of maternal inside of her. She's so beautiful."

Jason staggered, and Jamar held his brother's hand, looking ready to pass out.

"May we see closer how beautiful your eyes are?" Jason urged the small girl.

Jamiliah looked at her mother again, who nodded in approval, and then the little girl looked at both of the men. She put her arms out to Jason, who took her from Madison.

"Lift me! Lift me!" Merrick and Mason said, jumping at Jamar's feet.

Jamar knelt down and lifted both of the boys.

Madison went up to the porch and hugged Mercy, who also was trying not to cry.

"I think we need to talk about Joshua," Madison said in a low voice.

"Why? You said to keep my opinion about him to myself."

"Did you open the lab in the basement?"

"Yes," Mercy said obviously. "I found the files and drive in the locked safe room and put them out. Go look them over, and I'll stay here and watch them."

Madison went into the house and down in her basement. Punching in the code to the lab, she saw Mercy had done what she had asked for over the phone.

The files to the drive were lying on the desk, and she opened them to refresh her memory about the splicing techniques she had perfected.

If Nikki didn't know how to do this well, she wouldn't even be able to understand how the whole process worked.

Madison wanted to kick herself for never having challenged Nikki, but that day was a new day.

She put all the research in her bag and locked up the private lab, which she never let anyone go into, except Mercy.

Logging into her computer she was able to get through the VPN at her company and start lockout procedures immediately. If her suspicions were right, she had to secure her company so she wouldn't lose everything again.

Before joining everyone upstairs, she called Joshua's cellphone but was pushed to voicemail.

Going upstairs, by that time everyone had moved into the living room. Jamiliah, as was her usual, went back to playing her small piano, while the boys questioned their fathers to death.

"Do they always speak in unison?" Jamar asked.

"Most of the time. Mercy's been trying to break them of the habit, but there are a lot of habits Mercy's been trying to break them of," Madison answered, and then whistled.

The room went instantly silent and all the children looked her way. "Mommy has to leave again, but I promise to return tomorrow afternoon."

"Awww," Mason and Merrick said in unison, but they ran to hug their mom.

Jamiliah came to kiss her mother's cheek and whispered something in her ear. Madison kissed the little girl and nodded.

"We'll be back Monday," Madison promised them.

Merrick and Mason started jumping around, celebrating, while Jamiliah went back to her piano.

Jamar and Jason reluctantly followed Madison out of the house.

When they were down the stairs, Jason gave her a huge bear hug and swung her around joyously.

"Why? When? How?" he demanded to know.

Jason set her down in front of Jamar, who cupped her face gently and kissed her. "Would you be angry if I told you in this moment, you are the strongest, most intelligent and beautiful woman in the world, Madison?"

She loved hearing those words out of his mouth. "I know, but it's nice to hear you say it."

"I concur," Jason, said kissing her cheek.

"Let's head back," she encouraged them, holding up the keys to the car, knowing Mercy was looking at them.

This time Jamar insisted to drive, and after she was ensconced in the passenger side, the brothers got in on the other side. Jason got in the back again, but leaned forward to hear everything she had to say.

"I realized I was pregnant a month after everything was over with, and went into a deep depression. Mercy really saved me. She's a doula and she helped me through the whole thing. She's right. I wouldn't have been able to get up off the floor if it had not been her."

"But the nursing and care had to have been hard," Jamar pointed out.

"You have no idea, especially when it came to breastfeeding, and I really did want to do everything naturally."

Jason gasped. "You had them naturally?"

"Yes," she said proudly. "Mercy was awesome in helping me through the water birth. We have it recorded. I'll make sure you will be able to see the video."

"And how did you manage to produce milk for all of them?" Jason asked.

"I couldn't. Not enough for Merrick and Mason especially, who were always hungry, but with Mercy's help, it was easy."

"What did she do?"

"She was born with a pituitary gland problem. Early in life, she had to take medicine to correct the condition, but it caused her to start making milk before she was even nine years old."

"That's terrible," Jason sympathized.

"It was, and she was made fun of a lot at school, to the point where her mother kept her and her sister at home to homeschool them. Mercy told me she never remembered a time when her shirt was dry. As she grew, at least her mother was supportive, and by nineteen, Mercy was a wet nurse for several wealthy families in the metro-Detroit area. She decided to become a doula and, with her condition, has made her own fortune selling her breastmilk."

"The medicine doesn't taint the milk?" Jamar questioned.

"No, but for the past five years, I've worked on a natural pituitary tea to help her take less medicine. She's almost chemical-free," Madison said proudly. "She'll have to be like this for the rest of her life, but she's accepted her situation."

"Except she seems bitter about the fact she doesn't date," Jason pointed out.

"A lot of men don't think that's very attractive," Madison said.

Jason and Jamar looked at each other.

"What?" Madison asked, seeing a mischievous look.

"Not all men think that," Jason said with a weird grin.

"I think Mercy hasn't been looking in the right place," Jamar said, with the said weirdly wicked grin as they pulled back in front of the hotel.

Jamar took her hand and kissed her palm. "Are you ready for tonight?"

Holding her purse in her other hand, she nodded. "I'm ready, I think."

"You're ready," Jason said with assurance. "You got this, Madison."

Taking a deep breath, she nodded. Taking her life back meant pushing away a lot of fear, but she could do this.

She would do this!

CHAPTER 50

J AMAR AND JASON WALKED her to the elevator, but Jason didn't get on with them.

"From here on out, Madison, I have to appear like everything is okay in Nikki's world," he explained. "I don't want her to know I'm in on setting up tonight's confrontation. I won't be there. She'll never know you know the whole truth. If she knew, she would find a way to get out of the presentation to prove that she doesn't know what she's talking about."

Madison bit back her fear of going head to head with Nikki. Given the resources the brothers had equipped her with, and remembering the beauty of seeing her children with their fathers gave Madison strength. Due to Nikki's deceit, she and her children had been long denied happiness, and Madison wasn't going to allow another day to pass without Jamar and Jason in their lives.

Jamar held her tightly in his arms all the way up to their floor.

"Did Jason say anything to you about how long he has?" Jamar questioned.

"No, it was pretty much the same that he said to you, Jamar," Madison answered.

He kissed her. "I know it's wrong of me to ask if he's keeping anything else from me. Now I'm really worried about him."

She bit her lip because there was still the matter of the abuse Nikki had been administering to Jason. Keeping that back from Jamar was hard, but Jason needed her secrecy at that time. "He just wants you to focus on us getting back together and not on his sickness. It's the only reason he's kept anything from you, Jamar. He felt it was better that way."

"I know I shouldn't waste a moment being angry at him, but I'm angry at myself for the years I missed out on not forgiving him."

She hugged Jamar because she felt the same way, and loved that they were thinking the same thing. He walked her all the way to her hotel door. "We'll find a way to make everything up, Jamar. We'll figure it all out."

He held her hand for an overly long moment before saying, "Thank you for what you've given back to us and added to our lives, Madison."

She blushed from his praise.

"Tomorrow is a new day and I want to spend every moment with you. No excuses. Can we promise each other that?"

"Yes," she said without hesitation.

Her makeup artist came down the hall.

Jamar gave her a brief kiss goodbye and she went into her hotel room to prepare for her presentation at the awards ceremony that afternoon.

A beautiful plum dress and matching shoes were delivered after her shower, and she felt like a queen as she was made up beautifully.

Her hair was drawn up in a crown of curls with ringlets to frame her face. Her makeup matched her dress color flawlessly, and she was ready for the night.

"Are you going to carry that ugly bag?" Phylis asked in distaste.

"I need to carry this research."

Phylis went over to her suitcase and found a sequin silver purse Madison could roll up her research right into, along with some other personal items.

"You are awesome," Madison complimented, and tried to give her a tip.

Again, the stylist refused and left Madison.

Madison looked at her security log online to see if Joshua swiped his badge into the office that morning. She called his cell phone and emailed him. No answer from anywhere. She didn't want to alarm his wife, but knew if she didn't hear from him by that evening, she would. Instead, Madison put the security staff on alert and then changed Joshua's access level to just his office. His computer was locked down and she made sure all the passwords to high level labs were changed.

A few minutes later, Heidi appeared at her door. "Mrs. Gates has arrived and everything is going wonderfully."

"You look like you've gotten some rest, Heidi," Madison noted.

Heidi rolled her eyes. "I had, until I found out that bitch... I'm sorry... Jerrell's mother reported our youth science fair to the media and said it was rigged. I almost had a meltdown and even Mr. Golden and Mrs. Gates had to come help make media appearances all yesterday to salvage our reputation."

She exhaled. "That woman is so much trouble. She always has been. I was glad when Mr. Golden severed his relationship with his brother so that woman wouldn't be up at our offices anymore. Yet, now it seems since she's been denied entry into the building, she is trying to burst our bubble on the outside as well."

"She used to be there?" Madison questioned.

"All the time, trying to discredit and undermine Mr. Golden's right to the foundation. She was trying to look for anything she could use so her husband could run the foundation, but in my opinion, that woman would have ran this foundation right into the ground."

Madison could just imagine the hell Nikki must have tried to raise, and she admired Jamar for staying strong.

Now it was time to do something about Nikki finally, and the proof in her bag would certainly discredit her wicked former friend.

Heidi added forlornly, "I feel really bad for Mr. Golden's brother and their son. They both seem miserable. Plus, the way she uses that child's smarts is horrendous. Jerrell's a genius and he'd be so much more if it wasn't for his mother."

Changing the subject, Madison questioned, "Did my VP, Joshua arrive?"

"No. He was supposed to read the company information tonight, but since I can't find him, I got someone else to do it."

Madison sent another text to Joshua for him to call her. She also sent a message to Mercy to ask if she had seen or heard from Joshua.

Heidi guided Madison to the raised platform where Kimberly Gates was seated, ecstatic to see Madison again.

"Your husband couldn't make the festivities tonight?' Madison asked.

"No, he wanted to take the children to a villa in Canada for a friend's birthday party. They left last night. It's rare all the children are out of the house; he even took my brother and his wife. I almost didn't know what to do with myself," Kimberly said happily. "If it wasn't for his calls to just hear my voice, I would have been bored to death. I think that's why he suggested I run this foundation. I was probably driving him crazy at home."

"And from what I've read about the foundation, you are a wonderful addition to this organization, Kimberly," Madison complimented.

Kimberly touched her chest, endeared by the accolade. "I'm honored to present this award to you, Madison. The work you've done, your tireless commitment to making women look and feel beautiful, is something we don't see every day. You are much loved for the work you've done."

Madison felt proud of herself. For the first time in years, she could sit back for a while and listen to her accomplishments and not what she had failed at. People came up to the podium to let her know their deep appreciation of her work and her products she had created, and how she had changed their lives.

When she finally got up to speak, everyone in the audience, except Nikki in the back, stood and applauded. Jerrell tried to stand up, but Nikki jerked him angrily back down. Jason was oddly not in sight.

Madison didn't need to look at her speech notes. Her heart was so touched by the entire weekend. "Sometimes in life, we don't realize how strong we are until being strong is all there is left to be. These past few days, I've realized the power I have through the positivity and products I've given out. I wish I had realized it a long time ago, but I've decided to take a stand." She looked through the crowd and spotted Nikki. "I thank you for showing me that I deserve the happiness that was denied for so long in my life." Madison kept looking directly at Nikki, who looked very uncomfortable. "I don't blame anyone for denying me the happiness I should have been given. I only blame myself, because I should have realized that I am strong, I am powerful, and most of all I am beautiful, inside and out. And although others tried to tell me, it was really all up to me to make the realization for myself. Today, I have done that. Today, I am going to make sure that every day from now on, no one will ever take my strength, power, and beauty away again. No one!"

The crowd exploded in a glorious boom of applause as Madison thanked the foundation and, most of all the Golden and Gates families for honoring her with the award she was given.

Kimberly hugged her.

Looking in the direction of where Nikki and Jerrell had been sitting, Madison couldn't see them anymore. Nikki had apparently left with her son. Madison so badly wanted to confront her now.

CHAPTER 51

SHE QUICKLY CHECKED HER phone as Jamar made the closing remarks and benediction.

Mercy's return text read, *"No, I haven't heard or seen from Joshua in a day or so. Oddly, his wife texted me this morning to ask if I had heard from him. She also called me this evening to ask if you had heard from him right after your text. She sez she can't find his phone on GPS and no one has seen him all day. She didn't want to call you because she didn't want you to worry."*

"I alerted security when I didn't hear from him yesterday, and he wasn't where his appointments say he's supposed to be," Madison texted back. *"Keep me informed if you hear anything else."*

Madison pushed away her worry about Joshua in order to finish enjoying her evening. But she needed to confront her Vice President and supposedly closest friend with her suspicions.

After the ceremony, more people wanted to meet Madison, and she didn't mind talking to each and every one of them. Many of the guests had bought the books she had written about her natural beauty regimens and healthy lifestyle.

Heidi guided Madison over to a table where she could sign books right outside the dining area in the hallway. When the crowd was dispersing, Kimberly made her way over. Heidi took what was left of the books, as well as Madison's award, promising to return everything to her room before leaving.

Kimberly had a slightly disgruntled look on her face as she glanced across the hall at another doorway, where three well-dressed, very serious looking African-American men were standing.

"What's wrong?" Madison inquired, seeing Kimberly's displeased expression.

"Remember when I said there are some people that look upon research more for business, and not so charitably?" Kimberly nodded to the three men. "Those are the kind of people. They're called The Cytee Boys. My husband calls them 'strong arm con artist'. The best in the business, but I don't think that's a compliment."

Madison took a good look at the three men and was interested to see two of them were twins, dressed perfectly alike, and now looking at Kimberly. One of them whispered something to the large man behind them, and then both of the twins walked over to Kimberly and Madison.

"Well, if it isn't Mrs. Gates," one of the twins said with a serious look on his face.

"Careful, Trenton; Mr. Gates or the black minx might be around. He wouldn't leave his wife exposed for the likes of us," the other twin said with a twinkle in his eye. "Or would he?"

Trenton looked around, almost scared, despite the big guy who stood at almost seven feet tall in the doorway across the hall.

Jamar walked up on Madison and Kimberly just in time.

"Is that black minx here?" Trenton asked Kimberly.

"I don't know and I don't care," Kimberly snapped. "Jamar, I suggest you take Madison to her room. She really doesn't need to be around people like this."

Jamar only nodded. "I'll take good care of Madison, Kimberly."

"I can't stomach their proximity. Goodnight," Kimberly said in a huff and walked away.

"I don't think Mrs. Gates like you," Jamar said, amused, to the twins.

"Most people don't, Mr. Golden. Is it a surprise you're still here?" the other twin said. "You don't like us either, does he Trenton?"

Trenton nodded in agreement.

"I've never said that, Trenton," Jamar denied. "I just don't like what you do, Lincoln. Or the people your family associate with."

"Aww, but you can't deny we get things done," Lincoln, the other twin, said, smiling wickedly.

"And make a lot of money at it," Trenton chimed in happily.

Lincoln looked over at Madison. "You're even more gorgeous up close. I've heard about you. A lot. I didn't think a scientist could be so beautiful." He took Madison's hand and kissed her knuckles.

"Thank you," Madison said hesitantly, unsure how to accept the compliment. "How do you know about me?"

Jamar practically knocked Lincoln's hand away from Madison and said, "She's taken, Lincoln, you charming ass, and wouldn't be interested in your seductive ways."

"I don't see a ring on her finger," Lincoln pointed out.

"That'll be taken care of before the end of the week," Jamar promised.

"It will?" Madison was surprised.

"That still doesn't mean she's taken yet," Lincoln pointed out, with that same amused expression on his face. "We can be very persuasive." He winked at his brother and then licked his lips hungrily looking back at Madison.

"You're trying to get your face punched in?" Jamar asked, balling his fist up.

The seven-foot guy took a step forward and Trenton looked back at him. "It's alright, Kansas. Mr. Golden's just teasing. You know how Lincoln can be."

"I don't write a check with my mouth that my ass won't cash, Trenton," Jamar threatened. "And you know your brother has it coming, as many women as he's stolen."

"We have a meeting to attend," Trenton said. "A very important meeting."

Jamar looked shocked. "You moved the presentation up?"

Lincoln questioned, "How'd you know about our meeting?"

"Who do you think pointed Nikki toward you?" Jamar growled.

"Jason," Trenton answered. "We thought Jason contacted the company."

Jamar refuted. "I instructed how him to instruct his wife to get in touch with you. Why do you think she signed that agreement so fast? Because I told Jason how to tell you how to word the document. I knew the money would outweigh anything in that document."

"But you know it had to do with *Him*?" Trenton asked worriedly.

"That was the whole point. I knew she had to make a deal with the devil in order to make sure she'd lose everything."

"Who?" Madison questioned.

No one answered her.

"And he'll thank you for that, whether she fails or succeeds," Lincoln said. "And even though I don't have to tell you, *He* moved the meeting up."

Jamar looked around desperately.

"What's wrong?" Madison asked him.

"Jason should be here. Why isn't he here?" Jamar looked at the twins for the answer.

"We don't know why and we couldn't care less. *He* called us to tell us about the new meeting time. Most likely, he only contacted her, and she didn't care to tell her husband."

Jamar gripped Madison's hand more tightly, and for a moment looked at her.

Madison could almost read his thoughts. He needed to know if she was ready for the showdown.

Holding her purse close to her chest, she nodded to assure him.

"Jason was supposed to be here to let us into the meeting," Jamar said. "You need us to be there."

"Oh Really?" Lincoln and his twin walked back over to the doorway.

Jamar guided her to that side of the hallway. The big guy, Kansas, stepped closer to prevent Jamar from entering.

Jamar had to actually bend to his right to look at the twins around the huge man standing in front of him. Madison only stared at the menacing man and swore his arm alone was the same circumference as her thigh. She'd never seen anyone as large as this man in her life, and would bet he could rip Jamar in two with his meaty fists.

Trenton asked, full of sarcasm, "I think you need to stay out of our business, Mr. Golden." He said the name again in full disgust.

"Just hear me out," Jamar pleaded.

Lincoln made a loud snapping noise, and Kansas Cytee, which Madison believed the man was about the size of, finally moved to allow Jamar and her to follow the twins.

Madison was trying to grip Jamar's hand as tightly as possible, knowing what he was trying to do, ready to speak out when it was time.

"Why should we hear you out when you deserted your brother? You left him broke. You left him to die," Trenton snarled. "He wouldn't have come for our help if you had been there for him."

"I didn't know how bad it was," Jamar confessed guiltily. "Jason never told anyone how sick he really was."

"You didn't care enough to know," Trenton said, racking up the guilt on Jamar's shoulder. "Anger should never have kept you from him if you truly valued the connection the two of you had."

Madison was tired of just standing there and knew how much Jason's sickness pained Jamar's soul. "Please," she beseeched the twins gently. "There's enough hurt going around. Jason and Jamar have reconciled. Jamar's even given a kidney. Just listen to Jamar."

Lincoln looked at his twin, and they both finally nodded. "Why do we need you two in this meeting, Jamar?"

"Because I know what that evil bitch is trying to sell you, and I know you'd hate for it to be known she got away with selling the best con artists in Detroit a handful of magic beans."

The twins looked at each other again. "How do you know exactly what Nikki will be talking about?" Lincoln asked.

"I won't, but Madison will. You should have someone in there with you to help you make an educated decision."

"With us?" Trenton was clearly skeptical.

Jamar stressed, "I know your reputation is on the line, but your ass is, too. You're not doing this for just your company."

"You don't know shit," Trenton snarled.

"Oh, really?" Jamar countered. "I know if you bring back some magic beans to King Heart, he'll run you through like shish-kabobs and put your little sister out on the street to earn your money back. Hell, he might even get your moms out of jail just so she can work the street for him, too. He's bitter like that."

"You know nothing about King Heart," Lincoln said quietly.

Kansas Cytee cleared his throat.

Disgruntled, Lincoln conceded, "I heard you, big guy, but Mr. Golden hasn't given us shit to make us feel like we should allow him in the room. Only her." He indicated Madison begrudgingly. "We need her brains, but we don't need shit from him."

Jamar smirked and looked at the larger brother. "What if I have the solution to the big guy's problem?"

"Kansas Cytee doesn't have a problem," Lincoln denied.

"What solution?" Trenton asked at the same time.

"I know what your mother did to him," Jamar said with cold calculation. "I know deep down inside, that big-ass man hasn't gotten a wink of sleep, and even you worry what could happen if he continues without what he needs. I know what will save him and it's clean. I guarantee."

Trenton narrowed his eyes and looked at Kansas. "You trust him, big guy?"

Kansas looked hard for a moment at Jamar, then nodded.

Lincoln and Trenton moved out the way for Jamar and Madison to enter the room.

Jamar tightened his hold on her hand and led her into the dimly lit room.

Madison swore she'd find out what the big guy's problem was and how Jamar was going to solve it later. Right now she needed to concentrate on getting her research back.

Nikki was sitting on a small platform in front of a screen with a laptop open. Jerrell was sitting beside her, pointing at items on the screen, as if explaining everything to her.

Nikki was using him for his intelligence? Pathetic, Madison thought. Her heart went out to Jerrell.

Yet, he reminded her so much of herself when she was that age. She remembered explaining complicated things to her own mother.

As she looked hard at Jerrell, she noticed similarities; the nose, the shape of his eyes and the crooked smile...

There were about ten chairs in front of where Nikki was to present, and Madison sat almost at the end.

Jerrell almost jumped out of his seat when he saw Jamar and Madison, but Nikki's hand seemed to clutch down on the boy's shoulder viciously.

"What are they doing here?" Nikki demanded, offended. "Trying to steal my work again?"

Madison gripped the arm of the chair, wanting to jump over to the platform and scratch the evil bitch's eyes out.

CHAPTER 52

L INCOLN SPOKE UP, sitting down next to Madison, while Jamar sat on her other side. "She's here to make sure you aren't trying to sell us some magic beans."

Despite the twins dressing alike, Madison could tell them apart. She smiled at Lincoln. He winked back.

"Magic beans?" Nikki questioned, appalled. "I-I would like to request more time. With my husband's health issues, I've had little to no time to—"

Trenton cut her off. "Let's get this started now. Mr. Heart has given you more than enough time to deliver the results you promised for the large sum of money you took from him."

Angrily, Nikki asked, "Then why isn't he here? I don't think we should get started without him."

Kansas sharply closed the doors, making the room darker. He moved over and whispered something in Trenton's ear, then handed a phone to Lincoln.

"He's here," Trenton said, while Lincoln put the phone down on the desk and pressed the speaker button.

"I don't think you'd want him in body," Lincoln warned and returned to sit beside Madison.

Jamar shifted in his chair, bristling.

Nikki stared down at the phone with the sweat of fear culminating on her forehead and then closed her mouth.

Jerrell waved excitedly at his uncle.

"Does the child need to be onstage?" Trenton asked impatiently. "He's distracting me."

"Yes. I mean no," she said. "Go sit down in a chair, Jerrell."

Jerrell ran to his uncle, then waved to Madison.

Nikki looked like she wanted to snatch Jerrell back, but then looked back down at the phone, which made no indication at all that anyone was on the other line.

Picking up some index cards, Nikki's hand quivered. Madison could tell her ex-friend was stalling as she stared at the computer screen for a moment.

Madison tried to stay calm as Nikki began the same presentation Madison had been prepared to present so long ago. The woman spoke Madison's original notes almost word for word.

Jamar endured the torturous grip of Madison's hand squeezing his own.

Yet, where Madison would have continued after the discovery of being able to splice and change the DNA of the potato, Nikki changed and went into a different direction.

She began to speak about possibilities of fruit germination in various environments, but she never went into the innovative technology Madison had perfected and coined herself.

Jamar was right. If Madison hadn't been at the presentation, Nikki most likely could have sold these brothers some magic beans. Nikki spoke like she knew what she was talking about to the untrained ear, but in truth, Nikki was trying to make the impossible seem possible through words. Almost like a child's theory of possibilities.

Madison looked at Jerrell, and immediately could formulate what Nikki had done.

When Nikki was through with her presentation, only Jerrell spoke.

"Good job, Mommy."

Nikki shot him a venomous look, and Jerrell curled into Jamar's large body.

Lincoln leaned close to Madison and whispered, "What do you think, Madison?"

Jamar stiffened at Lincoln's proximity to Madison.

"Personal feelings aside, sir, Nikki only speaks of possibilities, when the gene splicing techniques to the plants she suggests would be impossible. They wouldn't adhere to each other and the seed growth would be little to none," Madison explained under her breath.

Trenton could hear Madison and said to Nikki, "These aren't the plants you promised us. We don't want berries and apples. You promised us pineapples and Shea trees. I hate apples and berries."

"You can't actually believe anything that whore says," Nikki snarled. "She's always been jealous of me. She's always wanted my life!"

"I think that's the other way around," Jamar corrected.

"I know you don't have shit to say to me," Nikki hurled out. "You're just jealous your brother loves me more than he's ever loved you."

Madison knew Nikki was trying to hurt Jamar, and she could feel Jamar stiffen.

"I love you, Uncle Jamar," Jerrell said encouragingly.

"Get over here, Jerry," Nikki snarled.

Reluctantly, the boy trudged over to his mother and she dug her nails into his shoulder until he sat down in the chair in front of the computer.

Madison had had enough. "I've never been jealous. I was just too silly and under-confident to realize I'm better than you, Nikki. I've always been better than you. Your presentation only explains promises, not what's possible. You have no idea how make the DNA sequences bind to each other properly."

"I do," Nikki insisted.

"Prove it," demanded Madison. "Please explain to these gentlemen how you perfected your gene splicing technique. No one does it the same. It's a variable that cannot be tamed, so I'd love to know how you perfected yours. How many hours in the lab did you spend? How many years did it take you?"

Nikki looked worried. "I don't have to explain myself to you, Madison Oliver."

"You don't," Trenton agreed. "But you do have to explain yourself to us."

Nastily, Nikki snarled, "You're nothing but *his* lackeys because he's too scared to step foot into this city. HE can't touch me, and neither can you." She started to walk out, but Kansas stood in front of her, and pointed back to the front.

Nikki stepped back to the podium with fear in her eyes.

Madison stood up, mostly worried for Jerrell. "Nikki, just explain yourself so you can leave."

"No!" Nikki railed. "You're just trying to steal from me."

"How? When you've already stolen from me!" Madison walked up to the presentation area and turned the computer around. Looking at the desktop, she saw her name on a file and clicked to open it.

The computer screen went dark and a box appeared, waiting for a password.

"Are those the files you stole from my flash drive, Nikki?" Madison asked. "You knew my science project like the back of your hand. You studied me. I understand. You had a lot of time. We've been together since junior high. You came to my every function more than my own dad did. Stealing my work was easy for you. Using my trust and knowing me, taking everything from me, was easy. And it wasn't Jason or Jamar, like you led me to believe. It was Joshua helping you, right?"

Nikki narrowed her eyes, but didn't say another word.

"He must've gotten the key to my room, right? You never returned the key to the office. You gave it to Joshua," Madison assumed. "He came back and took the result reports so you could placate the money people, while you waited to hack the password. Or, you got Joshua to stick around me, make me trust him, so eventually you two could figure it out." She rubbed her fingers on the keyboard. "All this time you've been trying to open these files, haven't you?"

Nikki stuttered guiltily. "I d-don't know what you're talking about."

"Then do it. Open these files, Nikki. Open this lone file on your desktop, because it's your computer, right? You've had this old, outdated laptop since high school. I remember when your parents gave this to you for your sweet sixteenth birthday. I bet with all the money you had, people have wondered why you never changed computers. I know why." She turned the laptop back around. "Because all my work is in that file, but you can't open it."

"No, it's not," Nikki denied.

"Then open it," Madison challenged her.

Jerrell looked at the screen and said, "Mommy, you said you couldn't open it. You forgot the password."

"Shut up," Nikki snapped, and slapped the child across the face.

Kansas Cytee leapt onto the platform, as did Jamar, but Trenton and Lincoln held both back. Lincoln was only coaxing Kansas to keep his cool, because Kansas was way too big to handle.

"Children should be seen and not heard," Nikki snapped.

Madison put the laptop in front of Jerrell. "Have you ever seen your mother open the file, Jerrell?"

He only shook his head, trying not to cry from his punishment.

"Has anyone ever opened that file?"

"She asked if I could get it open, but it's especially hard. If you type in the wrong code so many times in a row, the files will delete," the child explained.

Jerrell reminded her so much of Madison when she was child. Looking deep in his eyes, she smiled knowingly, and looked back at Nikki. "No one knows about him, do they?"

Nikki now looked frightened. "There's nothing to know."

"Really?" Madison asked with a smirk. "How many times did you try to open the file, Nikki? How many times?"

Nikki stiffened.

"Answer her," Trenton ordered.

"Seven," Nikki answered reluctantly.

Madison inserted the flash drive into the computer and then typed in the password.

The laptop clicked for a moment and then the screen brightly came to life and a large array of information started pouring down. Code after code drained down into the laptop for at least a minute.

"My research," Madison said, showing the screen to everyone else. "It has my name at the bottom and top of every page. The file can't be opened unless it has the original flash drive it was saved on. That was my fail-safe that I never told anyone."

"She's lying. Give me my laptop!" Nikki demanded, lunging for Madison.

Madison pushed her away and put the laptop back in front of Jerrell after she downloaded Nikki's entire drive to the flash drive. "Do you know how to wipe a file, Jerrell?"

He nodded.

"No!" Nikki screamed.

"Do it," Madison ordered, removing the flash drive, while still holding Nikki back.

"Stop! Stop it now, Jerrell, or you'll be sorry."

The child hesitated for a moment, looking at Nikki, and then his eyes landed on Madison. With a strong, determined look, he started to type in the sequence.

Madison knew anyone with a sense of the source code could figure out how to wipe the file from the computer.

"Any diligent scientist has backups, right, Nikki? You save your files somewhere else, but that was one file you couldn't duplicate. The file could only be chopped from the flash directly, which you couldn't get your hands back on." Reaching in her bag, Madison pulled out the old flash drive she had from high school – the one Nikki had stolen a long time ago.

"You bitch!" Nikki shoved Madison away, grabbed the laptop, and hurled the device against the wall.

Madison smiled. "*I should be angry at you. I should want to choke the life out of you,* but now I just feel sorry for you. You've ridden on others' shoulders to get to where you are, and you will never know how it feels to really create something of your own." She looked at Jerrell curiously and then back at Nikki. "Where is Joshua?"

"I don't know and I don't care," Nikki scowled.

"How'd you do it, Nikki? How'd you control him? What were you using to get him to do what you wanted him to do?"

"I don't have to answer to you, Madison."

Trenton said, "But you do have to answer to us."

"And you owe a lot of people a lot of money," Lincoln added.

Nikki said, feigning nonchalance, "My husband has more than enough property to sell to pay off Mr. Heart."

"No," Jamar disputed. "When Jason returned his foundation rights, he also signed over all the property we'd jointly owned solely to me."

Nikki gasped. "Impossible. We've used the property just last month for vacation."

"I own the property now. I let him keep access."

"So how do you plan on paying all the money back?" Trenton demanded of Nikki. "The agreement says if proof is not shown by today, you have less than forty-eight hours to return all the money you owe us."

Nikki looked lost for words. Madison could see her ex-best friend's world falling apart before her eyes.

"I-I..." Nikki was flustered. "I'll figure it out."

Kansas handed some paperwork to Lincoln, who came up to the platform and put the papers in front of Nikki.

"You can sign over the trust from your father that your husband didn't know about."

Desperately, Nikki said, "That's all I have!"

Trenton set a pen down on the table. "We have things to do, Nikki."

Nikki had the nerve to look at Jamar and Madison for help.

"And don't forget the intellectual lawsuit I'll be filing by Monday morning," Madison said, and let Jamar take her hand and to lead her to the hallway.

Seeing Nikki's mouth drop open in horror was the best.

Heidi was just coming down the hall from the elevator.

Jamar gave private instructions to his assistant and then said to Madison, "I need to find Jason. He wasn't answering his phone. Heidi's going to ensure you get back to your room safely."

Madison watched him leave the hotel, then followed Heidi to the elevators.

"Ms. Oliver," Lincoln said behind Madison, reaching out and touching her shoulder.

Heidi grabbed his arm and in one motion, flipped him over her body and stood in an Osae Uke karate position over him.

Kansas was right behind Lincoln and started to grab Heidi, but Lincoln stopped him.

"Whoa, big guy," he said, catching his breath.

Heidi didn't look scared. Matter of fact, the small intern looked ready to kick the big guy's ass too.

"I see Onyx Heart doesn't have to be around," Lincoln said, needing Kansas to help him back on his feet. "You're one of her trainees."

"She warned me about your family," Heidi said.

Madison was amazed at the woman's skills.

Lincoln took out a brown pill bottle. "I only came to give Ms. Oliver this."

"What are they?" Madison demanded to know.

"Pills, to help Jason. He promised if he could make sure his wife showed up at the presentation, King Heart would help him." He handed the bottle to Heidi, who handed them over to Madison.

Madison looked at the large white pills with nothing inscribed on them. "What do they do?"

"It's a black-market immunotherapy to help him live longer. It won't reverse the damage the cancer has done, but at least it won't be any day now, anymore. We'll supply him with all he needs. He'll see that little boy graduate from high school." Lincoln sighed. "And if you care more about that little boy in there than anything, you'll make that woman makes a deal and get full custody of him."

He turned and walked away. Kansas followed.

Madison looked down at the pills, then followed Heidi onto the elevator.

CHAPTER 53

AFTER HER LAB ASSISTANT picked up the medicine from the hotel in the morning, Madison spent the whole day studying the financial records for her company.

Mercy brought the children to the hotel, and they all attended closing ceremonies for the conference.

This also gave Madison time to express her feelings and concerns about the company and Joshua's roll in it.

"Don't hate yourself," Mercy admonished her.

"You told me not to trust anyone." Madison regretted not heeding her cousin's advice.

"I looked at the books myself, and there was never any time Joshua took from you."

"And that's what's confusing, Mercy. He could have stolen millions from me, ran off with Nikki and I wouldn't have been the wiser. Why wait all this time to expose himself?"

Mercy frowned, deep in thought.

Jamar and Jason walked up to their table. The closing ceremonies were winding down and Jamar must've come to deliver the final thank-you speech.

Madison hugged both of them as her children wrapped their arms around the men's legs. It was a funny moment for everyone before the seriousness set in. The brothers sat at the table.

Her daughter crawled in Jason's lap like it was natural, while the twins wiggled rambunctiously in Jamar's.

"Is everything okay?" Madison asked Jason.

"Yes," he assured her. "By the time I found out about the meeting, I'd missed everything, but Nikki had plans to leave town last night without me. There were two tickets for Switzerland with suitcases packed in the hall closet at the house."

"She was going to take Jerrell away?" Mercy questioned.

"No, the tickets were for two adults."

Mercy and Madison looked at each other. "Joshua?" they asked together.

"We don't know. Have you spoken to him yet?" asked Jamar

"No," Madison answered, disappointed.

"And neither has his wife since this morning," Mercy added.

Heidi came over to the table. "Mr. Golden, it's time for your speech."

Mercy helped the twins off Jamar's lap, but he promised them he'd return shortly.

Jason said, "I informed The Cytee Boys of her intentions and gave them the tickets. Kansas caught her trying to catch her flight last night at the airport, but Joshua wasn't with her."

"She really was planning on just leaving you all alone with Jerrell?" Mercy asked incredulously. "How could a mother do that to her child?"

"I don't know."

"Where's Jerrell now?" Mercy asked.

"The Gates' are taking care of him. Their children attend the same school." Jason looked at Madison with a little desperation.

"I can take the kids home," Mercy said, also noticing the intense look in his eyes.

Madison thanked her cousin.

When they were gone, Jason asked, "Can we go to your hotel room?"

She nodded.

***

He seemed anxious and nervous as they entered her hotel room, and waited until the door was fully closed before he started to speak.

"I thought about a lot of things last night, and I never told you how much I loved you," he declared. "How much I still love you."

She was speechless. "Jason, I don't think—"

"Don't think," he said. "I know you're very smart and you know I'm physically incapable of pleasing you like a man can please a woman. You know how severe my condition is. You know I can't... I think Nikki liked that I got sick. I don't think she ever wanted that from me. The prestige and the association of being with me was all she was after. That's why she easily agreed to the divorce."

"Divorce?"

"I proposed divorce the same time she agreed to prove her findings to the investors. Whether the meeting went well or badly, she signed another agreement that our divorce would be final the day after. I give her everything I own and walk away with nothing, except share custody with Jerrell."

"And now that you have nothing?"

He smiled. "Sometimes nothing is all a man needs to know he really has everything. I still have Jerrell, and that's what's important."

"Where's Nikki now?"

Jason answered strongly, "Most likely on her way to Chicago to explain herself to her investors."

"Did you know about her father's money?"

He shook his head. "That was a surprise to me. She's kept that a secret. I thought after her parents died, she was left with nothing from them."

Walking up to Jason, Madison said, "I'm glad you realized the truth about Nikki before it was too late."

"Some truths," he pointed out. "Not all the truths. I have a feeling that woman has more secrets."

She agreed.

There was a knock on the door and she let Jamar inside.

He pulled her into his arms and kissed her like he hadn't seen her in centuries. She enjoyed the kiss and returned her own embrace.

"Did you tell her?" Jamar questioned.

"Tell me what?"

"How we plan on making you happy for the rest of your life," Jamar stated, matter-of-factly.

Madison was speechless. Jason and Jamar were almost too good to be true.

***

Early in the morning, Madison unraveled herself from Jason and Jamar. They'd slept in one bed, just like old times.

Jason warmed her up; foreplay and lots of kissing, while Jamar sated her body. He apparently found so much pleasure seeing how much she enjoyed having Jason's touch and Jamar's body please her. She loved every minute of being with them, and knew a lifetime of love with them would be forever.

"Where are you going?" Jason asked sleepily as she dressed.

"To finish solving everything from the past," she said. "Last night kind of opened my mind to a lot of things."

"You're welcome," he teased, handing her his valet ticket. "You might need this."

She kissed Jason and left the hotel while texting Joshua's assistant. By the time she was inside of Jason's vehicle, she had a pretty good idea where she could find Joshua.

Finding Joshua was merely by coincidence, since Madison decided not to go down the main street, which was packed with parents dropping kids off at the private school nearby.

Madison had investigated the school a while ago, and was familiar with the exterior layout. Going down a residential street by the main entrance, she just happened to pull up behind Joshua's light blue, brand new luxury Cadillac.

He was leaning on the hood, sipping on a coffee, watching the front of the school like a hawk.

Standing beside him, Madison said, "You come here often?"

Joshua didn't take his eyes off the school, and didn't seem surprised by her presence next to him. "I was wondering when you'd figure everything out, Madison."

"I don't think I've figured everything out, Joshua." She leaned on the hood next to him and took his coffee to sip the warm, thick caffeine. "You've been here a while."

"I try to come when I can. I've always wanted to know the truth from her, but she's managed to still hide secrets after all this time."

"Who is *she*?" Madison demanded clarification.

Joshua tore his eyes away from the school and looked at Madison. "Nikki," he said obviously.

CHAPTER 54

JOSHUA LOOKED AT THE ground for a moment, then back at the school. When he spoke, his voice was heavy with sadness. "The truth of the matter is, the only reason she became involved with me was because I was working with you. Prior to that, she wouldn't even give me the time of day. I switched schools because I was so heartbroken over not being able to pursue her, and I started going to your school."

"That's why Mercy recognized you. She went to Nikki's college. She knew Nikki and most likely saw you along with all the other guys who hung around her." It took Madison everything in her whole body not to break down at this new information. "All this time… you've been disillusioned by her all this time, Joshua?"

He glared at her for a moment. "I've loved her all this time," he admitted. "She told me she loved me too, and made me believe we were going to be together as soon we got all the information from you. She even gave me some of her body. Just enough to sway me that it could be a possibility. Yet, I knew the truth. I loved her, but I wasn't stupid. I knew she was using me. I knew I wasn't good enough for her, but I thought if I became better, she'd see she should be with me. I helped your company because it gained me wealth and notoriety, all the while holding off on the information she needed to make her stolen research a success."

"You betrayed me, Joshua."

Joshua nodded. "Did you hear what I said, Madison? I loved her."

He said this as if that was supposed to make all the sense in the world, but Madison still couldn't understand his reasons.

"Joshua, you stole my research and gave it to her."

"I stole the research," he admitted. "But I knew from the beginning, she was only trying to get to your research through me. I knew she was going to use me, but I had power over her the whole time." He laughed triumphantly. "All the time she thought she was playing me, I was playing her and I was playing to win… And all I wanted to do was win her."

"And that's supposed to make me feel better? You knew she took my research and used it to get the grant. That destroyed my life!"

"But look what that did for you. You were able to find something else, right? When I went into the hotel room you were staying at and I saw what you were creating with the facial line, I knew it could be bigger than Nikki would ever imagine."

Madison slapped him in her anger, right across the face. "Don't act like I should be grateful, because you had every intention of selling me out in the end. Everything I created you were going to hand to her on a silver platter weren't you?"

Joshua leaned over the car from the impact and shame. "I only gave her a part of you initial research; never the whole thing," he tried to justify himself. "I knew the access to the rest of the research needed your flash drive. I had access to that all the time." He touched his face to feel the impact of her blow.

"Then why didn't you just betray me all the way? Finish the job?" she spat bitterly.

"I told you I was in love, not stupid. When she wouldn't tell me all her secrets, or admit whether she wanted to be with me, I let you put the research away. Remember, I even suggested the safe room in your house?"

"But if she had given you her body, her heart, or her love, you would have given her everything, right?" Madison sneered, letting her anger come to the surface.

"She… She promised… but I knew… all along, I knew…" His voice trailed off in a miserable tone as he wiped a tear from his eye.

Madison couldn't believe how pathetic he sounded. "You've waited all these years for her? All this time, Joshua? Does she know?"

Joshua wiped away another tear, shaking his head.

"And you know she's never going to give you her heart, her soul, or her body again, right? You know that will never happen," Madison pointed out. "She already tried to leave you last night; she tried to get out the country. She even left her own child. How could you love someone like that?"

He shrugged miserably. "I know how awful she is, but there was the baby. I thought at least we had that."

"Is that how she kept you strung along, Joshua? She told you Jerrell was yours?"

He looked back at the school. "So, he is mine, Madison? Is that what your lovers told you?"

She didn't want reveal what Jamar and Jason said to her. "What did she tell you, Joshua?"

"She said Jerrell's not Jason's, but then said she wasn't sure who the father was."

"But you slept with her during the time she became pregnant."

"He's got light skin. He could be mine."

There was so much hope in his voice, Madison knew Nikki had probably been stringing this man so long with what could be a lie.

Madison admitted, "He's not Jason's, but you have demanded a DNA test from her, right?"

"She wouldn't allow me to get near him. Threatened to file a restraining order against me if I set foot near Jerrell."

Madison now understood why Joshua had been at the school. He was looking for Jerrell. With Nikki in Chicago, doubtful to ever come back, Joshua could do whatever he wanted to prove if Jerrell was his son or not.

Spitefully, Joshua said, "She's always told me just enough to give me doubt, but he could be mine."

Madison had to agree Nikki had been manipulative. She had Joshua's heart and mind in a tizzy.

Moving in front of Joshua, blocking his view from the school, Madison declared, "Nikki is evil incarnate. She uses people. She hurts people. She's deceived people, all for her own selfish reasons. And you still have the nerve to love her?"

"The heart wants what the heart wants. Look at you with those brothers. Yes, I love her, but that's more normal than what you're doing. Loving two men?" he asked, disgusted.

She was going to deny she was in love until she felt something tugging at her skirt. Turning around, she looked down to see Jerrell. His eyes were bright and happy to see her, with reverence beaming from his face.

"Ms. Madison, it's good to see you. Are you here to talk at my school?" he asked hopefully.

She knelt down and closed the top part of his coat. "You shouldn't stray away from school, Jerrell," she gently reprimanded him. "Your mother wouldn't approve."

"Momma doesn't care," he said with a shrug. "Daddy might be upset. He'd understand in this case, because he knows how much I like you. But he didn't come pick me up last night."

She heard Joshua bristle, and knew he was upset by the boy referring to Jason as his dad.

Madison also felt awful keeping Jason away from Jerrell the night before, while she enjoyed herself. "I'm sure he'll be back with you soon," she promised.

"Whenever he would leave, Momma would say she didn't care if he ever comes back, but I haven't seen her in a couple of days. Uncle Jalen and Aunt Kimber's been helping my dad." He didn't sound as sad when he made this revelation.

Giving Joshua a side-eye, she asked Jerrell, "Your mother said this to you? What else did she say? Has she ever said anything to you about Mr. Joshua here?"

"I heard her say one time I was a bastard, and she didn't want me from the beginning, but as long as Mr. Josh believed I was his, she could get what she needed from him."

Madison looked back a Joshua, who was trying not to contort his face as the blood rushed to his cheeks in anger. "So you've met Mr. Joshua?"

Jerrell shook his head. "I've seen him at my mom's office when I had to stay and wait to go home. I had to sit at an empty desk but I don't think he saw me and I wasn't allowed to speak to guest or Mommy would get upset and pinch me."

"What else did your mommy say about me?" Joshua demanded.

Jerrell answered, "She said you've been wondering who the bastard's daddy was, and she might never tell him." The little boy looked at Madison with a frown. "I know she was talking about me, but I don't know what she means, Ms. Madison."

"He's coming with us," Joshua declared, before Madison answered Jerrell.

"Coming where?" Madison questioned Joshua. "This isn't your child, Joshua, to take anywhere you want."

Joshua grabbed Jerrell's arm and started dragging him to the back seat of the car. "That bitch knows his daddy isn't Jason. I need to know the truth."

"What truth?" Madison asked hysterically, not liking the maddened look in Joshua's eyes. "You can't just abduct a child, Joshua."

"Either you're coming with me or not, Madison, but the boy's coming back to the lab and I'm personally dissecting his DNA to find out the truth, even if I have to hurt him to take it."

"You're crazy. You can't do this without his parent's permission, and you can't get into the lab to do a proper test without me allowing you in."

"Then I'll take him somewhere I can extract his DNA. I'm going to do whatever it takes. Are you coming or not?"

She saw the crazed look intensify in Joshua's eyes, and worried about how much he could hurt Jerrell because of what Nikki was driving him to.

Knowing Jerrell would be upset going with a stranger, Madison jumped in Joshua's backseat with the small boy, while Joshua drove away from Jason's car. After locking up Jason's vehicle with the remote, she quickly texted Jason to let him know what was going on.

"Where are we going, Ms. Madison?" Jerrell inquired.

"To my lab, Jerrell," she answered calmly.

Jerrell brightened up. "Will you show me around?"

The boy was becoming too precious for words, and she vowed not to let anything bad happen to him. "Yes, Jerrell, I'll show you around after we help my friend." Drawing him into her closely as if she could just protect him from Joshua's rage, he leaned into her chest.

Jerrell nodded and relaxed. Joshua drove like a madman to get to the company's building and opened the back doors after parking near the lab.

She hesitated before getting out.

"I can either drag him out, or you can convince him everything's okay," Joshua threatened under his breath, so that only she could hear.

"Let's go see my lab," she said to Jerrell, who happily followed her out, holding her hand and staying close.

While they had been driving, she had also texted Jamar their location and an access code into the building, and let him know to bring Jason to get Jerrell.

Jerrell was so excited to be with her, but was clueless about Joshua's rage. Getting to her lab, she halted Joshua from grabbing a needle.

"There is a humane way to extract DNA," she said, getting an electronic needle from a cupboard and instructing Jerrell to sit in a high stool by her desk.

The child was asking a million questions and, with the patience of Job, Madison answered each one of them. He barely felt the prick and the hair sample she extracted.

"For faster results, we'll need a female subject as well," Joshua said knowingly. "We can use you."

"I'm not his mother," she protested.

"Let's not argue, dammit. Any female DNA will push the results out faster; you and I both know this. I've come this far, Madison," Joshua snarled. "I need to know the truth, now or never."

She sighed and took her sample after Joshua took his. "And if he's your son?" she questioned Joshua. "What are you going to do? Fight for paternity rights?"

"Expose her for the liar she is," Joshua said, feeding the results into the computer. "Finally, I'll know she can't use me anymore like she wants to. I need to stop giving her a reason to control me."

Rolling her eyes in exasperation, Madison said, "You're going off your rocker, Joshua. She's pushed you over the edge and you have no idea if she's ever coming back to Detroit; kidnapping, endangerment, conducting illegal medical tests without a legal guardian? How do you think all of this is going to go, Joshua?"

"Who the fuck cares?! You can't be on her side after all these years! And you certainly can't forgive her for what she's done to you. To your family! To your heart."

"I'm not going to hurt an innocent child to justify any harm I'd like to do to Nikki," she reprimanded him.

Insanely, Joshua cackled. "If I get caught, I guess you'll have to be the face of the company, finally." He refreshed the screen impatiently and slammed his fist on the desk because the computer was still calculating the results.

Madison knew whatever the results were to this test, Jerrell could be hurt because of the outcome. "You won't win anything, Joshua." She pulled her cell phone out to phone the police. "This is over and I'm going to protect Jerrell from you."

"Give me your phone," he ordered.

After turning the device off, she reluctantly handed Joshua the phone, then took Jerrell to her personal glass lab where she usually conducted her plant growth experiments.

Jerrell was fully consumed with taking small seeds that had sprouted and putting them into pods to be shipped to the many greenhouses she had all over the world to test their growth rates.

Joshua didn't follow them. He was too consumed with the results from the computer. He knew they couldn't get out of the lab without going past him.

But he couldn't hear them, because the growth room door was closed. Madison was secretly trying to get to the phone on the wall.

"You want a phone?" the little boy asked.

She looked at him, startled. "Yes, honey."

There's one in my backpack," he said, pointing behind him.

Relieved, she went behind him and secretly reached in his bag to find the phone, but didn't take it out because she was hoping her earlier message helped get Jamar and Jason in action to come save them. Joshua might've had ideas to search her, but he wouldn't search the child.

"Will he hurt us?" Jerrell sounded worried.

Telling the child the truth would only upset him. "No. He's just angry."

"At my mom, right?" he surmised.

She smiled at Jerrell's intelligence and cognizance of his environment. "She's caused a little trouble for you before?"

Jerrell smirked. "Mom causes a lot of problems."

"What other problems has your mom caused that you know of, Jerrell?"

"She lied to my dad about her research. She got five million dollars and said I had to help her because I liked plants, but a lot of it was really hard. She said Uncle Jamar was deliberately keeping money from us because he didn't like her. I know that's a lie."

"He could've helped her with some money," Madison pointed out, playing devil's advocate, while they continued to transfer seedlings.

"No, I told him the research wasn't Momma's. I told him she didn't know anything about what those reports meant and that she made me tell her what they meant. I told him Momma didn't know shit," he said proudly.

Madison gasped. "Jerrell, language."

He giggled. "Uncle Jamar says it."

She would definitely reprimand Jamar about watching his tongue around the influential young man and all the other children.

"But even I saw that Momma's stuff didn't make sense when she tried to explain what it was to me," Jerrell pointed out. "She has no knowledge of DNA breakdowns, and even though I don't know a lot, I've seen more intelligence in a YouTube video."

She snorted, feeling bad for laughing, but Jerrell was hilarious. Madison could tell Jamar and Jason had influenced him greatly.

Jerrell got serious suddenly. "She would smack me when I talked about you. First, she thought Daddy had told me about you, but I learned about you because of all the research you were writing and doing. I saw your videos on YouTube and would ask questions about you."

"Thank you, but I'm sorry you got in so much trouble. Why would she think your father talked about me?"

"Because they argued about how he 'fawns' over you. Momma said he was always gushing over Madison Oliver's shit every time she was on TV. That's why Momma made him pull out of the organization, because she thought Jamar talked too much about you to my dad." He flinched as if he remembered something bad.

"What's wrong, Jerrell?" she questioned, concerned.

"Momma hits Daddy a lot," he confessed. "I saw her."

Madison held Jerrell close, hearing Joshua cursing as the computer started printing out the DNA results.

Whatever Joshua was discovering, he was not happy.

CHAPTER 55

J OSHUA WAS FURIOUSLY GRIPPING the computer printout and looked up at her. "You knew, you bitch!" She read his lips. "Didn't you?!" He grabbed a scalpel off the shelf and started toward her.

She backed away from the door in fright, running toward Jerrell to save him. At the same moment, Jamar flew in the room and tackled Joshua to the floor.

In his anger, Joshua threw Jamar off of him and swiped at his body with the scalpel.

Jamar ducked away, then came forward to punch Joshua across the desk. Joshua leaped up and tackled Jamar to the floor, rolling across it, trying to get the upper hand with the scalpel still between them.

Using the opportunity of distraction to escape, Madison grabbed Jerrell's hand and went for the door to try to get out, but it wouldn't open. Joshua had poured acid in the lock. She picked up a chair and tried to break the glass, but that was useless, and she almost injured her hand.

Going back over to Jerrell, she held him close.

"I'm scared, Ms. Madison," he whimpered, hearing the awful commotion from the other room.

Madison looked over the desk to see Joshua grab a steel tray and knock it over Jamar's head. She pushed away the urge to scream for Jamar, not wanting to upset Jerrell anymore.

Joshua stabbed Jamar high in the shoulder with the scalpel. He then ran towards the doorway.

Jason happened to be rushing in at the same time, and Joshua slammed into Jason's large chest.

In one punch, Jason knocked Joshua in the face, hurling his body across another desk, knocking him out cold.

Jason went over to Jamar, who was just struggling to stand up, and was holding his shoulder. He wavered a little from the knot in his head, but straightened up seeing that Madison and Jerrell were fine.

"Tie him up," Jamar ordered his brother. "I'll go help her."

Madison pointed to the shelves where the zip ties were. Jason retrieved them and went back over to Joshua to tie him up, while Jamar came to the door. He used the ax from the fire box to knock the melted lock off the door.

Jerrell rushed to his uncle's waist, while Madison rushed into his good arm. Jamar winced in pain, but received the grateful hugs happily.

The police arrived and took Joshua into custody. He was disoriented, but would live. Madison hugged Jason for all his help as they went to Jamar's car. She made sure Jerrell was secure in the back seat, but overly worried about if Jamar was going to be alright.

EMS attended to Jamar, but he was being grouchy and insisted he didn't need to go to the hospital. He finally came over to them.

"I'm so glad you guys came to my rescue," Madison said as they started driving toward Jason's vehicle.

"Thank Jason for being the calm thinker," Jamar said, rubbing his shoulder bandage, wincing in pain. "I was hell-bent on just getting to you. Jason's the one who called the police to meet up here. I used your codes to get in the back, while Jason ushered them through the front."

"I just called Jerrell's school," Jason informed them, getting off his cell phone. "They said my car is safe and their security will meet us over there so no one will tow the vehicle before we arrive. Where you parked is a high-security patrol residential area. They were concerned about Jerrell and I assured them he was safe and we're on our way back together." They passed the police car where Joshua was in the back, looking worn. "He's going to jail, I hope," Jason said, taking a computer printout from Jerrell's hand.

"Yes, he is," Jamar answered. "I spoke to the detective while with EMS: child endangerment, kidnapping and felonious assault."

Despite everything, Madison hoped Joshua was going to be okay and would get the help he needed when incarcerated.

Jamar groaned a little.

"You should've gone to the hospital," Madison insisted to him.

"I was not going anywhere until I knew you were okay."

"Where'd you get this paper?" Jason asked Jerrell.

"From the man," the little boy said. "I saw the police rip it outta his hands when they put the handcuffs on him. He was screaming about lies."

"Madison, would you know what all this says?" Jason questioned, handing her the printout.

She immediately realized these were the DNA printout results for Jerrell. Speaking her observations aloud, she said, "Joshua is not Jerrell's father, but…" she hesitated, not believing what she was seeing. "It says the maternal match…" She looked at Jamar as he stopped next to Jason's car.

"What?" Jamar asked, worried.

"The results say the female contribution is a close relative of his."

"Meaning?" Jason asked, confused.

Astonished, Madison revealed, "Jerrell is my brother."

"Yours?" Jamar questioned. "How?"

She got out of the car to give herself air.

Jason took Jerrell over to his vehicle and put the child in the back after starting the car. When he returned to his brother and Madison standing nearby, she explained what the paper was telling her.

"According to this, my and Jerrell's DNA closely resemble each other's, meaning we have the same parent."

Jamar was about to say more, but a cab pulled up and Nikki jumped out of the rear. The security from the school held her back.

"Let her through," Jamar ordered them. "She can explain this."

Nikki walked over as if she had every right to be there. "I came for my son," she demanded.

"No, you didn't," Jason refuted. "You could care less about that child. You came back because Chicago was not what you expected."

Madison's ex-friend shifted uncomfortably. "He's my son, not yours!"

Throwing the results at Nikki's feet, Madison demanded, "When did you fuck my father, Nikki? Was it every time you came to my house? Is that why he only let you come? Why he curbed his rules just for you?"

Nikki picked up the results and looked at them, replying, "I don't know what you mean."

"Really?"

Nikki tossed the results back at Madison's feet. "That's my son."

"And obviously my brother too, Nikki."

Her ex-friend stiffened. "I never gave you or anyone permission to do a DNA test."

"Why? Because we'd find out the truth?" Jamar questioned. "We all knew he wasn't Jason's."

"You can forget about taking him, Nikki," Madison said. "My brother will never know a day of hardship or your punishment ever again."

"You can't do this! I'll go to the police!" Nikki threatened. "No one has rights to him but me." She smiled deviously. "Although, if you want to see him you can pay. Fifty thousand a month and I'll let you see him twice."

Madison had had enough of Nikki's greed. "You must be out of your damn mind." She stepped forward and slapped the taste out of Nikki's mouth.

Her ex-friend staggered back, clutching her face. "You'll never see Jerrell again! None of you!"

"How about you sign over full custody and I don't sue your ass for all you've got hidden in Switzerland?"

Nikki looked ready to break in half, she jerked her body so fast in guilt. "H-h-how do y-you know about my accounts there?"

Smiling triumphantly, Madison said, "I didn't, but with you trying to take off for Switzerland, and knowing how secretive and greedy you are, I figured it out. So how much can I get from you for copyright and patent infringement, Nikki? My pain and suffering alone, I'm thinking just ten million and then the years of struggling, the embarrassment and—"

"Fine! Take him. I'm moving anyway." She glared at Jason. "Now that I'm a free woman, I don't have to worry about anyone but me."

Madison was tired of listening to her. She returned to Jamar's vehicle to get away. As she waited, she called her company to make sure everything would be cleaned up and replaced by the following week in her private lab, and the security codes and protocols were changed completely.

She arranged with human resources to send Joshua's bonus and final paychecks to his wife, and then made sure he was no more on her books. Leaving a message for her lawyers, she hoped by the following week, she would have wiped Joshua out of her life.

A few minutes later, Jamar joined her, getting off his phone, and waved to Jason who was about to drive off with Jerrell in the backseat.

The security team had already driven away, and as Jamar drove away too, they left Nikki standing in the middle of the street alone. Her cab had left her and she was stranded.

Madison didn't feel one shred of pity.

"You aren't really going after her bank accounts in Switzerland?" Jamar asked when they pulled up to a red light.

"I won't, as long as she signs custody agreements," Madison responded. "I'm sure your Cytee Boys can get to her with the paperwork, but that doesn't mean I won't tell the university or the professor's widow about the money they could get out of her."

"Gawd, I love you," Jamar said, before reaching over and molding his lips passionately to hers.

Chills and heat seemed to fight on her insides as she whispered, "I love you too, Jamar. Now, let's get to the hospital."

He chuckled, agreeing.

CHAPTER 56

JAMAR INSISTED HELPING her pack her hotel room. With the conference over and Nikki taken care of, Madison could go home and start a new life with the fathers of her children.

On the way to home, Jamar asked, "Would you mind if Jason and I thought about moving everyone in together?"

"Would there be a house large enough?" she questioned playfully.

"The Boston Edison home would be perfect. It even has a cottage house for Mercy."

That home held a lot of good memories for her, and she smiled, holding his hand as he drove. "I think we could consider something like that."

Jamar smiled confidently. After they finished taking everything into her house, he pulled her in his arms and kissed her. Madison was becoming addicted to his kisses.

"You know I'm planning on an extravagant marriage proposal," he promised.

Madison laughed. "I figured you were."

It almost looked like he wanted to ask then, but he only gave her another peck on the lips before leaving her.

Madison closed her eyes for a moment alone as she leaned against the door. Mercy had sent her a message that she'd taken the kids to the park for a Sunday bike ride.

Having that quiet was really needed.

Loud frantic knocking at the door startled her and without even looking out, she opened the door, assuming Jamar had returned.

Joshua's wife, Shelby, looked frazzled, bombarding her way inside. She was a mousy black woman the same age as Madison, with unique silver-brown eyes hidden behind long bangs. Full-figured and highly intelligent, she seemed to have her own worries, but had always been a good helpmate to Joshua.

"What's going on?!" Shelby demanded. "Why is Joshua calling me from jail?"

Madison didn't know how to explain everything. "What did he say?"

"That's the problem, Maddie. He's not saying anything, but it sounds really bad," Shelby cried. "He just ordered me to get his lawyer and bring as much money to the precinct as I could."

Taking a deep breath, Madison was still indecisive as to how to advise the woman. "Sit down, Shelby."

They moved to the living room as Shelby questioned, "Does this have to do with that Nikki woman?"

Madison was shocked Shelby knew about Nikki.

"How do you know about Nikki?"

"I know enough. Just because I don't say anything doesn't mean I don't know what my husband is doing." She cut her eyes at Madison. "I know he only married me for show. I know he has true feelings for you and that Nikki woman." She straightened her back. "I know I'm not as smart as you or beautiful like Nikki is, but I was a safe bet. I could give him a family."

Her heart truly went out for Shelby living with Joshua all this time, despite the fact she was aware her husband's heart never was really there for her. "But how do you know about Nikki? I never knew he even knew her until recently," Madison questioned.

"I saw her. After we got married, he'd sneak to her and beg her to love him or tell him the truth, but she just played with him. He'd send her emails about how much he loved her and how he'd rather be with her. He'd give her bigger flower bouquets and send her really expensive gifts from bank accounts he thought I didn't know about." There was so much hurt in her voice. "I thought he was cheating with you, but when I saw who she was, I got so mad."

Madison felt awful for Shelby for enduring knowing what her husband was doing. "All these years, you've known about his love for Nikki and never said anything, Shelby?"

"Look at me." Shelby said in distress. "I'm nobody and Joshua's..." She sobbed. "And then there's you."

"Me?" What about me?" Madison questioned. "Joshua and I never did anything together."

"If I'd have gotten rid of Nikki, he'd just fawn more over you. He's always fawned over how intelligent you were. I'd never be able to get rid of you in his life."

"To me, it was just some college crush I never encouraged, Shelby. And now, considering what he did to me…"

"What did he do?" Shelby insisted.

Madison knew she should tell Shelby before this mousey woman had a nervous breakdown. "He was giving secrets to Nikki to undermine my college research."

Shelby gasped. "It was her! She was manipulating him! She was controlling my Joshua."

"He admitted he did it," Madison said. "I was just as hurt that he'd deceived me all this time. I thought I could trust him after everything that had happened. He had the nerve to act as if he was doing me a favor by not giving her all the information. But that was only because he knew she wouldn't ever love him. The fact that he used my research as bait to win that evil woman makes me sick to my stomach."

Shelby shook her head dejectedly. "I'm sorry, Maddie. I had no idea how bad it was. I can understand how hurt you are. I understand about being used." She took a deep, depressing breath. "Maybe if I had loved him more or done more…"

Madison shook her head. "There was nothing you could have done, Shelby. What's done is done. Jacob made that decision to deceive us on his own."

A message came in on Shelby's phone, and she deleted it.

"Who was that?" Madison inquired.

"It was Joshua's lawyer. He said people are waiting at the precinct to pick up the money."

"The money wasn't for him?"

"No, Joshua said he has to pay a Mr. Heart."

Madison was appalled. Joshua was still helping Nikki by helping her pay off the debt? "How much money, Shelby?"

"Two million is in our savings, and then there's the stocks he sold off, and the money in our retirement, which I was given when my parents died. That's about two million more," Shelby said innocently.

Madison didn't want to tell the woman not to support her husband, but couldn't be sure if Joshua really needed that money all for himself, or just to help Nikki. She forced out, "You should help your husband, Shelby." Saying those words left a sour taste in her gut. "Despite what he did."

Shelby sighed despondently. "I think the only reason Joshua wants me to bring the money is to help him." But she sounded as if she was really not considering it. "I don't think he wants me there for anything else."

"That's not true, Shelby," Madison tried to encourage her, but the sour taste was getting worse.

"I'm a realist now, Maddie. I know the truth of Joshua's heart and I know that man hasn't loved me since I gave birth to our only child."

Madison bit her tongue, trying not to look bothered. The baby had died shortly after birth, and she had thought they were still trying. "Whatever you decide, Shelby, I'll help you. You run a lucrative virtual assistance business. You can take care of yourself. You'll be okay if you decide to divorce Joshua."

Shelby snorted. "Like I said, Maddie. Look at me. What man would want this?" She stood up and closed her coat.

The woman's low self-esteem was her downfall, in Madison's opinion.

Madison walked Shelby to the door and paused as the woman stopped abruptly and turned to Madison.

"Did he ever find out if that child was his, Maddie?"

Madison didn't want to say anything at first, because she knew it would be the straw that could break the camel's back. But that sour feeling in her stomach was prevalent and she would throw up if she said one more lie.

"No, it wasn't his."

Shelby seemed satisfied by the answer. "You'll be okay, Maddie?"

"Yes, but I'm worried about you, Shelby."

"Don't worry. I'll be fine," Shelby assured her, but didn't make eye contact with Madison, as if there was something else on her mind. "I know there's no chance in hell Joshua will have a job when he gets out."

The woman sighed. "You know, before I met Joshua, I never went by my first name."

Madison thought it odd for the woman to reveal something like that to her.

"When I met Joshua, I thought I'd change my life and grow up. I thought I was smart enough to be with a man like that, but I guess I wasn't smart enough to keep him."

Just out of curiosity, Madison asked, "What name did you go by?"

Shelby looked delighted Madison asked and gushed, "My maiden name, Diamond. No one called me Shelby before I met Joshua. I pushed away all my friends because I didn't want them to get in the way of my new relationship. I guess I was the stupid one."

"Shelby, that's not true. Love is complicated, but don't hate yourself for loving."

Shaking her head, Shelby said, "I just hate myself for not being good enough, Maddie. But it's fine. Are you going to sue him? Or hurt him anymore financially? I know after this, he won't be able to get a job anywhere, and money will be tight."

Madison responded, "I've forwarded all I owe him to you, and that's really all I can say until I speak to my lawyer this week. You'll get the checks in a couple of days."

"Thank you, Maddie. I'm so sorry for everything."

They hugged, knowing they'd always be friends if one needed the other, but Shelby wasn't stupid. Joshua was going to be a burden to her if she stayed with him.

When Shelby was gone, Madison spent the rest of the day trying to determine what to decide for the children and Mercy, and how smoothly to incorporate Jamar and Jason into her future.

She received a text from Jason, inviting her to a private dinner Sunday at the Boston Edison home. Replying immediately, she accepted the invitation.

Going in her basement lab, she looked over the pills she had been given for Jason and decided Monday morning she would see how she could incorporate her own knowledge in improving his health.

When Mercy came in with the kids, her cousin looked rattled. But when Madison tried to inquire, Mercy just put a hand up in an "I'll talk with you later" way.

Madison respected her cousin's stalling, but worried something about Mercy's condition was bothering her. She pushed this worry away quickly, and enjoyed being home with her children. They'd missed her just as much as she'd missed them.

CHAPTER 57

SPENDING THE REST OF the night with her children was wonderful. Madison knew after that night things would change, and she still wanted to speak to Mercy about what happened that she was upset about, and about the prospect of moving into the Boston Edison home.

After putting the kids to bed, she softly knocked on Mercy's door. After a moment, Mercy gave her permission to enter.

Madison walked in to see her cousin putting the breast pump away. There was a small refrigerator in her room to keep the pumped milk fresh.

Despite Mercy's condition, Madison was proud her cousin made a way for herself and didn't let things bother her, although finding a man of her dreams was out of the question. Most men couldn't understand how breasts worked, and when they didn't work normally, they were baffled as to how to handle the whole condition.

"Are you okay?" Madison asked, concerned.

"Yes, I am now."

"What happened today?"

With a deep sigh, Mercy sat on the bed. Madison sat beside her and took her cousin's hand to show comfort.

"This guy at the park, he gave me the creeps. He was with his nephew and…" Mercy paused. "I just felt like he knew things about me."

Madison frowned. "What did he say to make you feel like that?"

Mercy shrugged. "I don't know. Maybe because… I felt… I don't know. Let me think it over before I try to verbally disseminate everything." She inhaled a calming breath. "You came here to just talk about why I'm upset?"

"Well, no, Mercy, I wanted to speak to you about Jamar and Jason."

"I'm cool with whatever you decide," she said with a noncommittal shrug.

"Really? I'd want you to come with us. You're family."

Mercy looked surprised. "Really?"

"Yes, Mercy. You're family, and I couldn't think of not starting something new in my life without you. There's a cottage house on the grounds you could move into, for privacy, and anything you need, you know I'm there for you."

Mercy hugged her tightly. "I know, and thank you, Madison. It's the same for me. Anything you and the children need, I'm there."

Madison smiled in relief, glad to have her cousin's support in choosing what to do for the future with her life.

"Goodnight," Madison said, kissing her cousin's cheek.

Mercy smiled and watched as Madison left out. When Madison closed the door, she could hear Mercy sighing and saying, "Might as well."

She prayed Mercy would someone for herself, like Madison had found someone.

Finally getting in bed, she took her own deep breath knowing the following night's dinner with Jason and Jamar would be life-changing.

***

After rising early in the morning, Madison kissed the kids goodbye and went to work. Getting things back together and going through her to-do list was exhausting. By lunch, she had gotten two messages from Jamar and one from Jason to confirm that night's dinner.

Instead of firing Joshua's assistant, Madison reassigned her to floor assistant for administration. To the assistant, this was a small promotion, but for Madison it was a way to see what the woman knew of anything Joshua had known, and what he had planned to do.

Usually, no one knew not to bother Madison during lunch, but when her new assistant peeked her worried face into the office apologetically, Madison motioned her to come in.

"A package arrived for you from Joshua's lawyer. I thought I should bring it to you right away."

"A package?" Madison questioned.

"Yes." She placed a brown wrapped package about the size of a toaster in front of Madison, with Joshua's handwriting on the front.

FOR MADISON'S EYES ONLY.'

"Should we call a bomb squad?" Madison joked.

"No, but I've asked Leah to come up. Whatever is inside that you don't understand, maybe she could explain."

Madison nodded. "Thank you."

Leah, Joshua's assistant, knocked on the door.

"Please come in, Leah," Madison urged, as her assistant walked out.

When they were alone, Leah asked, "Is there something wrong, Ms. Oliver?"

"Nothing that you can't help me with, Leah. Please sit down."

Leah nervously sat in front of Madison.

"Do you remember this package in Joshua's possession?" Madison questioned as she picked up her letter opener.

"No… well, yes, about a couple of months ago, he was angry after one of his Thursday afternoon meetings. He never explained why he'd go to these meetings, but I knew they had to be important to him because he'd get very upset if I overbooked him to where he would have to miss one." She shifted uncomfortably. "In honesty, he would become so enraged with me, almost like this monstrous being that was going to kill me if I overscheduled him, so I did my best to never do that."

Madison fought not to show how angry she was that she had never noticed Joshua and his secret meetings. "Do you know where he went for these meetings?"

"No, but I had a feeling he was having an affair with someone."

"How?"

Leah shrugged. "Sometimes a woman knows, and I knew his wife had a feeling about it too, yet he tried to keep her in the dark as much as he could. I'd hear them argue, but I never said anything because I really do like working for this company, ma'am. You've done so much for me and I always hoped having a job as his assistant would help me." There was worry all over her voice.

Madison didn't want to talk about Leah's future with the company until she knew this package was not going to blow them both up. "So what about this package?"

"He didn't come to the office that Thursday. He called me and said he had to retrieve something from a safe deposit box and then go to his standing Thursday appointment. I didn't think anything about it until he came to the office with the package after his so-called appointment. It was in a very old box with old tape. He slammed it on his desk and ordered me to find a better box so he could get rid of the old box. When I returned with a better box – that box, he wasn't around, so I took the initiative and opened the box, took the items out, and put them in that box and taped it up. When he returned, he didn't ask me anything. He actually thanked me for helping him and said he was going to return it to the post office in the morning and would be late coming in." Leah frowned. "When I had to turn in his receipts to payroll for his company credit card use, I saw he had driven to Lansing both of those days."

Typing in the computer quickly, Madison pulled up Joshua's company credit card records and saw the dates mentioned by Leah. Joshua had eaten lunch and gassed up his vehicle in Lansing both days.

"I see what you mean and how you came to that conclusion, Leah," Madison said, leaning forward. "Now the real question I need to know is, what was in the box?"

Leah took a deep breath, bit her lip for a moment, and then answered Madison's questioned. "I didn't really look through the pile of items, which were mostly file folders and a sandwich bag with a flash drive. I understand privacy, but I'm not stupid. I knew this was some kind of secret research he didn't want anyone to get their hands on."

"Details, Leah," Madison insisted. "What did you see?"

"There were file folders, each with a name of fruit on them, like pineapples, potatoes, and stuff like that. I knew it had nothing to do with company research, so I didn't think anything of it." She looked terribly worried. "Was I wrong?"

"No, Leah, you're fine." Yet, Madison still looked at the box in deep worry.

"I don't think Joshua would hurt you. He adored you. I mean, towards the end there were a lot of things that bothered him, but I think it was more personal than anything. If you don't feel comfortable, why don't you step outside and I'll open the box, Ms. Oliver?"

Madison didn't feel comfortable putting the woman in danger.

"Please," Leah said, reading her thoughts. "I insist."

She got up from her desk and put the box cutter in front of Leah on the desk. "Be safe, and if it feels suspicious, stop everything and leave, Leah."

Leah nodded. "Don't worry."

Madison left the office where her assistant was waiting outside. She let her assistant know what was going on, and they nervously waited for the door to open...or a bomb to explode.

A few moments later, Leah opened the door and smile. "See, I told you not to worry. It was duck taped to death, though. I think I cut my hand a little."

"Come to first aid," Madison's assistant encouraged.

Leah and the assistant left while Madison walked into her office where Leah had taken everything out of the box and placed it on the desk, just to be sure nothing was at the bottom of the box.

She opened each folder and gasped. Joshua had all the research Madison had thought had been destroyed.

Why hadn't he given this information away?

There was an envelope with her name on it.

Dear Madison,

If you are reading this letter, that means I didn't have the heart to do what I was going to do and give this to Nikki, or sell to the highest bidder. By the time you read this, I know the worst has happened, but I don't want you to worry. Obviously, I had a change of heart and decided against hurting you.

You see, from the moment I read about your research, I knew I would respect you. Nikki convinced me to change schools, get into your program, and then steal your work for "us." That's what she said—or rather, sadly, that's what I believed.

Yet, my head was stronger than my heart. I knew this was all for Nikki, and once she had the research, she was going to drop me like a bad habit, so I hid the research until I knew for sure I would have her love and devotion forever, just like I wanted to give her mine. When she became pregnant, I was sure it was mine, but Nikki would never confirm this. She dangled the knowledge in front of me to lead me to give her what she wanted.

She never knew I had everything. I wanted to wait. I thought that, at the perfect moment, I would take everything to her and then go away with her and be with her forever, with our child.

If you're reading this, that didn't happen and I, like all the other men in Nikki's life, paid the ultimate price, and that is misery.

I'm sorry. I'm sorry for my betrayal. I'm sorry for hurting you.

I hope with this box you can forgive me.

Thank you. Your friend and longtime admirer,

Joshua.

Madison touched the research Joshua had been keeping all that time, and wanted to cry. Her assistant entered the room quietly.

"Leah is fine, but I sent her home."

"Really?" Madison asked, straightening up so her assistant wouldn't see her upset.

"Yes, we just heard on the news that, ah…" She looked down somberly, trying not to cry. "Joshua committed suicide in his jail cell."

Madison turned away because she couldn't hide her grief anymore. Joshua had ended his life because of what Nikki had done to him.

"Ma'am, is there anything I can do?" her assistant asked.

"Call my lawyer. I need to meet with him by the end of the day. I plan to get all parental custody of my brother away from that witch, and I swear if she fights me on this, I'll take every penny she has and sell her blood for money."

"Ouch. I always knew I'd hate to get on your bad side."

When her assistant left her alone Madison, sat at her desk and cried. Joshua would have been a great friend if his heart had not been involved with Nikki. Her ex-best friend would pay dearly for her deceit.

By the time her revenge was over, Madison would make sure Nikki wouldn't have a pot to piss in.

CHAPTER 58

THE DAY HAD BEEN LONG, but knowing she was going to see Jamar and Jason brought her euphoria. They'd all made arrangement for the children, mostly by Jamar's doing. He spoke to Mercy, who seemed to have no problem taking on an extra child so Madison's little brother could get use to the triplets.

Madison drove to the Boston Edison home, where Jason came out to the driveway to greet her with a big hug and a kiss. They'd missed each other, and she was glad to see him first.

"We're going to get through this," she promised. "My private lab is already working on serums for you."

He kissed her fully on the lips. "Be gentle with me, Maddie."

She chuckled. "I promise." They walked in the house through the side, right into the kitchen.

The whole place looked as if it had been newly revamped. She knew the kitchen had been changed to combine the family room to the back of the house for more space. She had to wonder if those changes were reflective of the fact that they would have small children in the house and would need the extra space for running room.

Before she finished that thought, Jamar pulled her into a hug and kissed her. She was thrown breathless by the surprise of him, but enjoyed how much he showed he missed her as well.

"Did you tell her already?" he asked Jason.

"Tell me what?" she inquired, trying to get her equilibrium to return to her from their kisses, but glad Jamar didn't take his from arms around her body and continued to hold her close.

"That we're going to do whatever it takes to make the perfect relationship for you," Jamar stated confidently.

Those words knocked whatever control she had gotten right back out of her.

Jason added, "We won't promise you normal, but we swear, we can promise you perfect."

Madison knew the day would come when she would be faced with perfection yet the abnormal. She had planned for this moment, but nothing was ever like the real thing.

Clasping Jamar's lapels tightly, she tried to calm herself down, but he could feel her upset. "Madison, tell us what's going on," he demanded, guiding her out of the kitchen into the family room. There was a large, tan leather sectional couch.

Instead of sitting her down next to him, he guided her into his lap.

"Do you love us, Madison?" Jason asked, sitting beside them and taking her other hand into his.

"Yes!" she said without hesitation, looking back and forth between them.

"Do you forgive us for all that we've done?" Jamar questioned.

"Of course. It's just that I can't forgive myself for what I have done to you."

"From the time I first met you, Madison," Jamar said, "You've been the most loving, beautiful, giving person I've ever met. We've all made mistakes. You forgive us, and you have nothing to be sorry for."

The word 'beautiful' didn't anger her anymore. She loved hearing it from Jamar's mouth, and in her heart and soul at that moment, she knew she had healed from the past.

Jason added, "We don't want to spend another day apart from you. And we want those moments to be cherished with you, the kids and Jerry.

"And don't forget Mercy," Jamar said.

"As if she would let us," Madison chuckled.

"We'd make a wonderful, happy family. Jamar and I want that with you, and to make you happy the rest of your days," Jason promised.

Coming from him, she knew that meant a whole lot. Tears ran down her check, and Jamar kissed them away.

"Spend a lifetime with us, Madison. Please," Jamar insisted. "Marry us so we will not miss another day with you and our children."

"Please, Madison," Jason insisted caressing her thighs and arms. "We'll make you happy. We'll be everything you ever wanted."

She smiled secretly because she had gotten Nikki to sign immediate divorce papers and full custody of her little brother to Jason, which were in her purse as they spoke. "And you won't mind sharing me with Jamar forever, Jason?"

"As soon as I get myself out of Nikki's life, it'd be an exquisite honor to share you with my brother," he said excitedly. "I've waited all my life to have this kind of relationship, and I'm not going to ever be foolish and take it for granted, Madison. Ever! By next year, I hope to be a free man and we can go to Canada to have a commitment ceremony."

Before the night was over, Madison would let Jason know the good news. Madison would also tell them later the large amount of money Jason would receive, and the full scholarship her brother would be due, plus the lifetime trust. Nikki had a lot of money put away, and just as Madison had promised, she now had absolutely nothing.

"By that time, we'll be officially married, and living together as one family," Jamar promised her. "It's really up to you. You are what will keep our family together. You have the power here."

To be loved by these two wonderful men was any woman's dream come true.

How could she refuse? Madison hadn't been this happy in all aspects of her life, ever.

"There's nothing left for me to say, but yes." She kissed Jason, and then Jamar. "Yes."

They smiled, honored, as she accepted their proposal. Each one took turns kissing her deeply again, with promises in their embraces for an infinite amount of lovemaking, happiness and life to come for that night and the rest of eternity.

Madison knew she would be forever beautiful and loved with Jamar and Jason.

The End

201511280511-20161005062-20170620-949414

The Author thanks you for supporting her writing endeavor and invites you to write a review for this book at the place you purchased or in the comment section at

www.sylviahubbard.com/beautiful

Thank you in advance.

ABOUT THIS AUTHOR:

Detroit Native, Sylvia Hubbard, is a diehard romance/suspense author. In 2005, Sylvia Hubbard was the recipient of The Detroit City Council's Spirit of Detroit Award for her efforts in Detroit's literary community, voted Romance Book Cafe favorite author and her book Stone's Revenge was voted best African- American Mystery by Mojolist.com. The Author is also founder of Motown Writers Network, which offers literary education and events in Detroit, Chief Producer for The Michigan Literary Network Radio Show and speaks on Internet Marketing and Promotions for Writers and Authors.

She resides in Detroit as a divorced mother of three.

She writes a blog called How To Love A Black Woman, which is described as her manual for loving her, and speaks on Creative Intimacy for couples, being a busy single mom and more!

She's written over 40 novels with more to come and always available to speak at any event on literacy, writing, publishing and mommying!

Related Links:

http://MotownWriters.com
http://HowToEbook.org

This author thanks you for your support to her literary endeavors. There are more books to read especially the Heart Family and the Cytee Brothers. Kimberly & Jaelen Gates have their own love story in Stealing Innocence Check out and collect over forty stories for your reading pleasure. Visit her website now. http://sylviahubbard.com

Support this author, by downloading or purchasing more books from her, reviewing this book from place of purchase and/or then sharing this author on your social network to encourage your reading friends to purchase her work. Thank you in advance for your support.

Connect Online to Sylvia Hubbard:

Twitter: http://twitter.com/SylviaHubbard1

Website: http://SylviaHubbard.com

My blog: http://SylviaHubbard.com/blogs

Want another book to read now?

http://sylviahubbard.com/fictionbooks